As the jailer turned the key in the lock, Alienor risked a glance to her husband, her gaze caught by the intensity of his eyes.

"I would see you once before the end," Dagobert whispered, and tears began to flow down Alienor's cheeks.

"'Tis true, then, that they will kill you?" she asked, earning a slow nod from her husband.

"Aye," he acknowledged simply.

"But why?" Alienor demanded, her frustration with the inexplicable turn their lives had taken coming fully to the fore.

Dagobert regarded her silently for a moment before a rueful smile twisted his lips.

"'Tis a long tale, but I suppose we have time enough. And 'tis only fitting that you now know the way of things...."

Dear Reader,

June's *Unicorn Bride,* by Claire Delacroix, is truly a big book. This sweeping medieval tale tells the story of Lady Alienor, a young woman betrothed to a man veiled in secrets and legends.

Popular author Margaret Moore brings us the latest installment in her Warrior series, *A Warrior's Way.* Awarded an estate for his valor, knight Hu Morgan is doubly pleased to acquire a wealthy wife in the bargain. However, the lady in question is decidedly less enthused about the match.

Jonathan Harris and Polly O'Neil make an unusual pair of lovers in *Timeless,* by Western author DeLoras Scott. Jonathan has been given a second chance in life and love, thanks to Miss Polly, but she soon begins to wonder exactly who—or *what*—he really is.

Laurel Ames creates another romp set in the Regency era in *Homeplace.* Masquerading as a boy in order to keep her inheritance, Justine Mallory finds herself in trouble when her handsome guardian decides to make a man out of her.

And keep an eye out for the *Promised Brides* Historical short-story collection, with authors Mary Jo Putney, Kristin James and Julie Tetel.

Sincerely,

Tracy Farrell
Senior Editor

Please address questions and book requests to:
Harlequin Reader Service
U.S.: 3010 Walden Ave., P.O. Box 1325, Buffalo, NY 14269
Canadian: P.O. Box 609, Fort Erie, Ont. L2A 5X3

CLAIRE DELACROIX

Unicorn Bride

Harlequin Books

TORONTO • NEW YORK • LONDON
AMSTERDAM • PARIS • SYDNEY • HAMBURG
STOCKHOLM • ATHENS • TOKYO • MILAN
MADRID • WARSAW • BUDAPEST • AUCKLAND

ISBN 0-373-28823-9

UNICORN BRIDE

CLAIRE DELACROIX

An avid traveler and student of history, Claire Delacroix can be found at home when she has a deadline, amid the usual jumble of books, knitting needles and potted herbs.

For Tracy, Angela and Harriet,
without whom *Unicorn Bride* would not
be what it is.
Thanks.

Prologue

Pamiers, 1223

Well enough did Arpais know the world and its ways to recognize the sounds of swordplay when she heard them. And no game was this, she thought with growing trepidation, unless a warrior's daughter could be so fooled.

Had she not awoken to these same sounds countless times in the East when she rode with her father? How many times had she listened to the distant sounds of the Mongols claiming victory over yet another town? It could not be, she told herself wildly, not here, not in this sleepy village where Robert had *promised* she would be safe.

Desperately did she listen for some sign that she was mistaken, but the clink of steel could be no other than the echo of blade on blade, and her mouth went dry. The fighting was close, too close for her comfort, and Arpais gathered her babe to her breast protectively as she dared to peek out into the street.

A man swore and she ducked quickly back into the shadows, the sight of fresh blood between the cobblestones outside her door making her own blood run cold. She watched in horror as her doddering older neighbor came out to investigate, his violent dispatch before her very eyes stunning Arpais, despite all the horrors she had witnessed in this life.

When the knight responsible for the deed turned his steely gaze upon her, Arpais's heart fairly stopped. 'Twas impossible that he would strike her down while she clutched a child to her breast but still she did not dare to breathe lest she provoke him.

The knight stepped forward purposefully and Arpais panicked. She spun in terror, hearing the knight shout behind her in outrage, and ran blindly down the street.

Her daughter began to cry and she hugged the babe tighter, angry tears blurring her vision as she darted through the congested streets. Suddenly she tripped over a bloody corpse and fell to her knees, horrified at the glassy eyes so close to her own, and stumbled to her feet once more.

No safety was there here, for the evidence lay before her eyes on the cobblestones of every street and alley. 'Twas a wholesale slaughter. Arpais's mind went numb as she recognized yet another dead neighbor bleeding at her feet. Her bile rose at the sight and she ducked down a side street, desperately trying to think. No longer could she even look at the corpses, so frightened was she of seeing yet another whose laugh she knew and had heard of late.

Alone she was, not safe, and she silently cursed the men who had left her in this position. First her father had returned to the East, then Robert had shown the poor judgment to die and leave her alone in his homeland with their child. A pox on both of them and their grand plans. Arpais clutched the swaddled child convulsively, knowing that somehow, in some way, she had to at least ensure her babe's survival.

She stumbled over another corpse that was yet warm and knew in that moment that it might be too much to hope for her own survival.

Naught had her father's plans for launching a new royal bloodline to do with her resolve to see her daughter gain some sanctuary. This was her babe, beyond any lofty political aims, and Arpais would do anything to see her offspring safe.

The Pereille clan, she thought suddenly, immediately wondering why the obvious solution had eluded her so long. She had to get to Montsalvat where they could offer her child the protection of a safe haven. Arpais spared a quick glance for the distant peak where she knew the fortress loomed, refusing to be daunted by the distance. Alzeu and Iolande would see to her babe, indeed they owed her no less for the pledges that stood between them. Arpais had but to reach the fortress to see her beloved babe safe and her resolve grew with every step she took.

Somehow she must reach Montsalvat.

Filled with determination, Arpais burst into the town square and glanced up from the sickening carnage, the very stillness of one knight standing alone drawing her gaze like a moth to the flame. He looked puzzled, mayhap astonished at the chaos surrounding him, and that alone was enough to give her hope. Intuitively, she knew that one way or another, she would persuade him to help her. To help her child.

Indeed, she had little choice.

Guibert stood motionless amongst the melee, his blade still sheathed, his somber green eyes tracing the jagged outline of the distant hills beyond the town walls, his mind assaulted by almost forgotten memories of his childhood spent nearby. He could but close his eyes and the years would fall away, peaceful memories crowding out the wanton destruction surrounding him.

The sunbaked dirt, the smell of the familiar bracken, the brilliant hue of the sky all summoned lost recollections of the days of his youth and Guibert de Perpignan found himself wondering how far he stood now from his grandfather's old stone villa. Decades it had been since he had set foot in this area, years since he had heard his sister's mischievous giggle and he could not recall when, if ever, he had previously felt this emptiness from lack of family in his mercenary life.

The sounds of battle rose around him, the cries of the dying, the rhythmic thump of falling blades finding their mark, and Guibert's horrified gaze fell on the town now cast into disarray. Although normally amongst the first to the fray, Guibert found himself reluctant to participate in what had become his daily task, uncertain for the first time of the "justice" he and the other Crusaders meted out when he thought of his sister and her proximity to this carnage.

Children she should have by now, he realized, staring about the terra-cotta walls of the town with new eyes, wondering where his sister now made her home. Could she have fallen prey to an attack of this kind? The very thought turned his battle-weary heart to ice.

Deaf to the victorious cries of his companions, his eyes drawn again to the ragged peaks jutting toward the sky outside the town walls, Guibert recalled a tale of his grandfather's, his imagination conjuring an image of the bright-eyed old man huddled before a raging fire on the hearth. Well enough he could see those bushy white brows rising and falling and catching the firelight as the older man talked, his three tottling grandchildren silent with wonder as they hung on his every word.

Tales of the return of the rightful king to the throne they had been, stories of the king who would come from these very hills and restore his divine bloodline to the regal seat, Guibert remembered now. He looked about himself with new eyes, wondering whether the ancient legend had anything to do with the purge of this province ordered by the church.

Perhaps it was the uncertainty in his eyes that prompted the woman to trust him, but Guibert never knew the truth of it. No sooner had the woman materialized from nowhere and shoved the bundle of embroidered cloth into his arms than she was struck down, decapitated by a single blow, her fingers twitching where they lay lifeless across his boot.

Guibert barely glanced up at the other knight's victorious hoot, his troubled gaze caught by the woman's blankly staring almond-shaped eyes. Barely had he the chance to note her exotic loveliness before the bundle in his arms began to wail and his thoughts were abruptly swept away.

Chapter One

Montsalvat—January 1243

"The timing is terrible." Dagobert interjected his opinion in a low tone that drew the attention of the others and typically brought the raging argument to a full stop.

When the small room fell silent, he glanced up and met Eustache's quizzical gaze thoughtfully, some slight motion of Iolande's drawing his attention to her. His mother pursed her lips to suppress some biting comment and he saw that she had not yet had her say, in her own eyes at least.

Smothering a smile of mingled amusement and affection, he lifted his gaze to the third and last figure in the room, an older man conspicuously uncomfortable where he stood still by the door. Ignoring the other two, Dagobert smiled genuinely and gestured to the chair opposite him.

"I would apologize for the rudeness of my house," he said softly, beckoning to the older man, noting the flush that rose over his mother's features at her realization that she had slighted a guest in her anger. Appearing no more comfortable now than a moment past, Guibert cleared his throat hesitantly and stepped forward, sliding into the offered chair with evident relief.

"You must understand that this is an issue of much concern here," Dagobert added by way of explanation, watching the man relax slowly under his attentive eye. "We are not usually so remiss in our treatment of guests," he concluded with a rueful smile. Guibert nodded, apparently reassured, but when he might have spoken, words spilled forth from Iolande instead.

"Neither are we remiss in fulfilling our pledges," she shot back at her son, "and the honoring of this one is long overdue."

"We can afford no distraction at this late date," Eustache said, leaning his fists on the desk and bending toward Dagobert to make his point. "Even as we argue this issue, the forces of the crown are advancing upon us."

"The blood is of utmost importance! Surely even an addlepated warrior can see the truth in this," Iolande insisted hotly. Dagobert held up one hand with a shake of his head at the sight of the argument erupting before his eyes once again, and his mother snapped her lips closed mutinously.

"I must confess that I am most confused," the older man sitting opposite admitted into the terse silence that followed. His quiet words drew a grin from Dagobert at the contrast between the older man's perplexed air and the emotionally charged atmosphere in the room. Indeed they had done precious little to make the matter clear to him, Eustache and Iolande simply arguing rudely between themselves, and his agreement was central to this issue.

A quick glance to the pair assured Dagobert that his mother was well and truly embarrassed for having lost control of her tongue before a guest. For his part, Eustache had folded his arms across his chest in annoyance, the stubborn set of his lips telling Dagobert that he would not utter a sound until addressed. If the two did manage to hold their tongues for a few moments, perhaps this matter could be resolved, after all.

"As indeed you must be, sir. At issue is my marriage to your foster daughter." Guibert nodded that he had understood that much at least, and Dagobert arched one blond eyebrow in Eustache's direction. "From this knight's description, my mother has no doubt that she is the same as was betrothed to me at her birth."

"Very like she is to the woman who entrusted her care to me," Guibert confirmed, and Dagobert nodded thoughtfully.

"The woman...?" he began hopefully for Iolande's benefit, a question in his tone, but the older man shook his head sadly.

"Dead long past," Guibert said flatly, his mouth pulling into a grimace as if some grisly sight were before his eyes once again. "She gave me the babe but had not the time to utter a single word before she was struck down." Iolande expelled a shaky breath and Dagobert flicked a glance to his mother, knowing that she had been hoping, but for naught.

"There is no question that Eustache speaks the truth," he said now, addressing his concerns to her in an effort to divert her bittersweet reminiscences. "'Tis an unholy time to make this match."

Iolande blinked several times in rapid succession, amazing her son that her usually tightly controlled emotions were so openly displayed this night. She took a deep breath before fixing her gaze on him once more.

"Well you know that as matters stand, the line would die with you," she whispered, Dagobert watching helplessly as the tears rose unchecked in those blue eyes. "Should Eustache speak the truth..." Iolande valiantly tried to continue, but her tears rose and choked her words.

Dagobert frowned down at his folded hands, completing the thought easily in his own mind. Should they be attacked, the king would ensure that Dagobert was amongst those who lay dead when all was said and done. A chill passed over his heart and he acknowledged to himself that his mother's concern had merit.

"'Twould not have been your father's desire to see his line end thus," Iolande managed to add shakily, turning abruptly even as one pale hand lifted to her face. "And well enough you know that 'twas *this* match he wanted for you."

Not knowing what to say, Dagobert mutely watched her hurry from the room as an awkward silence settled over the three men. The candle flame sputtered in the tallow, drawing Dagobert's gaze, and he wondered how he could in good conscience bring a bride into this unholy mess. Even a bride his father had sworn he would take.

"'Tis a risk we needn't take," Eustache muttered under his breath, but Dagobert stared thoughtfully down at his hands.

Unlike Iolande 'twas to show her heart so openly, and he could only conclude that she felt strongly about the matter. A simple truth rang in her words that he could not deny, and he sighed, frowning at the top of his desk in dissatisfaction at the role he had drawn in life. Would that he had been born a man devoid of responsibilities, but the die had been cast and he would not shirk what needed to be done.

Always did Eustache talk of success, but Iolande was right. Should Dagobert fail, he left no heir and he had no brethren to take up the cause. No right had he to discard the future of the bloodline for the sake of his own convenience. This pledge of his father's he would keep. The woman had been pledged to him and she, too, must follow her destiny wherever their paths might lead.

The matter resolved in his mind, he gave Guibert de Perpignan an encouraging smile and leaned forward to explain the situation in full to the older knight.

The bright January sunlight did nothing to soften the foreboding facade of the fortress Montsalvat looming overhead, and Alienor shivered inwardly at the sight of the stone castle crouching atop the steep mountain like some great venomous toad.

Short and squat the building was, or perhaps 'twas just an illusion created by the contrast of the sharp incline of the mountainside with its brooding walls, its darkness highlighted by the light dusting of snow. As her horse climbed the steeply winding path and grew ever nearer, she refused to look up again, her first impression of the château that would become her home doing nothing to dispel her trepidation.

"Trust me," Guibert had insisted when she had balked at the restriction that she would not meet her bridegroom before the nuptials, and she had willingly done so, trusting easily in the man who had so often put her needs before his own.

But now, before the forbidding facade of Montsalvat, she could not help but question the haste with which her marriage had been planned, the secrecy and mystery surrounding her bridegroom. Her gaze fell on her foster father's back as he rode before her, still straight and proud despite his advancing years. How could she question this man who had given her so much?

Well enough did she know that Guibert had been hard-pressed to afford her tutors, well enough did she know that on more than one occasion he had unsheathed his blade as a mercenary against his heart to see her raised as he saw fit. Schooled as a southern lady she had been, tutored and taught in music, languages and mathematics, Guibert insisting that her mysterious origins gave her the opportunity to claim a finer destiny than his had been.

And now she was to wed the Count of Pereille himself, the most powerful man in the province, the ultimate vindication for all of Guibert's sacrifices, and all she could think about was the fact that she was deeply afraid. Too many rumors had she heard in the village of the ominous doings at this place, provocatively half-heard morsels of tales of magic, of legends come to life, of strange doings beneath the fullness of the moon.

Alienor glanced up at the foreboding edifice looming ever closer and allowed herself a grimace. Why would anyone build such a château? And why here, virtually in the middle of nowhere? Why was the stone not the pleasing dove gray from the local quarries? Why not build an elegant tower, a spire, an attractive curtain wall instead of presenting this dark menacing face to the arriving traveler? What secrets did Montsalvat so jealously guard within its walls?

Hours later, Alienor toyed with the seed pearls sewn to her crimson kirtle and surveyed her reflection in the silvered glass hanging opposite, unable to believe that she would be wed before the day was through, unwilling to accept that she was already ensconced in the building that would now be her home.

One secret already had she discovered about the château—its crusty exterior belied the wealth and opulence of the furnishings within, though that fact did little to ease her trepidation. This tiny antechamber near the gates had been offered for her use, as it was undoubtedly offered to countless other guests, but even its decor easily overwhelmed anything she had known before. Intricate tapestries hung on each of the four walls, a fire raged on the hearth beneath an elegantly arched and ornately carved stone fireplace. A bed draped in brocades and scattered with embroidered pillows dominated the far wall, a comfortable chair and table were placed invitingly before the hearth.

The mirror amazed Alienor in and of itself, as wide as she, it was, and nearly as tall, and shockingly expensive to acquire, without a doubt. She could not even imagine how it had been carried up that winding mountainous track and arrived here intact. Never had she seen anything like it and she touched it carefully as if her fingertip alone would shatter it, marveling at the smoothness of its surface. As she touched the glass, she marvelled again that *she* should be the one the count would take to wife, Guibert's ominous assurance ringing again in her ears.

"The count wills it" was all she had been able to coax from him and Alienor shivered anew in recollection.

The bells ringing in the chapel brought her head up with a snap, her heart tripping a staccato, and she summoned a cursory smile of encouragement for the sad bride reflected in the silvery expanse, rising to her feet to check her appearance one last time before donning her veil.

The red velvet kirtle was laced snugly to her forearms, the cuffs and high neck trimmed with pearls carefully removed from an old garment, the fullness of the skirt cascading over Alienor's knees and ankles. The pearl-encrusted hem stopped just above the floor, revealing a glimpse of the gold brocade trim on her chemise, which swept the ground.

The toes of her red kid slippers were barely visible and she spun around experimentally, checking that the narrowness of the band of brocade was not visible. Her nimble fingers were clever at making less look like more, the sliver of heavily embroidered gold hinting at an entire chemise of the cloth, when in fact she had only had the coin to buy a narrow strip. Alienor was not ashamed of her own circumstances, but in the open opulence of this château she was curiously loath to clarify the matter.

Only her groom's mother had she met so far, and that lady's intimidating presence alone would have sent a lesser soul scurrying homeward through the heavy gates. Icy perfection indeed was Iolande de

Goteberg, her fair brows, clear blue eyes and pallid complexion such as Alienor had never seen before in this land of dark-haired, dark-eyed people.

Both horses had paused of their own volition within the gates when Alienor and Guibert had first seen Iolande, her tall figure draped in pastel mauve velvet, the cold winter sunlight falling full on her fairness as she stood in the courtyard, one long hand trailing over the ears of a huge gray wolfhound at her side.

A deliberate pose, Alienor was certain, but an effective one nonetheless, and she turned to the mirror once again for reassurance, seeing no evidence of the regal bearing of her mother-in-law reflected there. Though Iolande's words had been carefully chosen, her welcome had not been warm and Alienor wondered yet again what future awaited her here.

She had plaited her dark hair earlier this morning, winding its length into an elegant arrangement of braids despite its unruly nature, more of the seed pearls gleaming from their perches within the ebony tresses. With a sigh of dissatisfaction, she carefully placed the linen circle of her fillet on her artfully arranged hair, draping her sheer white wimple around her neck with practiced hands and tucking the ends into the fillet. A whisper of golden veiling slipped over the entirety, covering her hair and the fillet and flowing down to her shoulders in a sheer cloud, her face a lonely oval in the midst of all the concealing cloth.

Married to a man she had yet even to see. Alienor met her own eyes in the glass, wondering what her husband looked like, panicking briefly at the thought that he might not find her pleasing. She scanned the reflection confronting her with a discriminating eye, the creamy skin of her face, the full rosy lips, the

tawny eyes with their uncommonly thick lashes that
tipped up at the outer corners, a scandalous hint of
some Eastern blood in her ancestry. That same Eastern influence seemed indicated in the honeyed hue of
her complexion, the heavy thickness of her dark hair,
though those tresses were defiantly wavy instead of
ramrod straight.

Though slender as a reed, she was tall for a woman,
Alienor acknowledged with a fleeting frown for the
umpteenth time since she had gained her stature,
hoping against hope that her husband was not a small
man, hoping that he would find her an attractive mate.
A misfit she had always been in this province of people who so closely resembled one another and who had
learned to regard foreigners as undesirable. Dark hair,
dark eyes, olive skin and compact bodies had confronted her at every turn, even her subtle physical dif-
ferences drawing attention amongst such startling
similarity.

Alienor clasped her hands together, fighting against
the tears that rose in her eyes at the thought of her
husband echoing the taunting comments she had endured for so long, the teasing when she had been a
long-legged adolescent towering over most of the other
women and not a few of the men in her town. She
clenched her fingers tightly and prayed to the powers
that be that her husband be anything but a short man
who thought her a freak of nature.

Alienor started at the sound of a light tap on the
door and turned away from the mirror, her heart
leaping wildly about her chest as she struggled to pull
on her gloves despite the trembling of her hands.
Pulling open the door, she met the admiration in her
foster father's eyes and managed to summon a smile.

Guibert stood framed in the portal, his mail gleaming from the enthusiastic polish it had received, his tabard carefully mended by Alienor's quick fingers and newly trimmed in crimson silk cording, his silver mane brushed to some measure of order.

He beamed at Alienor with pride, and as he offered her his elbow, her heart swelled with love for this man who had so gallantly seen to her upbringing. Guibert pressed her hand affectionately when she slipped it through his arm and her tears rose unbidden again, the older man gruffly tolerating the kiss she planted on his cheek.

Neither of them said a word as they stepped out into the corridor, the moment too fraught with emotion for them to trust their tongues. Alienor could hear her heart beat as Guibert steadily paced off the seemingly endless length of the hall, its walls lined with curious onlookers who murmured to one another confidentially as they passed. So many lived within these walls—would she ever grow used to it? She blocked her ears to their whispered comments, focusing her attention on the brightly colored light fanning out of the chapel doors at the far end of the hall, matching her pace to Guibert's.

Guibert paused in the chapel doorway moments later and Alienor took a shaky breath, forcing a tight smile when her foster father squeezed her hand encouragingly. But a glimpse of the open speculation in the eyes of the assembled crowd compelled her to lift her gaze to the stained-glass window that filled the wall behind the altar.

Rich in detail it was, and she studied the strangely entwined images of grapevines ripe with fruit as she walked ever closer to her destiny, finding the battle scenes between a unicorn and a lion an unusual choice for a place of worship. No crucifix was there, she noted with relief, refusing to so much as glance toward the spot where she knew her bridegroom must stand.

When Guibert paused, Alienor's gaze fell to the priest in customary black before her for the barest instant before she dropped her eyes to the floor, her nervous mind seeking some explanation for the impish glimmer she had seen in the cleric's blue eyes. A Celt he was by his coloring. No doubt he simply found the world a merry place, she thought sourly. Squaring her shoulders and taking a deep breath as the red-haired priest began the ceremony, Alienor risked a quick glance to her right to confront the inevitable.

The spot was empty. She stood alone before the altar.

Wide-eyed with surprise, Alienor looked up at the priest in panic, distrusting now the mischievous twinkle in his eye. He almost chuckled aloud at her discomfort, lifting his hand to beckon to someone at the side portal. Alienor followed his gesture, her mouth dropping open in shock when a shabbily dressed man appeared, coaxing a single-horned goat toward her. A garland of flowers and ribbons was draped around the goat's neck, the man tugging him forward by a scarlet cord while the beast chewed nonchalantly on a blossom it had apparently pulled from its ornament.

"'Tis a goat!" Alienor blurted in disbelief, and the goatherd glanced up sharply, the warm glimmer of humor in his slate eyes sending a tingle right to her toes.

'Twas hardly his place to look at her so boldly, she told herself indignantly, even as she felt the heat rise over her cheeks. As if he had had a similar thought, the man dropped his gaze, a secretive smile playing over his lips, and Alienor forced herself to look at her apparent groom, her ears catching an indignant shush from the priest and a sharp clucking sound from some woman's tongue behind her.

"A unicorn, child, a unicorn," the priest corrected her softly, admonishment in his tone. "You surely understand that he can only remain in the chapel for the ceremony itself," he added in a confidential undertone, and Alienor raised her gaze to his in shock.

The goat was truly her groom? What madness was this?

"But why?"

The priest tut-tutted indulgently under his breath at the folly of her question and leaned forward to respond. "We cannot have dung in the house of the Lord," he murmured, but Alienor shook her head impatiently, desperately trying to assemble her jostled thoughts in a world gone insane, uncomfortably aware of the goatherd's amusement with the situation.

"Nay, I would ask why must he be here at all?" she demanded in a terse whisper, and the priest regarded her in openmouthed surprise in his turn.

"'Tis his nuptials, lass," he hissed back, and Alienor's mind positively boggled.

Sturggling to assimilate this news, she stared down at the beast beside her, but it merely returned her regard calmly from alien yellow eyes. The goatherd who had led the creature handed her the end of the silken leash with a bow that seemed faintly mocking, his gray eyes twinkling with some barely suppressed amuse-

ment as she gaped at him and tried to come to terms
with her situation.

With the cord dangling loosely from her fingertips,
Alienor glanced over her shoulder to find the assembled group watching her without undue interest, as
though nothing untoward was occurring and this
wedding was proceeding as customarily as any other.

Incredulous, she sought Guibert's eyes, but he was
studying his toe with great interest. She glanced back
to the beast at her side, wishing now that she had not
prayed so fervently that her betrothed be anything
other than a short man.

"A goat," she whispered in disbelief, and the priest
shot her a warning glance.

"Unicorn," he pointed out reprimandingly. "Do
not be so foolish as to insult his family again." At his
words, Alienor stifled a chuckle with an effort.

Insult his family? And what of her family? Her
dignity? Surely she was not alone in thinking the situation bizarre. This was a joke, a prank, a test of her
good humor, a frivolity to allay her nervousness. It
simply had to be, for she could think of no other
plausible explanation. To wed a goat was beyond belief.

She giggled at the absurdity of it all, earning another quelling look from the priest, and bit her lip to
control her laughter, determined to play her role well
in this farce. No doubt her intended was a prankster
who enjoyed teasing others and she would do well to
learn to play along with his games.

'Twas the solemnity with which they all waited for
the creature to nod its agreement to the vows that first
triggered Alienor's suspicions that the joke was going

too far, but by the time she had worked up the nerve
to interject, the priest had slid a gold band onto her
finger. He threaded her husband's ring onto a length
of red cord from which already hung a signet ring,
handing her the makeshift necklace with complete solemnity. Alienor slipped it over the unicorn's neck with
numb hands, unable to believe that this was really
happening to her. Surely 'twas no more than a dream,
some contortion of her prenuptial nervousness by her
restive mind.

But the numerous hands pressing hers and the myriad kisses of congratulations forced upon her cheeks
were more than real, the slim cord in her fingers was
tangible beyond belief, the smell of the single-horned
billy goat unassailable evidence that it did in fact stand
at her side, mutely, endlessly chewing. Having extended their felicitations, the assembly filed out of the
chapel, laughing and joking in anticipation of the feast
the lady would spread to celebrate her son's nuptials.

The beast reached experimentally for the velvet of
her kirtle and Alienor instinctively slapped its nose.
Her rising panic made the blow harder than she had
intended and the creature sneezed as it backed away,
fixing her with an accusing glare.

"You wed me to this beast in truth!" she spat at the
priest, the horror of it all finally sinking in. "'Twas no
jest."

The priest shook his head slowly, apparently surprised that she was displeased. "No jest is there in
wedding the Count of Pereille," he answered calmly,
his russet brows drawing together in a frown. "Surely
you knew his circumstance?"

"No!" Alienor responded sharply, regarding the
docile animal with something akin to disgust. "No one

told me of this detail, for 'tis not one I would easily have forgotten."

The cleric laughed softly behind his hand, his eyes twinkling as he nodded in agreement, his good humor doing little to alleviate Alienor's frustration. "Aye, 'tis an affliction that would stick in one's mind."

"'Tis no doubt amusing for you," she shot back, feeling her tears rise once more. "Unreasonable was it then for me to expect to be wed to a man?"

"Oho," the priest replied with a chuckle, waving aside her concerns with an indulgent hand. "'Tis this form that worries you," he said, as if everything were clear to him now. "Cursed the boy is and condemned to the shape of a unicorn by day," he confided, patting her companionably on the hand and sparing her a wink, "but by night you will find him man enough to suit you."

"What Celtic nonsense is this?" Alienor demanded, her ire well and truly roused. Did this man honestly expect her to believe that her husband was a shape-shifter, like some ancient pagan god? "No tales of magical spells will I accept as explanation for this foolishness. 'Tis mad to be wed to a beast such as this." She took a deep breath and fixed the cleric with a determined eye.

"I demand an annulment."

The priest studied her thoughtfully, tapping one finger against his chin as he considered her request. "You must understand," he finally said, "that such would not be regarded with approval by my lady and patron. Indeed, you place me in a tenuous position by your very request."

"No less than you have placed me!"

"Indeed." The priest considered Alienor thoughtfully, all trace of humor gone now from his eyes. "Well you know that an annulment can only be granted if the match has not been consummated," he continued, "and in all fairness, I must give the boy an opportunity." He nodded silently with pursed lips as though pleased with his decision, then met Alienor's hopeful eyes.

"Should you wish the same in the morning, I shall grant your request," he concluded with an efficient nod, turning to stride toward the hall in the crowd's wake, leaving Alienor struggling against his evident meaning.

"You expect me to couple with a goat?" she demanded in disbelief, and the priest paused halfway down the aisle, glancing over his shoulder with that impish grin.

"Unicorn." He mouthed the correction, shaking one finger at her in gentle admonishment before striding out of the chapel and leaving Alienor at the altar with the complacently chewing creature. She bit her lip to hold back her tears of frustration, raising one hand to cover her eyes, overwhelmed at the prospects confronting her.

How could Guibert do such a thing to her? What folly her simple trust had brought! How could she hold up her head before the company in the hall, knowing that she was the laughingstock of the province? Wed to a beast! Could there truly be any worse fate than this?

"I will tend Dagobert," came a low voice from her side, and Alienor jumped, having thought herself alone in the chapel. She was surprised to find the servant who had led the beast to the altar standing beside her, some measure of sympathy for her predicament in his gray eyes.

"Should you wish to retire for a few moments," he added softly, and Alienor nodded, grateful for his understanding. A relief it was that someone else could appreciate that this situation was beyond normal, be he only a goatherd.

"Dagobert?" she asked doubtfully as she handed him the slim cord, and the man grinned, displaying a remarkably straight set of white teeth, the sight sending her heart lurching about her chest. Emotionally distraught she was, she told herself, off-balance from the events of the day, tired from her trip and definitely not susceptible to the smile of a servant.

"You did not listen to the ceremony," he chided her gently, and Alienor smiled ruefully in turn, feeling a faint blush heat her cheeks.

"I confess I was preoccupied," she admitted, stifling a giggle as she looked down at her groom. Dagobert, she thought, trying unsuccessfully to fit the name to the beast.

"Dagobert V de Pereille," the man supplied as if he had read her thoughts, and Alienor laughed aloud at the juxtaposition of name and beast.

"'Tis a lengthy name for such a humble creature," she commented, folding her arms speculatively across her chest, and the man chuckled with her, reaching down to scratch the creature's ears with something like affection. His hands were tanned and Alienor found herself noticing the lean strength of them, the length of his fingers, the gentleness with which he rubbed Dagobert's ear.

"No humble creature is he, but a unicorn, nobly born," the stable hand corrected her, flicking a warm glance in Alienor's direction that made her suddenly aware that the chapel was abandoned except for the three of them. Dagobert shook his head and eyed Alienor's kirtle assessingly again, reaching tentatively for the red velvet and sending her scurrying backward, away from both man and beast.

"Touch me not," she admonished the beast with a warning finger, the stable hand's deep chuckle reminding her that he had overheard the priest's words and sending a hot flush over her cheeks.

"'Tis said the unicorn comes only to a woman pure and true," he observed quietly, and Alienor felt her color deepen yet again, her mortified gaze falling to the floor at his teasing. Too often for her taste was the subject of her wedding night being breached by strangers, and she gripped the back of a pew with shaking fingers, wondering how on earth she would manage to get through the rest of this day.

She started when the stable hand brushed one fingertip gently across her chin, tipping up her face with the simple gesture. Her eyes flew to his at his familiarity, the tremor that tripped along her veins at the imprint of his fingertip beneath her chin startling her with its intensity. Too aware was she suddenly of the warmth in his eyes, and she found herself caught in his regard, powerless to move beneath his gaze.

"Fear not the night, lovely lady," he said softly, Alienor watching with fascination as his mouth pulled into that reassuring grin again. Somehow his words assuaged her fears, his quiet confidence restoring her own resolve to hold up her chin and see what she had begun through to its finish. Unthinking, she smiled shyly back at him, and he blinked as if disconcerted, his gaze dropping to her lips and back to her eyes again.

"'Tis good to see the bride smile," he murmured under his breath, his words reminding Alienor of who and where she was, of how singularly inappropriate it was for her to be studying the hard outline of this goatherd's lips. She felt herself flush scarlet at the realization, managing to mumble some inarticulate excuse as she turned and fairly fled the chapel.

If Alienor thought she had managed to regain some of her composure by the time she reached the hall, dinner quickly demolished those hard-earned illusions. Iolande handed Alienor a chalice brimming with mulled wine when she reached the head table, her mother-in-law's hands icily cold when the two women's fingers brushed. The pewter chalice was clearly of some ceremonial value, its decoration too ornate for an oft-used piece, the design an echo of the branching grapevines laden with fruit that Alienor had noted in the stained glass.

"To the fruit of the union," Iolande said as Alienor lifted the warm brew to her lips, and she stifled a twinge of annoyance that yet another mention had been made of the impending intimacy of her wedding night.

"Blessed be the fruit!" the company intoned, and Iolande arched an imperious eyebrow at her new daughter-in-law.

"Blessed be the fruit," Alienor managed to say, wondering at the words, and Iolande summoned a smile that did not quite reach her eyes. Sensing someone behind her, Alienor turned slightly, startled to find

the stable hand's bemused gaze upon her as he led
Dagobert to his apparent place at the table.

Iolande bent now and offered the chalice to the
beast, making the same enigmatic blessing as it lapped
at the wine with its startlingly blue tongue. Alienor
barely stifled a grimace and shot a glance at the previously sympathetic stable hand to find his lips twisting in an effort to suppress his mirth, his gray eyes
twinkling at some hidden joke.

"Blessed be the fruit," he repeated along with the
company, and Alienor felt a hot flush steal over her
cheeks, the words curiously intimate when they fell
from his lips.

She opened her mouth to make some retort and
found herself without anything clever to say, closing
her mouth with a snap as she turned and took her seat
at the board in ill humor. A quick glance to her right
confirmed that Dagobert was indeed still ruminating
complacently, and Alienor blinked back silent tears of
frustration at her predicament, lifting her gaze to
study the stonework in the ceiling.

"I thank you, but I will take no meat." Alienor's
soft refusal seemed to draw the attention of everyone
at the head table. A quick glance down the board revealed Guibert looking grim, and Alienor regretted the
impulsive words. To her right, Iolande inhaled
sharply, muttering something unintelligible under her
breath, and Alienor's heart sank to her toes. Truly she
had erred, but the dangerous declaration had left her
lips before she thought.

Too long had she been blessed with the tolerance of
her neighbors and now she would forget herself at the
board of a count undoubtedly pledged to the king's

will. A king pledged to exterminate the Cathars, who were known to spurn the consumption of meat. To spurn meat was to be Cathar; to be Cathar, an enemy of the crown. How could she have been so foolish? The response of the others at the head table left no doubt in Alienor's mind that her religion had been suspected and was not appreciated. Could anything else possibly go wrong this day?

"I have little taste for venison after the day's ride," Alienor clarified, shooting a sharp glance at her new mother-in-law to see her response.

Iolande sniffed with what could have been relief, and Alienor watched the other woman carefully over the goat's head, uncertain whether her fears had truly been dispelled. The look in the older woman's eyes when she turned to Alienor made her heart sink to her toes in anticipation of the worst.

"I would assure you, my *daughter,* that we have a fine cook and I would not wish to insult his abilities," Iolande murmured, a thread of steel underlying her words.

"I truly meant no insult," she responded carefully, "but the day has been long and I have little taste for food."

"Understandable, indeed," Iolande said smoothly, and Alienor realized that she had been given a reprieve, "but you must eat something, my child. Come, the meat is good."

"Venison, milady?" the servant at her elbow encouraged once more, pushing a steaming bowl of stew helpfully toward Alienor's trencher, and she fairly gagged on the smell of the roasted meat. Not for her was this, but while searching for a polite refusal in her mind, she happened to glance up and met the hostile speculation in the green eyes of the knight seated on her left.

Eustache, Alienor recalled his name. Any thought of refusal evaporated as she confronted the accusation she saw in the man's eyes. Alone she would be in this household on the morrow, alone with her new relations and the politics of their hearth. She swallowed slowly and glanced down at the chunks of meat in the stew, bracing herself for what she must do.

"I thank you for your thoughtfulness," she murmured to the servant, helping herself to half a dozen morsels of meat, the dark gravy slipping over her fingertips.

"If I may suggest, milady..." The knight beside her gestured politely to a large and particularly succulent piece of meat, the open challenge in his narrowed eyes leaving Alienor no other option.

"You are indeed too kind, sir," she managed to reply, taking the piece of meat and granting the servant a polite smile, indicating that she wished no more, turning to confront the seven pieces of meat reposing on her crust of bread as if they were the hounds of hell themselves.

"The meat is very fine," the knight at her side prompted, his eyes knowing, and Alienor hated him in that moment with every fiber of her being.

Never had she denied her faith, but she knew she must do it now to ensure her safety in this household, this household allied with the king who had decreed that to be Cathar was to die. Alienor stared at the offending meat and wished she could rely upon herself to swallow it and not make a spectacle of herself here in front of the entire company.

Trying not to show her hesitation, she picked up a piece with her fingertips and popped it into her mouth, willing herself to chew in a normal manner, all the time aware of the older knight's and Iolande's watchful scrutiny. When Alienor swallowed without incident, she was so pleased with herself that she granted the knight an unexpected and perfectly cheerful smile.

"'Tis indeed wondrously well prepared," she agreed wholeheartedly, taking another piece and repeating the gesture, pleased to see some measure of surprise settle in his eyes. Her stomach rolled threateningly and she knew that she could not eat a third piece of meat so easily, but the knight seemed reassured by her consumption of the stew so far.

Evidently thinking himself unobserved, Eustache flicked a meaningful glance across the room and she followed the gesture covertly, certain that she had misunderstood when Dagobert's goatherd, leaning against the far fireplace, nodded as if in acknowledgment. Alienor frowned to herself, wondering why the knight would seek to communicate with the stable hand, sneaking a glance to her left from beneath her lashes to find him calmly consuming his meal as if nothing untoward had happened.

Truly she saw meaning where there was none, she reasoned, feeling a gentle nudge against her knee. A peek beneath the table revealed the large dog who had accompanied Iolande in the courtyard, or one much like him, his tail thumping genially when Alienor rubbed his nose. He licked the gravy from her fingertips enthusiastically and she smiled to herself, knowing how she would make the remainder of her meat disappear.

Chapter Two

The candles were burning low when the women escorted Alienor to the nuptial chamber, their confidential giggles doing little to ease her growing fear of what the night would bring. Somehow she had managed to retain her composure throughout the seemingly endless meal, holding her chin high and slipping her dinner carefully to the great dog sitting on her feet, barely sparing a glance for the goat tethered at her side. A vegetarian that creature seemed to be, as well, for it had no taste for the meat, preferring instead the flowers arranged upon the board, and Alienor was appalled to feel a curious kinship growing between herself and the beast.

Too soon she sat with drawn-up knees on the green brocade coverlet spread on the wide bed, hands clenched in her lap, the bed curtains drawn back and tied to the bedposts. The women fussed over her sheer nightgown, a nightgown she and her thoughtful neighbor had stitched carefully in anticipation of a man's pleasure, that recollection making Alienor reflect on the irony of it all. The women remarked on the luster of her hair as the braids were unfastened and the lengthy tresses brushed out, but Alienor was deaf to their comments, blind to the splendor of the room around her, her heart fluttering in fear of what lay ahead.

A light tap and the goatherd himself opened the door, leading the shaggy white unicorn, his quick glance to the bed reminding Alienor what had passed between them earlier. One of the women scolded him outright for entering the chamber unannounced, and Alienor looked quickly away, painfully aware of how little her garment concealed and imagining that she could feel the heat of his gaze upon her, the warmth of that finger beneath her chin once more.

She blinked back her tears bravely as the entire party departed, refusing to meet the eyes of any one of them, closing her mind to idle speculation, nodding dumbly in response to their encouraging words. The door closed with finality, leaving her alone with her husband.

Alienor regarded the beast with distrust, her frazzled nerves slowly settling as she watched it methodically chew its cud, apparently completely disinterested in her presence now that she had discarded the red velvet kirtle it had found so tempting. The fire crackled in the grate, the light of the dancing flames glinting off the rings dangling against the creature's chest, the golden circles half obscured in the thick hair.

Her tension easing as the creature remained oblivious to her, Alienor sighed and rose to turn the lock in the door, returning to stretch out full length on her stomach on the bed, propping her chin in her hands as she studied her husband, pursing her lips thoughtfully.

Perhaps an annulment would be hers after all. And what then?

Dagobert. He was not very tall, for her hand could have just barely brushed the top of his head when they had stood alongside today, had she wished to reach out and touch him. Thick white hair hung from his sides and chest, thinning and shortening on his squat legs, dwindling to a fuzziness above his black hooves. The hair hung heavy on his neck, making almost a mane in the back, progressing into a definite beard below his relentlessly ruminating chin.

His ears flicked now as he looked back at her in apparent thoughtfulness, moving not unlike those of a horse, his tail swishing despondently behind him. A single pearly horn rose from his forehead to a height roughly the span of her outstretched fingers, though it seemed slightly closer to his left ear than his right now that she studied his features more carefully.

'Twas his eyes that disturbed her the most, she realized, the yellow orbs with their dark vertical slit unspeakably inhuman, their otherworldly gaze sending a shiver down her spine and making his reputed nightly transition impossible to believe. She flicked a glance to the darkness pressing against the shutters, concluding that Dagobert's metamorphosis must not be tied to the rising and setting of the sun as one might expect, if indeed the count was a shape-shifter, as they had seemed to expect her to believe. She folded her arms before her and dropped her chin to rest on them, feeling the exhaustion seeping through her bones, resolving to watch for his change just before she fell asleep.

The room was dark as pitch when Alienor awoke groggily, sensing the presence of another even as she slept. She started to rise to rekindle the fire but a man's arm closed surely around her waist, halting her progress as he pulled her back into the warmth of the bed.

Who invaded her chamber?

Alienor struggled as firm lips closed over hers, swallowing her attempt to scream before it started, that strong arm pinning her arms effortlessly to her sides. She panicked and writhed within the man's embrace, thinking someone came to take advantage of her situation, but the man merely rolled her effortlessly beneath him, guiding her fingers unceremoniously to the cord encircling his neck and the rings that dangled from it.

The ring, the cord, the unicorn, her husband.

"Dagobert," she breathed in surprise, all the fight dissipating from her as she tried to discern his features in the darkness to no avail. It was true, it had happened, he had truly changed from beast to man, as incredible as it seemed.

"Alienor," he whispered in response, his voice as deep and resonant as a caress, his callused fingertips sliding exploratively over her face, his thumb caressing the full curve of her lips.

Alienor closed her eyes at the tenderness of his touch, a grateful teardrop squeezing out of the corner of one eye. 'Twas true, she knew not how or why and cared nothing for the explanation right now, the masculine scent that filled her nostrils setting her nerves atingle.

She felt him bend toward her and parted her lips, sighing with satisfaction when that firm mouth closed possessively over hers again. Strong hands slipped over the length of her, broad palms cupping her breasts, the edge of a thumb drawing a gasp from her as it slid over her nipple. Emboldened by the darkness, Alienor reached up, running her hands over the smooth warmth of her husband's broad shoulders, discovering the corded strength of his neck, her fingers tangling in the thickness of the mane of hair hanging long down his back.

He was nude, she marveled as she ran her hands over the warm satin of his skin, almost purring beneath the surety of his touch, her heart singing at the realization that he was strong and tall, her toe stretching down and barely caressing his ankle. His knee slipped between hers and he rolled to his side, gathering her up against him without breaking his languorous kiss, his tongue nudging at her teeth as his fingertips nibbled at the softness between her thighs.

Alienor shuddered when he unexpectedly found the sweet spot beneath her nest of curls, his arm tightening fiercely around her waist, his lips falling to taste her jawline and tease her earlobe as he caressed with slow, sure strokes. His hair fell across her face and Alienor breathed in the clean scent of wind and sun and masculinity. His questing lips eased aside the sheer confection of her gown, finding her turgid nipple, and she arched instinctively to his touch, his embracing arm moving immediately to support her, those long fingers curving possessively around her buttocks.

Alienor moaned as the storm gathered within her, her hand sliding through the wiry curls on his chest and across the taut strength of his abdomen, closing experimentally around the hardened thickness of his manhood. Dagobert gasped against her breast and she parted her thighs even wider, wanting to feel his strength within her, wanting his possession to be complete.

Needing no other invitation, he lifted his weight between her thighs, pulling the skirt of her sheer chemise carefully out of his way. Alienor heard the husky rasp of his breathing in the darkness as he fought for control and trembled involuntarily, suddenly fearing the pain that would accompany their union. Dagobert murmured something low and reassuring against her throat, then his hands were on her again, the warmth of his touch easing her trepidation as no words could.

He cupped the back of her neck, bracing himself on one elbow as he lowered himself atop her, his lips tasting her eyelids, her nose, her cheek, her lips in an endless caress. The slight weight of his rings fell against her breast and Alienor closed her eyes at their smooth warmth. His other hand returned to stroke her softness, one finger sliding within her as his thumb teased her hidden pearl. Alienor raised her hips to accommodate his exploring finger and he kissed her leisurely, the intoxicating taste of his tongue diverting her attention as his manhood replaced his finger at her portal.

She gasped when she first realized his bulk and he paused, kissing, caressing, relaxing her as he made easy, incremental progress. When his length was buried within her, Alienor shivered with relief, wrapping her legs around his waist and her arms around his neck in complete surrender. Overwhelmed by sensation, she pressed her lips to his throat.

Dagobert shuddered from head to toe at her submission and held her close, his teasing fingers managing somehow to caress her yet again while he pressed kisses into her ear and along her length. Alienor felt the heat gather in her veins and arched against his weight, tightening her grip on him as if she would meld their very flesh together, the encroaching wave setting her writhing beneath him. Dagobert groaned and she felt the tension grow in him, his arm like a vise around her, his hand gripping a fistful of her hair as he moved within her with deft deliberation.

Suddenly, the universe exploded into a thousand stars, the blood rushing hotly through her veins, and Alienor cried out her husband's name as he thrust emphatically now, his strong hands clasping her buttocks as he rose above her. A shadow against the shadows he was as he stiffened, lifting her bodily from the bed as he spilled his seed within her, a roar erupting from his throat at his release.

Alienor awoke with a satisfied smile teasing her lips, rolling over and reaching across bed linens redolent with the scent of lovemaking for her husband's form. Finding the straw-filled mattress cold and empty beside her brought her eyes open with a shock.

She sat up abruptly and stared around the room, squinting against the brightness of the morning sunlight, momentarily disconcerted to find the white unicorn standing before the barren hearth.

But of course, she chided herself. Was it not fully morning? The golden rings that had brushed against her skin so many times the night before hung from the beast's neck as they had the night before, a quick glance confirming that the door remained as securely latched as she had left it.

Could she truly have dreamed her husband's relentless and tender lovemaking? A flush rose over her cheeks in recollection of the things they had done, the pleasure she had felt beneath her husband's hands, and she shook her head in mute denial.

She certainly felt as though she had barely slept, Alienor acknowledged, lifting the weight of her dark hair away from her face, noting her nakedness, the sheer wisp of her gown draped over the end of the bed. She frowned to herself, remembering well how Dagobert had removed the garment before he had made leisurely love to her the second time, the dull ache between her thighs evidence of the persistence of his passion throughout the night.

Her perplexed gaze fell to the sheets, the incriminating bloodstain on the snowy linen summarily dismissing any remaining doubts.

Unwillingly, Alienor turned to regard the unicorn, the beast returning her speculative look unflinchingly as it calmly and methodically chewed its cud.

Had he truly changed form in the night? And reverted back to this goatlike form with the morn? Too whimsical was that tale to be believed and she regarded the unicorn thoughtfully, as though she would will it to confide in her the truth.

Mayhap the tale was true. Or mayhap Dagobert had secrets to hide from prying eyes. Well enough could she understand that for she, as a Cathar, had some secrets of her own. She rose from the bed and bent to scratch the docile creature's ears, surprised at the softness of the white fur.

And truly what need had she to know his secrets? She had the security of hearth and home and well enough was Alienor used to being practical about accepting what was her due. Lucky she was that her spouse desired her, despite her common status and she would not so readily cast aside her fortune. Should

Dagobert respect her privacy, 'twas only fair that she respect his.

She smothered a satisfied smile as she shivered in the morning chill and wrapped her arms about herself. And should her spouse insist on loving her with such breathtaking thoroughness, Alienor decided that she might well make a concession to the rigors of her faith and bear him a child to assure his line.

"Fool!"

Dagobert spun on his heel at the indignant cry, his eyes narrowing speculatively when he met Eustache's derisive sneer.

"Did I not warn you that naught of merit would come of this whimsy?" Eustache demanded sharply, and Dagobert spared a quick glance around the deserted stables to confirm that they were alone before he spoke.

"What is this nonsense you speak?" he shot back, deliberately keeping his voice low. "And what recklessness prompts you to address me now?" he added, jerking his head toward the golden rays of the morning sun spreading across the stable floor from the courtyard. Eustache had the grace to look momentarily sheepish, but Dagobert saw that he would not be easily deterred from his argument.

"Are you truly not angered with the woman's folly?" the older knight demanded in an angry undertone, and Dagobert shrugged in response.

"Tell me and be done with it," he insisted, running one hand tiredly through his hair. Eustache's eyes narrowed to dangerous slits of jade at his friend's gesture and Dagobert wished the man were less perceptive.

"Aye, one night of bedding the wench and already you cannot see the danger she poses," Eustache observed with a snort of disgust and a shake of his head. "In truth, I had expected better of you."

Dagobert couldn't stop the impulsive thought that he could hardly have expected better of his new wife and fought the smile of tender reminiscence that struggled to curve his lips.

"Tell me what disturbs you, Eustache," he offered again, relieved when his old friend spared a smile. "I vow the woman will not make me soft," he added humorously, only to see that vestige of warmth leave Eustache's features.

"Soft would be naught compared to dead," Eustache shot back, and Dagobert's brows rose in surprise. "Surely you did not fail to note that she refused the meat last night?" he countered at his lord's apparent lack of understanding.

"Aye, she did," Dagobert acknowledged. "What of it? Even if she is Cathar, she would not be the first such in this household."

"Hardly," Eustache snorted, "but rotten luck 'tis, and that you cannot deny."

Dagobert dropped heavily to sit on a bale of straw, frowning at the stone floor as he considered the implications should Alienor prove to be Cathar. Eustache was right, he acknowledged to himself, surprised that he had not seen the full import of the situation earlier.

"Indeed you may speak the truth, my friend. This match could be construed as an alliance of the house of Pereille with the Cathar sect." He scowled briefly before lifting troubled eyes to his companion. "Perhaps we read too much into naught, for she did finally take the meat.''

"Mine were not the only eyes to see her feed it to one of Iolande's beasts," Eustache scoffed, dropping to sit beside the younger man, glancing up when Dagobert chuckled unwillingly.

"Verily she did?" he asked, and Eustache nodded ruefully. "Perhaps she is more clever than you would give her credit, my friend," he added good-naturedly, earning a sour glance from the knight.

"But one night in her bed and your brains are addled," Eustache muttered. "Truly this does not bode well for the future."

"Ah, Eustache, always do you see trouble lurking in every shadow," Dagobert replied dismissively, rising to his feet and brushing off his chausses, pausing to stretch and yawn luxuriously.

Indeed he doubted that anything could ruin his spirits this morning. Alienor's religion was but a suspicion, one that he could easily dismiss after the exhausting night they had spent together. Did not the Cathars take a vow of chastity? Clearly that trait was not among his willing wife's innocent charms. He glanced at his companion to find him no more appeased than before and smothered a smile, certain that news of Alienor's sweet loving would do little to improve the other man's humor.

"Aye, ogres at every turn," Eustache agreed dryly. "Crusading season but two months away, the king's troops fairly knocking at our door and his spies dining at our board. Pope and king persisting in a Crusade purportedly against the Cathars, which we both know to be a hunt for your sorry hide. Truly I overreact."

"Spies?" Dagobert demanded sharply, his attention captured by the apparently casual comment. This was much more serious than he had thought. Rumors in his own home or among his own people were one thing, rumors in the king's court quite another. Eustache studied him for a moment, then nodded sagely, rising more slowly to his feet.

"Perhaps you have not completely forgotten your responsibilities, after all," he observed under his breath. "There were those at the board last eve who I have seen in close company with the king at Fontainebleau." Eustache shot Dagobert an appraising look. "Interesting 'twas to see them dressed as troubadours, not the nobles I know them to be."

"Certain you are?" Dagobert challenged, a chill settling around his heart at Eustache's affirming nod. "Spies at my own hearth," he mused almost to himself. So it had come to this. How much did the king suspect? Well enough did he know that the king had no qualms of conscience in using the threat of the Cathar heresy as an excuse to hunt his family, and that put new light on Alienor's slip.

The tale of his new bride's refusal of meat would be certain to travel now and he could not even speculate what rumors it would prompt. Surely one simple gesture could not manage to send all their plans into disarray, but Dagobert knew better. The road was long to Paris and who knew how convoluted the tale would become before it reached the court.

And there was so much at stake. Should suspicions of Alienor reach the king's ears, no longer would the verbal assurance that his house agreed with the king's Crusade against the Cathars be enough. His participation in the attack on his friends and neighbors would assuredly need to be enthusiastic, for the king would welcome any excuse to attack Montsalvat itself. Only thirty years it had been since the crown had last declared the Pereille lands forfeit, ironically enough as penance for the flat refusal of Dagobert's father, Alzeu, to join the Crusade, and the regaining of Dagobert's rightful legacy had been arduous, indeed.

The merest whisper of acceptance of Cathars in the house of Pereille at court would send Crusaders and papal legates swooping down on Montsalvat come summer, intent on repossessing the lands. And what disastrous timing! Just as years of planning were finally moving into place with such precision.

"Quietly ensure that the curtain walls are in good repair," Dagobert insisted softly, "and keep a close monitoring of those who demand accommodation."

"I have already sent a few trusted men into the villages," Eustache added with a confirming nod, and Dagobert sighed, hoping against hope that this summer would not shape up to be worse than he had already anticipated it would be.

"Let me know the moment we receive word from Anjou and Brabant. We cannot take the risk of sending envoys," Dagobert added, and Eustache nodded, ducking out of the stables and into the morning sun.

Dagobert remained behind, tipping back his head as he recalled the image of his new wife's features soft in sleep when he left her this morning, regretting with all his heart that she had to be thrown into the midst of all this trouble.

A tap on the door sent Alienor scrambling out of bed for something to cover her nakedness and she

tugged her chemise over her head before she turned the
key in the heavy door. Iolande stood in the hallway, as
icily aloof as the previous day, her bemused gaze
sweeping over Alienor's disheveled state as she curtsied.

"I trust all was well last night," the older woman
commented, flicking a disparaging glance to the beast
at the hearth before she stepped smoothly into the
room. Her obedient hound dropped to its haunches in
the doorway, awaiting its lady's command.

"Indeed...indeed yes, milady," Alienor stam-
mered, feeling every inch an idiot before this woman's disconcerting perfection. To her further
discomfort, there was a positive gaggle of women behind her new mother-in-law, jostling and joking, their
faces wreathed in expectant smiles as they awaited the
sheets. Alienor swallowed convulsively at the knowing smirk that would surely curve the short priest's lips
at the evidence of her broken maidenhead and hoped
she would not have to face him this day.

"Dagobert always sought to do his rightful duty,"
Iolande murmured ironically as she stared down at the
stained sheets, and Alienor flushed, folding her hands
before her nervously. With one elegant gesture,
Iolande flicked the linens from the bed, tossing the
evidence of the consummation of the match to the excited women, her startling blue gaze fixing discon-
certingly on Alienor.

"It seems that you will not receive your annulment," she said softly, and Alienor flushed scarlet. So
the priest had told of her request.

"I meant no offense, milady," she offered with
quiet boldness. "You must understand that the situation was most irregular."

"Indeed." The single word seemed to hold a wealth of meaning when it fell from Iolande's lips, and Alienor waited, knowing instinctively that her mother-in-law was not done.

"I would that you not hinder your natural processes," Iolande murmured finally, her voice so low that no other could hear. Alienor's eyes flew to meet those knowing blue eyes in surprise. Surely Iolande could not be so certain that she was Cathar, Alienor told herself, the older woman's next words dispelling all doubt.

"I would not have my husband's line without one male heir," Iolande added, and Alienor managed to nod once.

Only the Cathars held procreation as a sin, but Guibert had warned her that she would be expected to bear her new lord sons. 'Twas the way of things, her duty to Dagobert, and she had delayed taking her final vows when she had learned of her pending nuptials.

"I was told 'twould be thus," she confirmed quietly, and one blond brow rose a fraction in apparent surprise. Alienor met her mother-in-law's gaze steadily, hoping her nervousness at being so easily discovered did not show. "I will not shirk my duties to my husband's house."

Their gazes held silently for a moment, then Iolande turned abruptly to the women still chattering outside the door.

With an imperious snap of her fingers, she summoned a young dark-haired girl from the group clustered outside the door. She was not much younger than Alienor and her brown eyes flashed with barely suppressed merriment, her expression prompting Alienor's welcoming smile.

"Giselle will see to your needs from this day forward," Iolande said simply, imbuing the words with a formality Alienor could not have suspected was possible.

"I thank you for your generosity, milady," she murmured, surprised to see something in those blue eyes soften, like snow melting before the spring sun, and she wondered fleetingly what Iolande would say. One of the women laughed in the hall, drawing the older woman's startled gaze, and abruptly, as if she recalled her place, Iolande turned away.

"We await you at the board to break our fast." She tossed the words over her shoulder in a voice devoid of inflection as she strode from the room, the women in the hall instinctively scattering from her path. Before Alienor could speculate on what her mother-in-law might have said, she glanced up to see Giselle's excited expression, mere eye contact loosening the girl's tightly checked tongue.

"Oh, milady, I know we shouldn't gossip, but everyone is talking about the wedding and the old servants say that Dagobert was the finest man you ever saw before he took this curse, and you must tell me, you simply *must*, was he absolutely *everything* you ever dreamed of?" Giselle demanded without taking a single breath, her eyes shining in expectation while she waited for her lady's response.

Alienor parted her lips to answer, her gaze unwillingly drawn to the unicorn before the hearth to find its knowing yellow eyes upon her. Was it only her fancy that the creature seemed to smirk in anticipation of her words?

* * *

Dagobert watched from the far side of the hall as Alienor descended the wide stone stairs to the great room, the unicorn's silken cord twined around her slim fingers. The saffron-colored pelisson his wife wore highlighted her tawny coloring and Dagobert felt a surge of pride that she was his, that she was tall and finely wrought, as gracious in manner as a princess. All stood in the hall before the cursed form of their lord and his new bride, and Alienor dropped her gaze modestly, the very gesture sending Dagobert's heart surging.

Perhaps Eustache spoke the truth and he was indeed bewitched after a mere night in this lovely creature's bed. Indeed, 'twould be his pleasure to fulfill his mother's desire for grandchildren. Smothering a smile at the thought, he stepped forward to take the unicorn's tether from Alienor as was his duty.

The company stood immediately at her appearance and Alienor found it slightly disconcerting to be the center of attention in such a large gathering. She scolded herself inwardly as she concentrated on the steps. She would simply have to get used to such courtlike pomp and splendor, as well as be more aware of what she said and did, for nothing would be missed by so many observant eyes.

Feeling the intensity of someone's gaze upon her, Alienor looked up to find the goatherd before her, predictable amusement lingering in the depths of his gray eyes. He smiled at her encouragingly while he reached for Dagobert's tether and she surrendered the silk cord readily, a tingle launching along her flesh when her fingers accidentally brushed the warmth of his. Feeling the color rise over her cheeks, Alienor dropped her gaze and made to step past him, his words bringing her to a stop.

"I pray I did not mislead you," he murmured, and Alienor's eyes flew to his in surprise.

"I beg your pardon," she demanded softly.

"Did I not assure you that you had naught to fear from the night?" he explained patiently, the intensity in his gaze holding her captive as she stared up at him.

"Indeed you did," Alienor answered shakily. What interest did this goatherd have in her conjugal relations? Or was it merely some obsession of these people to constantly discuss such delicate matters?

"And did I mislead you?" he insisted, surprising Alienor anew with his audacity. She would have brushed past him, but something in the sharp focus of his attention tugged at her heart, convincing her that he was sincere in his concern, and she answered, albeit unwillingly.

"Indeed you did not," she confirmed, surprised to see some of the tension ease from his features. As if he were suddenly aware of her surprise at his interest, his lips pulled into a wry grin that made Alienor's heart pick up its pace.

"I would that you were happy, milady," he confirmed by way of explanation, and she could only nod mutely, completely confused by the warm regard that she saw in his eyes. Alienor nodded more crisply to regain her senses and stepped past him to take her place at the table.

"Madame, I must apologize to you for my failure to eat last evening despite the splendor of the meal," Alienor said smoothly to Iolande as she took her place, making sure her voice was loud enough to be heard by others at the board. 'Twas her duty to avoid bringing any difficulties upon her husband's house and she could think of no other way to rectify her foolish error of the night previous. "'Twas nervousness over the nuptials that stole my appetite away and today I mean to do justice to your generosity."

"Glad I am that your health is restored," Iolande returned calmly, her bright blue gaze capturing Alienor's regard for a long moment before she summoned the servers with a regal wave.

Alienor barely suppressed a smile of delight at her victory, a quick glance at Guibert revealing that the set of his shoulders had noticeably relaxed. The gaffe could not be undone, but she certainly had done her best to rectify her error. She glanced sidelong to find the knight Eustache eyeing her speculatively and her heart sank with the realization that not all were convinced.

That thought gave her the strength to load her trencher with a variety of leftovers from the repast of the night before, cold venison, duck, pheasant, boar, an egg soufflé, each and every morsel forbidden for consumption by her faith. Alienor steeled her resolve, feeling the eyes of the company upon her, and thought of her husband's tenderness with her the night before. She owed him this loyalty, she told herself, daring a perky smile to Eustache before bending to the task before her, her stomach rolling in silent mutiny as she lifted the first piece of cold meat to her lips.

An hour later, Alienor was running, the weight of her skirts catching at her knees as she struggled to put distance between herself and the keep before she was ill. A cold wind danced over the curtain walls and snatched away her veil and fillet, her loosened hair cascading down her back, and still she ran, leaping over stones in the high bailey as the north wall grew ever closer. Her shoes crunched in the last vestiges of snow, the chill that reached her as she gained the wall making her shiver from head to toe.

As she had suspected, there was a narrow staircase carved out of the heavy stone, the steps leading to a tiny sentinel post on the wall, a post currently unmanned and perfect for her purposes. Without another thought, Alienor climbed to the post and crouched down to ensure that she was out of sight.

Moments later she looked up and took a deep shaking breath of relief, surprised to see that the land dropped straight down below the sentinel post. Uncompromising outcroppings of rock far below threw dramatic shadows in the winter sun, the wind that swept up against the walls on this side sending its icy fingers up her sleeves and under the hem of her pelisson. Alienor shivered slightly and sat down against the cold stone, taking great gulps of the icy air to regain her composure as a tiny smile began to curve her lips.

She had done it! She had eaten of the meat without embarrassing herself and hoped she had allayed any outstanding doubts that could reflect poorly on her husband's house. She folded her hands over her stomach and breathed with satisfaction that she had made it this far, unable to speculate whether she could ever repeat her feat even to uphold her husband's honor.

The wind lifted her hair, sending the thick waves against her cheeks, and she realized, too late, that her veil and fillet were long gone. With a grimace, she tugged off her wimple and tossed it impatiently aside, her gaze drawn to the craggy peaks of the mountains surrounding the fortress on this side while she savored the moment alone.

A tread sounded on the stairs directly interrupting her thoughts and Alienor almost gasped aloud. Who came here? Did someone follow her, suspecting what she had done? Foolishness, she chided herself. 'Twas probably just a sentry checking this post. Her hands automatically rose to her hair. How scandalous 'twould be for any of her husband's men to see her thus. She looked wildly around the small enclosure, but amazingly no veil awaited her in the sentry tower.

Alienor bit her lip and scooped up her wimple, managing to drape it around her throat before a man's figure appeared in the narrow opening, his head and shoulders silhouetted against the sun so that she could not distinguish his features. He paused as if surprised to find her there, sitting on the floor no less, and Alienor's heart stopped in her throat.

"I thought 'twas yours," the goatherd commented, and a wave of relief washed over Alienor.

"'Tis only you," she said before she could check the words, and he chuckled as he ducked into the tiny room.

"Aye, 'tis only me." He held out Alienor's discarded veil and fillet, and she fell on them gratefully.

"I would thank you," she murmured breathlessly under his regard, uncomfortably aware of his gaze drifting over her disheveled state as she attempted to put herself to rights. He crouched against the opposite wall, still watching her intently, and Alienor was uncomfortably aware of how tiny the sentry post actually was.

"'Twas rolling across the bailey," he told her, making a circular motion with his finger when Alienor looked up and caught his grin.

"Rolling?" she asked skeptically, and he laughed.

"Aye, a fillet so stiff as that could fairly turn a broadsword aside." He laughed and Alienor laughed along with him, experimentally tapping the hard linen circle that held her veil in place before putting it back on her head.

"I should hope to never put it to such a test," she jested, but his gray eyes sobered at her words. He turned and looked pensively to the mountains stretching toward the sky, his lips thinning slightly before he spoke.

"Why came you here?" he asked, but Alienor shook her head silently, unwilling to answer him, fussing with her headdress in the hope that he would abandon his question. As the silence grew between them and she could do nothing further to adjust her veil, he turned and met her eyes again, compelling her to speak. Certain that he would not abandon the subject, Alienor took a deep breath and tried to lie.

"'Twas merely a short walk I took," she began, and made to rise, but he blocked the exit easily by raising his arm. Alienor met his eyes tentatively and he shook his head. Too close was he now, this intriguing man whose gray eyes sparkled and whose words coaxed her laughter, and Alienor's heart accelerated, her nostrils picking up the scent of wind, sun and honest labor from his tanned skin.

"I would have the truth, milady," he insisted softly, and she was hard-pressed to deny the determination in his eyes.

"By what right do you question me?" she demanded more sharply than she intended, and his eyes narrowed briefly at her tone before he glanced away.

"Should I find your meal on the rocks below if I but looked, milady?" he asked quietly, his words such a surprise to Alienor that she gasped before she could stop herself. His gaze swiveled to hers again but she lowered her eyes, frustration welling up inside of her. Had it been so obvious that she had put on a facade this morning?

"Well you know that you would," she admitted, sinking into a dejected heap against the wall.

"Are you Cathar?" The question came quietly, the words shocking Alienor even though she had expected them.

"How dare you ask me this?" she demanded, hoping against hope that he had seen no glimmer of her fear. Before she could continue, he held up one hand for her silence and Alienor was surprised to find herself obeying him. Such presence the man had for a mere goatherd, and she found herself too aware of him as he crouched before her.

"I would not betray you," he insisted in that low voice she was growing used to, and Alienor fought against her instinctive urge to trust him. "Sworn am I to the protection of this house, and I would know if there is any potential threat to my lord." 'Twas a reasonable request and well she knew it. Tears rose unbidden to Alienor's eyes and she shook her head helplessly.

"I would not bring disgrace to his house," she insisted, tangling her fingers together nervously. "Too good indeed has he been to me for such ingratitude," she added, flushing at the unwitting implication of her words. "'Twas a foolish mistake I made last evening and I would that I could undo the deed," she concluded in a rush, jumping with surprise when the goatherd's warm hand closed over her trembling fingers.

"In truth, your performance this morn has fair undone the damage," he assured her quietly, and Alienor's eyes flew to his, relief settling over her when she saw the sincerity in those gray depths.

"Verily?"

"I believe I alone observed your hasty departure," he assured her, and Alienor took a deep breath to steady herself anew. And why had he noticed? an errant voice prompted in her mind, but she shoved away the thought.

"I know not your name," she confessed, and he squeezed her hand gently before lifting the warmth of his palm away.

"Alaric."

"No more than that?" Alienor asked, and he grinned that mischievous grin that her heart responded to so instinctively.

"'Tis all." He rose to his feet and extended one hand to her. "Come, before you are missed." Alienor nodded and accepted his help to rise to her feet, brushing her pelisson with deliberation as she realized how much she had revealed to this goatherd. Alaric.

As if he understood the reason for her sudden hesitation, he touched one fingertip beneath her chin, tipping her face so that their eyes met once more.

"Your secret is safe with me, milady," he assured her, and Alienor believed him. "Soon the guests will leave and you will be able to eat however you desire."

"Truly?" she asked in surprise, and he smiled crookedly.

"There are others here," he said quietly, and Alienor's heart leapt. Others of her creed here? Was Alaric himself Cathar?

Before she could summon the nerve to ask, he ushered her toward the portal and she had no choice but to descend the narrow stairs. The unicorn waited placidly at the foot of the stairs, busily devouring some early growth.

"Yes, milord?" Alaric bent and scooped up the unicorn's cord, dropping to one knee with an inquisitive expression as though the beast actually spoke to him. "Indeed?" he asked of the creature with apparent surprise, and Alienor almost laughed aloud.

"Certainly I will ask the lady of her desire." Alaric looked up at her with a twinkle in his eye and Alienor could not restrain herself from smiling back at him. "Milord Dagobert suggests that he and I give you a tour of Montsalvat. Time it is, he says, that you learn about your home."

"And a fine idea 'tis," Alienor agreed, not fooled by Alaric's charade for a moment but curiously unwilling to lose his friendly companionship. Alaric grinned, then bent back down to the unicorn with a frown of concentration, holding up one finger for Alienor's silence while he nodded thoughtfully.

"As you wish, milord," he said to the creature, flicking a glance to Alienor. "Dagobert suggests we visit the kitchens first, in deference to his lady's needs," Alaric told her mischievously, and Alienor fairly laughed aloud, wanting to swat him for teasing her so.

"A fine thought," she retorted playfully as she darted ahead of him and gathered the fullness of her pelisson in her hands, "and I shall race you there!"

Alienor stretched luxuriously back against the clean bed linens, her hair brushed out and strewn across the pillows, her muscles tired and relaxed from the hot bath Giselle had brought her this night. Too luxurious indeed was this life, she marveled, smelling the sandalwood soap on her skin. Dagobert chewed complacently before the fire burning merrily in the grate and she watched him through her lashes.

She noted the falling darkness and felt a tremor of excitement despite the languor stealing over her body. So many questions she had for her husband, so much to tell him, so much to give him. Tonight she would stay awake to see this shape-shifting, Alienor told herself firmly, her eyelids growing impossibly heavier despite her resolution.

Alienor awoke to teasing kisses against her lips, recognizing immediately the musky scent of her husband's skin. The fire had burned low and the room was dark as it had been the night before. She reached up to Dagobert and felt him smile against her lips, the solidity of his rings falling against her breast as she moved into his embrace. His hand slid up her back to grasp a fistful of hair at her nape, his other hand cupping her breast as he deepened his kiss, and Alienor trembled against him.

"No pain will there be," he murmured against her ear, and she shivered at his breath there, already knowing that she had naught to fear this night.

"'Tis not fear but anticipation," she confessed softly, grateful that the darkness hid her flush when he chuckled under his breath.

"Would that I please you, milady," he growled, nipping at her earlobe and making her giggle before his fingers dived between her legs. Alienor gasped at the sure intimacy of his touch, reaching to stroke the planes of his face, to know him even better.

To her disappointment, he pulled his hand out from beneath her and trapped both of her wrists in his grip, her dissatisfaction fading as he stretched her out across the mattress and caressed her sensitive pearl. Alienor writhed as she began to tingle all over and arched toward the shadow that loomed over her in the darkness, fancying she could see the glitter of his eyes in the night.

"Dagobert," she murmured sleepily some hours later, and he tucked her even tighter against his side, his long fingers fanning out around her shoulder. Fighting her exhaustion, Alienor struggled to one elbow, her tangled hair falling over her bare shoulders and against her husband's chest as his hand slipped to the indent of her waist.

"I would talk to you," she protested when he would have pulled her back down beside him, and he stilled immediately, Alienor feeling the weight of his gaze upon her in the darkness. "So many questions have I," she confessed softly, wishing he would speak, surprised when the pad of his thumb pressed against her lips and silenced her words.

"Hush," he insisted, his thumb moving slowly across the softness of her lips in an intoxicating rhythm.

"I know not whom to trust in your house," she managed to whisper before her response to his touch overwhelmed all else, not knowing why those words should rise to her lips before all others.

"Trust those I trust," he murmured against her lips before his mouth closed over hers possessively. She reached for his shoulders, savoring his strength, tangling her fingers in his hair, filling her nostrils with his scent. Dagobert groaned, his thumb and forefinger closing around her nipple as she opened her mouth to welcome his tongue. Alienor sighed in capitulation, the battle against sensation already lost, and he rolled her beneath him yet again.

Chapter Three

"I would take my leave this day should you be settled here," Guibert said to Alienor as they broke their fast together the next morning.

Alaric had spoken the truth and many of the guests had left the previous day, the fortress apparently returning to its usual routine and the morning meal becoming a fairly casual affair. There was leftover stew for those who desired it, but Alienor was relieved to note that most took only bread and cheese, as was her usual fare.

Guibert had beckoned her to join him in a quiet corner when she entered the hall and she had expected this news. Never could he rest long in one place and she smiled at him affectionately.

"Too long at one hearth?" she teased, relieved to see him smile in return instead of looking so solemn.

"Indeed," he answered restlessly, making her remember that he liked to be on his way with the first rays of the sun. If only she had known he was chafing to go, she would not have taken so long with her toilette this morn.

"Back to Perpignan, is it then?" she asked, surprised when Guibert shook his head with determination.

"Nay, child. Naught is in Perpignan for me these days," he insisted gruffly.

"The house?" Alienor asked in surprise, but Guibert shook his head again.

"'Tis sold," he reported. "I would not return to a cold hearth there. 'Tis to Montsalvat I will turn now." Alienor hugged her foster father impulsively, her eyes glazing with tears, knowing what it cost him to speak of his emotions.

"And welcome here you will always be," she assured him, earning a sidelong smile from the older man that seemed almost sly.

"I should hope so," he declared emphatically. "My blade is sworn now to your lord's service."

"Guibert!" Alienor felt her mouth drop open in surprise. "Naught did you say of this to me." Guibert colored slightly under his tan and shot her a sheepish look.

"A fine man he is, straight and true. I would see his cause win the day," he concluded enigmatically, and Alienor frowned in confusion. What cause? Before she could ask anything further, Guibert shot her a sharp look from beneath his brows and rose suddenly to his feet, seemingly having sensed that he had said too much.

"Already the sun rides high," he protested when Alienor gripped his arm and would have held him for another moment by her side. "Be happy, child. 'Twill be soon enough that our paths cross again."

"Be safe, Guibert," she responded, as had always been their fashion. Never had either uttered a farewell to the other, and so it would continue. Alienor pecked the man she had known as a father against his weathered cheek, blinking rapidly to stay her tears while he strode from the hall.

Never had he tolerated tears on his departure, and by tacit agreement, never did she actually witness his riding out. 'Twill be soon enough, she repeated to herself, cherishing the familiarity of the words. How many times had he taken his parting thus?

"'Twas my mistake that we missed the gardens yesterday," came an increasingly familiar voice from her side, and Alienor glanced up through her tears to find Alaric beside her, sympathy in his gray eyes. "He shall return soon enough," he assured her quietly, his words an unconscious echo of Guibert's own.

Alienor nodded in agreement, realizing that she was now well and truly alone in her husband's home. Suddenly needing some sort of reassurance, she reached out and patted the small shaggy beast standing beside Alaric, wishing her husband was not lost to her by day.

Trust those I trust. Dagobert's words echoed in her mind again and she glanced up to find Alaric's steady gaze upon her. This man Dagobert entrusted with the unicorn's care and safety each day, surely there could be no greater trust than this. With an effort, Alienor banished her tears and summoned a smile, rising to her feet to face the goatherd.

"I would like very much to see the gardens," she confessed, and he grinned, urging the unicorn forward and ushering Alienor toward the door.

"Careful we shall have to be, for Dagobert shows little discretion once he is amongst the herbs and flowers," Alaric confided with that troublemaking twinkle in his eyes that she had grown to distrust. "My hide would be forfeit if he became ill and was compelled to abandon your bed for even one night."

His words sent a scarlet flush rising over Alienor's cheeks and she quickly stepped ahead of him that he might not witness her embarrassment, his knowing chuckle doing little to dispel her discomfort. Why were these people so intent on discussing such private matters?

"Worse than a rutting goat you are," Eustache grumbled under his breath as he and Dagobert climbed the stairs together to the lord's chamber. The keep was quiet, the hour late, and the sound of snoring rose from the hall below as Eustache's torch cast a flickering light over the stone.

"'Tis jealous you are and no more than that," Dagobert retorted, unwilling to let his friend's sour mood affect him. Truth indeed there was in the assertion that he was more and more anxious to seek his lady's bed after but two nights, her willing response to his touch and her warm companionship each day together weaving a web around his heart that was proving difficult to deny. Blessed he was indeed to draw such a wife by pure chance and well he knew it.

"'Tis undoubtedly these nights in the company of a chewing goat that improve my humor," Eustache observed, and Dagobert threw him a crooked grin.

"All for the greater good, I assure you," he joked, and Eustache looked skeptical.

"Would that you got the woman with child that we might get back to more pressing matters," he muttered. Dagobert smothered a chuckle, knowing that if Alienor were to conceive, he would be the last to tell the household lest he be compelled to abandon her bed.

"Have you heard tell of Brabant?" he asked, forcing his mind to return to more practical matters as they reached the top of the stairs, his heart sinking when Eustache shook his head firmly. Could something have gone amiss in their carefully laid plan?

"Nay, but he has yet a fortnight to confirm," Eustache conceded. "Unlike him 'tis indeed to wait until the last moment but perhaps 'twas unavoidable."

Dagobert nodded in agreement, frowning slightly as he opened the antechamber door and pulled a heavy brass key from his pocket. He heard Eustache close the door to the hall behind him, enclosing the two of them in the small outer room of the lord's chambers before slipping his torch into an iron sconce on the wall.

Dagobert fitted his key easily into the lock on the inner door and the tumblers rolled with a barely detectable sound, the door swinging open on carefully oiled hinges. He breathed a sigh of relief when he saw that Alienor did not stir. His namesake looked up from the hearth with interest and, apparently having seen the way of this nightly event, strolled toward the door with a wag of its short tail, evidently anticipating the treat Eustache always brought it.

While the goat chewed deliberately on some nicety from the kitchens, Dagobert removed the cord with his wedding ring and signet ring from around the beast's neck and slipped it over his own head, nodding to Eustache before he stepped into his chamber and closed the door, his heart pounding in anticipation.

Alienor. She rolled sleepily to her side, as yet unaware of his presence, and Dagobert watched the firelight play over her features for a moment. How he wished that he could love her in the light, that he could watch the pleasure wash over those amber eyes instead of merely hearing her gasp of surprise. Her arm fell to the mattress in her sleep, her fingers extended toward him as though she would beckon him to bed, and his breath quickened, even as he knew she slept soundly.

His heart wrenched and he wondered how long this game could continue. How long until Alienor suspected that the cup Iolande offered her each night contained more than wine? How long until a trusted member of the household slipped and revealed his true identity? He fidgeted uncomfortably at the thought, the time that he had spent in his wife's company convincing him that she was no fool in her own right.

How long until she guessed his dual identity herself? Already he thought he had seen speculation in her eyes, and her attempts to touch his face the previous night had surprised him. How long could he curtail her curiosity? Should he fall asleep when Alienor did not, she would surely find him out. And should he speak overmuch to her, she would surely recognize his voice.

Could he trust her with the truth of it? The thought stunned him with its insistence, the temptation of doing just that almost overwhelming his usual caution. So little he knew of Alienor and her loyalties, of her ability to hold her tongue under duress, of her commitment to his house. His heart urged him to trust her fully, but he knew there was too much at stake to take such a foolhardy risk.

Years of planning and buying alliances, almost two decades of hiding, of preparations for this one at-

tempt to regain his heritage. Even now the days were
rapidly slipping away before his final test, a test failed
by each generation of his family for centuries past.
Would he manage to regain the crown wrongfully sto-
len from his ancestors? What had he to offer a
woman, a man pledged to this seemingly futile battle? What had he, indeed. At best, he could give her a
son who would take up this same task in his wake.
With a heavy heart, Dagobert turned to extinguish the
fire that he might join his wife.

"Dagobert," Alienor murmured sleepily when he
had shed his clothes and stood beside the bed, and he
smiled sadly to himself. Would that he had been born
a simple man bereft of such responsibilities. Would
that he had, and could love this woman with the fullness dawning upon his heart.

"Dagobert," Alienor breathed in the darkness, her
body exhausted from her husband's tempestuous
lovemaking. Never yet had he been so demanding, so
passionate, never had she thought she could ride out
such a storm of ecstasy and survive to tell the tale,
never had she given him so much of herself. The regular sound of his breathing filled her ears, the rapid
pulse of the heart beneath her ear telling her that he
was not yet asleep, and she determined she would talk
to him this night of all nights.

"Dagobert," she repeated slightly more urgently,
and she sensed that he fidgeted inwardly as if he would
avoid her questions. "I would speak with you," she
whispered, her heart sinking when his thumb landed
unerringly against her lips.

"Nay," she insisted, pushing his hand away determinedly. "We have but a few hours together each

night and I would talk to you, I would know more of you."

Alienor felt him shift beside her and sensed that he rose to prop himself on one elbow. She felt his gaze upon her and hated the fact that she could not see him, that he would not permit her to touch his face, that she knew not even the color of his eyes, that she was unsure what happened to him each day.

His thumb landed again on her lips and tears rose unbidden in her eyes at his refusal. 'Twas too much to know such physical intimacy and be denied any other knowledge of the man who carried her to such great heights each night. How could he refuse her something so simple as a few words? Had he so little respect for her as his wife? Or did he see her merely as a breeder for his babes?

Too cruel was that last thought and Alienor rolled abruptly away, her back to her husband as the tears that had welled up in her eyes tumbled over her cheeks. 'Twas the only explanation for his unwillingness to talk to her, his lack of curiosity about her. He saw her only as a means to an end; his passion was all for the pursuit of a son and naught for her. Unreasonable indeed she had been to expect more from this match.

A yawning silence filled the space behind her as Alienor sobbed quietly in the darkness, certain she had never felt so alone in her life. Had not Iolande made her promise that she would not interfere with conception? Had not everyone who spoke with her been most concerned with the events in her nuptial bed? Did the entire household know her womb was all that was desired here? 'Twas too much to be borne, and she wept as though her heart would break.

She thought she heard a sigh just before Dagobert's strong arm closed around her waist, but she could not be sure. Alienor struggled briefly but he drew her easily back against him, curling her into his warmth and pressing gentle kisses into her hair. She halfway thought that he might speak, but he did not, disappointment welling in her chest that he could not even manage a few words to console her.

Despite her turmoil, Alienor's exhaustion won the day and she eventually fell asleep cuddled against Dagobert's warmth, the pillow wet with her tears, while her husband stared unblinkingly at the ceiling throughout the long night.

"Madame, I would ask for some small labor to busy myself." Alienor managed to summon the nerve to make this request of Iolande the following morning at the board. She had more of value to contribute to this household than her womb, and the morning light had brought a new determination to prove that fact. Too soon was it to tell if she could conceive, but she would plan for the worst case and ensure that she maintained a place in the household, that she contributed so significantly that they would be hard-pressed to turn her out even should her body fail to fulfill its task.

"Indeed?" Iolande asked archly, her pale blue gaze slipping assessingly over her son's wife. "Have you talent with a needle?"

"Of course," Alienor responded with confidence, uncertain why she would be questioned on such a basic skill. "'Tis my understanding that most women do." Iolande raised one eyebrow at her audacity and almost smiled.

"Most women are not reared single-handedly by a knight," she retorted sharply, the twinkle in her eyes belying her tone. Alienor took a chance and smiled at her mother-in-law, reassured when some measure of the frost in those blue eyes slipped away in response.

"Guibert was oft away and our neighbor took me under her care. As a seamstress she earned her trade and I learned early to assist her."

"Then your skills will indeed be welcome here," Iolande asserted calmly, and Alienor breathed a silent sigh of relief. The wolfhound resting at the lady's feet stood up and shook himself, apparently anticipating its mistress's intent.

"Should your fast be adequately broken, you are welcome to join us," Iolande invited as she rose, her tone less formal than usual, and Alienor readily abandoned her crust of bread, following her mother-in-law to the stairs.

Alienor quickly saw why her presence was so welcome in the lady's solar, for there were only a handful of women who came to sew for all the inhabitants of the fortress, and even she had seen that at least two hundred souls made their home here. Assigned to piece a man's tunic, she worked carefully and silently, realizing only now how few women she had actually seen in the keep once the wedding guests had left.

The weight of the fabric she stitched was considerable, the weave of the wool heavy, and she knew that this was no ornamental garment but a tunic designed solely to keep a man warm in battle. A quick glance around the room confirmed that all of the women worked with similar cloth, wool woven thick enough to block a wind as chill as the stiff breeze that had accosted her in the sentry tower.

Suddenly the pieces all fitted together in her mind, the design of the castle with its heavy curtain walls, its location atop a craggy peak with only one road winding to its gate, the vast number of knights and men at arms within its keep, a population of warriors that seemed to be slowly increasing as each day passed.

A fortress Montsalvat was in the true sense of the word, a fort, a bastion to be defended against invaders. The authoritative ring of the smith's hammer in the forgery far below rose to her ears, a second and remarkably a third smith's blows chiming in with the first, and Alienor wondered suddenly whether Montsalvat prepared for battle.

"Your work is fine," Iolande commented quietly from behind her, and Alienor fairly jumped, surprised as much by the older woman's proximity as her praise.

"I thank you," she murmured under her breath, daring a glance upward to find Iolande frowning thoughtfully.

"Can you stitch pictures?" she demanded suddenly, and Alienor nodded immediately.

"Aye."

Iolande nodded curtly and summoned a stiff smile for Alienor.

"My son needs a new banner and 'twould be fitting for you to take the task," she revealed abruptly, striding across the room to open a trunk.

Barely able to take in her remarkable and unexpected words, Alienor trailed in Iolande's wake, her eyes widening in surprise when the older woman dropped a length of heavy red samite into her hands. The cloth gleamed with the luster only silk can give, and Alienor ran one hand across its softness in open admiration.

"This I have saved but do not trust myself to the task," Iolande confessed quietly, and Alienor looked up, a warmth settling around her heart when she met the expression in those blue eyes. She was being granted an honor and well she knew it.

"I shall do my best, milady," she vowed, and Iolande smiled.

"Aye, I know it," she affirmed, and Alienor smiled in response. "His insignia is a crowned unicorn on a red field such as this. I will call for his old standard that you might learn the design."

"I thank you, madame." Alienor curtsied and clutched the beautiful fabric to her chest. Indeed, she would make a place for herself in her husband's home, even if Dagobert did refuse to speak with her as his wife.

The sun had passed its zenith when Iolande called for a harpist to entertain the women, and Alienor sensed without turning that Alaric had entered the solar. She glanced up in time to note Iolande's lips thin in disapproval, another of the women smiling secretly to herself before she met the warm regard in the goatherd's eyes and all else was forgotten.

Guiltily feeling a telltale flush rise over her cheeks, Alienor bent quickly back over her work to hide her discomfort. Would that her husband spoke to her as this man did, would that her heart tripped at his very presence in the same room.

The other women's voices rose as they requested different songs and vied for Alaric's attention, but Alienor concentrated on the evenness of her stitches. Despite her valiant efforts, she was unable to keep her

ears from burning when Alaric finally strummed his
harp and began to sing a romantic ballad, his deep
voice setting a resonance around her heart.

"Sidon has been attacked—Anjou will not come."
Eustache greeted Dagobert in the hall with the unwelcome words and Dagobert cursed under his breath.
His gaze went immediately to the knight following his
friend; 'twas a man he knew and whose word he
trusted. With a last longing glance up the darkened
stairs leading to his chambers, he turned his attention
to the two men.

"Sidon was lost?" he demanded sharply, and the
tired knight shook his head, giving Dagobert's worst
fears a momentary reprieve.

"Nay, but they have taken heavy casualties and are
loath to march out so soon."

Dagobert nodded in understanding, frowning
slightly at the import of this news, his mind immediately exploring the alternatives. "How long ago?"

"Two weeks past," the knight replied, shuffling his
feet for a moment as though unwilling to continue, his
gesture drawing the attention of both Dagobert and
Eustache.

"Out with it," Eustache demanded sharply, and the
knight flicked an apologetic glance to Dagobert.

"'Twas but a rumor," he confessed uneasily, but
Dagobert nodded encouragingly.

"I would hear the tale," he insisted, and the knight
nodded.

"'Twas said the attackers headed for Montsalvat."
Eustache and Dagobert exchanged a glance of open
surprise at this unanticipated development.

"To parlay?" Eustache asked, but the knight shook his head adamantly.

"To lay siege," he confirmed flatly, and Dagobert's heart sank.

"'Twould be madness," Eustache muttered under his breath in disbelief, but Dagobert saw the concern in his friend's eyes when their gazes met. Truly things were turning for the worst and he sighed with dissatisfaction. No leisure would there be for him this night.

"I would speak with you privately," he said to the knight, gesturing along the passageway when the man nodded. Despite the proven loyalty of his household, the hall was no place to discuss such delicate matters and he must learn more of this development.

Her turbulent stomach had not been able to bear the thought of Iolande's evening draft of wine and Alienor had refused the chalice politely. The flicker of panic that lighted her mother-in-law's eyes for an instant struck her as odd, for 'twas not that great a breach of the lady's hospitality. The expression was gone as quickly as it appeared, leaving Alienor wondering whether she had imagined it even being there as she lay for the first time unable to sleep in her marital bed.

She supposed it had been only a matter of time before she had an uneasy night, especially now that the excitement of the nuptials was behind her. The unicorn chewed complacently before the hearth, consistent if nothing else, and she wondered if she would actually witness the "transformation" this night. As much as she intended to hold to her vows to respect her husband's privacy, 'twas only natural that she was

curious. Or so Alienor told herself as she studied the
beast and waited.

The sky outside her window grew ever darker, the
fire flickered low in the grate as the sounds of merrymaking in the hall below faded into oblivion, and still
Alienor stared wide-eyed at the canopy over her bed.
Without a doubt the hour was late, the air outside
thick with the expectant silence of the night. The
moon rose and climbed into the indigo sky, casting its
silver rays into the room, and still Alienor did not
sleep.

Still Dagobert did not change. She rolled over restlessly and stared at the unicorn, who returned her regard unblinkingly as it lay calmly before the fire.
Alienor propped her chin on her hand and, recalling
their disagreement of the night before, wondered if her
spouse had the power *not* to change, just to spite her.

A tap at the door disturbed Alienor's fitful slumber, her heart leaping in her throat at the sound before she opened her puffy eyes and noted the full
brightness of the morning.

"I would light the hearth, milady, for the morning
is chill," came Giselle's voice through the thick wood
door, and Alienor nodded to herself in mute agreement.

The unicorn lifted its head at the sound of the other
woman's voice and she fairly scowled at the beast as
she clambered out of bed. The linens, her hair and her
chemise seemed to be conspiring against her, the lot
tangling around her and fairly sending her tumbling
face first to the floor. With a defiant kick and a curse
she freed herself and stomped to the door, her foul
mood not improved by the incident.

Giselle bustled about with typical efficiency and in the twinkling of an eye the fire was made, the bed linens pulled up and hot water poured for Alienor's bathing. When the younger girl made to take the unicorn's lead and escort it to the stables as she did each morning, Alienor stayed her with one hand, fixing the unicorn with a steady glare. Enough was enough. Had she not kept her side of their bargain? Well enough did she expect Dagobert to keep his, and if he would not grant her the opportunity to tell him, then she would tell this beast.

"I would have a word with my husband afore he goes," she said softly, and Giselle looked momentarily startled.

"But, milady—" she attempted to protest, the look of flat determination Alienor sent her way stilling the words in her throat.

"I will speak with him," Alienor reiterated, and the maid's glance darted from one side to the other as if she sought some escape.

"Aye, milady," she agreed doubtfully, and reluctantly let go of the lead.

"Alone," Alienor insisted stonily, and Giselle hesitated only an instant before she bobbed a curtsy and ducked out of the room.

"Waiting in the hall will I be," she said, and Alienor nodded slowly, never lifting her gaze from the unicorn's disconcerting yellow eyes.

"Oh, milord!" Dagobert looked up as Alienor's young maid charged down the stairs and fairly flew down the hall to the room where he had held council throughout the night. Giselle burst into the room and

pushed past a surprised Eustache, her brown eyes wide
with surprise.

"Milady would speak with the unicorn," she whispered breathlessly, and the men's eyes met over the
girl's head. Dagobert shook his head in disbelief.

"Explain yourself," he demanded curtly, and Giselle took a deep gulping breath, nodding in affirmation of her own words even before she spoke.

"A moment alone with him she would have, she
said, to *talk* to him."

To talk to him? Alienor was talking to the goat?
Never had Dagobert imagined that she truly believed
the tall tale she had been told, her inquisitiveness of
the past few nights convincing him that she sought his
daytime identity. Apparently he had been mistaken.

But what on earth was she telling the creature? His
eyes widened in surprise at the realization that *he*
would be expected to know what she had confided in
the creature, Eustache's chuckle telling him his friend
had come to the same comical conclusion.

Dagobert swore under his breath and darted out of
the room, taking the stairs three at a time with tiny
Giselle trotting along in his wake, Eustache laughing
uproariously far below.

When the girl was gone, Alienor approached the
beast slowly, bending over to grip the tufted beard
beneath its chin that it might not turn away from her.
Her fingers tangled in the kinky white hair and she was
momentarily surprised by its silky texture before her
resolve hardened anew. Ineffective this was certain to
be, but she *had* to talk to someone. And who knew the
truth? Mayhap some element of Dagobert's tale was
true, unlikely as that seemed.

"So, you would punish me for my curiosity, milord, for demanding more of you than your touch in the night," she murmured, and the creature stared fixedly at her, its chewing miraculously stilled for the moment. Surprisingly, she didn't feel silly addressing the unicorn and had the sense that it was actually listening to her words with rapt attention.

"I would have your touch rather than naught of you at all, milord," she confessed, finding herself rubbing the hard nub of its chin beneath the beard. "Should you return this night, I vow I will ask no more than you would willingly give."

Alienor fairly held her breath while the creature looked over her features as if it would discern whether she spoke the truth, her shoulders relaxing when it began to chew once more and tugged impatiently against her hand to free himself. She could only interpret the gesture as one of acquiescence and she smiled at it as its beard slipped through her fingers, certain in that moment that her ardent lover would be back in her bed this night.

Too late, too late. Dagobert's heart sank when he crossed the threshold and saw Alienor's satisfied smile as she stepped away from the unicorn. Would that the miserable creature could talk and tell him what it had heard! His chest tightened as he recalled his mother interrupting his councils with the news that Alienor had refused her draught of wine, and he studied her speculatively, wondering what she had seen, or *not* seen, during the night past.

She evidently sensed his presence now, darting a glance over her shoulder toward him, and he saw the dark shadows etched beneath her tawny eyes, the tired droop to her full lips. Her sleepless night was echoed by his own exhausted body and he stifled the urge to gather her up and carry her back to bed.

Their eyes met and she flushed scarlet, her shielding hands drawing his attention to the sheer gauze of her chemise and how little of her delightfully feminine form it concealed. He caught a glimpse of one rosy nipple hardening to perfection and felt his maleness respond in kind, wondering now how he had managed to spend even one night without her beneath him.

"Do you not knock?" she demanded imperiously, and he almost smiled at the breathlessness in her voice. Truly they were each as aware of the other and he was amazed that she had not guessed the game. He inclined his head now, playing the role of meek goatherd as well as he was able, gesturing with one hand to his four-legged ward.

"My pardon, milady, my concern was that Dagobert see the stables in time to avoid you embarrassment, and as the door was open, I thought you gone," he explained smoothly. "I will be but a moment," he added quietly, his heart pounding as he realized that his path to the unicorn would take him within an arm's length of his lady.

"I would that you were quick about it," Alienor said, and turned her back to him, making great pretense of holding her hands out to the fire in the hearth. Dagobert took a deep breath and stepped quickly across the stone floor, the intoxicating waft of sandalwood that teased his nostrils as he passed making him grit his teeth.

He spared one glance to her and immediately regretted it, the thick ebony mane that tumbled down her back calling to his fingers to tangle in its wavy length, the pale curves of her buttocks visible through the fine cloth inviting his caress. Even the delicate bones of her ankles fed his desire this morn and he had trouble grasping the unicorn's leash as he made his way from the room.

Tonight, he vowed to himself, tonight his wife would learn the meaning of passion.

It seemed all went awry for Alienor that day, Alaric's barging into her chambers and seeing her virtually nude and her telling response to his presence setting the tone for the day. Her needle seemed cursed as she worked in Iolande's solar and she was certain she ripped out three stitches for every one she made.

The unicorn's failure to change troubled her more than she might have hoped, and as the day progressed, she found herself growing more skeptical of the tale. That, in turn, led down a dangerous path, one that left her wondering where her husband secreted himself during the day and why he did so. Both of these thoughts were disturbingly inconsistent with her vow to honor his privacy, but Alienor knew not how to still her mischief-making mind.

Alaric did not come to sing to the women this day, which was a disappointment to Alienor, for despite the embarrassment of this morning, she had looked forward to seeing him again. To top it all off, one of the knights had killed a boar at the hunt and all were compelled to partake of the meat and salute his skill at the board that eve.

Alienor excused herself early from the celebration, barely noting how many watched her departure with avid interest, crawling bone tired into bed and dropping into a motionless heap on the mattress. All day long she had fretted inwardly about Dagobert's agreement to her vow, hoping against hope that she had not misread her husband's intent, and now her fears came back to haunt her anew even as she dozed.

If he was not truly the unicorn by day, how would he know her desire?

What if he did not come to her again?

Alienor's heart leapt when the bed curtains were pulled open unceremoniously and she sat up startled amongst the linens. A tall, broad-shouldered man stood at the foot of the bed, silhouetted against the dying embers of the fire as he surveyed her silently, his long hair streaming over his shoulders. Something about him struck a familiar chord in her mind, but then a circle hanging against his chest caught the light and Alienor threw herself on her husband with glee.

"You came," she had time to breathe exultantly before his arms closed around her and his lips claimed hers hungrily. The intensity of his kiss made her head spin and she gripped his shoulders, closing her eyes against her instinctive response to his touch. His tongue was in her mouth, the sure grip of his hand on her nape holding her captive beneath him, his other arm binding her against his chest as he crawled to the center of the mattress without breaking his kiss, and his demanding embrace was all she had ever wanted and more.

It was too much, this passion of his, it was everything, and she feared she would melt in the heat of it, melt into a boneless puddle on the floor. Her skin was on fire, her blood turned to molten lava as it rushed through her veins, her heartbeat echoed in her ears.

She struggled to return his caresses, to touch him as boldly as he touched her, but she was lost to sensation, stretched to endurance to merely respond to his demands.

Before Alienor could think, she was pinned to the bed, Dagobert's weight between her thighs, his pelvis imprisoning hers as she squirmed beneath his endless kiss. He ripped her shift away with one abrupt gesture, his strong hands exploring her hills and valleys in one unceasing caress. The pulse pounding in his manhood thumped against her secret lips and Alienor moaned softly, wrapping her knees around his waist to welcome him closer.

He slipped lower, his elbows bracing her knees wide, his hands capturing her wrists, his tongue lighting on that pearl hidden between her thighs, laving, teasing, caressing so that Alienor thought she might lose her mind. She writhed against his strength, but he would not let her twist away from his touch despite her entreaties.

The heat built to a crescendo within her, onward and upward till she thought she could stand it no more, and still it grew. Suddenly, abruptly, light ran through her veins to her fingertips in a bright explosion of color. She thought she screamed as her back arched off the bed, every muscle extended in ecstasy while deep inside her undulations marked the light's passing.

She gasped for air, her arms clasping Dagobert's neck when he rose to nuzzle the soft spot beneath her ear, the weight of his hands as they slid over her breast quickening her blood again. Almost dizzy from her release, she felt her body begin to respond anew and moaned softly as his fingers slipped into the dampness between her legs, knowing that he intended to cast her over that precipice again.

His thumb landed on that still-swollen bud and Alienor jumped at the jolt that tripped through her, but his touch was gentle and she readily parted her thighs for him. He kissed her gently, almost reverently, his lips grazing a path down her throat, nibbling at her collarbone, unerringly making their way to the hardened point of her nipple. He pulled the tip into the warm wetness of his mouth and Alienor groaned, grabbing a fistful of his hair even as he slid one finger within her.

Never had she felt so cherished and adored, and she positively purred beneath his touch, the thought occurring to her that he was begging forgiveness for his stubbornness of the night before. Too foolish that was, but she would keep her own vow and ask him no questions this night. The storm rose anew within her and she pulled his lips to hers, twining her fingers into his hair as she rained kisses all over his face. Too much did he give her by pleasuring her alone; she would share this ride with him.

"Come with me," Alienor urged, and she thought she felt him smile against her lips before he leaned back and rolled her to her stomach, his teasing fingers splayed flat beneath her now and wound into the nest of curls at her crotch. His fingers moved there and she giggled as they tickled, gasping when his finger stretched to touch that sensitive bud once more.

Dagobert rolled smoothly atop her, his hips against her buttocks, his other hand sliding beneath them to cup her breast, his breath on her ear as he slowly licked the sensitive spot behind the lobe. She wriggled with delight and his manhood hardened still further against her backside, Dagobert lifting his hips quickly and sliding his shaft along her wet folds. Alienor pulled up her knees and he groaned into her throat while his fingers caressed her more urgently, his heartbeat pounding against her shoulder blades as she heard herself begging for his possession.

He melded their bodies together with one long stroke and Alienor lifted her hips against him that she might take even more of his length. He gasped at her move and she undulated her pelvis, the curse that tumbled from his lips and the way his arm tightened around her filling her with a curious sense of power. His fingertip teased and she was lost herself, writhing beneath him as he began to pump, hardly noticing that he grabbed a fistful of her hair and bared her face to his gaze as they climaxed together.

And so Alienor's days fell into an easy rhythm, her needlework filling her days and her husband's ardor filling her nights. Every night did he come to her without fail, and every night did she keep her vow to ask of him no more than he wished to give. Of his body, he gave her all, but naught of his mind or soul was she apparently to have.

Her foolish hope that more would grow between them dwindled now as the white unicorn took shape beneath her fingers on the precious red samite. Iolande often commented on the piece and Alienor saw the pride in her mother-in-law's eyes at the work she evidently stitched for the love of her husband, a labor that she was sure would be no more or less appreciated than her willingness to welcome him to her bed each night.

Perhaps she would not have minded Dagobert's silence and single-minded pursuit of a son if Alaric had not been so often in her presence. The contrast between her husband's reticence and the goatherd's interest in her was marked and made her heart sad on those days that she indulged her emotions.

It seemed the goatherd was always nearby, his warm gaze upon her, his encouraging smile at the ready. 'Twas true enough that he teased her mercilessly and laughed aloud when he managed to make her blush, but he kept her confidence about her faith and indulged her fancies. When guests arrived at dinner and she was forced to eat meat at the board for appearance' sake, she would find fruit, bread and cheese in her chambers when she retired and he would wink conspiratorially at her when next their paths would cross.

Mere friendship, though, was less than she wanted of Alaric, and the thought alone set her feeling guilty. Too often now, Alienor found herself aware of him as a man and not a servant, too certain was she that he was finely wrought, too often did she fantasize of how he would tease a woman in bed.

'Twas unseemly for her to think thus and undoubtedly wrong, yet the matter was not helped by the fact that her husband had no face in her mind. His body she knew well, its smell and taste, the hard curve of his muscles, the texture of his hair against her lips, but she would know the man and he refused her that one indulgence.

'Twas probably inevitable that Alienor's frustrations would come to this, but when the deed was done, she was as shocked as her husband. For stunned he undoubtedly was when, in the midst of their lovemaking one night in early March, Alienor called out "Alaric" as she climaxed instead of gasping "Dagobert," as was her wont.

Immediately she realized what she had done, but 'twas too late to make amends, her husband recovering from his frozen shock to climb abruptly from the bed and stalk across the room. Alienor called out some inarticulate apology, her hands pressing to her lips when her words were answered by the slamming of the oaken door to the room. Her tears spilled down her cheeks unchecked and she threw herself across the bed, sobbing inconsolably into her pillow.

'Twas only much later, as the sky tinged pink and he did not return, when she realized that Dagobert had not had to unlock the chamber door.

Chapter Four

"Get up," Dagobert angrily whispered in the darkness of the antechamber, too furious to be polite. Eustache roused himself with some difficulty, cocking one skeptical eye at the darkness still enfolding them.

"Can you not make merry a little longer that a man might have a decent night's sleep?" the older man growled crossly, gathering a blanket around his shoulders against the chill of the early hour.

"She knows," Dagobert spat, pacing the length of the room and back while his friend absorbed the news, barely restraining himself from kicking the one-horned goat that was at the center of the entire mess, his temper not improved by the timing of Alienor's declaration. Eustache ran one hand through his rumpled hair and squinted at his lord in the shadows.

"And what of it?" he demanded offhandedly. "Most others know within the keep."

"You do not understand," Dagobert insisted hotly, spinning on his heel to confront the other knight, his fury almost burning out of control. Never had he felt so betrayed, never had he made himself so vulnerable to another. "I was *certain* she did not know. The woman has deceived me and, like a besotted fool, I believed her.''

He watched as Eustache's eyes narrowed thoughtfully, somewhat reassured that his companion's normally suspicious mind had also been taken in by his wife's charade. But too close were they now to the critical moment to allow anyone to stand in their way: just today another messenger had come from Brabant. 'Twas only a matter of weeks before they departed themselves for this last confrontation and not a good time for unexpected revelations about one's immediate household.

"How else has she deceived us, I wonder?" Eustache mused almost to himself, and Dagobert's heart sank at the implications. How else, indeed?

"God knows. I only pray she holds her tongue," he muttered.

"And if she has already loosened it?" Eustache asked the inevitable question and Dagobert's lips thinned to a harsh line. He could not even bear to think of what Eustache was suggesting. Was their cause truly worth the sacrifice of anything—or anyone—that lay in their path?

A pang of guilt twinged him with the recollection of Alienor's desire to talk and he could only wonder whether he had forced her into this deception by refusing to speak with her. He shook his head in confusion, unable to think clearly so soon after his lovemaking had gone awry, knowing he needed a draft of wine and a few moments away from the muted but unmistakable sounds of Alienor's sobbing to collect his thoughts.

'Twas unsettling, that soft painful sound, and Dagobert knew that if he stood here any longer letting it fill his ears, he would be certain to return to bed and console her. Duty bound as always, he did permit himself to wonder briefly whether he was overreacting, but quickly schooled his emotions.

What other explanation could there be for that name springing from her lips? He gestured impatiently toward the stairs and Eustache rose to his feet with a nod of agreement.

"What of your namesake?" the knight asked, indicating the sleeping goat. "Should he not be back in your chambers?"

"I care not where she finds him," Dagobert said dismissively, shrugging into his chausses. "More important matters are there at hand now. We must review what she might have overheard."

Eustache nodded and scooped up his belongings, not even sparing a backward glance as he followed his lord out into the hall and down the stairs.

The news that came with the morning sun confirmed Dagobert's worst suspicions, although he gritted his teeth painfully to keep from showing it. A delegation from the king himself rode toward Montsalvat and he heartily doubted that 'twas coincidence or fancy bringing them so far afield. He met Eustache's eyes steadily when the sentry brought the message, his gut twisting at the coldness that settled in his friend's eyes.

Eustache had no space in his heart for spies.

Alienor! Dagobert screamed to her in his mind. How could you have betrayed me thus? Unthinkable 'twas that he had taken her to his hearth, his bed, his very heart, and she rewarded him only with deceit, she who held his own heart so surely in her hands.

* * *

To say the hall was in uproar by the time Alienor finally dragged herself out of bed would be vastly understating the flurry of activity that confronted her. Rushes were being swept out, trestle tables set up, a fire set in the second and seldom used fireplace, new herbs carried in from the garden by the armload. It seemed to Alienor's nose that only mint was sprouting so early in the year, and she heartily doubted that even a scrap of it had been left outside.

Iolande strode through the melee, imperially dispatching servants this way and that with a stern eye and a wave of one long white hand. Clearly guests of merit arrived, for Iolande wore a sweep of royal blue silk, its hem rich with silver embroidery the like of which Alienor had never seen. She glanced to her own olive and gold, knowing 'twas the finest she had other than her wedding kirtle and curiously loath to change after the events of the previous night.

Would Dagobert ever forgive her blunder? Upsetting enough 'twas that she had found the unicorn sleeping in the antechamber this morning, but now it seemed that the whole household knew of her error, for they avoided her like the very plague.

Foolish whimsy. 'Twas naught but the busy nature of this morning, she told herself firmly as she heard the cook raise his voice at a clumsy assistant in the kitchens, and she stepped forward, determined to make herself useful.

"Madame, how can I be of assistance?" she asked Iolande, stunned when the woman gave her a look of such hostility that her blood chilled in her veins. Had Dagobert told his *mother?* Surely this could not be.

"I doubt that we shall need your assistance this morn," Iolande responded in clipped tones. "I trust you will find some way to amuse yourself," she concluded before Alienor could speak, and spun away to oversee some task on the far side of the room.

So that was the way of it. Alienor watched the bustle of activity for an instant, knowing now that she had not imagined that the usually talkative Giselle was quiet this morning. She spotted Alaric and would have stepped forward to speak to him, certain that he at least would have a kind word for her, but he looked up and met her gaze squarely, a frost in his eyes not unlike that in Iolande's.

Alienor was certain she could not have hurt more if someone had buried a knife in her chest, and she spun on her heel abruptly, running unsteadily to the stairs. Tears glazed her vision as she gained the abandoned ladies' solar and closed the door behind her, her tears spilling anew down her cheeks as she leaned back against the solid wood.

Sometime later when she had cried her eyes dry yet again, she wiped the last vestiges of tears from her cheeks and picked up the banner where she had left it the day before. She ran her fingertips over the white embroidery of the unicorn's coat, as soft as the down beneath the real beast's chin, and the silken floss that she had wrought into the twisted spire of its glossy horn.

How could such cruel words have fallen from her lips? How could she utter words that wounded a man who had been so considerate of her in his bed, a man who already bore the weight of a secret so burdensome that he was forced to hide within his own keep?

Truly she did not deserve the respect of his household for her thoughtlessness.

Tears pricked anew at the back of her eyelids, but Alienor blinked them back resolutely, uncoiling a golden thread from the basket of floss. With care, she threaded a needle with the bright gilt and bent to her task, plying the gold into the curve of a regal crown around the unicorn's shining horn.

Dagobert struggled to remain outwardly calm even as the awaited hoofbeats of the knights' chargers rang in the courtyard, knowing that his household expected him to keep his composure, expected him to set the tone that all was perfectly normal in Montsalvat. The sound of footsteps and men shouting to one another came in the hallway, and he took a deep steadying breath. Already he knew he was stretched too far, short of sleep and under unbearable pressure as the deadline for their departure approached, but even as he made the excuse, he knew 'twas none of those things that lay at the root of his unease.

'Twas Alienor and the shock she had given him that sapped his strength and ate at his resolve, the arrival of the king's men prompting Eustache's assertion that she must be a spy. His lovely, laughing Alienor a spy, a traitor to his cause and his very life.

This could not be. His heart fought against the evidence even as his intellect insisted that it must be so. Truly everything had gone wrong since her arrival, the painful loss of Anjou's support, indeed the sudden attack on Sidon after their betrothal, and now the king's knights rode right into his own keep.

He scanned the company assembled in the hall and realized with a frown that Alienor was not among them. Did she avoid watching the trouble she had brought upon his house?

Even if these knights had only suspicions, Dagobert feared 'twould not be long before they knew the way of things. Though his staff were loyal to a fault, they were many and all knew of the conspiracy. 'Twas only a matter of time before someone made an inadvertent slip, or two, and all would be lost. God knew the king did not suffer fools in his close retinue. With trepidation speeding his heartbeat, Dagobert met the concern in his mother's eyes, then the steely resolve shining in Eustache's.

The knights swung into the hall with a positive gaggle of squires and retainers and Dagobert inhaled sharply at their insignia of azure and gold. They sported the fleur-de-lis itself, just as he had been warned, and he regretted that his sentry had not been incorrect. There was no way that Iolande could turn away the king's own knights without severe repercussions.

The largest of them swept off his helmet and pushed back his coif with dramatic flair, revealing cropped jet black hair as he doffed his gloves and dropped respectfully to one knee before Iolande. Dagobert watched his mother struggle with her emotions, knowing he was the only one who saw the subtle signs of turmoil in her lovely features, before she extended her hand to the knight, indicating that he might rise.

"Welcome to Montsalvat," she said coolly, and one of her dogs came to sit against her leg, the beast's eyes surveying the soldier as icily as those of its mistress. The knight, seemingly unperturbed, inclined his head and kissed the back of Iolande's hand, rising slowly to his feet. They looked each other right in the eye, the willowy countess of the estate and the broader warrior, each clearly assessing the other.

"I would request your hospitality, milady," the knight began in a clear deep voice. "We ride through these lands on the business of the king."

"The road to Montsalvat leads no further," Iolande commented, a challenge in her tone, and Dagobert fancied that the knight stiffened a little under her regard.

"Indeed," he confirmed. "We make a census of all the lord's châteaux for the king that he might know the full extent of his vassalage."

"Vassals we are to Isarn de Foix," Iolande countered as Dagobert watched warily, wondering if his mother pushed too far.

"And thus to the king. Whether your allegiance be sworn directly or through another is of no import to me." The knight shrugged, apparently too tired to pursue an argument. "Again, I would request your hospitality, milady. We have ridden hard this day though the sun is yet high."

"Of course," Iolande conceded with a regal nod, as though there had never been any doubt, clapping her hands for servants to make the men comfortable.

"Oh, milady, here you are!" The light was fading and Alienor's eyes were aching when Giselle ducked into the solar, the concern on her round face easing momentarily into relief when she spied her mistress.

"Aye, here I am and here I stay," Alienor asserted, certain she had not the wherewithal to face the household again this day.

"Would you not sup this evening, milady?" Giselle demanded shyly, a hint of apology in her voice.

Alienor merely shook her head and returned to her work. Truly, joining the company below was the last thing she wanted to do now. Besides the greeting she was likely to receive, her stomach had been unsettled all day and she was loath to eat anything that might set it further askew. When Giselle did not leave, she glanced up and met the girl's troubled gaze.

"I would have only a lamp when you have the chance," she commented, making the last stitch of gold into the crown and surveying it critically. Rubies it needed round the circlet, Alienor decided, rooting in the basket of floss for a length of crimson silk, a jewel of kings. Were not unicorns said to have a red carbuncle of great healing power embedded at the root of their horn?

"The board fairly groans with fine dishes to tease the palate," Giselle offered, and Alienor threw her a smile, pleased when the girl smiled back and advanced into the solar.

"Not this night, Giselle. I fear I have no taste for food," Alienor explained, her mind occupied with the shape and placement of the rubies she would stitch. So caught up was she in her thoughts that she barely noted Giselle's presence beside her.

"Oh, milady, 'tis the loveliest banner ever I saw," the young maid cooed, and Alienor smiled to herself.

"'Tis not done as yet," she said quietly, and threw Giselle a wink, sensing the girl wanted to return to the festivities downstairs. "Now off with you to fetch me a lamp, else crusading season be upon us and my lord be without a banner!"

"Aye, milady." Giselle grinned and darted to the door, bobbing a curtsy before she turned back. "He does not crusade, milady," she added softly from the portal, and Alienor looked up with surprise. Does not crusade? What manner of knight was this man she had wed?

"Then the keep shall need a banner," she countered weakly, pleased when the girl grinned anew and bobbed out of sight.

Did not crusade, Alienor mused as she settled on oval rubies, like the cabochon stones she had glimpsed once embedded in a chalice at the monastery in Perpignan. A knight who did not partake of bloodshed readily and at every opportunity was a rare man indeed, she thought to herself, unable to suppress a swell of pride that this rare man was hers.

Hers if she could but win him back, Alienor corrected herself angrily, and promptly stabbed the needle into her index finger beneath the cloth.

Dagobert carried the lamp carefully down the hall to his mother's solar, the silence from that chamber making him doubt Giselle's word that Alienor was there. The shadows were falling long in the room and he hesitated in the doorway when he caught sight of his wife seated on the window ledge, turning toward the fading light that she might have some illumination for her work.

The red samite spilled over her olive green linen kirtle, the golden light that washed over her from the sinking sun making her warm coloring even more exotic, the shadows making her lashes appear more luxuriant, her lips more richly red. He stepped farther into the room and she started at his movement, her tawny eyes wide with surprise as she watched him like a doe about to fly, clearly uncertain of his manner.

"'Twas said you had need of a lamp," he offered by way of explanation, the words sounding like an excuse for her company even to his own ears.

"Aye," Alienor said simply, and stood, putting her work aside that she might come to him for the vessel filled with oil and wick. "I thank you for your trouble," she said with soft formality, and he noted that she made sure their hands did not touch when she took the lamp. Nor did her eyes rise to his, and so great was her discomfort that he wondered for just an instant whether he had misjudged her.

"Your presence in the hall has been missed this day," he commented quietly, and she threw him a surprised look over her shoulder.

"I should think not," Alienor shot back as she placed the lamp down carefully on a chest and dropped to the ledge to take up her work again.

"Why would you say such?" He braved the question, almost taking a step back at the hostile glare she slanted his way.

"I should think it clear that all know I have insulted my lord." She bit out the words and Dagobert felt a surge of optimism.

"Indeed?" he asked politely, surprised when Alienor tossed her work aside abruptly and stalked toward him with intent in her eye.

"Indeed?" she mimicked. "Play not these games with me. Do I truly seem so sluggardly in intellect that I would fail to note the entire company holding me in low esteem? 'Tis more than clear that all of you know the slight my lord endured last night and there is naught that I can do to make amends."

She turned and faced the window resolutely, folding her arms across her chest, and Dagobert thought he heard her catch her breath.

"Would that I could take back those words," she murmured emotionally, and 'twas all Dagobert could do not to fold her into his arms.

"What words?" he demanded softly, and earned himself another hostile glare.

"Do not make me say it," she whispered fiercely.

"I would hear it from your own lips," he countered cautiously, undeterred by the way she pursed her lips in dissatisfaction. He thought he heard her mutter *"Men"* under her breath in a disparaging tone, and he could not help but be encouraged by her words.

It truly seemed as though she had not guessed the truth of it, a fact that by itself would have made him want to laugh aloud to see Eustache proven wrong. But additionally there was the tempting implication that Alienor must have some tender feelings for him as a man and not just a lover in the night. 'Twas almost too good to be true.

She fidgeted now and studied her toe as if 'twere of great interest, then suddenly took a deep breath and blurted out the words. "Surely you know that I called him by your name," she confessed, and Dagobert wanted to scoop her up and kiss her breathless.

"Aye," he admitted, and permitted himself a mischievous grin. "But I know not when, milady." To his delight, Alienor blushed absolutely scarlet.

"'Twas a most inopportune moment," she mumbled, and he could not help but laugh aloud.

Aye, it had been that, my precious Alienor, he thought to himself, it had been that. The very sight of

her soft and defenseless before him prompted a recollection of just how inopportune it had been.

"I take it milord was vexed?" he asked in a teasing
tone, lingering on the last word as if he could not
choose an adjective. Alienor regarded him with
something vaguely akin to horror, her amber gaze
holding him captive for one endless moment, then she
unexpectedly chortled with laughter, her cheeks suf-
fusing with color.

"*Vexed?*" she repeated with an involuntary giggle.
"Aye, milord was sorely vexed."

"Did he raise a hand against you? Is that why you
would hide this day?" Dagobert demanded quietly,
determined to play his role as well as he was able.
'Twould not be uncommon for a lord to beat his wife
should she displease him, and well he knew that he had
found her utterance displeasing enough.

"Nay, nay," Alienor replied with genuine concern
that he had apparently misjudged her husband.
"Never would he lift a hand against me, I am sure of
it." She bit her bottom lip then and tears appeared
suddenly in her eyes, her hands rising to her lips as her
next thought overcame her with emotion.

"He merely left the chambers," she confessed
shakily, "and slept in the antechamber." She took a
deep breath and fixed Dagobert with an imploring eye
that shook him to his core. That look alone would
send him scaling mountains and fighting dragons to
coax a smile to her lips.

"I fear he will not come back to my bed," she added
quietly, and he almost proved her wrong then and
there.

"Perhaps you should speak with him," he suggested wildly, his mind thick as he fought against his

more basic desires, a memory shoving itself suddenly into his thoughts. "I believe you did thus once before and I trust all went well." Alienor smiled a secretive woman's smile at his reminder and her cheeks stained with a gentle flush.

"Aye," she admitted softly, "it did indeed work well enough." Dagobert breathed a silent sigh of relief, knowing that somehow the fates had smiled upon him and he had fulfilled her desire without even knowing what it was, the soft luminosity in her golden eyes at the memory making him wish he knew what she had asked of the goat.

"'Tis settled then and as good as done," he concluded brightly, extending his hand to her gallantly. "Would you sup this night, milady?"

"In truth, I have little appetite," she demurred, but Dagobert insisted, wanting to ensure she spoke with the creature this evening. Eustache would have much to say about the risk of him joining her with so many guests in the keep, but risk be damned, Dagobert meant to sleep with his bride.

"Lady Iolande has ordered fish prepared and a *cassoulet*," he tempted, knowing how she loved the baked bean dish. Alienor hesitated, and seeing that she was changing her mind, he pressed his advantage. "A vegetable *ratatouille* with the first few herbs from the garden awaits you, milady, and fresh strawberries from the coast."

"Truly?" she demanded in surprise when he mentioned the strawberries, and he grinned victoriously, beckoning to her with one tanned finger.

"You must see the repast for yourself," he cajoled, his heart fairly stopping when she gifted him with a sunny smile.

"Aye, it seems I must," she conceded, taking his hand and letting him usher her from the room. Dagobert retrieved the lamp, not wanting to leave it burning untended, and followed Alienor down the hall, stopping with surprise when she spun around to address him.

"I would thank you," she said softly, and he wondered if he could truly drown in the golden depths of her spectacular eyes.

"I do not understand, milady," he admitted, knowing that he understood little of anything at this moment, watching with fascination as she colored once again.

"You did not make me feel the fool for my words last night," she explained quietly. "'Twas most gallant and I would thank you for your kindness."

To his complete shock, Alienor stretched on tiptoe and pressed a chaste kiss on his cheek, her flush deepening before she turned and fled his presence. Dagobert was left standing thunderstruck in the hall with a maelstrom of emotion raging loose in his gut, not knowing whether to let jealousy, pleasure or satisfaction win the day.

Alienor felt the weight of someone's perusal upon her as she descended the stairs into the crowded hall, easily picking out the bright gaze of the man who watched her from where he sat on the dais. His ebony hair was cropped short at the nape in the manner of knights, its waves sticking damply to his head, his dark eyes intense in their survey of her, his jaw and neck reddened undoubtedly as a result of the wine he had imbibed.

A mockery of convention and polite society was the knight's boldly appraising stare, but Alienor saw with embarrassment that none rebuked him for looking her over so openly. Not for the first time she wished that Dagobert could or would stand openly in his own keep that he might defend her place in his household, for there were no others to take her cause.

Truly she had waited too late to join the company, and she briefly considered flying back upstairs from this ruckus of men, when her stomach voiced its objection to that idea and growled in discontent. Iolande was nowhere to be seen, the ever vigilant Eustache deep in discussion with another knight attired in the same azure and gold as the rude one who watched her. Even Alaric had seemingly become lost on the stairs behind her.

Resolving that there was nothing for it, Alienor strode across the room with a confidence she was far from feeling and took her place at the unicorn's side, steadfastly ignoring the insolent knight's intent gaze. Trouble this man was, to be sure. Would that she could eat quickly and return to her chambers.

"Milady!" Giselle exclaimed with surprise from beside her elbow, and Alienor turned with a smile to find her maid's eyes bright with wine, as well.

"Alaric said there was *cassoulet*," she explained over the din of the company, and the girl nodded, expertly evading pinching fingers as she trotted to the kitchens to fetch something warm for her mistress.

The unicorn nuzzled against her knee and Alienor rubbed its chin almost absently, noting how similar in texture its silky beard was to the banner she worked upstairs. Would her spouse be pleased with her stitching? She could only hope 'twas so. Recalling her vow to talk to the unicorn, she bent down, stopping cold when she met the speculative and amused gaze of the knight who had been watching her.

"And where has this tasty morsel been hidden away?" he drawled, Alienor's spine straightening with an almost audible snap of indignation. Before she could make some sharp retort, she felt a cool hand rest lightly on her shoulder and watched a certain wariness land in the knight's eyes.

"'Twould be most rude to devour my daughter-in-law, Chevalier Jordan," Iolande commented icily from behind, and Alienor breathed a silent sigh of relief. One of Iolande's wolfhounds hunkered down beside the two women, its knowing eyes fixed steadily on the visiting knight.

"No harm meant I," he confessed with outspread hands, lolling unsteadily back on his bench, and Alienor stifled the urge to tell him she knew he feigned the extent of his drunkenness.

Her last silver denier would she bet that he was not the least drunk, despite his show to the contrary, and she barely restrained herself from curling her nose in disgust at his game. Such cowardice 'twas for a full knight as broad as this Jordan to be afraid of a woman and her dog, even should those be the formidable Iolande and her great wolfhound.

Giselle appeared in that moment with Alienor's meal and she thanked the maid prettily, settling to the food with a hunger she had not known she possessed. Iolande strolled away gracefully when the knight seemed to have diverted his attention to his companions, giving Alienor's shoulder a tiny squeeze of encouragement before she parted, the dog a bulky shadow in her wake.

The unicorn seemed hungry and she fed it some of her trencher, smiling to herself as it licked her fingers with his blue tongue. Truly she must find a moment to speak with the unicorn for she had no desire to sleep alone this night. She knew not what magic permitted her husband to know what she told this beast, but it had worked before and she would try again. Her blood quickened at the thought of her husband keeping the chill of the early-spring air from her skin, and so caught up in her thoughts was she that she jumped with surprise when the knight addressed her abruptly again.

"'Tis you then who are wed to the beast," he commented, and she saw the open assessment in his eyes of a perfectly sober and calculating man.

"Aye," she answered simply, and took a deep draft of the red wine in her chalice, painfully aware that he watched her every gesture.

"A sad waste 'tis that such a fine lady be wed to a rutting goat," he goaded, and Alienor turned on him with flashing eyes.

"A sad excuse for chivalry 'tis that such a rude boar earned his spurs," she shot back, surprised to see his neck grow ruddy as her barb hit home.

"I beg your pardon, milady," he said with apparent contrition. "'Tis the wine that loosens my tongue."

"I think not," Alienor responded with clear disbelief, momentarily startled when the knight threw back his head and laughed till the tears gathered at the corners of his eyes. When he had composed himself, she flicked him a cold glance and commented, "I fail to see the humor in deceiving others."

"Indeed," he agreed, sobering with an immediacy that told her he was mocking her. "'Tis a rare woman indeed who takes the time to look closely or has the intellect to understand." Alienor merely arched one brow so as not to encourage him but to indicate that she had heard, feeling herself grow increasingly uncomfortable beneath his scrutiny.

"Chevalier Jordan de Soissons," he murmured in a deep voice that Alienor was certain had brought many wenches to his bed, but she merely sent him a cold sidelong glance.

"Alienor de Perpignan," she countered politely, rising immediately from her bench to quit the hall, determined to give this man no more of her time. Jordan climbed to his feet and she saw that he stood eye to eye with her. Alienor took the opportunity to give him a cold glare as she shook off his hand discreetly from where it had landed on her elbow.

"If you will excuse me," she said icily, scooping up the unicorn's tether as she made to brush past this insolent knight. In some corner of her mind, Alienor acknowledged that she was learning much from Iolande and almost smiled at the errant thought.

"This time, milady," Jordan murmured as Alienor drew alongside him, but she refused to look up and meet his gaze. "But should you grow tired of coupling with a goat, I should be glad to teach you the ways of men."

That last comment earned Jordan a glance that would have pierced armor on the battlefield but he only chuckled to himself, raising one hand in farewell as Alienor gained the stairs.

"Sleep well, milady," he called, feigning his drunkenness again as he raised his voice above the clamor of the hall, and Alienor's cheeks burned with humiliation. "Until the morrow."

"I like it not," Eustache muttered under his breath as he mounted the stairs alongside Dagobert, and the younger man smiled wryly to himself in the darkness at this expected argument. "'Tis not worth the risk with so many strangers in the keep," he added in a disgruntled tone.

"Little enough is there that you find worthy of risk," Dagobert commented quietly, shooting his friend an assessing look. "Mayhap I should find you a bride to show you the way of things." Eustache snorted indignantly, the sharp sound echoing in the silence of the hall, and Dagobert was pleased to see the older knight's lips curve into a reluctant grin.

"Should she muddle my mind as much as this one does yours, I should indeed be better without," he parried quickly, and Dagobert sobered slightly at the truth of it. "Unconvinced am I as yet that she is not at the root of our troubles this hour," Eustache began, and would have continued, but Dagobert silenced him with one hand.

"I will hear no more of it," he commanded, what remained of his buoyant mood evaporating at the reminder.

"Hear no more of it if you will," Eustache countered as they entered the antechamber, his voice dropping to a mere whisper, "but mind you still *think* upon it, ere you face yet another surprise."

With that and a grunt of approval for his own wisdom, he dropped to sit on the floor, drawing his blanket around himself as he fixed the younger man with a knowing eye. The words set a chill around Dagobert's heart as he wondered whether Alienor could indeed be playing him for the fool. He stood motionless for a moment, suddenly less certain of his own conviction in her innocence. Eustache jerked his head toward the inner door impatiently when Dagobert hesitated.

"On with you, then," he said gruffly, settling himself into the wool blanket with great ado. "Well you know that I have always been afflicted with a suspicious mind, but I would have some semblance of rest this night."

Dagobert moved then with a terse nod of agreement, knowing that that would be the full extent of any concession he might hear from Eustache's lips. Perhaps 'twas enough to know that this man who saw shadows lurking at every turn was not entirely sure of Alienor's guilt, either, regardless of the uproar in their plans since her arrival at Montsalvat.

The door swung silently inward when he pressed it with his fingertips and he cast an appreciative eye over the domestic scene within, the comfortable tapestries, the glowing embers of the fire burning low in the grate, the padded seat on the window ledge where one could look out over the hills in daylight.

The bed curtains were drawn against the coolness still clinging to the spring air, the soothing sound of Alienor's breathing while she slept filling Dagobert's ears and prompting him to smile softly to himself before beckoning to the goat with an outstretched morsel. Would that he could openly retire and awaken in these rooms, would that he could be done with subterfuge once and for all.

This wish chilled him with its implications, for surely he would be done with this plan and its execution within the year, and he shuddered in sudden trepidation of the unknown. Had he not regained his rightful heritage in twelve months' time, he undoubtedly would have died in the attempt, and the reality of his situation, which had never troubled him before, now filled him with dread for the future of the woman who would become his widow.

What bargain had Alienor unwittingly made with him, even now unaware that she would spend her life on the run, with or without his babe? But there could be no turning back at this late date and he sighed, feeling anew the ache of dissatisfaction with his lot that seemed lodged so firmly in his chest these days.

Moments later he slipped between the bed linens and pulled the dozing Alienor into his arms, her skin smelling of the sweet warmth of sleep and sandalwood, her lips soft and tasting faintly of wine. She sighed with contentment as she became aware of him and twined her arms affectionately around his neck, Dagobert's heart melting at the flurry of kisses she pressed gently against his throat and jaw.

"However did you know?" she murmured drowsily, her breath a sweet caress against his ear, and Dagobert's heart leapt in panic at the import of her words. "I had not the chance to speak to you before I fell asleep." This last sent his mind into a whirl, but he nibbled gently on her shoulders and neck as if unperturbed as he desperately sought some plausible excuse.

"Always will I know your secret heart, milady," he whispered gruffly, feeling the explanation was hopelessly inane even as he uttered the words, fairly sagging with relief when she chuckled under her breath and pulled him ever closer.

"That indeed must be the way of it," she agreed easily, and Dagobert claimed her lips with a triumphant surge of passion, amazed that he had once again managed to leap some invisible hurdle that she set.

Jordan watched the keep of Montsalvat from the window of his room over the stables, carefully ensuring that he remained in the shadows cast by the moon so that none might note his presence there. Little enough had he learned this night, naught indeed had he heard of the persistent rumors that the old line of monarchs rose again from this remote fortress to challenge the king, but Jordan de Soissons was a patient man. Some sixth sense told him that the confirmation of his suspicions would come all in good time and he was more than content to wait here in the Pyrenees. To wait and to listen.

Interesting indeed 'twas that the old countess herself was so openly hostile to his arrival, he recalled, knowing that she had not been completely fooled by his act, narrowing his eyes speculatively as he scanned the impassive walls of the keep. A sentry walked the curtain wall and he watched the man's progress with a dispassionate eye, making note of the high level of security maintained here, a remarkable vigilance considering Montsalvat's extreme distance from any other settlement in these parts and the fact that only one fairly arduous road approached its gate.

For years there had been tales of the Cathars' gold and jewels presumably hidden somewhere in Languedoc. Did Montsalvat house those precious valuables? Was that the reason for the close guard? Even though they had served meat at the board, Jordan's experienced eyes had noticed that there were precious few children among them, his quick peek into the chapel revealing that no crucifix hung over the altar, as was the Cathar way.

Was Montsalvat merely a last bastion of the Cathar sect, determined to defend itself against the almost certain onslaught of Crusaders this summer? If so, there could be naught behind the rumors of the lost king returning and Jordan was wasting his time. Without a doubt, the Cathars were virtually extinct already, expedited along their path to meet the Maker by the violent response to the pope's call to exterminate these heretics. Already the battle was lost as Jordan and anyone else with a wit of sense knew, a season or two more of crusading certain to flush out the last of the infidels.

It occurred to Jordan as he stood in the inky shadows that the rise of the rumors of old kings and the Crusade against the Cathars might be interrelated somehow and he marveled that the thought had not come to him before. Nigh on thirty years the crusading knights had ridden into Languedoc, slaughtering all who came across their path, be they faithful or heretic.

And to what purpose? Already the sole issue of Raimon de Toulouse had been forced to wed the king's own brother, already the lands that should pass to her were forfeit to the crown should she die without issue herself. It would take a greater fool than Jordan to miss the inevitable conclusion that the king's brother would be amply rewarded should his wife prove barren. Did he not know of his own experience how these matters were contrived?

'Twas almost as if the pope and king sought to exterminate someone whom they knew to be in these parts, someone whose identity or location none had been able to pin down. Why else these decades of senseless killing?

Too well did Jordan know the old stories of the stewards of the royal line stealing away the power of the throne, killing their lords that they might wield the scepter themselves. As a child left to the resources of the monastery, he had read the old romances that maintained the original line survived, fired by the hope of regaining their legacy.

Old stories they were, no more, no less. Romantic tales of fantastic quests and spiritual enigmas to haunt the dreams of a young boy abandoned by his family, a young boy growing to a man beneath the oppressive yoke of heavy labor and ceaseless beatings for naught, a young man who earned his spurs not through his heritage or the goodwill of his family but solely through his own hard work and perseverance in the face of adversity. A boy who had become a man determined to look after himself alone.

Foolish stories, Jordan thought dismissively, almost lifting his hand to brush the thoughts away. No time had he for such flights of fancy these days, but no fondness had he for those who would use such tales to their own advantage. 'Twas a travesty he found particularly repugnant, mayhap because he, despite the hardship of his own life, could still feel the magical allure of those tales.

He would have to have been a simpleton not to have noted the seething hostility against the presence of the king's knights here, the quartering of his men and especially himself over the stables and not within the keep, itself a definite snub, despite the countess's polite assurance that these rooms were the only ones available at present.

Something was afoot, Jordan could practically smell it in the air. Perhaps the Cathars used the old tale of lost kings as a means of concealing their true intent. His lip curled, something deep within him despising the very idea that anyone could twist such a magical tale to support his own grab for power and glory.

He folded his arms across his chest and tapped his bottom lip thoughtfully, recalling the Lady Alienor's insistence that he was not drunk. Which naturally he was not, but her perception of that and resulting indignation were intriguing to say the least. Had she not warned the hall of his true state with her open challenge, as if she wanted none to be fooled?

As that had been precisely his intent, Jordan had been torn between annoyance and a grudging admiration for the lady's boldness. 'Twas not soon after she left the hall that he became aware of the knight Eustache's attention fixed solely on him, a skeptical regard that never wavered until he retired to his room.

And to be truthful, 'twas that interest the lady sparked within him that made Jordan curiously reluctant to leave Montsalvat. A quickness of mind she had, the like of which he had seldom seen in a woman, and the exploration of that trait was definitely worth a few days' wait. Unusually featured she was, to be sure, her ancestry undoubtedly one of mixed blood, but he found those tilted amber eyes oddly compelling, intriguing, exotic as some foreign fruit that he longed to sample.

And wed to a goat without complaint. Surely that was beyond belief in itself. A unicorn they called it, he thought scornfully, as if such a beast truly existed. 'Twas but another foolish tale. 'Twas plain enough to anyone who ever tended livestock that this creature was merely a single-horned goat, though whether the other horn was missing by accident or design was impossible to tell.

A goat that changed to a man in the fullness of the night. Truly they thought him no better than a drooling idiot to trust in such nonsense. A goat that satisfied a lovely woman's carnal desires, indeed. His blood quickened at the thought that Alienor might yet be a virgin and he savored for a moment a fantasy of taking her, his daydreams halted by an inability to picture her hair. Assuredly 'twas dark, but fine and straight or thick and wavy or fine and sleek he could not decide, and shook his head in annoyance.

But to what purpose did they tell the tale of the unicorn? 'Twas clear the countess had a son and Jordan shrewdly wondered what the man had to hide. Perhaps he was dead and the countess did not want to face any threat of the lands becoming forfeit.

Or perhaps the Count of Pereille fancied he had a legitimate claim to the throne. Presumably a more legitimate claim than the king currently enthroned there. Perhaps he merely wanted the throne and was prepared to use any means to attain it.

Perhaps Jordan's arrival had been anticipated.

He shook his head abruptly at the thought, dismissing his musings as too farfetched, but an unshakable vestige of doubt remained.

A light bobbed in the keep, visible first here, then there, the moving light attracting Jordan's eye as someone climbed the stairs to the solar. Who moved about so late when all were long asleep? Who carried a torch so openly in the darkness of the hour? Jordan pursed his lips as he tracked the light, making careful note of the last window where it was visible before the flame disappeared. Nodding silently to himself, he turned to his straw pallet.

No, things were not as they would appear here at Montsalvat.

Chapter Five

Alienor lay back against the pillows and closed her
eyes, letting the faint calls of the birds on the early-
spring air waft across her while she caught her breath.
'Twas no coincidence that she had been ill again this
day, she was sure, and she forced herself to face the
truth.

She had not bled since her nuptials and 'twas the
third morning in a row she had been ill. Her stomach
was even more temperamental than usual regarding
food, her emotions twisting and turning with an unpredictability that made her own head spin, her tears
seemingly always close to the surface. True to her
promise to Iolande, she had not interfered with conception, and it seemed indeed that Dagobert's seed
had taken root within her.

Without a doubt, Alienor was pregnant.

She sighed and gazed out the window at the clear
blue sky, her heart filled with conflicting emotions.
Much as she adhered to the tenet of her faith, disliking the fact that another soul had been trapped in flesh
and was doomed to walk the surface of this earth,
Alienor could not suppress an insistent thrill of pride
that she bore Dagobert's child, that he would have an

heir so soon after their nuptials, that they together had created something that would endure beyond their own days. 'Twas beautiful in a way and she could not honestly deny her own pleasure in the completed deed.

It took but an instant for her thoughts to turn to the worst, as had been typical of her lately, and she recalled her own suspicion that Dagobert wanted her only that she might provide a continuation of his lineage. Alienor bit her trembling lip, not liking the unassailable fact that he continued to avoid speaking with her at night. In truth, she knew that he had uttered less than a score of words in her presence since their nuptials, and that did not bode well of the possibility of his having any feelings for her.

Would he cease to come to her bed now that she was with child? The thought sent a chill through her and she knew 'twas not a remote chance. She shook her head mutely, resolving in that fleeting moment that she would not go without Dagobert's caresses and feel completely abandoned in this household. She would not speak of it to him. Did he not prefer that they loved silently? 'Twould be a fitting response for her not to share this news. Soon enough indeed would the truth of her condition be inescapable.

Filled with a new resolve, Alienor swung her feet energetically from the bed and rose to perform her toilette. Her bubble of determination burst abruptly when a frightening thought elbowed its way resolutely into her mind.

Would the child share his father's cursed predicament and be forced to hide all his days?

"Rise, gentlemen, rise." Jordan's drunken voice assailed Alienor's ears as she descended to the hall that

evening and she glanced up to find his bright regard
fixed upon her. Truly she had awakened from her afternoon nap too late this day, for many had already
left the hall and those who remained were clearly well
into their cups.

There was naught for it, Alienor resolved grimly.
She had to eat for the babe and 'twould be churlish to
retreat now and force Giselle to fetch her meal upstairs. If only this Jordan had taken his leave, 'twould
have been much easier to bear the normal rowdiness
of the late evening hall.

With a mocking little bow, he now lifted his chalice
to her, a coy smile playing over his lips. As he gestured to the few other men assembled in the hall to
join him, Alienor's heart sank. It seemed he would not
abandon her easily this night.

"A true flower graces us with her very presence," he
continued, and Alienor felt hot color rise in her face.
Had she not been the very center of attention, she
surely would have turned and run back up to her
chambers, regardless of what the others might think
of her manners.

Giselle hissed something uncomplimentary under
her breath behind her and Alienor restrained herself
from agreeing wholeheartedly with her maid. 'Twas
clear the man was a menace to polite society and most
in the keep would cheer when he finally took his leave.

"I drink to your health and beauty, milady Alienor," Jordan crooned, and Alienor frowned at his
impropriety even as he drained his goblet. No maid
seeking a match was she but a married woman already rounding with child.

She glanced across the hall for assistance, noting
that none there looked as though they would come to

her aid, most of those remaining being from Jordan's own retinue. How much did these men drink here at the keep? she thought indignantly, calculating the cost of their visit and realizing just how long they had been in residence. One would think a simple tally of the household could not take so long.

"Your comments are most inappropriate," she restricted herself to responding tightly, her very words lost in the roar of agreement that rose from the remainder of the king's knights as they hoisted their own chalices to join the salute.

"Not so inappropriate as my thoughts," Jordan confirmed with a broad wink that convulsed his men with laughter. Alienor scanned the dais only to find Iolande absent, as was Eustache and even Alaric. 'Twas abundantly clear that she was on her own in defending her virtue this night.

"Then I would suggest you keep those thoughts to yourself," Alienor retorted primly, her chin rising one defiant notch. This man would not drive her from her own board, she resolved to herself, sitting at her place with newfound determination. Giselle spared her an encouraging smile and darted away to the kitchens, apparently intent on making her mistress's time in the hall as short as possible.

"Ah, milady, my heart demands to be heard," Jordan continued, and Alienor flicked him a look of open dislike. How dare he take it upon himself to embarrass her so in her husband's home? She met his gaze for an instant, barely surprised to find sharp lucidity in his brown eyes. She gritted her teeth as she turned away, but she could not hold her tongue.

"What measure of a man would feign drunkenness where he is but a guest?" Alienor demanded, a quick glance to the knight confirming that she had completely taken him by surprise. A curious stillness fell over the hall and Jordan straightened with care before he responded.

"What do you mean, milady?" he asked cautiously, his brown eyes narrowing in assessment, and Alienor was uncannily reminded of a cat about to spring on an unsuspecting mouse. Undaunted, she lifted her chin and stared him down.

"I call you a fraud, Chevalier Jordan," she confirmed quietly, and the hall grew even more deathly quiet.

"Surely you jest," Jordan countered smoothly, his insinuation that she should retract her words bringing Alienor to her feet in one angry move.

"If any jest, 'tis surely you," she shot back, "for any fool can see that you are not in the least drunk. And this is not your only deception, for truly no census could take so long as you have tarried here." Jordan leapt to his own feet, his anger bringing him across the floor to Alienor with alarming speed.

"Do you call me a liar?" he rasped, and Alienor met his gaze unflinchingly.

"Aye, clearly I do," she confirmed, watching fury flare openly in his eyes. "And further, I would know your purpose."

"As I would know yours," Jordan seethed in return, the drop in his tone ensuring that none could overhear. Alienor took a reluctant step backward, wondering now whether she had made a wise choice in confronting this man.

"My purpose?" she repeated, her trepidation mitigated by her confusion at his words.

"Aye, milady, for no fool is Jordan de Soissons," he muttered under his breath, his handsome features twisting into something unrecognizable. "Would you have a clever man believe you are truly wed to a goat?" Jordan asked pointedly, and Alienor found that she had no answer.

"What evidence is there of this magical conversion save your word, milady? Who *truly* warms your bed each night? Which of the men in the keep come to you?" His eyes glittered with something undefinable and he took another step forward, compelling Alienor to back into the wall.

"Or do they each take a turn, milady?"

Alienor slapped his clean-shaven face with an abruptness that sent his head jerking hard to one side. With horror, she watched as he only grinned and continued as if she had not interrupted him, even as the reddened imprint of her hand flamed against his jaw.

"If so, milady, I would take my own turn," he fairly growled, and Alienor gasped in disgust, the bile rising in her throat at the sexual intent gleaming in the man's eyes.

"Milady," Giselle's stern voice interrupted, and Alienor stepped around the surprised Jordan with relief, her cheeks burning as she met the young girl's incredulous eyes.

"I would dine upstairs," she managed to reply, and Giselle only nodded, her puzzled gaze flying to the knight Alienor felt still standing behind her. "It seems that I am more tired this night than I had thought."

Dagobert stood silently staring down at his sleeping wife in the wee hours of the morning, wishing he knew why she had been speaking with that Jordan and what had passed between the two of them. Too sketchy indeed had been the reports he had received, and he found them unsettling to say the least. Would that he could trust this woman; would that he could simply ask her the way of things and trust in her word.

He sighed and ran his fingers through his hair, wondering if they were ever destined to have the rapport common between man and wife. Would there always be secrets and distrust? Or would his days be cut so short that there would be no time for anything else? Truly it seemed that everything raced toward some mysterious destination these days and he had barely the time to speculate before he was swept along the course. Where would it all end? Would it ever end?

Dismissing his thoughts impatiently, Dagobert climbed into bed and pulled Alienor into his arms, the only smile of his long day curving his lips as she snuggled against him with some incoherent murmur of welcome. Her warmth spread through him and he leaned back against the pillows, closing his eyes and savoring the delicate scent that rose from her skin. She stirred no further and he had not the heart to wake her, knowing that holding her alone was all he needed in what precious little remained of this night.

No matter what else happened in his day, it seemed he could always sleep here with Alienor, that she alone could draw the anxiety from him and give him ease to rest. She alone demanded nothing of him, she alone gave to him instead of taking, and Dagobert was forced to praise the day he had taken her to his side. Inconsistent it seemed that Eustache could suspect her of being the source of the betrayal within the house, but truly Eustache had never experienced the peace Alienor gave him. 'Twas in the quiet hours of the night that Dagobert had no doubt of his wife's trustworthiness.

If only such conviction would not fade so readily before the harsh light of day.

His thumb drew rhythmic circles against the smoothness of her shoulder and he stared down at her curled against his chest as if he would see right through to her very heart. Dark lashes splayed against the smooth golden contour of her cheek, her rosy lips pouted even fuller in the relaxation of sleep.

Waves of her hair fell over her bare shoulders in joyous disarray and he lifted his hand through the dark tresses, watching the ebony strands catch on his fingertips. He clenched his hand over the thick softness of her hair and he lifted the long strands to his nose, inhaling leisurely of his wife's scent, feeling the tension of the day ease from his muscles.

Alienor sighed, her breath a soft flurry against his skin, and her hand drifted across his chest, her fingers tangling in the springy curls there. Dagobert smiled into the darkness and tightened his arm around her shoulders, bending to brush a kiss across her forehead as he felt exhaustion rise within him. His lids drooped and he pulled Alienor yet closer into his embrace, knowing that he would not trade these moments for all the riches in Paris.

The days passed, the winds of March that wailed around the keep growing steadily warmer and less insistent in their cries. New grass unfurled itself in the bailey and a few intrepid flowers dared to poke their heads from the chill of the earth.

Alienor's stomach grew more steady and she fancied 'twas in concordance with the passing of the

equinox in mid-March, though she doubted that that
could actually be the case. In truth, she sadly missed
the festivities of Bema and the celebration of the
equinox that she had grown accustomed to within the
circle of Cathars in Perpignan, but the holiday was not
marked here at Montsalvat and she was hardly in a
position to encourage it.

None other in the household had learned of her
state. Even Giselle was ignorant of the soft curve of
her mistress's belly as yet and Alienor could not help
but wonder how long this fortunate condition could
continue. Iolande commented idly one day in the solar that the spring had put roses in her cheeks and
Alienor's hands had frozen over her work, certain her
secret had been detected, until the other women
laughingly agreed and talked of losing their own fairness of complexion in the blush of the warm winds.

Iolande seemed preoccupied these days, concerned
with matters in another sphere, and Alienor wondered at the cause of her mother-in-law's distraction.
More than once did she glance up and find the lady
frowning down at her work as though she saw not
what lay before her. Perhaps 'twas as much Iolande's
preoccupation as Alienor's cleverness that kept the
older woman from learning of the babe's existence.

Alaric seemed touched by the same mood that
struck Iolande, and Alienor was disappointed to find
him distant on those rare occasions when their paths
did cross. Amply occupied he seemed to be, the care
of the unicorn entrusted often to a young squire and
Alaric himself seldom to be seen around the hall or
stables. Only Eustache seemed much as usual, his appraising eyes darting from one face to another around

the hall as if he sought some hidden piece of a greater puzzle.

And that Jordan. No gallant was he despite his spurs, of that Alienor was certain. Ever did he threaten that he would show her the way of real men should she so much as crook a finger in his direction, never did he cease his cajoling and sexual commentary. 'Twas improper and disgusting and Alienor could only be amazed that none seemed to have noticed that, either. 'Twould be a fine change of events indeed if she had a husband who could take issue with such insult within the light of day.

'Twas near the end of March that Alienor awoke one morning and found that Dagobert was not with her in either form. To her surprise, the chamber door was still locked and she rose hastily, unable to shake a feeling of dread.

A quick survey of her rooms revealed that the unicorn was not hidden there, the brightness of the morning sun fueling her disquiet. With alarm, Alienor turned the lock and hauled open the heavy door, fairly bumping into Giselle in the darkened antechamber in her haste to find her husband.

"Milady, the floors are too cold for you to be barefoot," Giselle began to scold as she attempted to usher her mistress back into her chambers, but Alienor interrupted her abruptly.

"Where is Dagobert?" she demanded, and the maid looked up at her in surprise.

"He is not within?" Giselle asked, gesturing to the open door, and Alienor shook her head quickly, panic settling in on her. 'Twas not a good omen that Giselle had not seen the unicorn outside the room.

"Nay, he is not there and the door was locked when I awoke." Alienor heard her voice rising but could not seem to check the haste of her words. "Giselle, something has gone amiss, I know it in my heart."

"Milady, certain I am that all is well," the younger girl asserted with an authority that belied her years, but one that did not settle Alienor's fears. "I would have you return to bed while I send someone to seek Dagobert and return him to you," she coaxed soothingly, but her mistress shook her head determinedly.

"Nay, Giselle, I would know the truth of it, now," Alienor insisted, and pushed past the girl into the hall.

"Not without your pelisson, milady," Giselle scolded from somewhere behind her as Alienor advanced on the stairs, and she barely noticed the weight of the silk-lined garment settling over her shoulders. Her heart picked up its pace as she gained the hall below, a quick scan of the common room enough to convince her that the unicorn was not there, and Alienor made to head to the stables.

"Milady, you have no shoes!" Giselle wailed, but her words fell on deaf ears, so focused was she on learning the truth.

"Milady," came a firm voice that caught Alienor's attention, and she halted in the hall before an obstacle, fairly sagging with relief when she met the concern in Alaric's eyes. Truly she had missed him these last few weeks.

"What is amiss?" he demanded softly, and she barely restrained herself from breaking into tears in the face of his evident concern.

"'Tis the unicorn," Alienor confessed, her fingers entangled before her in her distress. "Have you seen him this morn?"

"He is not in your chambers?" Alaric asked carefully, and she shook her head adamantly, realizing that he had not answered her directly.

"Nay, and the door was still locked," she confessed, the narrowing of Alaric's gray eyes making her fear the worst. "He is not in the stables?" she demanded, certain that she knew the answer even as she spoke.

"I thought not," Alaric admitted, "but perhaps I am mistaken. Let us look again, milady. I am certain he cannot be far." With that, he took her trembling hand within the warm breadth of his as if she were but a child and led her toward the stables.

"A dreadful feeling have I," Alienor said in a small voice, and Alaric shot her a sharp look.

"Have you the sight, milady?" he demanded, and she was forced to shake her head in denial.

"Never before," she responded, knowing her face reflected her concern, "but this portent of trouble is most strong."

"Indeed it seems an odd occurrence," Alaric added with a troubled frown. He said nothing else but squeezed her fingers tightly in reassurance and Alienor was inordinately glad that he was with her in this task.

A cry of alarm rang out from the smithy just as they gained the stables and Alienor's mouth went dry with fear. She glanced up to see Alaric's lips thin into a grim line, the expression making his visage more harsh and forbidding than she had ever seen before. She shuddered inwardly and he must have felt the tremor, for his grip tightened on her hand and his gaze dropped to hers.

"Fear not, milady," he murmured, but she heard the lack of conviction in his tone and knew she was not alone in her trepidation of what they would find.

'Twas in the smithy that they found the slaughtered unicorn.

Even fearing the worst could not have prepared Alienor for the grisly scene, the profusion of blood, the smell of freshly killed meat, the senseless violence of the creature's death. That the beast had been brutally killed was obvious to the most casual observer. Its head was fairly decapitated from its body, the long slash that split its ribs leaving its innards spilling out onto the packed dirt floor in the smith's shop.

Its single horn was predictibly missing, the place where it had been crudely hacked out of its skull still oozing red. Had it been killed for the reputed healing powers of the horn alone? It seemed as though the killer would have them believe that was the only justification, but the sheer brutality of the killing imprinted the single word *hate* in Alienor's mind and she could not dislodge it.

When she spotted the silken cord and its golden rings lying amidst the bloodstained white fur, memories of her wedding day assaulted her. In that moment, Alienor fancied she could feel the smoothness of that silk cord beneath her fingers once again, could feel the sunlight filtering through the stained-glass windows in the chapel with their enigmatic pictures. She recalled the warmth of the cord when it lay against her husband's neck as he came to her in the night and the bile rose uncontrollably in her throat.

She gagged at the very sight of the red blood marring the soft white fur, not caring that she fell grace-lessly to her knees in the bailey and vomited, feeling nothing but the heat of her own tears scalding her cheeks. The reassuring strength of Alaric's hands closed over her shoulders in a sure grip and she welcomed his support even in her despair. When her retching finally stopped, Alaric left her side for an instant and Alienor knew instinctively that he fetched the cord, but she had neither the strength nor the will to ask him for the token.

Her heaves turned quickly to sobs and she buried her face in her hands as she knelt on the new grass, uncaring of who saw her in this state, paralyzed with grief that she would not know her husband's gentle touch again. Without the premise of the unicorn, it took little to see that Dagobert would truly disappear into hiding.

She was effectively a widow now, a widow who bore a babe. Too late she regretted not sharing this news with Dagobert, knowing instinctively that the pregnancy would have pleased him, not caring now that the source of his pleasure might have been only in the continuation of his line.

Alienor heard not the anger and dismay expressed by those gathered around her, felt not the knowing regard of that knight Jordan, and was only dimly aware that 'twas Alaric who swept her up into his arms and carried her back to her chambers.

"She must be told," Dagobert insisted hotly when he and Eustache finally had the opportunity to meet without the threat of being overheard.

"We cannot risk it," Eustache shot back. "Already the stakes have been raised and your claim must be suspected."

"The woman is beside herself and I would not have her so pained," the younger man argued, but his companion shook his head sadly.

"Still you do not see the import of this, so fogged are your wits with this woman," he complained, and Dagobert threw him an exasperated look.

"She thinks me dead!" he exclaimed, throwing out his hands in frustration, and Eustache sprang toward him with an outstretched finger and a light in his eyes.

"Aye, that she does, and she has more sense than you for that," he asserted, earning a frown of confusion from his lord. "The lady thinks you dead because someone has tried to kill you," Eustache stated slowly and lucidly, his words finally sinking in through Dagobert's concern for Alienor. "Make no mistake, my friend. Someone is trying to force you into the open."

Someone had tried to kill him.

The battle had already begun.

"I would still confide in her," Dagobert insisted quietly, sinking slowly beneath the weight of his realization to sit in the straw on the stable floor.

"Aye, and you would regret the telling," Eustache asserted firmly. "Naught but trouble have we had since you took this bride, and I would not jeopardize what meager hope we still have of emerging alive from the field."

Dagobert closed his eyes and dropped his head to his hands, rubbing his temples with his thumbs. Much as he would contest the point, Eustache was right. The loss of Anjou's assistance greatly reduced their chance of success and he suspected from Brabant's reports that that knight brought fewer blades to the cause than he liked to confess.

'Twas all going awry, this intricately laid plan unraveling before his very eyes, the brutal murder of the goat leaving no doubt that his identity was suspected by someone who did not sympathize with his cause. Too much risk was there in bringing another soul into the circle of conspiracy, let alone confiding in his wife, whose arrival here seemed to coincide remarkably with the beginning of their run of bad luck.

As much as he loved Alienor, would he risk his very life to confide in her the truth?

If only he could hold her close once again before he was forced to ride out, he told himself wildly, but even as the thought formed, Dagobert knew 'twas not to be. His very presence would prove the unicorn fable false, would prove that he did still draw breath and he could not take the chance. Better that she remain ignorant of these dark doings and perhaps she might escape unscathed.

But bittersweet 'twas indeed to know that he must ride out to what would surely be his last battle, now sooner than he had anticipated and without the blessing of his bride.

On the second day that Alienor lay inconsolable in her chambers, Iolande came to visit, the subtle clicking of a great dog's nails on the flagstone floor betraying her presence even before she spoke. Alienor managed to rise to her feet to greet her mother-in-law, her limbs weak from her refusal of food, her eyes swollen from countless tears, her hair hanging in tangled disarray around the pale oval of her face.

"Milady." She forced the word past dry lips and performed a serviceable curtsy beneath Iolande's assessing gaze.

"'Tis said you do not eat," Iolande accused flatly, sparing no time for pleasantries, and Alienor nodded weakly in acknowledgment.

"Aye," she agreed quietly, and felt herself waver unsteadily on her feet before Iolande's fingers gripped her upper arm mercilessly and steadied her.

"Endura is for cowards," Iolande hissed, and Alienor's eyes flew open in shock at the reference to the Cathar practice of elected suicide by fasting. The older woman shook her roughly and glared down at her with determination in her eyes.

"None would be so fool as to tell you there is no evil in this world, but daring to live is the greater challenge, child," the older woman continued in a scathing tone, her eyes burning with passion. "'Tis by living alone that any of us can affect a change and diminish the power of Rex Mundi."

Alienor shook her head mutely, stunned to hear such familiar words falling from her mother-in-law's lips, amazed to hear the familiar name of the Dark God himself uttered in this place.

"Cathar," Alienor proclaimed softly, the way Iolande eloquently arched one brow telling her all she needed to know. Indeed. Had not Alaric told her in her first days here that she was not alone?

"I took the consolamentum vows when my husband died." Iolande confirmed her taking of the final pledge tonelessly, her sapphire gaze compelling in its intensity.

Alienor nodded and licked her lips carefully, understanding now the abrupt loss of love that would prompt a woman to take those final vows of poverty and chastity. Alienor herself had plenty of time to consider making such a vow, for she could not begin the required year of preparation before her babe was born and weaned. Evident it was by now that Dagobert indeed did not intend to return to her, as the last two markedly lonely nights would attest. Alienor feared for his safety, for the threat against him could not be misinterpreted after the unicorn's death. Too late was it to wish he had taken her with him into hiding, but Alienor wished for that, all the same.

"I did not pursue endura," she corrected quietly, seeing the flicker of relief light Iolande's eyes before the emotion was suppressed.

"Indeed," Iolande said skeptically, and the word hung between the women for a moment before the older woman turned and strode a few paces away, speaking now in a clipped tone that brooked no argument.

"Two deaths I will not tolerate under my roof in so short a time," she commanded, and Alienor felt the full press of the older woman's resolve.

At Iolande's impatient gesture, Alienor slipped tiredly into one of the chairs before the hearth, feeling the relief flood through her body after the effort of standing. Despite Iolande's determination, she knew not whether she had the strength to complete this task. Without her spouse, truly it all seemed meaningless. Alienor sighed and would have closed her eyes, but firm fingers gripped her chin and tipped her face upward, compelling her to meet her mother-in-law's steady blue gaze.

"Unseemly 'tis for you to wallow in your sorrows so," Iolande reprimanded harshly, and Alienor almost gasped aloud at the other woman's callousness. Her very son was lost to them all, hunted if not already dead, and she showed no more emotion than she might for the passing of a stag planned to grace the board this night.

"Truly, I did not think you this cold," Alienor retorted, her physical discomfort giving her words a bite she would never have permitted normally. To her surprise, Iolande smiled with what appeared to be genuine amusement.

"Aye, a cold and heartless bitch am I," she confirmed as though savoring a private joke, then her eyes narrowed and she studied the younger woman's complexion critically.

"Better color have you now—perhaps I should vex you more," Iolande observed dryly, and Alienor felt an indignant flush flood her cheeks. Before she could make any response, the older woman released her chin and strode to the door, summoning a servant to build up the fire and sending Giselle to assemble a hot bath and a meal for her mistress.

"You will lie abed no longer," Iolande told Alienor over one shoulder, arching one blond brow when the younger woman shook her head in adamant denial.

"I have no reason to rise," she declared limply, sagging back against the chair. What meaning had any of this without her husband by her side? Who would rejoice in the birth of her child in this hostile keep? To Alienor's surprise, annoyance flickered across Iolande's features at her words and the woman strode impatiently back to her side.

"More sense have you than this," the older woman hissed, gripping Alienor's upper arms and giving her a little shake. "What foolishness invades your mind that you think it finer to fade and die rather than survive the fight and emerge victorious? Take not the easy choice, child, for I was not alone in expecting more of you."

Alienor clenched her hands in her lap and looked up at Iolande defiantly, daring the woman to challenge the assertion she would make.

"No victory is there for a babe born without his sire." She fairly bit out the words, pleased to see that she had completely stunned Iolande with her admission.

"A babe?" the older woman breathed, and Alienor nodded, watching Iolande's lips work for a moment. "The fruit indeed is blessed," she seemed to whisper, her lips curving into a genuine smile. "When?"

"Before *Toussaints*," Alienor admitted, the color rising in her cheeks at her mother-in-law's open glee at the news.

"October," Iolande confirmed. "Aye, 'tis a good month for a babe, well before the snows and after the heat of summer." She spun around in a flurry of blue silk, her eyes sparkling as she whirled to a stop and shook an admonishing finger at Alienor.

"Sooner than this you should have told me, for there is much to be done and certain foods that you should be taking. New goats will we need so that there is ample milk for you, and runners must be sent to the coast for fish."

"Aye, milady," Alienor conceded agreeably, the first glimmer of hope she had felt in days lighting in her breast, this tenuous alliance with Iolande lifting her chin to the fight. "Your approval surprises me," she dared to comment, feeling the full focus of Iolande's attention land upon her.

"You would say 'tis unfitting for a Cathar to rejoice in birth?" Iolande demanded.

Puzzled by her attitude, Alienor nodded. "Aye."

"And of your role in this..." Iolande's voice dropped to a whisper. "Are you ashamed, Alienor?" Alienor flushed awkwardly, not yet having come to terms with her part in bringing this child into the world. Had she not sinned in the eyes of her faith? Her own eyes filled with tears and she was surprised to find the older woman's hand covering her own with a sympathetic squeeze.

"No perfect are you, child," Iolande murmured, "for your vows lie far ahead, if indeed you ever take them. Consolamentum is for widows, ascetics, those who have tasted the fullness of life's pleasures and found them wanting."

"But I have tried to follow the faith," Alienor objected, seeing Iolande shake her head sharply even through the haze of her tears.

"Be not so hard on yourself," she admonished. "There are many amongst the believers who do far less than you do even now. You are young, Alienor," Iolande said firmly, and the two women's eyes met. "Do not deny yourself your natural pleasure in this child's arrival. 'Tis a miracle, a triumph of love. Feel no guilt for your part in the deed."

Alienor took a deep breath and considered Iolande's words thoughtfully, hoping that the older woman did not tell her nonsense just to ease her heart. She dared to look up to Iolande's intent blue gaze, watching as her mother-in-law arched one brow regally.

"Make no mistake," Iolande murmured with a wry smile, "my counsel will change drastically should you bear six more."

Alienor laughed at the unexpected jest, feeling closer to the cold countess than she ever had before. Perhaps 'twould work out after all, perhaps she and Iolande could raise a warrior straight and true. A shadow of sadness crossed her heart again and she withheld her tears with difficulty. No way was there to bear six more children with Dagobert gone, she recalled, the fear that had plagued her since she became aware of her conception haunting her anew.

"Tell me, child," Iolande insisted, her voice warm and close, and Alienor could not halt her tears from falling at the heartfelt compassion she heard there.

"The fate of the babe concerns me," she confessed softly, and heard the long release of Iolande's sigh. Out of the corner of her eye she saw the older woman shake her head as if with regret and knew her meaning had been understood. Would her child be forced to hide all of his days?

"Look to me, Alienor," she said, but Alienor had not the strength to see the confirmation of those fears. "I would have you know that I tell no tales," Iolande insisted in a firm but quiet voice, and Alienor looked up finally, blinking at the stark sincerity she saw in those sapphire depths.

"'Tis unhealthy for the babe that you worry yourself unnecessarily," Iolande said. "Rest your mind, for Dagobert's affliction was indeed a recent one, a burden placed upon him when he gained his manhood."

"I understand," Alienor said after a long silent moment, certain that her mother-in-law spoke the truth. She closed her eyes and took a deep breath, feeling the weight of her concern slip from her shoulders. Truly now she had nothing more to mourn than the loss of the babe's sire.

When next she opened her eyes, the light had changed in the room and she felt less strained. Iolande smiled in friendly greeting from the chair opposite, a fire burned merrily in the grate despite the early hour and a wooden tub reposed before the hearth.

Alienor caught a whiff of something hot and savory and her stomach made its wishes known. The demanding rumble drew a chuckle from both women simultaneously, a convivial sound that seemed to underscore the bond growing now between them. In unison, they smiled at each other across the hearth and Alienor knew that she had no fear of being turned away from Iolande's hearth.

"I would have you renounce your quest." Iolande's words rang with quiet conviction amongst the three gathered in the small darkened room. Dagobert flicked a glance to Eustache to find his own shock at his mother's request mirrored in his friend's eyes.

"Surely 'twas not you, milady," Eustache began with a confused frown, making a dangerous link between Iolande's objection and the goat's death. Dagobert winced in anticipation of the tongue-lashing that would certainly come and busied himself with flattening a hopelessly curled parchment that he might not be caught in the battle.

"I?" Iolande demanded archly as she drew herself up to her full height, and Dagobert suspected that Eustache was already regretting his hasty words. Indeed, the stalwart knight looked more than a trifle cowed before Iolande's righteous indignation.

"*I* do such a thing?" she demanded. "Truly you have lost your mind for once and for all, Eustache de Sidon, should you believe such nonsense. Well you know that I abhor the killing of *any* creature, even to fulfill the duties of the lord's board. 'Twas the workings of Rex Mundi's hand you witnessed in the smithy, a calculated display of evil intended to strike fear into those who viewed the carnage."

Dagobert glanced up to see his mother leaning over his companion purposefully, the light of battle in her eyes, and stifled a smile when Eustache actually flinched before her.

"I only thought..." Eustache managed to say before Iolande interrupted him with icy precision.

"Of thinking you know naught. Should you have the poor judgment to truly believe your accusation, Eustache de Sidon, well I know that you have no place at my hearth," she grated, and Eustache immediately held his hands up in apologetic surrender.

"Impulsive words they were, milady, and sorely regretted ere they left my mouth," he conceded gruffly. Iolande sniffed and folded her arms across her chest, her anger only moderately appeased by his apology.

Perceiving that the moment was ripe for a change of subject, Dagobert cleared his throat and drew their attention back to the matter at hand.

"Why would you make this request now?" he asked, surprised by the pain that flickered through Iolande's eyes when she first looked to him, though the expression was smothered quickly enough as was her wont.

"A dream I had," she explained unsteadily, and Dagobert knew that this was not the true reason. Indeed she sounded as though the thought had just occurred to her. "A vision of your demise," Iolande confirmed, her voice more confident as she warmed to her theme. "Truly I would not have you ride to your death when all odds seemed stacked against you."

Dagobert folded his hands together carefully on the well-worn tabletop, considering his mother's words for a moment even though he knew 'twas impossible to grant her request at this late date. Unlike her 'twas to show reservations about any plan of action and he wondered what had prompted her demand.

"Well do I appreciate your concern," he began diplomatically, but Iolande let him say no more.

"You *cannot* go!" she cried in exasperation, extending one imploring hand toward him, and Dagobert met her gaze with bewilderment.

"What has changed?" he asked quietly, and his mother retreated quickly.

"'Twas the dream," Iolande countered weakly, but Dagobert shook his head with finality, determined to get to the root of this despite her apparent unwillingness to tell him the whole of the matter.

"No dream was there," he asserted, noting that though she glared at him, Iolande had not the gall to assert her lie again. His eyes narrowed briefly when she defiantly offered no new explanation, his expression softening when he recalled something she had said just moments before.

"'Twas the murder of the goat that frightened you," he said, not knowing what to believe when Iolande looked momentarily blank before she nodded slowly. Had he only succeeded in handing her some new excuse?

"'Twas an evil death," she agreed in a low voice, the conviction Dagobert heard in her tone making him wonder if he had imagined her hesitation. "I would have better for you."

"No death will there be for milord in this battle," Eustache asserted valiantly, but all three knew he spoke not with confidence. Truly so much had gone wrong that it seemed their mission was doomed before it was fully under way. The chances were indeed slim that Dagobert succeed in his quest or even return unscathed.

"I ask you only to step back from the fray," Iolande implored one last time, drawing her son's gaze to hers. Dagobert ran his fingers through his hair with frustration and stood up to face his mother.

"I have not that option," he stated firmly, seeing that she had anticipated his response. "A vow I took many years past, a vow to my sire no less, and I would not break my word at this late date."

Son and mother stared at each other for a long moment across the heavy table in a silent battle of wills, until Iolande's lips thinned and she turned abruptly away. She walked stiffly to the door, pausing with her hand on the handle to cast one last glance over her shoulder.

"Your father regretted his folly," Iolande said, the softness of her tone belying the cruel words. Dagobert gasped at her audacity before she turned and strode from the room, leaving her statement hanging in the silence behind her.

His father had regretted his path?

Inconceivable 'twas, for the man had died blade in hand, surviving by will alone long enough to extract a vow to continue the quest from his twelve-year-old son. Vividly did Dagobert recall the image of his father's eyes blazing with passion, his left hand clutching the shoulder of the young Dagobert that he might hold himself upright. The blood had been running from his midriff, that huge hand heavy on his shoulder with the weight it supported, but those pain-filled gray eyes had brimmed with conviction and determination.

Never would Dagobert forget that moment when he had sworn the oath to his dying father, and in this moment he hated Iolande with all his heart and soul for daring to cast aspersions on the nobility of the man he had worshiped all these years. How could she state such a thing?

How dared she challenge his recollection of his sire to twist him to her own purposes?

"Milord, I would counsel you to..." Eustache began all in a rush, but Dagobert silenced him with a single burning glance.

"I will hear no more of it," he snapped with uncharacteristic sharpness. "We ride to Paris one week hence to meet Brabant, be the king's knights still here or not."

Chapter Six

"That will be all, Giselle," Alienor told her maid, nervously and pointlessly checking the tightly laced cuffs on her kirtle once more. Time enough 'twas that she showed her face at the board, and Iolande's attention had given her the only encouragement she needed to leave the solitude of her chambers.

"Sir!" Giselle gasped from the doorway, her startled exclamation drawing Alienor's attention. She fairly gasped herself at the sight of the knight Jordan standing in the doorway, resplendent in his azure-and-gold tunic and polished mail, his hair neatly combed. Did these knights of the king still linger at Montsalvat? To stay so long was an indecent intrusion on Iolande's hospitality and she had assumed them gone during her convalescence.

"Milady, I would beg a moment of your presence," he began prettily, but Alienor shook her head, her patience well and truly expired with his impudence.

"I should think not," she countered sharply, backing away when he took another step into the room as though he meant to stay. A frisson of dread tripped over her skin and she wondered at his intent.

"I would request but a short interview," he cajoled, his manner feeding all of Alienor's suspicions.

"The forum is most inappropriate," she shot back, but Jordan only smiled, a slow, calculating smile that made Alienor suddenly fear for her well-being.

She flicked a panicked glance to Giselle when Jordan seated himself in one of the chairs before the hearth, but the girl was gone. Confound the girl for her hasty departure! Alienor swore silently under her breath, bracing herself for what would surely be an awkward interview.

"I should think the setting most fitting," Jordan commented smoothly, his voice deepening with seductive intent that did naught to assuage Alienor's fears. She clasped her hands together and regarded him mutinously, knowing she could not dislodge him from the room herself, resolving that she would simply keep her distance.

"Indeed?" she inquired, barely able to keep her mind on his words.

"Indeed," he confirmed with assurance, gesturing gallantly to the chair opposite him. "Would you join me, milady?"

"I think not," Alienor refused tersely, noting too late how his eyes narrowed, trepidation setting her heartbeat running. Jordan frowned slightly at his hands and slowly stretched out his legs, crossing them at the ankles, before he spoke, as though he chose his words with care.

"As a widow, I would expect your manner to an eligible knight to be more accommodating," Jordan observed, the slight emphasis he placed on the last word fueling Alienor's suspicions. She took a hesitant step backward and he was on his feet in a moment, closing the space between them with sure steps.

"Be not afraid, milady," he said under his breath as he grew ever closer. "I would not have such strain between two who would spend the remainder of their years together."

"No desire have I to wed again in the near future," Alienor argued breathlessly, but the knight merely shook his head as if he argued with a foolish child and smiled that maddeningly confident smile once more.

"What other options have you, Alienor?" he demanded quietly, the caressing way he uttered her name making her shudder and take another step back.

"I shall stay with Iolande," she managed to object wildly, but Jordan only shook his head sagely as if he well understood the ways of the world and she did not.

"Until she chooses another for you, Alienor? A month of peace you have, perhaps two, before your burden on the household becomes clear." He looked her full in the face, his dark eyes glittering. "And who would the noble Iolande choose? A wealthy man from within her own domain? A man in his dotage with drool on his chin? Be sure that she will be thinking of alliance, not your physical pleasure."

He stood back with a knowing smile and gestured to himself with pride, the slight movement of his hand drawing Alienor's glance unwillingly over his form. Conceit he undoubtedly had, but the man was young and not offensive looking. 'Twas his manner alone that Alienor despised.

"Choose another for yourself, Alienor," Jordan urged as though he saw encouragement in her eyes, and he took the last step remaining between them. His hands rose quickly to trap Alienor's shoulders before

she could move away and he fairly lifted her toward
him.

"Let no other make your choices for you this time,
for they would not make the selection best for you. I
have adequate wealth, a fine home, a title, a place at
the king's own court. No finer suitor will you find in
this backward province, milady," he asserted, and
gave her a little shake. "You have but to reach out and
accept me to see the deed done."

Alienor shook her head in denial, not even needing
to consider the idea to know she could not wed this
man. But two days her husband had been lost to her
and now this heartless cur expected her to take him in
Dagobert's stead.

What travesty of fate would ask her to trade the
tender compassion of one man for the cynical self-
motivation of another? This man had no feelings for
her, indeed he knew naught of her. 'Twas her form
alone he desired and his own desires that concerned
him to the exclusion of all else. And that desire would
die a quick death when he discerned the faint begin-
nings of the rounding of her belly.

"Nay," she said quietly, and Jordan's eyes darkened still further as his jaw tightened in anger. She
would not do this thing, did not need to make this
match, for Iolande had ensured her place here at
Montsalvat.

And mayhap, she dared to hope, when the threat
against him was gone, Dagobert would return to her
side.

"What say you, woman?" he demanded sharply,
and Alienor's anger sparked at his tone. How dare he
assume that she would fall easily into his plans? How

dare he approach her in her own chambers? How dare he press his suit upon her when she refused?

"I say nay," Alienor shot back, shrugging off the weight of his hands and darting across the room. Fury erupted in the knight's eyes and suddenly she wondered how much more he would dare. Her heart pounded in her throat as she backed away and Jordan stalked her with silent intent, no sounds of salvation carrying to her ears from the stairs.

Did no one come to help her? Did no one note her absence in the hall? Did Giselle not wonder what took her so long to descend? Fear made her voice rise higher than usual and she barely recognized her own tones when she hotly protested his advance.

"I will *not* have another! I will not have *you!*"

'Twas undoubtedly the worst thing she could have said. Jordan's features distorted with rage and Alienor turned to flee, knowing now that he would stop at nothing to see his suit accepted. She thought briefly of the babe within her and prayed that his attack would not hurt her child.

"Naught difference does your will make in this matter!" Jordan roared, and lunged across the room after her.

Alienor's adrenaline soared and she dived across the flagstones for the door, certain she would be safe if she could but gain the hallway. The iron handle was but a span away and she savored a fleeting sense of victory when her fingers brushed against it. Jordan's booted foot landed on her trailing hem in that moment and her heart sank.

She twisted desperately as the weight of his hand fell on the cloth and the kirtle tore with a resonant rip. Alienor's heart leapt with the brief respite from his grip, but she managed only another half step before Jordan's hand closed on her hair. She cried out in anguish at the pain in her scalp and came to a full stop, certain he would tear the hair from her head if she did not.

"More than one way is there to force a match," he gritted into her ear, and Alienor struggled against him, her worst fears finding confirmation in his words.

Despite her desperate fighting, Jordan easily trapped her with one arm and ripped the remainder of her kirtle aside with the other. He shoved her unceremoniously to the floor and the coldness of the stone pressed through her chemise to her buttocks and bare legs. Alienor rolled immediately in a last bid to escape, but he fell directly upon her, fumbling with his chausses while his sheer weight held her captive.

No! This could not happen here in her own chambers! Helpless to do anything else, Alienor tipped back her head and screamed loud enough to bring the very roof down upon them.

"Bitch!" Jordan had time to swear, his eyes flashing with dangerous fury, before his weight was suddenly hauled from atop her. Alienor scrambled to sit up even as she disbelievingly watched her attacker's bulk fly across the room and land in a crumpled pile against the far wall.

"My wife's services are not for hire," Alaric declared coldly from above her. Alienor's head spun at the import of his words, her gaze flying to him, but she barely glimpsed his grim expression before he stalked the other knight down.

His wife? Clearly she had misunderstood what Alaric had said, her fogged mind assured her as she watched him stride purposefully across the room, blade in hand. He paused, looking expectantly down at his prey, the sunlight silhouetting his form, and some inkling of familiarity nudged Alienor's heart at the sight. Easily she recalled her husband's silhouette as he stood outlined before the fire and she swallowed now with difficulty, unable to accept the evidence before her.

Dagobert?

"Your wife?" Jordan demanded sharply, his words echoing Alienor's own confusion. Alaric nodded once firmly and held up his left hand, the gold wedding band on his third finger glinting in the sunlight even as Alienor's breath caught in her throat. The signet ring that had also been on the cord was now placed on his middle finger.

"Dagobert, Count of Pereille am I," he asserted calmly, one impatient gesture indicating that the other man rise. Alienor thought that she saw something remarkably like satisfaction flicker through Jordan's eyes. "Rise and defend yourself," he demanded, but Jordan shook his head.

"But, milord, I assure you I meant no harm. Had I but known you drew breath," he argued, but Dagobert cut off his words abruptly.

"Harm you did indeed intend," he corrected, and Alienor fairly shuddered at the coldness in his tone. "Harm to my lady and harm to my house. Defend yourself, sir."

"Dagobert," Alienor whispered to herself in shocked disbelief, unable to absorb the revelation that had just been laid before her. Confirming images flooded her mind too quickly to be studied individually, suspicious happenings that she had ignored to her own folly. Too easily she recalled her ready attraction to Alaric, the twinges of familiarity when she glimpsed some shadowed detail of her husband's build and visage.

All too much sense it made now; his refusal to speak or let her touch his face in the night had clearly been to ensure that she not recognize him during the day. Dagobert, she marveled, her eyes running over her husband's form, seeking reassurance. Dagobert was truly alive and stood whole before her. She trembled at the realization, relief spreading tenuously through her that she was no longer alone.

"Aye, 'tis he." Eustache's gruff tones came from beside her and Alienor lifted her eyes to find his workworn hand proffered. She put her shaking hand in his and rose unsteadily to her feet, accepting the pelisson he offered and slipping it over her shoulders with a grateful smile, still unable to accept that Alaric and Dagobert were one and the same.

A number of household members clustered in the doorway, their expressions bright with curiosity and expectation, but Alienor saw not a flicker of surprise among them. Was she then the only one who had not known of this deceit? Her hurt at that thought was quickly followed by confusion.

To what purpose had Dagobert enacted this charade? Why had the unicorn been killed? And by whom?

"En garde." Dagobert's words echoed across the room and Alienor's gaze flew back to the two men.

"It need not be this way, milord," Jordan said, and Alienor held her breath for an instant, wondering at his game even as she hoped Dagobert would abandon the fight and not endanger himself.

"What manner of man does not face the consequences of his actions with a steady hand?" Dagobert demanded scornfully.

Jordan straightened with bad grace and pulled his blade from its scabbard, his gaze running assessingly over his opponent.

Alienor unconsciously did the same, her fear for Dagobert taking some measure of relief from the fact that he stood taller than the other man, his shoulders broader, his muscles coiled with tension like that of a wolf poised to spring. Instinctively, Alienor realized that his skill with a blade would be sure and deadly, but her fingers gripped one another in trepidation when she realized that, unlike his opponent, Dagobert wore no mail.

"What manner of man masquerades within his own keep as a goat?" Jordan sneered, and Dagobert stiffened, lifting his blade even higher in silent challenge. Jordan snorted as he touched the tip of his blade to Dagobert's sword tip and the battle began.

"Is it truly your lady's honor that prompts you to challenge me?" Jordan taunted as he lunged at Dagobert's middle, the taller man parrying the blow expertly and stepping quickly aside.

"So you would doubt my word, as well?" Dagobert countered calmly, and Alienor saw the cold determination in his eyes as the men circled each other cautiously.

Jordan jabbed again with lightning speed and the room filled with the sound of clashing steel. Back and forth across the floor the battle continued: thrust, parry and counterthrust, the two men's skill virtually equal.

The tip of Dagobert's blade caught Jordan's cheek and the shorter man growled in annoyance at the nick. Jordan sprang toward Dagobert with a renewed ferocity and backed him into the wall, his blade lingering dangerously close to Dagobert's throat. Alienor gasped, Eustache reached for the scabbard of his own blade beside her, but Dagobert jammed his knee upward defiantly. Jordan groaned and fell back in pain, the two men circling each other cautiously once again.

"A fetching bitch she is, but you do not challenge me for the woman," Jordan goaded, but Dagobert's attention remained riveted on the other knight's face.

"Do explain," he invited indulgently, and Alienor saw his fingers tighten imperceptibly on the hilt of his sword.

"I could not have left your keep without this challenge," Jordan murmured confidentially. "For I know too much, do I not, milord?" This last word was uttered mockingly and Alienor could not follow the knight's meaning.

"You speak gibberish," Dagobert affirmed, his blade catching the light as he attacked with sudden ruthlessness. Alienor's hands rose to her face at the ferocity of this exchange, the broadswords clanging high over the men's heads and again between them.

Again and again and again they clashed, the men fairly dancing back and forth across the flagstones. Jordan jabbed and Dagobert parried in the nick of time, barely managing to deflect the sword point from his heart. They parted reluctantly, their breathing echoing heavily in the room.

"How much do I know?" Jordan panted, his eyes wild as he lifted his ebony brows quizzically, and Alienor felt Eustache stiffen beside her. "How far

have I seen behind the facade? Have I discovered what
you would aspire to hide, Dagobert de Pereille?"

"I have naught to hide," Dagobert maintained
tightly, but Jordan only smiled.

"Perhaps not now," he conceded. "A curious act
'tis for a man to place a goat in the hall in his stead. I
can only surmise that your reason was compelling."

"'Twas a jest, no more," Dagobert argued, the
forbidding lines of his face belying his words. 'Twas
deadly serious, this game.

"No jest was the creature's death," Jordan countered, diving forward only to have his thrust deflected
and turned back against him.

"And no jest would your house have seen if it had
been truly your own blood royal spilled in the smithy,"
he continued, his unexpected words sending a curious
stillness over all the occupants of the room. Jordan
smiled with self-satisfaction. "So, you have convinced them all that you are the key to the tales of
old," he mused almost to himself, scanning the
shocked faces of the household members gathered in
the doorway.

Jordan's perusal was his undoing, for Dagobert
moved with quick deliberation, his blade catching
Jordan's beneath the hilt. A flick of his wrist and the
broadsword danced out the window, catching the
sunlight before it spun and fell to the bailey below. A
quick look of terror flickered across Jordan's features before a knowing expression settled in his eyes.

"'Twould not be chivalrous to strike down a man
who had not a blade," he murmured confidently. Dagobert's chin snapped up, his eyes blazing. Alienor
saw that the king's knight spoke the truth and that her

husband would not strike him down now, despite the anger flowing hotly through him.

"'Tis fortunate indeed 'twas not you in the smithy," Jordan hissed as he leaned toward Dagobert. "For 'twould be nigh impossible for your line to continue through your Cathar mare."

Murderous intent gleamed in Dagobert's eyes, but before he could move, Jordan had jumped to the window ledge. He blew Alienor a cocky kiss, then turned and leapt from the ledge.

The assembled company gasped as one and ran to the window, incredulous at the risk the man had taken, but Dagobert was there first. His lips tightened and Alienor knew before she saw that Jordan had survived the three-story fall.

"Eustache!" he called, stepping away from the window even as the others crowded to it. Alienor caught a glimpse of Jordan far below in the bailey, running unevenly toward the stables and clearly favoring one leg. "We ride in pursuit! He will not be far ahead of us."

"Aye, milord, he must be stopped," Eustache agreed wholeheartedly, and turned from Alienor's side to hasten away.

He had gone but a step before he swore under his breath, and Alienor spun around to find six knights in azure and gold closing ranks in the portal with blades at the ready.

"As must you," the lead knight commented with assurance. "'Twould be most distressing if the king did not receive word of this conspiracy."

"As you wish it." Eustache audibly gritted his teeth and drew his blade before Alienor's eyes. Dagobert shoved his way through the surprised retinue of his

household to stand beside his companion and Alienor's heart began to pound that they should be so
outnumbered in their own keep. She pressed back
against the wall with the others, barely feeling Giselle's tiny hand slip into her own as the men stepped
forward of one accord and the sound of fading hoofbeats carried from the courtyard below.

Barely had steel tasted steel than one of the servants standing against the wall tugged a short dagger
from his jerkin and joined the fray. Alienor gasped in
surprise when a second and a third followed suit and
the numbers became more evenly matched.

A young boy who usually ran errands throughout
the keep braved the swinging broadswords and side-
stepped his way through the fight, darting out into the
hallway to summon help before any could impede his
progress. In the blink of an eye, only Giselle and
Alienor stood against the stone wall as the room
erupted into one large battle.

A servant fell right before Alienor and she gasped,
making to step forward and assist him. Her movement drew the unwelcome attention of the knight who
had fought with him, and with deadly precision, the
mailed man in azure and gold turned his attention on
the two women remaining in the room.

Alienor's heart raced when he took a step toward
her and she felt Giselle slip away from her side. A chill
weight remained in her hand despite the girl's departure and Alienor risked a glimpse behind her, surprised to find that the maid had given her a short
dagger. Truly the girl was clear of thought for her age
and Alienor felt a wave of mingled gratitude and admiration wash over her, even as she met the knight's
gaze squarely.

Let him come and taste the bite of her blade.

No need had she to reveal her weapon however, for just when the knight leapt toward her, Dagobert dispatched his own opponent with one fell swoop of his broadsword. He spun on his heel with the impact of the blow and immediately saw the other knight's intent, cutting the man down before he could move any closer to Alienor.

Alienor exhaled shakily as the knight measured his length across the floor as though he would kiss her very toes, the sound of another falling bringing her alarmed glance to a victorious Eustache. A servant held a third knight at dagger point in the far corner, a fourth had lost his blade, and the remaining two threw down their weapons in concession.

At that moment, the cook, the ostler and the chatelain leapt through the door looking dangerous, and Alienor almost laughed at their evident disappointment that they came too late to the fray.

"To the dungeons with them," Dagobert decreed, and the men of his household nodded in agreement, setting immediately to the task of incarcerating the defeated knights. With a worried frown, he turned anew to Eustache as he resheathed his blade, summoning the older man with an imperative glance.

"We must go," Dagobert insisted, and Eustache nodded in agreement, following suit and heading for the door.

"And where would you go, milord?" jeered the king's knight who had led the five others, drawing the surprised glances of those remaining in the room. "Jordan's path is an hour cold and you have yet to saddle your mount and don your mail. Think you that his destination was that obvious that any could dis-

cern it? Under secret orders he was, and you would be
skilled indeed to divine his path this day.''

Alienor caught the quick look that flashed between
her husband and his companion and knew that there
was some measure of truth in the man's words.

"Much did I learn of coercion at my former master's knee," Eustache muttered slowly, and Alienor
shuddered at the thought of anyone being tortured
within the keep. The knight who spoke so boldly was
undisturbed by the thinly veiled threat and grinned
broadly at the older man.

"Aye, and a time-consuming process such coercion
can be, indeed. Especially when practiced on one so
young and well rested as myself," he added confidently as he fixed Dagobert with an assessing eye.
"Even should I know Jordan's path, he would surely
have arrived there before you could learn the truth of
it from me."

"Remove him," Dagobert ordered curtly, and 'twas
clear to all that he was annoyed by the truth in the
young knight's words. The servants departed with the
knights in tow, Giselle and the other women carrying
their discarded weapons and leaving Alienor alone and
apparently unobserved with the two men.

"Tracking dogs have we," Eustache suggested quietly when the footsteps on the stairs faded, but Dagobert shook his head in slow refusal.

"'Twould be futile and well you know it. The road
goes leagues before it forks clearly and is cursed by any
number of goat paths that could be used by a cunning
rider."

"And the way is traveled by so many who would
muddle the scent," Eustache concluded glumly, earning an answering nod from his lord. Eustache frowned

down at the blood on the flagstones, his expression thoughtful when he lifted his head. "'Twas almost as if he deliberately drew you out," he mused, and Dagobert laughed a dry sardonic laugh.

"'Twas exactly thus," he admitted heavily, throwing a sharp glance in Alienor's direction that chilled her heart.

'Twas not her fault that Jordan had used her as a pawn in his game! But the coldness in Dagobert's eyes told her that he thought she had had some part in his uncloaking, a quick glance to Eustache revealing the open hostility that lurked in that knight's eyes.

"A dark day 'twas..." Eustache began, but Dagobert waved him to silence, gesturing toward the hallway.

"Come. We will decide our plan in confidence," he interrupted coldly, his eyes raking over Alienor once more before he stalked purposefully from the room. The door closed with finality behind the two and Alienor fell bonelessly against the wall, the dagger clattering from her limp fingers to the floor, her stomach rebelling as the adrenaline released its grip upon her.

"'Tis the woman who has brought all of this upon us," Eustache asserted, as he paced Dagobert's office in agitation for the umpteenth time. "Never should you have wed the woman, knowing so little about her, never should the match have been made on the basis of her similarity to Arpais."

"You would question my recollection of one of my closest friends?" Iolande demanded archly from her chair across the room, and Dagobert closed his eyes in annoyance, certain that he was doomed to hear this argument run its course yet again.

"I would question your wisdom in promoting this choice!" Eustache shot back, but when Iolande's eyes flashed, Dagobert rose to his feet tiredly.

"As I would question the two of you for wasting time so scandalously," he commented dryly, noting with satisfaction the way both of them flushed in embarrassment. "Fortunately, you have unwittingly given me time to reflect upon my path. I have decided to ride out this day into hiding."

"No!" Iolande declared, rising to her feet in horror.

"No!" Eustache asserted in the same instant, stepping toward his lord in concern.

"There is no need," Iolande added, but Dagobert shook his head in denial.

"There is every need," he insisted. "Jordan knows the way of things and makes his way to the king or some trusted messenger of the crown. When news of our plan reaches Paris, a sortie will undoubtedly be sent to Montsalvat to ensure my demise." Both blue and green eyes dropped away from his regard and Dagobert knew they had reached similar conclusions.

"I will not endanger the keep thus with my continued presence," he concluded softly, dropping back into his chair with the sense that he was completely alone in the world.

Alienor, he thought, but pushed her image away, not having the courage even to imagine her response to the surprise she had had this morn. Ironic it was indeed that Eustache spoke so often of her deception, as yet unproved, when the evidence of his own deceit was right before their eyes.

"Where will you go?" Eustache demanded hoarsely, and Dagobert frowned.

"I had thought to seek out Brabant," he began, but the older knight shook his head.

"If Jordan truly knows the way of things, 'twill be the first place they look. Let me send a messenger to Brabant that the hunt for your hide is not made so easy."

Dagobert nodded in agreement, tired before he even began, all his energy sapped by the knowledge that he was now on the run and 'twas only a matter of time before he was tracked down like an animal and killed.

"Do you ride alone?" Iolande demanded sharply, and he nodded immediately, not seeing the point of her question. "Would you not protect your own, then?" she asked, and Dagobert looked up with surprise.

"Milady, you and Alienor are in no danger with my presence gone," he pointed out, bewildered when his mother shook her head adamantly.

"Nay, my son, 'tis not so. Alienor risks as heavily as you in this endeavor."

"I do not understand," Dagobert confessed, a quick glance to Eustache confirming that he was not alone in his confusion.

"She bears your child," Iolande asserted as she folded her arms across her chest, and the silence that fell in the small room fairly hurt the ears. "Should the king truly seek to exterminate the blood royal, she also will die."

A child. Dagobert ran his hand through his hair in frustration, shoving to his feet and pacing the length of the room himself now. His child. Even in the face of such difficulties, the thought that he and Alienor had conceived a babe launched a bubble of excitement within him. He envisioned Alienor ripe and rosy with his child and fairly grinned at the prospect, sobering immediately when he recalled the danger she was now in. Danger he had squarely placed her in.

"I cannot ride with a pregnant wife," he protested, knowing in his heart that that was exactly what he must do, but still surprised when his mother's eyes flashed and she poked her finger uncompromisingly into the center of his chest.

""Twas your pleasure that made her thus and your seed 'tis that grows in her womb," she fairly growled. "Should you think you can walk away from her in this regard, then I have surely erred in bringing you forth into this world." Dagobert swallowed with difficulty, knowing these were the sternest words Iolande had ever had for him. "The pledge your sire and I made is fulfilled in this child and you *will* not cast the babe aside."

"You have not erred, milady, for already did I know my duty to Alienor and intend to keep it," he admitted quietly, before lifting his gaze to Eustache. "See that our mounts are made ready," he added, and turned to stride from the room.

Liar!

Alienor's surprise had turned to full-blown anger by the time the sun rose high in the sky and she threw trinkets around her chamber in unparalleled frustration. Any relief she had felt that Dagobert survived the bloodshed in the smithy had quickly been eclipsed by the realization that she had been deliberately deceived.

He had lied to her, the miserable wretch! Alienor launched a brass candlestick across the room with all the vehemence she could muster. The hours she had spent scolding herself for her awareness of Alaric had been all for naught, for they two were in reality one and the same! Would that she could take a strip off his hide for daring to give her no clue, however minute, that might illuminate her to the way of things.

And when the unicorn had been killed and she had been so distraught, certain she was never to see him again, could he not have spared a kind word for her then? Oh, nay. A discarded shoe came to hand and she hurled it at the fireplace, enjoying the way it bounced off a brass plate left by the hearth. Could he not have come to her bed to reassure her with his presence, even if he had continued to refuse to speak? What little 'twould have cost him to assuage her fears!

Would that she could recall the hours she had futilely fretted over the future of their unborn babe. She spied the mate of the shoe that had just flown across the room and kicked it instead with an unparalleled viciousness. A full score years had she worried from her life over the past three months and 'twas all for naught!

Not only had he deceived her, not only had he let her agonize about her apparently disloyal interest in Alaric, not only had he caused her to fret over her unborn child, not only had he ignored her weeping over the death of the goat, but now he blamed *her* for Jordan's discovery of his deception.

'Twas ridiculous, to say the least, that she, an unwilling participant in these games of men, should be considered the master conspirator behind it all. That he should be blessed *stupid* on top of it all was too much to endure. Not only was she wed to a lunatic, but 'twas clear the man's thinking was addled, as well.

And did he simply ask her about her involvement? Was she questioned, given the opportunity to explain? Nay! Alienor punctuated that thought with the hurling of a hammered brass trinket box. He simply drew his conclusions and painted her with the blackest brush, granting her nary a chance to defend herself!

As if that were not enough, it well appeared that she was the only one within the keep who did not know the truth of things. Clearly a mere woman such as herself could not be trusted to know her own mind, let alone be privy to a "secret" that it seemed everyone knew but her! Yet another insult to be endured, that he did not find his own wife worthy of his confidence.

And had she chosen this match? Nay! She had not even been willing for it, yet everyone seemed conveniently to forget *that* aspect of things. Quite ready she had been to begin preparations to take the consolamentum vows and pledge herself to a life of piety and chastity, but these fine-minded individuals had had other plans for her.

As if to compound the matter further, she carried the deceiver's babe within her belly. Argh! Alienor shoved the chest at the foot of the bed across the floor and it hit the far wall heavily, something inside jangling with the impact.

Another unsettling thought occurred to Alienor and she gritted her teeth once more. Even Guibert had conspired against her of necessity, for he must have known the fullness of the tale before committing her hand to this madman. Truly that man would receive a

tongue-lashing when next she saw him that he would
not soon forget.

Men! Alienor cast a glance around the chamber,
seeking something that would shatter satisfactorily
when she threw it, only to find her husband standing
quietly in the portal, watching her steadily. He folded
his arms across his chest as if he faced a defiant child,
and Alienor's hackles rose, her chin lifting a notch as
she confronted her spouse.

Nay, she realized, 'twas a forbidding stranger that
stood before her in her husband's form, showing neither the tenderness of Dagobert, who came to her in
the night, nor the lighthearted good nature of Alaric,
who teased her each day. Under his steely gray regard, Alienor's anger evaporated and she grew suddenly afraid of the man she had wed, uncertain of his
true nature beneath the facade.

"We depart with the darkness," the tall man in the
doorway informed her with a toneless hauteur. "I
would that you packed lightly, milady, and speak of
this to none other than Giselle."

Before Alienor could demand an explanation or ask
whither they went, he had turned away, his footfalls
fading as he descended to the hall. For a moment she
stood completely bewildered by this turn of events,
then the explanation came to her and her lips set in
angry defiance.

Send her back to Perpignan like some sort of dam-
aged goods, would he? *Fine!* And she would ensure
that he never laid eyes on the babe she bore him.

Pack lightly? *Fine!* She would take no more than she
had brought to Montsalvat herself.

And may the lot of the Pereille clan rot in hell!

* * *

Dagobert's gut twisted when a clearly mutinous Alienor descended the stairs as the sun sank over the mountains, her lips thinning as she tugged her gloves on impatiently. What had he let himself in for? 'Twas evident to even the most casual observer that she was still furiously angry with him for not confiding in her and he knew not what to say to console her.

He scanned her attire and noted with relief that she had dressed sensibly for traveling, her clothing warm and unadorned, the bundle of possessions Giselle carried for her smaller than he had anticipated. When she drew alongside him, he offered his hand politely but Alienor made as though she had not noticed the gesture, her attention apparently fully captured by the cuffs of her gloves. Dagobert almost spoke sharply to her, then stifled the impulse when he caught a glimpse of humor in Eustache's eyes.

"May Dame Fortune ride with you," the older knight commented dryly under his breath, and Dagobert almost grimaced.

"To be sure, she does not as yet," he responded, encouraged when Alienor shot him a dark glance. He winked boldly at his wife and she spun on her heel to stalk toward the stables, but not before he caught a glimpse of the color rising on her cheeks.

"Your travels should indeed be interesting," Eustache remarked, and Dagobert shrugged noncommittally, unwilling to speculate on what tempestuous road lay ahead of him.

"Forget not our plan," he muttered under his breath, noting that his companion looked momentarily surprised.

"You would continue then?"

"It seems 'twill be our last and best chance," Dagobert confirmed grimly, and Eustache nodded in thoughtful agreement.

"I would have you ride with us," he suggested tentatively, and the younger man nodded in the affirmative.

"I will find you," Dagobert asserted, and he shook hands with Eustache in the darkness of the hall before he strode away.

Shadows were stretching long across the courtyard and the stables were unnaturally silent when Dagobert stepped outside into the cool bite of the evening air. Alienor stood waiting for him, her back turned to him and unnaturally stiff, and for a moment he thought her the only one there.

She fingered the reins of the smaller saddled steed as if she were nervous and he knew by that fact alone that she sensed his presence. He almost stepped forward and clasped the narrow span of her shoulders within his hands, almost whispered an apology in her ear, but pulled himself up short, knowing that each moment they lingered in the keep endangered them yet further. Ample time there would be for explanations on the dusty road ahead.

Gradually his eyes adjusted to the light until he could pick out the inky silhouettes of other members of his house standing quietly, here the chatelain, there the ostler, there the smith, the farrier, the marshal, Iolande and two of her dogs, the squire he had trained these past three years. Each of their shadowed faces was etched with a mingling of hope and disappointment, each brow burdened with some measure of fear of what lay ahead.

No secret was his departure now, but he could not summon an iota of displeasure, the concern of these people he had lived with and the send-off they gave him more important than any escape that would not hold secret until the dawn.

Dagobert acknowledged each with a nod, a slight smile, an easy wink, hoping that he could ease their trepidation at least a bit by his own apparent confidence. In truth, he did the best thing for the safety of all by leaving Montsalvat, and he saw in the eyes of more than one servant and friend an understanding of this simple fact.

Iolande stood tall with downcast eyes and Dagobert stepped to embrace his mother last, brushing an affectionate kiss against the smooth coolness of her cheek.

"All will be well," he quietly assured her, and she nodded emphatically, evidently not trusting herself to speak. "I leave you with the responsibility of the keep," he added unnecessarily, and Iolande nodded again, straightening her spine.

"Take care," she managed unsteadily, lifting her eyes to meet his with a shaky smile. Well might it be the last time they saw each other, Dagobert knew, and he squeezed his mother's shoulders tightly once more before he stepped away, his own vision none too clear in this moment.

To his surprise, Iolande turned to Alienor and pulled the younger woman into an impulsive hug. He watched Alienor close her eyes against the shimmer of rising tears in those amber depths, the long lashes spiky and wet against her cheeks as she returned Iolande's embrace. Dagobert glanced away to find wistful expressions on the surrounding sea of faces,

more than one member of the household wiping away
an indulgent tear at the two women's leave-taking.

Iolande whispered something to Alienor that Dagobert could not catch and he watched his wife nod in
agreement and force a smile to her lips. She darted a
glance in his direction and her color rose slightly,
making him wonder what his mother could possibly
have said. He glanced impatiently at the deepening
shade of the sky and extended his hand to Alienor,
knowing that they had to ride out, despite their wishes
to the contrary.

"I will, madame," Alienor vowed, and turned to
place her hand in Dagobert's, her gaze flicking immediately downward under his perusal that he might
not guess her thoughts.

Annoyance rippled through him, followed closely by
a wave of possessiveness that had him lifting her into
his own saddle before he had the chance to check his
own impulse. Alienor opened her mouth to protest,
but he cut off her words before she could even speak,
tying her horse's reins to the back of his saddle with
one abrupt gesture.

"You must rest for the babe, milady," he said
curtly, watching with satisfaction as his wife bit her lip
and the color rose in her cheeks. Behind him, a murmur of approval rippled through the crowd of well-
wishers, but Alienor's back was straight and stiff when
he swung up into the saddle behind her.

"You make the road longer with your anger," he
dared to murmur into her hair, closing his arm around
her waist in that same moment and pulling her resolutely back against his chest.

To his immense relief, Alienor did not fight him, but
she did not relax until long after Montsalvat had faded

in the distance and she fell into a fitful slumber. Only then did Dagobert pull her even closer, permitting himself the luxury of inhaling the delicate sandal-wood scent of her hair, of letting his gloved hand curve proprietarily over the soft indent of her waist.

Chapter Seven

The smell of wet metal greeted Alienor when she awoke groggily, closely followed by the scent of soaked leather and sodden wool. Momentarily disoriented by an incessant motion that did no favors for her unsettled stomach, she opened one eye tentatively, only to be confronted by a solid wall of red wool, her raised hood letting little light onto the scene. Judging by the rows of tight circles impressed against her cheek, 'twas red wool over chain mail, both of which were stretched over her husband's broad chest. She stirred and his arm tightened around her waist, though the horse did not ease its pace.

"'Tis but dawn," Dagobert murmured, and she felt his chin graze against her hooded temple as he inclined his head to speak to her. Only now did Alienor become aware of the rain pounding against her shoulders, realizing that she sat completely sideways before Dagobert, her face buried in his chest, her arms wrapped around his waist beneath his mantle. And his destrier was galloping at a relentlessly steady pace despite the rain.

"And the weather is most foul," he continued formally. "I would that you go back to sleep, milady."

"Have you slept?" she dared to ask, tipping her head back to venture a glance through the wet cloaks to her husband's stern visage, seeing the lines of tension etched alongside his mouth. The sky was an endless expanse of gray above his head, his eyes were narrowed against the chill rain dashing against his face, and he barely spared a downward glance at her move.

"Nay, milady," he replied, confirming her suspicions grimly. His tone discouraged any further inquiries and she wondered at this total stranger who held her so uncompromisingly close to his side.

No less forbidding did he look now than when he had greeted her last eve at the foot of the stairs, a strange and hostile warrior clothed head to toe in his mail, his coif leaving only the matching coldness in his eyes visible. Who was this man? Not one inkling of the lover who had warmed her bed illuminated him, nor did a glimmer of the lighthearted companionship of Alaric touch his face. Was this then the true Dagobert? Was this the man whose seed bore fruit within her? Was this the man with whom she would spend the remainder of her days?

She squinted up into the silver onslaught of rain at that rigidly set chin, conceding that he undoubtedly saw her as a burden to his travels. A woman who would slow his pace and block the swift thrust of his blade by her very presence. Why then had he insisted she accompany him?

The answer followed quickly on the heels of the question: 'twas the babe she bore him and no more. Indeed, Alienor admitted to herself sadly, she had seen the whole truth of it when she had first thought that the man desired her only for her womb. A fool she had been to dare to hope he might learn to feel differently, but the taste of her folly in her mouth was no easier to swallow for having been anticipated.

Would she be abandoned then as soon as the child saw the light of day? The thought was chilling. But 'twas clear to even the most casual observer that this man bore no softness in his heart for her, that she was being protected solely that his heir might be born strong. Alienor fidgeted, wishing to put some distance between herself and this remote man who had claimed her for his own, but his arm tightened like a steel band around her waist and he flicked her a quelling glance.

"'Tis warmer for you thus," he commented tersely as his fingers fastened unceremoniously around her hipbone and held her intimately captive. Alienor gasped at his move but his grip trapped her easily and she struggled to slow the rapid pace of her heart. Too aware was she of the shape of the man beneath his mail, too well did she recall those strong thighs clenched beneath hers, too easily did she remember the safety she had felt with his weight pressing her into their soft mattress back at Montsalvat.

And the scent of his skin. Even through the over-powering smells of wet clothing and armor, she could detect that tantalizingly musky scent of his skin. Too strange it seemed indeed to have such intimate recollections of a man who seemed now to be a virtual stranger.

Uncomfortable with the turn of her thoughts, Alienor pursed her lips, steeling herself with the confirmation of her fears that she found in his sharp words. She must not sicken and lose the babe, 'twas the only significance to his mind. Had she not been pregnant, she would without a doubt have been left behind to her own fate.

"Where do we ride?" Alienor asked, uncertain what else to say, her heart sinking as his lips thinned still further.

"Away," Dagobert conceded tightly. Not knowing what to make of this response, Alienor glanced up, seeing his gloved hand rising in her peripheral vision. She flinched instinctively, thinking he meant to cuff her for her insistence on asking questions, aware more than ever that she knew not the man who rode behind her.

He noted the gesture and glanced down at her with what seemed to be genuine surprise, the look in his eyes making her wish she could have controlled her inadvertent gesture. The wet reins he held brushed against her hot cheek for an instant as he pulled her hood further forward once again, enclosing Alienor in the cocoon against his chest and effectively ending their conversation.

"'Twill be a long day, milady," he said, and his tone was distant now, a tone of defeat underscoring his words that Alienor had not heard before. "Rest for the babe if you can."

Despite her best efforts to the contrary, Alienor felt her heart yield to this remote knight, and she felt his disappointment as keenly as if it were her own, though she knew not its source.

Instinctively wishing she could comfort him in some way, she tightened her arms around his waist and leaned more fully against him as if she would gather him to her breast for consolation. For an instant, no more, it seemed to her tired mind that his fingers tightened around her waist, and she thought she heard him sigh softly before she drifted back to sleep, the pounding of the destrier's hooves and the drilling of the rain an incessant lullaby.

So she feared he would beat her, Dagobert acknowledged to himself, unable to believe that his life had taken so many turns for the worse as he gritted his teeth in frustration. Only a woman could come to such a conclusion when he had done nothing but see to her comfort so far on this journey. Did she think he cared for her health and rest only so that there might be more sport in the beating? Did she honestly believe that he could touch her cruelly after so much tenderness had passed between them?

Not that he hadn't the right to beat her as her legal husband. Or more than adequate justification, should she truly have been at the root of all his recent troubles. Dagobert spared a quick glance down to the damp softness tumbled against his chest, barely suppressing a smile as he heard her slow breathing. He pulled her a little closer and she snuggled against him like a cat before the fire, her sleepy murmur fueling a warm glow around his heart.

Could she truly have betrayed him thus? Could she have engineered his unveiling with Jordan de Soissons? Now that his temper had cooled, he found the thought harder and harder to accept, despite the wealth of evidence ready to support the accusation.

At the very least, this voyage would eliminate her ability to communicate with anyone but him, for they would not have the luxury of stopping at inns and taverns. And she could not know their path for he knew it not himself. Away from Montsalvat, 'twas all.

Away from those he loved and trusted that their lives might be spared.

And what of this one he loved but could not trust? He spared another glance downward at Alienor's sleeping form. And what of the babe she bore him? Did his son not deserve better from him than a life of endless traveling? What else did he have to offer her when the comfort of his own hearth was denied to him?

A ray of hope stirred within his breast and he thought of carving a new life for his family, away from the politics and demands of Montsalvat, away from the intrigue of his heritage. Perhaps to Normandy or Germany they could go when all this was done and he could make his way with his blade. Perhaps to Iolande's family in the north, or perhaps over the seas to Outremer, to what remained of the Latin Kingdoms in the East.

Perhaps, but probably not, he conceded with a sigh of defeat, the brief bloom of hope fading as abruptly as it appeared. Should he acknowledge the truth, he would be forced to admit that there were but two ways for this matter already set in motion to resolve itself. One left him king. One left him dead. And the second seemed far more likely at this point.

Alienor had been awake for an hour or so when the horse's pace slowed, although she had not dared to speak during that time. The rain still pounded on her back and beat on the new leaves of the trees around them; Dagobert still held her tightly against him. She pulled back her hood as the destrier's pace changed, risking a curious glance beyond the curtain of wool to find the sky darkening already around them, and looked up to Dagobert with surprise.

"A storm," he explained shortly, never sparing a downward glance but clearly having felt the weight of her regard. "'Tis best we stop until it passes."

Alienor nodded but he had already swung out of the saddle, leaving her feeling cold and bereft on one side. She shivered as she twisted to grip the pommel, seeing that he led the horses inside a cave directly before them, the rain falling away from her shoulders abruptly as they gained the shelter.

Before she could slide down to the ground, Dagobert was before her, his long fingers fitting comfortably around her waist as he lifted her from the saddle. When she would have stepped away, he held her silently there, and she caught her breath, knowing that he looked down at her steadily. A pulse rose in her throat at his proximity and her knees began to weaken when his thumbs leisurely stroked her waist.

"You are certain about the babe?" he demanded softly, and Alienor glanced up at him, her surprise making her take the risk of looking into his eyes before she thought better. A flicker of warmth lighted their gray depths and she wondered at the concern she saw there. Still he did not release her and her heart tripped at the intensity of his expression.

"Aye," she acknowledged, uncertain of his point. Did he mean to leave her here?

"October?" he asked, and Alienor nodded slowly in agreement, warmth flooding her veins as his thumbs slid slowly back and forth over the barely curved expanse of her stomach. He shook his head and glanced down, as if unable to believe what she said, and his lips twisted in a semblance of a wry grin before those gray eyes met hers again.

"In truth, you seem smaller than before," he murmured speculatively, and their gazes caught and held. Alienor's breath froze somewhere in her chest and she felt pinned beneath his scrutiny, the continued smooth motion of his thumbs doing mysterious things to her equilibrium.

"Iolande says 'tis often thus when the mother is ill early on," she explained breathlessly, uncomfortably aware of the way his gaze slid to her lips as she spoke, then rose slowly to meet her eyes again.

"And have you been ill?" he prompted, his voice as soft and fathomless as silken velvet, and Alienor could only nod mutely in response.

He leaned closer and she had nowhere to go, trapped as she was between him and his horse, the realization that she had no desire to evade him stunning her with its intensity. Too long it seemed now since she had tasted him, too long that she had hungered for his lips on hers.

Thunder rumbled ominously in the distance and she barely heard it, so focused was she on her husband's intent. Dagobert scanned her face as if he would memorize her every feature, his fingers spreading across her back as he lifted her unerringly toward him, and Alienor thought she heard herself moan when his lips closed gently over hers.

His kiss was tender, one of his hands sliding up to cup the back of her head with infinite care, and Alienor sensed that he meant to reassure her. She realized instinctively that her flinch had offended him, that he meant her no harm, that the way he touched her now, almost reverently, was his means of telling her so.

Unspeakably relieved to find some measure of her husband's gentle touch in this warrior, Alienor slipped her hands around his neck and opened her mouth to him, telling him as well as she was able that she understood.

Dagobert lifted his head leisurely and stared down at her, the brightness in his eyes making her wonder what he saw that fascinated him so. Before she could ask, the fleeting expression was gone, his attention fixed on the removal of his gloves for an instant before the warmth of his fingers framed her face. Alienor relaxed against him, welcoming his touch, and he almost smiled as he leaned over her anew, his fingers slipping over her ears and into her hair as he kissed her.

Her veil and fillet tipped askew, then fell away beneath his gentle assault, but she barely noticed their departure or the whisper of her sheer wimple joining them on the ground. A barely audible click revealed the undoing of the clasp on her pelisson, the sliding of its weight from her shoulders the only other clue of its departure.

Alienor's entire universe focused on Dagobert's coaxing lips, on the kisses pressed to her temples and eyelids, the tip of her nose, her earlobe, the burning trail etched down her throat to the neckline of her kirtle. The thunder rumbled closer now, more ominously, the leaves of the trees outside the shelter of the cave whipping in the flurry of wind before the storm.

Her hair fell loose from its braid somehow, the long tresses spilling over her shoulders, and Alienor felt Dagobert's fingers slowly combing through their length. She glanced up to find his regard warm upon her, his eyes bright with fascination as he looked at

her. As she watched, he lifted one hand and kissed a
tendril of her hair that had wound around his palm.

Alienor smiled at the gesture, warmth replacing the
chill in her bones when he smiled back, a mingling of
Alaric's easy humor and Dagobert's passion burning
in his eyes. He tipped her chin with one finger and she
parted her lips in silent invitation, reveling in the surety of his touch when his lips closed firmly over hers.
No gentle tribute was his kiss now but an ardent demand, and Alienor responded with the ferocity of her
own pent-up passion, matching him touch for touch.

Strong fingers carefully unlaced the neck of her
dress, but she only arched back to grant access to those
questing lips, loving the feel of his kiss on her throat.
He kissed the flickering pulse below her collarbone as
if acknowledging it, his lips caressing and teasing as
they continued on their downward path and fastened
unerringly on one nipple.

Alienor cried out at the fire that raced through her
from that aching point and Dagobert's hands gripped
her waist like a vise, granting her no escape from his
touch. He lifted her up as he suckled her breast, laving the nipple with his tongue, kissing and nibbling
until she twisted against him in desperation, writhing
toward that elusive flash point she had missed since he
left her bed. He lifted his head and threw her a mischievous grin, dipping mercilessly to take the other
nipple in his mouth despite Alienor's protest, his
teasing and suckling arousing her impossibly further.

Just when she thought she could bear no more, he
released her, his lips taking hers again, his hands slipping up to bracket her ribs. Alienor inhaled sharply
when his thumbs brushed against her swollen nipples

and she felt him smile before they stroked the tender tips again, sending her arching toward him.

The rough edges of Dagobert's thumbs stroked across her again and she thought she would go mad from the pleasure. And again and again. And impossibly again. Lightning flashed somewhere in the hills and the cave was briefly illuminated, the answering crack of thunder astonishingly close. The rain fell with renewed vigor, pounding into the ground an arm's length and half a world away, the horses stirring slightly as they sensed the rage of the storm, but Alienor was safe within Dagobert's embrace.

She gasped his name and gripped his shoulders as he caressed her, stumbling slightly when he squatted suddenly. Removing her kirtle and chemise in one clean upward sweep, he stood once more and tossed the garments aside.

The chill of the air struck Alienor's bare skin but she was oblivious to its bite, so amazed was she at the delight in Dagobert's heated gaze as he looked upon her nudity. Her nipples jutted still tighter at his attention and the cold, her color rising as he met her gaze with a tender smile.

"Let me look but for a moment," he cajoled in a deep tone, and in that moment Alienor could not have refused him anything. He offered her his hand and she took it, his warm fingers closing resolutely over hers as he lifted her hand high, turning her in a tight circle once before him. Rain fell in sheets right outside the cave, effectively closing them off from the world and sealing the two of them in a separate universe where none other could intrude.

"You are beautiful, my Alienor," Dagobert breathed, and her heart sang at his pleasure with her form. She stepped toward him happily and he lowered his arm to close protectively around her waist, his eyes dark as he bent to kiss her gently. Alienor shivered against the cold press of his mail and Dagobert lifted his head with a fleeting frown, swinging his fur-lined mantle from his shoulders.

"Too easily do I forget your health, milady," he murmured by way of apology. She could take no offense at his carelessness when he sighed with such regret and wrapped the cloak securely around her. The fur was still dry despite the inclement weather and Alienor snuggled within it, knowing that 'twas the residual heat of her husband's body that clung to the pelts and now touched her skin.

Dagobert slid his thumb across the fullness of her bottom lip as if he could not restrain himself from touching her, then moved quickly to retrieve a pair of dry blankets from his horse's packs. He spread one on the dry ground against the cave wall and scooped Alienor up to deposit her upon it like an ancient queen reclining before her subjects, then draped the second over her. Immediately Alienor felt newfound warmth spread through her and she smiled up at him, earning herself another sweetly thorough kiss that did not satisfy the ache within her for his touch.

"We shall go hungry this night should you regard me like that much longer, milady," Dagobert threatened teasingly, and Alienor laughed, watching with pleasure as a mischievous grin curved his lips.

"Indeed, I am hungry," she countered, flushing when Dagobert scanned her draped form appreciatively.

"As am I," he responded with a suggestive leer, and they laughed easily together once again. Would that this moment could endure, she thought wildly to herself; would that things were always so comfortable between them. But even as the thought formed within her mind, Alienor knew 'twould not last.

"I should help with the meal," she protested as she began to rise, but Dagobert placed a heavy hand on her shoulder.

"You should stay warm," he advised, his deep tone revealing his seriousness. "There is little enough to do this night."

When she would have argued further, he pressed his finger gently against her lips to silence her, replacing that touch with his lips as she smiled in acquiescence. His lips feathered over her eyelids and Alienor left her eyes closed for just a moment, surprised when she opened them again to find a merry fire blazing just inside the lip of the cave.

That some time had passed was clear, for the two horses stood unsaddled against the far wall and the darkness of the storm had been replaced with the shadows of early evening. Her wet clothes had been spread out before the fire to dry and Alienor propped herself up on one elbow to look around. The rain still fell but its pace was more fitful now, and of Dagobert there was no sign.

Dagobert's euphoric mood did not even last until he reached the shallow stream he had noted earlier, the incessant rain overshadowing his fragile hopes for the future. What sort of fool was he to think of days ahead with Alienor and their child? he demanded of himself as he ferociously sharpened a stick. 'Twas most likely that he would never lay eyes on the babe, should things continue to go so poorly.

He glanced back up the hills, checking that the smoke from the fire was not discernible against the flat gray of the overcast sky, and mentally shrugged. What matter if Alienor softened to his touch so invitingly? Less than a day's ride from Montsalvat had given him neither affirmation nor denial that she had betrayed him. He flicked another speculative glance upward, wondering whether she truly slept, and returned his attention to his fishing with a vengeance.

What matter if it was she or some stranger who betrayed his presence ultimately? For Jordan's shrewd guesses and hasty departure had numbered his days as surely as those of the summer itself. 'Twas only a matter of time until he was brought before the king, for in his heart, Dagobert knew that the rallied attack they had planned these years past would never succeed now.

What manner of man was he then, to court the favor of a lady who would soon be widowed? Was it not better that Alienor be left with a son to love and no tender feelings toward the babe's departed sire when all was said and done? Would it not be easier for her to find satisfaction then with another?

Dagobert's gut tightened at that last unwelcome thought and he impaled the shadowy outline of a fish in the creek with more ferocity than the task required.

A fortnight had passed since they had left the fortress, fourteen days and nights of grim silence, and Alienor thought she might scream at the relentless tension between herself and Dagobert. The curt warrior had returned that first night, replacing the tender lover of whom she had had but a telling glimpse and remaining resolutely lodged in her presence. Alienor slanted a look beneath her lashes to her husband's straight back where he rode ahead and stifled a childish urge to stick out her tongue at him.

Not a kind word did he spare her, nor even a word that was not absolutely essential, be it tender or not. 'Twas not the weather that ailed him, for the rain had ceased after that first night, the tentative spring sunlight liable to warm any heart, any heart but the stone that was placed where Dagobert's heart should have been.

Alienor had ridden alone since the first day, unwilling to have so little distance between them that her vulnerability to her husband's touch would show so readily. He had made no objection, not even a comment, a fact that did little to assuage Alienor's wounded feminine pride.

As they rode steadily northward, she thought frequently about taking the final pledges of the perfect, the Cathar vows of poverty and chastity, once her babe was born. No right would he have to touch her henceforth, and that seemed somehow a fitting punishment for his complete ability to ignore her presence. Days passed without acknowledgment between them and Alienor's heart drooped with despair at the thought that Dagobert might not care to touch her again. Perhaps one child would be enough for him.

One thing it was for her to decide to deny his conjugal rights, quite another for him to appear to have no interest in them.

Dagobert stopped for the umpteenth time this morning, peering up and down the road with narrowed eyes, listening. Alienor sighed with dissatisfaction, annoyed that he was dallying so much this day, knowing that he would not change his activities should she trouble herself to complain.

Enough of the road! she wanted to shout at him. Let us simply reach whatever destination we ride for, that I might have a bath and a decent night's sleep!

But she kept silent, knowing that he would simply give her that slow, thoughtful regard as he had so often of late, then silently climb back into his saddle and continue as he would had she not spoken. He frowned now and pursed his lips, Alienor's heart taking a sudden lurch when he deigned to speak to her.

"'Tis a fortnight since we left, am I correct?" he demanded, and Alienor nodded in amazement.

"Aye," she responded simply, and he nodded in turn, frowning anew at the road.

"'Tis most curious," Dagobert commented quietly, almost as if he spoke to himself. Alienor glanced down the road, only to find the very predictable sight of leaves unfurling and spring flowers rising from the new grass. She looked back to her husband in time to see him shake his head dismissively, then swing up into his saddle again and put his spurs to his destrier.

To Alienor's increasing puzzlement, this little scene was enacted repeatedly with slight variation over the next few days. Dagobert stopped often to listen at the road, his expression clear evidence that he did not hear what he sought. He even made the unprecedented move of leaving her concealed in the forest while he rode into a small village for some mysterious purpose, his brow furrowed yet deeper when he returned.

And even Alienor, with her limited skills in the woods, could see that they had been traveling repeatedly over the same terrain for more than a week, remaining within a tightly defined area on seldom used paths. Never did they encounter another soul, for when the breaking of twigs or sound of footfalls betrayed another's presence, Dagobert immediately hauled both horses into the brush, where they waited with bated breath until the sounds passed.

The paths themselves were a tangle of undergrowth even this early in the season, the brambles tugging at Alienor's skirts when the sun grew hot in the afternoon, dewy new fronds of trees slapping wetly against her face each misty morning. Not a word of explanation was she granted for her discomfort, nor could she fathom a plausible reason for their circuitous path. If they meant to leave Montsalvat for some remote sanctuary, why did they not ride as fast and as far as they were able?

After four days of Dagobert's apparently futile peering at the ground, despite the fact that his countenance had grown even more grim and forbidding, despite her certainty that her question would not merit an answer, Alienor dared to ask.

"What do you seek?" she demanded without preamble one afternoon, earning a sharp glance from her companion when she boldly drew up alongside him.

"What do you mean?" Dagobert returned, his blank expression not appearing quickly enough to hide his surprise. He halted the horses with a deft gesture, fixing his attention on her and sending Alienor's heart into a nervous flurry of activity.

"Clearly you seek someone," she continued, emboldened by the rarity of a word from him that did not urge her to silence. "Even the most simple soul could not fail to see that we have been riding in circles these

past days. It would seem that you await another here
and search for some sign of their passing.''

Dagobert lifted one brow slowly, his steady eyes
scanning her face as if he sought some clue to her in-
nermost thoughts. When he did not respond, Alienor
plunged on bravely, taking his silence for permission
to continue.

'''Twould seem that if you sought another rider,
they might be more apt to use the main road,'' she
suggested, ''and we would be more like to miss them
on these backward paths.''

''Indeed,'' Dagobert responded tightly, but there
was no thread of censure in his tone. He gazed
thoughtfully into the lush green woods surrounding
them and Alienor fairly held her breath, knowing that
he was considering her suggestion. He nodded once,
curtly, and flicked a glance in her direction before
touching his spurs to his mount.

''The main road 'twill be, milady,'' he confirmed in
clipped tones, and she could only follow his lead along
the narrow pathway.

The orange rays of the sinking sun were just brushing the tops of the trees when they gained the road, its
comparatively wide surface a relief to Alienor. She
raised her face to the cool breeze with pleasure and her
mount seemed to feel much the same way, the horse's
pace increasing once they were free of the cloying vines
in the undergrowth.

Dagobert turned his charger away from the mountains still looming behind them and toward a town
nestled in the shadows of a valley far ahead. Few
travelers were on the road at this hour and Alienor
took the opportunity to draw up alongside her hus-

band, not failing to note his quick sideways appraisal
of her move.

She focused her attention on the town ahead,
watching it grow to considerable size as their chargers
closed the distance. Easily she imagined the luxuries
of civilization that she would soon enjoy, knowing she
would savor even warm bathing water and a hard
straw pallet after these days of bathing in cold streams
and sleeping on the ground.

The walls of the unnamed town became discernible
in the twilight shadows and formidable barriers they
were indeed, with high smooth faces and watchtowers
aplenty. She wondered how far they had ridden before Dagobert began biding his time in the woods, but
never having left Perpignan before her nuptials, she
could not recognize this town.

"Toulouse," Dagobert supplied unexpectedly from
beside her, and Alienor glanced to him in surprise that
he should so easily read her mind. She thought he almost smiled, but in the half-light it was hard to be sure
before he turned his attention back to the road and
continued. "We shall seek an old friend of my sire.
Raimon is his name, and be he still the man who rode
with my father, but a glimpse of your smile, my love,
will have his entire household at your disposal."

Alienor fairly gasped at his casual endearment and
its import before she realized that it meant nothing at
all from her remote spouse's lips. She dared not look
at him again, even knowing he had called her his love
without second thought, the heat rising over her
cheeks making her want to draw her hood even further over her face.

Raimon, it seemed, was gone from this earth, but
his son, a man some twenty years older than Dago-

bert and named Raimon, as well, welcomed the two travelers with open arms. The new count was a likable man, drawing out Alienor's laughter and earning her infinite gratitude by offering to order a hot bath to the chamber she and Dagobert were to share. If a certain wariness lingered in the gray depths of Dagobert's eyes, Alienor was certain that 'twas no more than his exhaustion taking its toll.

In but a twinkling of an eye, their horses had been tended and stabled, a chamber prepared for them, a bath summoned for Alienor and a blazing fire set within the hearth in their room. By the time Raimon joined them, Alienor had scrubbed the grime from her skin and donned cleaner clothes. Dagobert likewise had shed his mail and bathed, his posture as he sat before the fire more relaxed than Alienor had seen in some time. With relief she noted that tinge of suspicion had abandoned his features and he seemed, surprisingly, on the verge of lightheartedness.

A trio of servants followed in Raimon's wake, moving a table and spreading hot fare upon it for their evening meal, the smells rising from the covered platters making Alienor's mouth water in anticipation.

"Please excuse our fare," Raimon apologized smoothly, though in truth the uncovered food looked splendidly tempting. "'Tis well past the hour of our evening meal and I regret having naught but remains to offer."

"'Tis most generous of you to be so hospitable at so late an hour," Dagobert responded, sparing a glance for Alienor as he filled a trencher for the two of them. He looked inquiringly to their host, but Raimon waved him off, sitting back in his chair with a cup of warmed wine.

"I have already partaken too heartily of the board this day," he confessed with a grin and a pat of his flat stomach, coaxing a smile from Alienor. Dagobert dropped to a seat beside her and she shared the smile with him, surprised when he casually slid his arm around her shoulders beneath Raimon's speculative eye.

Alienor turned her attention to the meal, noting with pleasure that Dagobert had taken some of every dish but somehow contrived that a minimum of meat had made it to the trencher. He took one of the few morsels of meat and popped it into his mouth and she immediately understood that he was still being cautious.

Tentatively, she took a smaller piece and willed herself to eat it, congratulating Raimon on the skills of his cook as she sampled each dish. Dagobert ate most of the remaining meat on the trencher quickly while she savored the vegetables and she wondered if he had intended her to eat any at all.

The two men began to talk about their sires and events of their childhood, mentioning people that they knew and sharing anecdotes while Alienor ate. The room was blessedly warm and she found herself relaxing as she sipped her wine and listened to the men, the dance of the flames in the hearth almost lulling her to sleep.

"Recently wed are you then?" Raimon asked pleasantly at one point, the marked interest in his tone drawing Alienor's attention.

"Aye, it has been but a few months," Dagobert responded with what could have been haste for him.

"I can only assume you hope for an heir soon," their host remarked, something about his level of curiosity making the hairs prick on the back of Alienor's neck.

"Perhaps we shall be so blessed one day," Dagobert returned cheerfully, his hand slipping from Alienor's shoulder to stroke her gently beneath her jaw.

She turned and glanced up at him, at his uncharacteristic show of affection, knowing she would look the adoring wife but wondering why he had not spoken of her pregnancy. 'Twas far enough along that there was little danger of her losing the babe, and she almost parted her lips to mention the fact before the warning in his eyes brought her up short. Instead she pressed a tiny kiss against his chin and spared a smile for Raimon.

"Perhaps someday," she confirmed, knowing that the blush that pinkened her cheeks at her falsehood did naught but enhance the tale.

Raimon chuckled to himself and raised his cup in salute. "I toast your health and happiness," he said, and all three drank deeply of the wine.

Perhaps 'twas because she fell asleep before Raimon had departed or perhaps 'twas simply that she had imbibed less of the wine that the sounds of heavy footfalls on the stairs woke Alienor in the darkest hours of the night.

A veritable army was assembling outside their door from the sounds of clanging steel and Alienor reached for Dagobert across the mattress. He was not there. She sat up abruptly in bed, the contents of the room spinning dizzily around her at the sudden move, and she pressed her fingers to her temples. Dagobert sprawled in his chair before the fire, snoring softly but not awakened by the riotous noise, and Alienor suddenly had an uneasy sense that all was not well.

The men's footfalls outside made her head pound so that she wanted to scream at them to stop, but she forced herself to stagger across the room to her husband and shake his shoulder insistently. The walls bobbed and swam around her and she marveled at the difficulty she had in such a simple task as walking. Surely she could not be this sleepy.

"Wake up," she insisted, but to no avail. Dagobert's arm fell loosely from his lap so that his knuckles brushed the floor, but otherwise he did not stir. Never had she known him to sleep so heavily. The volume rose in the hall as more men arrived and Alienor's heart began to pound in fear.

"Something is amiss, milord," Alienor cried as she shook her spouse again, this time more roughly. Dagobert murmured something incomprehensible under his breath and tried to brush her hands away.

The latch on the door jiggled, the sound echoing loudly in the silent room, and Alienor froze in shock. Her gaze was riveted on the iron latch as it wiggled again. Something was definitely wrong.

"Milord! Wake up!" In desperation, she slapped Dagobert as hard as she could across the cheek and his eyes flew open immediately, his hands closing hard on her upper arms.

Before Alienor could explain, the latch rattled more insistently and the men's voices carried clearly into the room. Dagobert was on his feet in an instant, shoving Alienor behind him even as he reached for his blade on the floor.

"Touch it not," came a dry voice of warning from the portal. Both Alienor and Dagobert looked up to find Raimon framed in the doorway, a large retinue of knights with blades at the ready behind him.

Knights attired in the king's gold and azure.

"You'll have no need of the blade now," Raimon added coldly, and Alienor shivered at the open hostility in his eyes.

"Why?" Dagobert demanded simply, enfolding Alienor's cold hands in his as he shielded her from the view of the men.

"Surely you know the fat price on your head?" Raimon remarked. In despair Alienor dropped her forehead to lean against Dagobert's broad back even as she heard the first knights step around their host and into the room. Raimon named a price and her eyes widened briefly.

"'Tis a fair sum, is it not, and more than adequate to restore my coffers to their former state. 'Tis proving most expensive, this lording of lands we were taught to regard as an honor. Though you would know little of such responsibilities and troubles at Montsalvat," he added bitterly, and Alienor felt the warmth of Dagobert's hand tighten around her trembling fingers.

"Tell me, Dagobert de Pereille, do the locals still pay homage and tithe to the lost kings of Rhedae?" Raimon sneered, and Dagobert straightened his stance.

"Our fathers fought together," he pointed out calmly, and Alienor felt his voice as a rumble beneath her ear. "Would you so readily discard the loyalty of your own sire?"

"Our fathers were fools," Raimon stated. "Naught did they gain by upholding the supposed claim of your birthright but humiliation and terrorization. 'Tis the

foolish daydreams of your line that we have to thank
for the ongoing presence of the Inquisition, the rav-
aging of our fields, the death of our vassals, the pil-
laging of our wealth. A heavy price has Languedoc
paid already, my own daughter among them.''

"Indeed I heard tell of your Jeanne's nuptials,''
Dagobert commented. Alienor barely had time to note
the thread of caution in his voice before the other
man's eyes narrowed angrily.

"Nuptials, indeed,'' he snarled, sparing a hostile
glance over his shoulder to the king's knights arrayed
behind him. "No easy task was it to sign that agreement,'' Raimon growled warily, and Alienor thought
she saw the glimmer of tears in his eyes before he continued tiredly. "No longer need we support the unbearable cost of harboring your kind in our midst.''

He turned to the knights now and gestured broadly
to Alienor and Dagobert before turning away for
good. "Take them now from my abode and wait not
until morning. I have no desire to play host to such
treachery any longer.''

Chapter Eight

"We must search your persons for weapons," a man said, and Alienor looked up to find a knight before Dagobert, a contingent of other knights backing him up with their swords drawn. Raimon was nowhere to be seen. Dagobert squeezed her hand tightly once more before he began to remove his shirt, and Alienor watched a knight bundle up her husband's mail and tunic.

'Twas truly happening, she thought dully, unable to believe that they were being arrested. To what purpose? And where did they ride in the midst of the very night? It seemed her brain was fogged from the wine and she had difficulty thinking things through, her pounding headache reducing her to a mass of raw fear.

Dagobert stripped to his very skin, standing with dignity while the knight checked his garments carefully for hidden weapons. The two men exchanged a meaningful glance when the knight demanded Dagobert's signet ring, Dagobert's lips thinning to a harsh line as he pulled the ring from his finger and handed it over. Finally satisfied, the other man handed Dagobert back his chausses, shirt and boots, his attention turning immediately to Alienor.

"And now the woman," he said impassively, and wide-eyed, Alienor took a tentative step backward.

"None will look upon my wife's nudity," Dagobert asserted flatly, stepping between the knight and Alienor.

"You must understand, sir, that 'tis but our duty," the man began, but Dagobert summarily interrupted him.

"Aye, and you must understand that my wife will not stand bare to an audience like some tavern whore," he retorted coldly. "Fetch a screen that she may disrobe out of common view if you must examine her garments."

Much to Alienor's surprise and relief, the deed was managed thus, though still she was absolutely scarlet by the time she was fully garbed again. She and Dagobert were permitted their own garments, though his mail, weapons and any evidence of his insignia were long gone. To her relief, Dagobert resolutely held her hand as if he sensed her complete terror at what was happening to them, and she wished that they had but a moment of privacy.

His horse had been saddled when they reached the dark courtyard, though without its caparisons, and the knight gestured that Dagobert might ride the destrier. "Where is my second beast?" Dagobert demanded in the quiet air of the night, and the knight pointed to Raimon's stables.

"We cannot let the woman ride alone," he explained, and Dagobert nodded, his grip tightening once again on Alienor's hand.

"Then bring the beast with us or set it free to run," he argued quietly. "The count has earned enough reward for his betrayal of a neighbor without the gift of such a fine horse.''

The knight studied Dagobert's stern countenance silently for a moment, then nodded as he turned and summoned another to release the beast. That done, the man indicated another mount with a knight already astride to Alienor, but Dagobert shook his head definitively, refusing to release her hand.

''My wife rides with me,'' he insisted. When the knight looked as though he might contest the point, Dagobert indicated the way his charger's reins were securely tied to two other knights' saddles. ''You do not mean that I should escape and I would not watch another fondle my lady on this last ride.''

The knight exhaled wearily and shook his head, sparing Dagobert a wry grin. ''An argument you have for everything and I cannot refuse you something so simple at this late hour.'' With that, he waved Dagobert toward his horse and strode away in the velvety darkness to seek his own mount.

Last ride. Dagobert's enigmatic words echoed through Alienor's mind, drawing a shadow of dread over her heart. What had he meant? Their last ride together or last ride ever?

''Where do we ride?'' Alienor managed to whisper nervously as Dagobert lifted her up into his saddle, and he shot her an appraising look.

''To Paris of course, love,'' he murmured, swinging up behind her and anchoring her tightly against him with one arm. ''To await the judgment of the king.''

''Judgment for what crime?'' she demanded softly, trying to quell that delicious quiver that tripped through her again at his casual endearment.

"Disloyalty to the crown," Dagobert confirmed grimly, his next words confirming Alienor's worst fears. "'Tis a hanging offense and one of which I am most assuredly guilty."

The journey to Paris was ponderously slow, the combination of Dagobert's destrier being linked to two other mounts and the large retinue of knights that traveled with them making daily progress almost nonexistent to Alienor's mind. It seemed that each morning she could see the town on the next hill where they would end up stopping that night, and the on-going monotony of the days fairly drove her mad.

That the drawn-out journey extended Dagobert's life was the only consolation in all of this. Despite the fact that they rode together, however, they had precious little time to talk privately, since another knight almost invariably rode close beside them. At night their hands and feet were bound and anchored to some heavy piece of furniture or post in a common room of the taverns where they stayed. They were permitted the luxury of sleeping beside each other, though the others surrounded them tightly, but mercifully Alienor could still curl up against Dagobert's warmth.

Occasionally as they rode together silently in the daylight she would feel his hand steal over her stomach, his gesture hidden from all by the fullness of her pelisson. Dagobert's fingers would spread as he secretly felt the barely ripening curve of her belly, and should she glance up at that moment, she would catch the faintest glimmer of a smile playing over his lips. Often now, she would turn to burrow her face against his chest, wrapping her arms around his waist and

feigning sleep after such a moment, briefly content to
feel his arms tighten securely around her.

'Twas the end of May when the troupe crested a hill
and Alienor saw the dark snake of the river Seine for
the first time, crowned with the cluster of buildings on
the Ile de la Cité that was the fortress of the Capetian
kings. The buildings of Paris spread out as far as the
eye could see around the island in concentric circles,
shops and homes, markets and merchants' stalls.

As the knights urged their steeds forward, doubt-
less glad to be within sight of home again, the details
of the city became more readily distinguishable and
Alienor was intrigued by the sight despite her fears for
the future. Never before had she seen such a vast settlement and the practical implications of its size were
overwhelming. At Montsalvat, there were merely several hundred souls living within the keep, but adequate water and food could be a problem. Like the
fortress, Paris had no crops and pastures within its
walls and the road grew ever more crowded with carts
of perishables being hauled to market as they approached the city gates.

So much was there to see that it seemed only moments had passed before they were within the sprawl
of the city, the smell of the streets temporarily de-
stroying Alienor's interest. Well now did she understand Guibert's old jest that an experienced traveler
could tell whether he rested one league or two from
Paris simply by the pungency of the smell.

Far ahead, the double towers of Notre-Dame Ca-
thedral rose against the cloudy sky, their heavier
square shape a sharp contrast to the delicate spire of
the newly completed Sainte Chapelle Church within

the king's palace, the dark gray stone of both temples etched against the soft gray of the clouds. A light drizzle fell on the party of knights as they made their way to the citadel, the mist seeming an ominous portent of what was to come.

They made slow progress through the city streets, giving Alienor the opportunity to watch the bustle of bakeries and *boucheries*, the throngs of people returning even at this early hour from the markets. Children darted back and forth across the cobbled streets, their mothers shouting recriminations while a variety of mongrel dogs barked at one another in feigned aggression.

Horses' hooves echoed on the stone roadway, the sounds of the troop's mounts blending with the footfalls of numerous other knights' and squires' steeds, plow horses and elderly beasts pressed into service to pull farmers' carts, pigs and goats being herded relentlessly toward the market. Pigeons and swallows swooped over the crowd, cats disdainfully ignored everyone from their window-ledge perches, a man's voice raised in lusty song carried to their ears from some hidden courtyard.

They crossed the bridge to the island, the Seine rolling beneath them on its rapid path northwestward, its dark surface hinting of mysterious secrets lurking in its depths. Alienor looked up with amazement at the smooth stone face of the fortress that the king of France called his palace. The buff-colored stones fitted together so expertly that the seams between the stones were barely visible, the smooth expanse rising high above the river and bridge, topped by soaring conical towers. Flags sporting the king's insignia fluttered above the towers far overhead, the deep blue and gold that she had grown to distrust snapping in the fitful breeze.

What fate awaited them here?

They were stopped at the gate by the king's guards and dragged from the saddle, their hands bound once again. Alienor was shoved forward and she almost panicked, a quick glance over her shoulder confirming that Dagobert was right behind her, his expression positively thunderous at their treatment.

The Great Room of the Capetian kings was built entirely of stone, the vaulted ceiling rising from sturdy, gracefully rounded columns, the supporting bows arching to meet at elaborately carved keystones. Fireplaces were evenly spaced along the two longest walls, fires blazing in two of them despite the early hour, the smell of roasting meat already rising in the air, but Alienor scarcely had the chance to notice her surroundings.

The low rumble of myriad voices filled her ears, the warmth and noise telling her that the hall was full of men, the smoke from the fires stinging her eyes as she was ushered through the hall. A great portal with a barred opening swung wide at the far end of the room and she was urged down dark stairs. The air grew damper and she shivered, feeling for each step with her toe despite the prodding of the man who pushed her onward. The darkness and inability to use her hands struck terror in her that she might fall, and the fathomless shadows gave her no clue as to how long the staircase was.

A clang echoed coldly down the staircase and the voices from above grew more distant as the heavy door swung closed. Keys jingled below, a lamp bobbed ahead, and Alienor's eyes adjusted to the darkness enough to pick out a careworn older man sitting at a ledger. He spared a disinterested glance for Alienor and Dagobert, continuing steadily with his scribbling.

"'Tis a casual pace you take, Imbert," the jailer observed dryly, making a note in his ledger. "And with one the king is most anxious to entertain."

"Too many of us were there for the task," the knight who had arrested them snapped, "and well you know it, Otho." The jailer spared him a wry smile and flicked a thumb to Alienor.

"Who might the woman be?"

"His wife," the knight responded tightly, and the jailer's eyebrows rose, his gaze now assessing as it slid over her. Alienor felt Dagobert stiffen beside her but she kept her eyes downcast, hoping that things would not become worse than they already were.

"'Tis no wonder you would have her to the last," the jailer commented to Dagobert with a friendly wink. "'Twill not be me who spoils your pleasure." He picked up his keys and fingered through them until he found the one he sought, shooting a sharp look to the other knight as he stood.

"Have you naught better to occupy yourself, Imbert?" he demanded. "'Tis a foul smell you bring to my dungeon, truth be told." The other knight's eyes narrowed slightly but he stepped away, permitting himself a small smile as he met the jailer's eyes once more.

"'Tis the king that plots my path, not I, and well you know it, Otho," he said by way of a parting shot.

The jailer nodded thoughtfully and watched the knight climb the stairs stiffly before turning his attention back to the two that stood before him, his gaze lifting to meet Dagobert's steadily. The two men regarded each other silently for a moment, the shorter man finally bowing his head in the slightest gesture of deference.

"From Mirepoix am I," he said, naming a town near Montsalvat, and Alienor's heart leapt.

Might he assist them to escape? Some of her hope must have shown in her eyes for the older man shook his head slowly, sparing her an indulgent smile.

"No, lady. I am not selfless enough to exchange my family's lives for yours." Hope died a quick death in Alienor's chest and she blinked back her tears as the jailer took a few steps along the stone hallway and gestured for them to follow.

"'Tis not luxurious accommodations," he observed as they trailed behind them, "but a larger, drier cell you shall have, and each other's company for this night at least."

Metal grated on metal as he turned the key in the lock of one heavy door, the door swinging open to reveal a dark stone room. Alienor thought she caught a glimpse of something furry running away from the light before she was ushered inside the small space. She shivered at the dampness that seemed to reach inside her very bones and she glanced around the barren chamber.

The ceiling was oppressively low, the stone walls sporting a meager growth of lichen, the floor unswept and dirty. An iron shackle hung from a chain in one corner and she looked abruptly away, not even wanting to imagine being chained thus. The jailer undid her hands and she wrapped her arms around herself against the cold, barely daring to wonder what manner of infestation they would pick up from this foul place.

"Might we have a light?" Dagobert asked quietly while the jailer untied his hands, and the man looked up at him speculatively.

"You might set the pallet afire," he pointed out, and Alienor tried to keep her lip from curling at the dirtiness of the straw pallet reposing in one corner.

"You have no reason to unlock the door should I do so," Dagobert returned reasonably, and the jailer nodded slowly, his gaze traveling over the cell and noting that nothing else in the small room could burn.

"Truth indeed do you speak, but I should not take the chance," he demurred, and Alienor caught a flicker of impatience rippling her husband's jaw.

"I give you my most solemn word that I will not start a fire," he insisted firmly.

The jailer studied Dagobert for a moment, then mutely handed him the oil lamp he carried and left the cell. The key turned in the lock and Alienor risked a glance to her husband, her gaze caught by the intensity in his gray eyes.

"I would see you once before the end," Dagobert whispered, and tears filled Alienor's eyes.

"'Tis true then that they will kill you?" she asked, earning a slow nod from her husband.

"Aye," he acknowledged simply.

"But why?" Alienor demanded, her frustration with the inexplicable turn their lives had taken coming fully to the fore. Dagobert regarded her silently for a moment before a rueful smile twisted his lips.

"Would you know the full truth of it, milady?" he asked, and she nodded immediately, her heart twisting when he sighed and ran one hand over his forehead. "'Tis a long tale, but I suppose we have time enough. And 'tis only fitting that you know the way of things now."

With that he turned and spread his cloak over the straw pallet so that the fur might be against them rather than the harsh straw. He offered his hand to Alienor and seated her there, dropping down beside her and pulling her into the crook of his arm. Dagobert pulled the warm cloak over her and Alienor snuggled contentedly into his warmth, pulling up her knees to ward off the chill.

"Cold feet?" Dagobert asked softly. When Alienor nodded against his chest, he pulled her feet into his lap and rubbed them with his left hand until they tingled.

"You are stalling, milord," she teased when her warm feet were nestled in his lap and his hand had grown still.

"I am deciding where to begin," he corrected as he settled her more comfortably and leaned back against the wall. Alienor watched him frown into the darkness for an instant before his eyes met hers and he began his tale.

His voice was low as he began to tell her of a race of kings who had ruled France centuries past in the north, when the tribes of the Franks had stretched eastward into the lands of the German princes and southward beyond the palaces of the popes. Priest-kings they were, their bloodline divinely chosen, their powers beyond the ordinary widely accepted, their mysterious link to Christ hinted at among those who knew the way of things in those days. Not so different was his tale from those Alienor had heard as a child, and she relaxed against him, wondering where this tale might lead.

Soon enough, his story took an unexpected turn, for Dagobert spoke of the assassination of a king of this line, a regicide committed under the orders of his own steward, the manager of the king's household. Killed also were the children of the king that afternoon in the forest, all murdered save the youngest boy. Secretly the boy was brought to Rhedae, the home of his mother, and Alienor's ears perked up at this mention of the ancient ruins so near to her own home.

Dagobert explained to her then how the stewards had taken possession of the crown, placing it upon the brow of one of their own within a generation, even while the rightful heir gained his manhood amongst his mother's family. Her husband's voice dropped lower as he recited a long list of battles over the centuries, attacks launched from Anjou, Lorraine, Languedoc, all of which had failed, many of which had resulted in exiles, all of which Dagobert claimed had been attempts to regain the crown by these divinely appointed kings.

It was with evident satisfaction that he told her of the betrayal of the usurpers some three centuries past, yet another line of wrongful kings seizing the crown and holding it from then until now. He spoke of yet more battles and his voice grew sad as his tale neared their own time, his eyes focused on some distant point as he named alliances, towns, individuals, many of which sounded familiar even to Alienor's unworldly ears.

When Dagobert mentioned his father, Alienor suspected the truth, his words confirming her fears. Pledged to the fight of regaining his heritage as his father before him and so back across the span of years, Alzeu de Pereille had seen the invasion of his beloved Languedoc and the wholesale slaughter of those around him. Though the attack was purportedly to eliminate the Cathar sect, 'twas clear to those in Dagobert's family that 'twas they who were hunted.

"I thought the lost kings was but a tale told to children," Alienor ventured to interrupt, and Dagobert smiled sadly.

"Aye, 'tis far more difficult to find the source of a child's tale than a man who openly declares himself before his time." He paused and frowned at the floor, absently stroking her shoulder with his thumb. "'Tis perhaps why they killed so many these last years." Alienor nodded and frowned herself.

"Always did I wonder why the Crusade continued," she mused, and Dagobert's grip tightened briefly on her shoulder.

"Pledged to the cause of the Roman church we were in days long past," he explained, and his voice grew hard, "and they to ours. 'Twas thus until they chose to betray our line."

Alienor pulled back in surprise and met his knowing gaze. "Truly?"

"'Twas the pope who offered the steward the crown as reward for killing the king," Dagobert confirmed, and Alienor sagged against him, her mind filling with questions. "'Twas another pope," he added softly a moment later, "who called for the Crusade against Languedoc."

"But why?" Alienor demanded, watching Dagobert consider her question.

"Many theories there are," he acknowledged finally, glancing down to meet her eyes, "but I suspect 'twas because we did not bend so easily."

"Aye, stubborn enough you are," she teased, wanting to lighten his mood, a smile of victory curving her lips when Dagobert grinned. He hugged her briefly, pressing a kiss against her brow, and she felt his searching fingers curve gently over her belly.

"Tell me about your father," she prompted, sensing the path his thoughts had taken, and Dagobert cleared his throat.

"A fine man he was, noble and strong with a vision true," he said thoughtfully. "'Tis more than fifteen years since he died on the field near La Bessède and still I miss him."

"Guibert has told me of that attack," Alienor offered tentatively, and Dagobert spared her a glance.

"Not a pretty tale does such viciousness make," he commented, and Alienor nodded in agreement, recalling Guibert's disgust at what had been done to the inhabitants of the fortress by the king's attacking force. Days later it had been when Guibert and his company of knights had arrived and there had been nothing they could do save bury the numerous dead. She shivered slightly in recollection and Dagobert's arm tightened reassuringly around her.

"I saw the carnage with my own eyes, Alienor," he admitted, and his voice wavered ever so slightly, "for I was one of the few among our forces who left the field alive that day." He shook his head, lost in his own memories. "'Twas not my choice, but my father would have it no other way."

Dagobert fell silent and she did not prompt him, giving him a moment with his recollections, feeling his

pain as he thought of his father. Wanting to comfort
him somehow, Alienor nestled closer, reaching up to
stroke the uncompromising line of his jaw.

He captured her hand almost absently in his, then
realizing what he had done, he opened his fingers
slowly and examined her smaller hand trapped within.
His thumb ran over her palm in a smooth caress before he lifted her hand to his lips and kissed it, his
composure restored when he began to speak again.

"He knighted me on the field," he admitted, not
without a trace of amazement. "I was but twelve and
green as new grass when he took his fatal blow. On my
knees I was and knighted, pledged to the fight before
I knew what I was about, then we stood together
amidst the fray. His knights surrounded us, protected
us." Dagobert smiled softly. "Eustache was there,
young and brash, and my father leaned on my shoulder, bleeding, demanding that I commit to the family
cause. He made me swear it."

A silence fell between them before Dagobert continued. "He made me swear that I would take up the
cause," he added softly, clearing his throat before he
spoke again.

"'Twas then I realized that he would die. There on
the field, far from home, and that my mother would
not have even that bittersweet moment of parting as I
did."

Silence reigned again in the shadowy cell, Alienor's
mind whirling with the implications of what Dagobert had told her.

"Why the unicorn?" she asked quietly, and Dagobert's lips tightened in recollection of that creature's
miserable fate.

"Some cover did we need," he confessed with a frown. "Time it was that I came out of hiding, but there were plans to make, alliances to guarantee before I could fully declare my presence. Time we needed, time to pull the pieces together. There were tales aplenty of mysterious doings at Montsalvat already being whispered in the area and shape-shifters are common in them."

He shrugged, as if dissatisfied with the explanation himself and spared a glance for the dank stone walls. "Long has the unicorn been not only the emblem but the guardian of our line. When this goat was born with but one horn, it seemed a divine sign." He fell silent and Alienor reached up to touch his face in compassion. "It seemed a sign that victory was to be ours," he added, his voice fallen so low as to be barely audible.

"You could not have foreseen its fate," Alienor whispered, wishing there was some way she could make matters turn right for him and knowing full well that she could not. Dagobert shook his head and spared her a sad smile.

"Nay, I could not, " he admitted heavily. "But 'twas on that morning that the shadow was cast over my heart. No good omen can it be for a man to find his talisman and protector slaughtered within his own keep."

He swallowed and cleared his throat, staring at the flickering play of light on the ceiling and Alienor momentarily knew not what to say. She gave him a moment to come to terms with his thoughts, wanting to ask one more question but unwilling to press him overmuch.

Even if it might be their last chance to speak thus.

"There are no others?" she asked finally, feeling him shake his head.

"I am the last," he confirmed flatly, and Alienor heard the despair in his voice. Without another thought she placed his hand once more upon her belly, surprised when he almost smothered her within the compulsive tightness of his embrace.

"They must know *naught* of the child," Dagobert warned, and she looked up with confusion at the tension in his voice.

His eyes glittered with a sharpness that could have been either anger or fear, but Alienor shook her head in mute incomprehension. "I will not have your life forfeit because you bear my babe," he added tightly, and she felt the color drain from her face.

Of course. The babe in her womb would continue Dagobert's bloodline, and as long as she was pregnant with that child, her own life could be in danger.

"Do they not mean to kill us both then?" she asked uncertainly.

"I shall claim you know naught," Dagobert promised with rare fervor, but Alienor's heart weighed heavily in her chest. His passion was only for the babe, for the survival of his line and the continuance of his quest after he was gone. Too foolish she had been to think he carried some tender feelings for her.

As if sensing her change of mood, he drew her ever closer, unbraiding her hair with gentle fingers and setting the dark mass loose over her shoulders. Dagobert combed his fingers through its thickness, lifting the ebony tresses away from Alienor's face, but still she sat with downcast eyes.

"Eustache you can trust with your life," he told her quietly, apparently thinking that she was concerned for her own safety in his absence. "And Iolande will aid you with the babe."

Alienor nodded against his chest and he tipped her chin up with one finger, pressing a gentle kiss to her lips. A tear trickled from the corner of her eye and he kissed it away, framing her face between his hands as he bent to taste her once more.

"I would love you in the light," he murmured against her mouth, his eyes darkening to slate even as Alienor's heart chilled at the unspoken thought that trailed immediately behind his words. The jailer had promised them this night alone, but who could tell what the morrow would bring?

Alienor nodded and blinked back her tears, standing to remove her pelisson. This night they would have for loving and she would take the meager gift while she had the chance. Her fingers grew clumsy as she heard Dagobert's boots strike the stone floor and she bit her lip, unaccountably nervous. A rustle of cloth and she struggled to keep her mind on her task, striving to avoid imagining the sight of her husband's bare broad chest.

Silence behind her and a gentle breath on her neck alerted Alienor to Dagobert's presence, her spine tingling as she felt him lift a lock of her hair. Something inside her melted as she felt the weight of his warm fingers on her nape, his touch sending tingles along her skin as he gently lifted her hair and spread it over her shoulders.

Dagobert's hands slipped around Alienor's neck and unfastened her kirtle, his fingers sliding beneath the wool and easing it over her shoulders. With nary a word, he unlaced her sleeves, pulling the cloth from one arm, then the other, while she resolutely kept her

eyes on the flickering lamp. The laces at her sides were
undone quickly and he paused only to cup the fullness of her breasts in his hands for a moment before
coaxing the cloth to fall to the ground.

Her chemise was disposed of with similar thoroughness and intent of purpose, Alienor feeling the
tickle of Dagobert's chest hair against her back the
instant the sheer cloth cleared her shoulders in its descent. Already she felt the dampness gathering between her thighs and the quickening of her blood
though he had yet to touch her intimately.

When her garments lay in a puddle at her feet, Dagobert picked her up and settled her back against him,
his arms wrapping securely around her waist. The hard
rod of his masculinity impressed itself on her buttocks and she arched back, all else forgotten when he
licked the very tip of her earlobe with slow deliberation and the whisper of his breath fanned across her
throat.

"Dagobert," she breathed as she leaned back
against him, and an instant later she found herself lying atop the softness of the miniver-lined cloak, her
husband bending over her with gleaming eyes.

"Alienor," he murmured in response, unable to
believe that this splendid creature would let him love
her, had in fact let him love her night after night already. The firelight played over her golden skin and
Dagobert savored the chance to look leisurely upon his
bride for the first time, marveling that she was more
stunning than he had dared to imagine.

And now there were no secrets between them, no
deception however goodwilled, and Dagobert felt a
contentment welling in his heart that things were finally as they ought to be. Worthy of his trust Alienor

had been from the first, her shock and incomprehension at their arrest in Toulouse, her wide-eyed amazement as he told her the truth tonight confirming what he had long suspected in his heart. He had wronged her with his suspicions, but perhaps this night he could begin to balance the scales more favorably.

The ripe curve of her breast filled his hand to perfection and he tested the fit once more, a thrill tripping through him when Alienor responded with a beautiful arch to his touch. What he had sacrificed all these nights of loving in the dark! Her nipple hardened to a dusky raspberry beneath his thumb and she writhed with closed eyes within the dark tangle of her hair, her rapturous expression urging him on that he might see her so beneath him.

Dagobert slid his hands over the slender perfection of her ribs and waist, sparing a soft brush across her stomach where his son grew, caressing the full flare of her hips to the tops of her slim thighs. With gentle fingers, he but touched the apex of dark curls before she trustingly, willingly, parted her thighs and invited him onward.

Dagobert inhaled sharply and glanced up to find her smoky regard upon him, his own arousal reflected in the tawny depths of eyes that tipped up so exotically. Magnificent she was and he could never have found her equal had he traveled the known world over.

He found the pearl hidden in the dampness between her thighs with two fingers, watching with fascination as Alienor arched backward, the tip of her tongue slipping over the rosy fullness of her lips. She trembled beneath his caress and Dagobert wondered how long he could maintain his own control before such temptation.

In the darkness of their chambers, it had been difficult enough to rein himself in that she might find the fullness of her pleasure, but here, seeing her passion before him for the first time and beleaguered by their recent chastity, he knew not where he would find the control.

Alienor reached for him now with a muffled moan and he could not have refused her siren's call to save his life. Dagobert watched her eyes widen as he loomed over her, finding himself smiling crookedly in response to her welcoming smile. He settled himself with care in the cradle of her thighs, a space that seemed exactly contoured to accommodate him, pride searing his heart when she gasped with pleasure and took him within her tight sheath.

She opened her eyes and murmured his name again as he slipped his length inside her, and he paused, savoring this moment in the fullness of the lamplight, knowing even now that he would recall it willingly when he was once more alone.

Alienor reached up and touched his face, running her fingertips over his cheekbones and the bridge of his nose, skimming her fingers across his lips, running her hands through the thick length of his hair. He noted her delight, realizing that 'twas the first time for her to see him in this intimate moment as well.

Her touch feathered over his shoulders, hesitating for a moment before continuing down his arms, and he knew that she had noticed his birthmark. Her golden gaze did not lift to meet his, but he felt the softness of her fingertip slowly trace the outline of that mark on his chest. Alienor glanced up to him now with understanding in her lovely eyes, and he smiled ruefully down at her.

"'Tis incredible that such tales are rooted in truth," she murmured, and Dagobert nodded in silent agreement as she came to terms with the revelation. Beyond belief, indeed. Alienor's eyes were wide as she glanced from the mark to his face again, her hand leaving his shoulder to slip between them and tentatively touch her stomach.

"And the babe?" she asked, her words more a statement than a question, and Dagobert nodded once more.

"The mark he bears will be much the same," he confirmed, watching her nod in comprehension. "'Tis said it appears on the shoulder blade of some but my father's was exactly thus."

"No idea had I," Alienor began, her gaze slowly finding its way back to meet his as something evidently occurred to her. "Why me?" she asked in confusion, and he knew she wondered how she had been chosen to bear his seed.

"Your hand was promised when you were but a babe," he explained, and her dark brows drew together in a quick frown.

"But Guibert . . ."

"Knew naught of it, for he found you quite by chance. When Pamiers was attacked and your mother disappeared, Iolande feared you lost forever," Dagobert explained, anticipating Alienor's next question before she could form the words. "She saw you in Perpignan last Yule and knew you to be your mother's child."

"Guibert always said I looked much as the woman who gave me to him," Alienor mused thoughtfully, her smile sweet when she met Dagobert's gaze again.

"Pledged we were as babes, then?" she asked, and he smiled that the thought pleased her so.

"Aye," he whispered, bending to brush a kiss across her lips as he felt an uncharacteristic rush of possessiveness.

"Always were you mine," he added, and Alienor opened her mouth to him, lifting her hips beneath him in silent encouragement. 'Twas all the urging he needed to carry them both onward and upward, a joyful shout dispelling the quiet of the dank cell when Dagobert finally saw Alienor peak beneath him, her golden eyes widening with amazement as a flush suffused her cheeks.

The morning came too soon for Alienor, the increased activity outside the locked door the only clue that another day had begun. She rolled over to find Dagobert already on his feet and listening at the door with a worried frown between his brows. Alienor smiled at the sight of him and snuggled contentedly within the folds of the fur cloak, convinced that his lovemaking had kept her from all but an hour's sleep. Her eyes drifted closed again, the imprisoning walls dissolving around her at the recollection of his caresses.

"Dress yourself," Dagobert ordered urgently, and she opened one eye speculatively to find him hastily tugging on his chausses. She propped herself up on one elbow and ran a sleepy hand through her hair, unable to see any reason why she should hurry.

"Someone comes," her husband prompted impatiently.

Briefly she considered arguing that she would stay wrapped in his cloak, but the blaze in his eyes told her he was in no mood to argue. And that she would undoubtedly lose the battle. With a heartfelt sigh, Alienor reached for her discarded chemise and pulled it over her head.

"You must hurry," Dagobert urged, even as he dropped the weight of her woolen kirtle over her head. Before Alienor fought her way through the neck, he was lacing the sleeves, and she began to pick up some of his urgency. While she laced the sides, he deftly braided her hair, then slipped on her shoes while she adjusted her wimple, veil and fillet.

The key turned in the lock and Alienor scampered for her pelisson. She was dressed and not a moment too soon. The door swung inward and she heard her pulse in her ears, her gaze flying to Dagobert, only to find his expression stony and unwelcoming. He had withdrawn from her again even after the intimacy they had shared the previous night, and the recognition of that fact sent a cold shudder down her spine. Who came to their cell? Did Dagobert know something she did not?

The jailer stepped into the room then, followed by a precisely dressed little man who flicked a cursory glance in their direction, his very manner and the ledger he carried betraying his occupation as a clerk. Dagobert folded his hands carefully behind his back as if bracing himself for bad news, and Alienor stepped a little closer to his reassuring solidity, not certain she would be pleased with the outcome of this interview.

"Matthieu de Tours," the unknown man introduced himself with a terse nod. "You are Dagobert de Pereille?" he demanded with a piercing glance to Dagobert, who nodded mutely in agreement. "And your wife, Alienor." Alienor nodded even though the man did not look up from his ledger for confirmation.

"I will be brief," Matthieu addressed the silent Dagobert. "The king has been petitioned with a pledge of Alienor's innocence in your household's treachery. Should you but confirm her lack of involvement, the king is willing to release her to the petitioner's custody."

"Alienor is indeed innocent," Dagobert asserted without hesitation, and Alienor's gaze flew to him in shock. He would send her so abruptly from his side without knowing anything further of this mysterious petitioner?

"And the lady also will confirm this?" the clerk demanded curtly, but Alienor could not drag her eyes away from her husband, let alone form a word with her parched lips. Dagobert turned slowly to face her and she was surprised by the intensity that burned in his eyes when she did not immediately speak in the affirmative.

"Who petitions the king?" she asked quietly, feeling the instant disapproval of all three men at her impertinence. Dagobert glared openly at her and she folded her hands nervously before her.

"'Tis not my business to speak of this," the clerk sniffed. "Suffice it to say that his word is considered reliable here."

Who would speak in her defense here in Paris? Alienor could think of no one, the anonymity of the petitioner making her loath to leave Dagobert's side, even tempted as she was with the possibility of gaining her own freedom.

"The gentleman awaits." Dagobert fairly growled the reminder, and she risked another glance in his direction, feeling the weight of his will upon her. Whether his interest was in the babe or herself, she acknowledged with a sinking heart that she must trust his instincts in this. Clearly Dagobert wanted her to agree and 'twas true that she had not conspired against the king.

"Aye," she assented in the barest whisper of a voice that was all she could manage around the lump in her throat. "The petitioner knows the way of it." Relief settled in Dagobert's eyes and she thought some of the tension eased from his shoulders, the sight convincing her that she had done as he desired.

"Fine." Matthieu marked her response in his ledger and gestured to the door. "The petitioner awaits upstairs, madame, if you would accompany me."

"Of course," Alienor agreed, momentarily jarred by the realization that she was expected to leave Dagobert right this moment.

Impulsively, she stretched up and pressed a kiss to his cheek, murmuring "God bless" under her breath as she was sure was expected. He made no acknowledgment of her gesture, softening not at all toward her, the single word he uttered when her lips pressed his stubbled cheek sending a wave of relief coursing through her.

'Twas all she could do not to smile at the clerk and jailer with her newly lightened heart, but she controlled herself with an effort, sparing not a backward glance to her incarcerated husband as she was certain he desired. Not a shadow of doubt must she cast on herself or her petitioner, for 'twould be impossible for them to engineer Dagobert's release should they, too, be imprisoned.

That Dagobert's release would be obtained, Alienor had not a doubt, for the word he had whispered to her was "Eustache," and she knew well that that loyal knight would not have ridden all this way alone or without a plan.

Chapter Nine

With an apologetic smile, the jailer picked up the flickering lamp, the cell plunging into darkness as the door swung closed behind him. Dagobert slumped onto the straw pallet and leaned his head back against the cold stone, feeling as though he had just lost a particularly hard battle. Tiny feet scurried in the darkness and it seemed the small room was danker, more miserable without Alienor's presence. He shivered at the dampness invading his lungs and pulled his cloak over his shoulders, taking consolation in the fact that Eustache was in Paris.

How he had missed the party of his knights on the road he could not imagine, and he would not speculate on what that must mean about their numbers. 'Twas enough that Eustache was here and that Alienor was out of this foul place. Even under the weight of his suspicions, Eustache would take care of her, out of respect for her station as Dagobert's wife if naught else.

Dagobert propped his elbows on his knees and his chin in his palms and sourly considered the state of his life. Naught else, indeed. The phrase was an adequate enough summary of what he had to offer Alienor other than his name. And when he had been executed for conspiring against the king, even that would be worthless to his widow.

To be shunned by polite society would not have been such a burden for him, for he cared little of such matters and suspected Alienor felt much the same way. Iolande would care for her and the babe should Eustache manage to get her back to Montsalvat, and well Dagobert knew that that old fortress was completely unassailable. His family would be safe there, even without his protection.

And finances should not be as much of a problem as they would have been here, he admitted to himself, knowing that the Languedoc showed more tolerance than these northern provinces. Somehow Iolande would find a way to pass his inheritance on to his wife or his son. Even should she be unsuccessful, there were enough who believed in his legacy that the two would be cared for adequately.

Indeed, it seemed the woman was better off without him and that was a bitter pill to swallow.

She had given herself with abandon their last night together and he treasured his memories already, caressing each recollection like a pearl on an infinite string in his mind, savoring the images impressed on all five of his senses. Sadly, 'twas not enough to fully warm his heart, for Alienor had made no declaration of love. Though he had not noted its absence at the time, now the thought sorely vexed him as he realized that he knew not how she truly felt.

Had she loved him purely out of compassion for his fate? Dagobert resettled himself on the hard pallet as if adjusting his posture would make that possibility easier to face. Would Alienor mourn his passing or praise the riddance of the trouble that seemed to follow him?

A pang went through his heart when he realized that he would never see his son. No consolation was it that he knew not what Alienor would tell the boy about him, whether she would call the boy's sire a fool or a noble knight. That the babe was a boy, Dagobert had never had any doubt, and he wished now that he had confided his knowledge in Alienor, that he had made her pledge that the boy not take up his family's cause.

Perhaps five centuries had diluted the blood royal too thin, for well he knew that he had not proven himself man enough for the task of regaining the throne and 'twas not for lack of trying. 'Twas evident that he had not the ability to heal by simply laying his hands on the ill as had his forebears, and he could not help but wonder whether that was the only skill lost to his kin over the years.

Truly the time had passed for restoration of the crown, the futility of the quest proven over and over again, each time costing the lives of more great men. Too much dying had there been over the years and the cause could not be worth the price it exacted. Would that his son could live a life devoid of this sort of responsibility.

Would that his son could live to hear the lady who held his heart say she loved him.

'Twas not Eustache that greeted Alienor upstairs, but Jordan de Soissons.

Jordan? How could this be? Alienor's eyes widened incredulously as Jordan calmly placed his mark on the clerk's ledger, clarifying his role as her petitioner beyond all doubt, and wondered how the fates could have turned on her so.

Where was Eustache?

Dazed at this turn of events, Alienor scanned the hall, seeking a familiar face. The great hall was filled with traveling knights and their squires, evidently guests of the king, the myriad colors of their tunics and tabards dim in the subdued light. Trestle tables were scattered around the room and the men sat talking, eating, playing chess, but not a one looked even vaguely familiar to Alienor. She flicked a glance back to Jordan to find him watching her with an indulgent twinkle in his eye, the clerk already scurrying away.

"Yes, 'tis I," he confirmed with a smug smile, and she recoiled from the knowing glint in his eyes. "Have you no pretty words of gratitude for me?"

Why on earth had he petitioned for her release? The very question made Alienor conclude the worst and she took a step backward.

"Should your intentions be the same as they were at Montsalvat, I see no reason to thank you," she snapped, the way Jordan's smile widened doing nothing to improve her temper. What was she going to do? She knew no one in Paris and had not a denier to her name should Jordan turn and walk away, but she could not, would not, share his bed in return for her freedom.

"'Tis my company or the cell," Jordan prompted, as if he had read her very thoughts. When her options were stated so plainly, her decision seemed inescapable.

"You make the choice most clear," Alienor retorted, turning back toward the oaken door that sealed the dungeon stairs. What manner of woman did he

think her to take another while her husband was imprisoned?

She cringed when Jordan's hand closed over her
arm and brought her to an abrupt halt, though she
could not have said that she was surprised by the gesture. Stubbornly she refused to look up and meet his
regard.

"Should you return there, you will die with your
husband," he said in her ear, and Alienor could not
argue with the truth of it. 'Twas her place, though,
beside her spouse, even in the face of his trial. "Think
you that Dagobert would not wish to see you far from
harm?"

These last words brought Alienor's mutinous
thoughts to a full stop. 'Twas clear enough that Dagobert would have said anything to see her free of the
tiny cell and she felt her resolve waver slightly at that
admission. She recalled the stubborn look in his eyes
when she had not answered the clerk immediately, as
if he would will the very words from her mouth, and
her determination crumbled.

Did she not owe him his child? Should she remain
at his side, the heir he so greatly desired would not see
the light of day. Even should she survive until the autumn, did she not owe the child the chance to be born
free of a prison's walls?

Seeing the neat fix she was in, Alienor cast a sidelong glance to Jordan, only to find him watching her
closely. He smiled, looking a little less like a predator,
and she fought a temptation to smile in response,
knowing that he alone could see to her survival in this
city of strangers. And, she was forced to acknowledge, he truly had taken a risk to speak for her defense. Should she prove guilty later or disappear from

his care before Dagobert's trial was completed, 'twould be Jordan's neck on the block.

"Why do you do this?" she demanded softly, but Jordan looked away evasively, answering only with a slight shrug. Had the hard edge of cynicism dissolved in his eyes for just an instant before he looked away? Alienor could not be sure and she almost forced him to look her in the eye that she might be certain. "'Tis not unreasonable for me to expect an explanation," she commented.

"'Twas an impulse, no more," he said offhandedly, still not turning to face her.

"You wish to lie with me." Alienor stated the obvious flatly and Jordan nodded, staring resolutely down at his toe. Was that the fullness of it then? There was no way to be sure. Alienor took a deep breath and studied the tip of her own shoe as she composed her negotiation in her mind. Would that he would agree.

"I will not be unfaithful to my husband while he yet draws breath," she said finally, feeling the weight of Jordan's gaze upon her again but unwilling to look up in her stead.

Inwardly she prayed that he would accept her excuse and stay his demands at least for now. She knew not what she would do when Dagobert was executed, but that was a bridge to be crossed when she reached it, for still she could not believe that day would come. Eustache was somewhere, she was certain of it, for Dagobert must have had some reason to expect his friend's presence here. And she could not plan a rescue should she be securely imprisoned along with Dagobert.

"'Tis futile to hope for his release," Jordan argued quietly, and Alienor nodded in acknowledgment, letting her fear for Dagobert's future take command of her heart. Let Jordan think that she grieved, if he so desired, let him think that she but needed time to come to terms with her husband's fate.

"I do not fool myself," she said dispassionately, "but I gave my vow at my nuptials and I would honor him to the end."

Jordan cleared his throat and stepped away for a moment, leaving Alienor to await his response with bated breath. The silence stretched between them, the sounds of the groups of men gathered nearby finally impressing themselves on Alienor's ears. Would he never decide? Her nerves pulled taut as he still considered, and she thought to shake him when he finally looked up with a half smile of concession.

"My quarters are small, milady," he said in a low voice, "but I would have you share them." Alienor flicked him a questioning look, needing things to be absolutely clear between them, and Jordan smiled ruefully back at her.

"My most sincere oath I give that I will not touch you while Dagobert de Pereille draws breath." Alienor blinked back her tears at these words and pressed a grateful kiss on Jordan's cheek, seeing surprise at her impulsive gesture light his dark eyes.

"I thank you for your kindness," she murmured, and Jordan reddened beneath his tan, tucking her arm into his elbow and leading her through the crowded room.

"Make no mistake, milady, 'tis not kindness that propels me," he fairly growled, but Alienor ignored his gruff disclaimer, sensing that she had seen a glimmer of the true man beneath Jordan's brittle crust.

* * *

Jordan kept a second-floor room in the home of a widow, the unmistakable dissatisfaction that crossed the woman's face when she met Alienor leaving little doubt in Alienor's mind as to what their arrangement had been. She thought to reassure the woman, though such words would clearly be beyond her place, her own uncertainty in Jordan's intentions not yet fully laid to rest.

The room was clean if small, its single glass window opening out over a relatively quiet street that ran behind the building, admitting a comparatively fresh breeze. The widow ran a bakery on the ground floor, the shop itself fronting the larger street on the other side of the house, the warmth of the wood floor beneath Alienor's feet evidence that the ovens rested beneath Jordan's room.

Any trepidation that she might have felt at the arrangement was quickly dispelled, for Jordan seemed perversely determined to show himself the gentleman. He conceded the bed immediately to Alienor, pleasing his landlady enormously when he requested a straw pallet for himself.

He left her for the remainder of that day, and though it took her the better part of an hour to convince herself that he was truly gone, Alienor was amazed at how deeply she finally slept. Weeks it had been since she had had the luxury of a bed or a full night's rest and she awoke to the aroma of fresh bread the next morning, feeling completely refreshed.

No time had she to dwell on her misfortunes, for no sooner had she completed her toilette and scrubbed the souvenirs of her night in prison from her skin than Jordan whisked her off to the markets.

Trinkets and baubles from all over the world glinted within the dark stalls but Alienor was blind to them all. Here she might find Eustache and she anxiously sought a glimpse of his stern countenance. Bolts of brilliantly hued sendal silk from Canton, hammered brass bowls and urns from the realm of Prester John, emerald samite from Persia, oranges piled high from Valencia, fluffy balls of woolen roving still pungent with the scent of sheep dung from Saxony, headily perfumed damask roses from Provins, early onions and chervil from local gardens, none could capture her attention as she searched hopefully for a familiar face.

Over the next few days they visited the market often, for Alienor confessed that the variety of goods and bustle of people fascinated her. In truth, still fueled by the belief that Eustache was near, she found herself examining other than the goods for sale, studying the crowd streaming through the streets in the hope that she would catch a glimpse of a friend. Once in a while, she would spot the back of a man who stood just as Guibert or catch a whiff of scent like Iolande's and her hopeful heart would leap to her throat, but each time the person would turn and she would see the fullness of her error.

She had even tapped an older knight on the shoulder one afternoon while Jordan was otherwise occupied, thinking him the very image of Eustache. He had turned slowly, just as Eustache would have done, but Alienor found herself looking into the eyes of a total stranger, the color rising in her cheeks at his open disgust at her audacity.

And each night as she lay alone in bed, she watched the night sky through the open window and caressed the fullness of her belly, her thoughts entirely with

Dagobert as the sound of Jordan and the widow's merrymaking carried to her ears. She had no way to know if her husband was fit or ill, even alive or dead, though she imagined there would be a great public fuss over an execution. She wondered if Dagobert thought of her, if he waited impatiently for her and Eustache to assist him. When she thought thus, her eyes filled with tears at his plight, knowing she had no way to help him alone and that Jordan would not assist her.

She thought often of that last night together, his tenderness and possessiveness, the magic of loving him in the soft lamplight and seeing his face etched with passion above her. Never, she knew, would she find another to dislodge him from her heart, and she wished in the darkness over the bakery that he had found room in his heart to think of her as more than the mother of his child.

"You are indeed most kind," Alienor said weeks later as she turned and admired the fall of her new ocher kirtle, checking that the fullness of the wool adequately hid the ripening of her belly.

Jordan watched her from the doorway with his arms folded across his chest, an indulgent expression in his eyes that Alienor was rapidly becoming used to. For nigh on three weeks he had treated her with polite deference, insisting now on presenting her with new garments.

"I thought the color would suit," he commented now in response to her gratitude, and Alienor threw him a smile.

"No need had you to spend the coin," she chastised him lightly, and he shook his head.

"Sorely in need of a garment were you and I saw you take no measure to see yourself suitably attired," he explained, and the color rose in Alienor's cheeks. No coin had she and well he knew it, or she would indeed have seen to the matter herself. The kirtle she had worn from Montsalvat was all she had left prison with and it had been in need of replacement before that arduous journey.

"Aye, you speak the truth," she conceded, "and well enough you know the way of it. Still, you had not the need to acquire a new chemise and shoes for me."

"The dressmaker assured me that always did a lady shop thus," he argued.

"Oho, always did her favorite customers shop thus and line her purse with silver," Alienor corrected hotly, seeing too late from the twinkle in Jordan's eye that he had not been fooled by the woman's pitch. Embarrassed that she had taken him for a fool, Alienor sent him a grateful smile.

"I would thank you again for your generosity. 'Twas most unnecessary but greatly appreciated," she added, and Jordan looked momentarily discomfited.

He fumbled with something in his pocket and Alienor realized that she had never seen him so clumsy, even when he had feigned drunkenness at Montsalvat. The color rose on his neck as he produced a finely wrought tumble of gold and handed it to Alienor all a-jumble.

Puzzled, Alienor lifted the slim links and the girdle fell out to its full length, the cabochon topaz stones set along its length catching the light. She looked up at Jordan, certain he only asked her approval before presenting the finery to some lady he held in high regard, the compliment on his selection dying on her lips when she met his eyes.

Too late she realized that the stones matched the wool of her new kirtle almost identically, the warm regard in Jordan's brown eyes leaving no doubt in her mind that the girdle was intended for her. Her mind whirled as she realized her mistake, the sounds of Jordan coupling with the widow each night having convinced her that he no longer had any interest in her.

"I cannot accept this," she said hastily, shoving the girdle back into Jordan's hands.

"I would ask you why," he demanded, but Alienor was too distraught to note the current of anger beneath his tightly controlled tone.

"'Tis inappropriate," she argued wildly, backing across the room to put some distance between them.

A fool she had been to think that Jordan wished only to see to her safety, an abject idiot to think that the point would not come when he would demand compensation. To think that she had been addlepated enough to learn to trust this man who had once attacked her in her own chambers. Had he not stated his intention to lie with her when he had won her release?

The way Jordan's eyes glittered and hardened told Alienor that she had made a mistake by inadvertently insulting her benefactor, but 'twas too late to call back the refusal.

"They will not come, you know," he shot out suddenly, propping his hands on his hips, and she looked at him uncomprehendingly. "From Montsalvat," he clarified harshly, and Alienor managed to look blank, her expression apparently feeding Jordan's frustration. He crossed the room in two strides and hauled her up to his face, his hands fastening heavily on her upper arms. Alienor tried to step back but his fingers only tightened as he leaned closer toward her.

"Only a fool could miss your hopeful scanning of the crowds in the market," he rasped, and Alienor's heart sank that she had been so transparent. "'Tis clear you expect someone from Montsalvat to ride to your husband's rescue, but you deceive yourself, milady."

"What do you mean?" Alienor managed to ask, her voice a mere whisper.

"They cannot come, even should they be willing," Jordan growled, and she suddenly dreaded his next words. "Montsalvat has been under seige since the first week of May."

"No, it cannot be!" Alienor argued hotly, pulling away so savagely that she managed to break free of his grip.

"'Tis so," he confirmed darkly, but she still shook her head. It was impossible, unthinkable for anyone to attack Montsalvat.

"Why attack Montsalvat?" Alienor demanded impatiently. "It has no wealth that another might covet."

"But its inhabitants have value," Jordan argued, his meaning taking a moment to come clear to Alienor. The first of May, had he said? But a week after she and Dagobert had ridden out of the courtyard? A chill stole around her heart as her mind leapt to an unerring conclusion.

"'Twas Dagobert they sought," she breathed, the steadiness of her companion's regard the only confirmation she needed before her mind skipped ahead once more.

"But he is here," Alienor argued. "Will they not retreat?"

"Too many men are there assembled," Jordan told her, and she saw with some measure of satisfaction that he was unable to meet her eyes.

How many men? she wanted to ask, the grimness of Jordan's expression making her suspect that she would not like his response. "Too much gold expended to turn back so soon," he added, and her heart sank like a stone. A considerable force would be needed indeed to encircle that fortress on its lonely mountain.

Even with Dagobert gone, Montsalvat remained under siege. Did the attackers not believe the truth when they were told that Dagobert was not in residence?

"Even should they have word that Dagobert is captured, they will undoubtedly ensure the destruction of Montsalvat so that this threat cannot rise again," Jordan supplied as though he had read her very thought.

Hope surged within Alienor as she wondered whether Dagobert had anticipated the attack. Was that truly the reason he had taken to the road, and not to return her to Perpignan? But had he known, why would he leave his friends and family to face the king's army without the assistance of his blade and leadership?

She would not even speculate on the fate of her child, should the king learn of its existence. Her mind whirling with questions, Alienor stared blindly out the window, struggling to come to terms with what she had just learned. How had the king known to send his forces to Montsalvat? Her anger rose as she fitted another piece into the puzzle and she turned furiously on her heel to confront Jordan. Too easy it was to lay the blame at this man's door for the travesty her life had become.

"'Twas you who sent them," she accused, and Jordan's lips tightened into a thin line.

"A task I had and 'twas fulfilled honorably." He bit the words out, earning a harsh laugh from the woman before him.

"Honorably?" Alienor demanded, hearing her voice rise hysterically. "What honor is it to betray a noble knight's hospitality? More than a fortnight did you sit at our board, with your squires and knights alongside and your steeds stabled comfortably before you betrayed my lord and husband. 'Tis clear that northerners are raised to a far lesser standard."

"What honor is there in exploiting the folktales of a vassalage?" Jordan snarled. "Explain to me the honor that prompts a lord to urge simple people to throw themselves to their death defending his fictitious claim to the throne."

Anger rose red-hot in Alienor's chest at Jordan's conviction that Dagobert lied about his heritage, but she checked herself with an effort. Should there be others who thought his ploy merely the result of blind ambition, not divine birthright, he might well live through this ordeal. She would not be the one to enlighten those around her.

"You know naught of what you speak," Alienor retorted, but Jordan shook his head.

"Old enough I am to see opportunism for what it truly is. A commission from the rightful king, in contrast to the claims of a poseur, is above rebuke," Jordan growled, but Alienor only glared up at him as her anger flared.

"And above mere ethics are his actions," she spat. "Should Dagobert be a liar, why then is your king so intent on executing him? Why is his trial so delayed?"

"Who knows the power of a magical king over a superstitious people? After all, did he not turn himself to a unicorn when he so desired?" Jordan demanded with a sneer. "As for the rightful king, perhaps he wishes to give your Dagobert no more or no less than is his due."

"The unicorn!" Alienor murmured, facing Jordan with new understanding in her eyes. "'Twas you who killed that gentle beast!" Jordan folded his arms across his chest and nodded sagely.

"'Twas I, indeed," he conceded without a trace of regret, and his eyes narrowed slightly. "No longer could I afford to dally and wait for someone in your loyal household to inadvertently slip. 'Twas time to call the matter into the open."

"And your visit to my chambers?" Alienor demanded, a sick feeling growing in the pit of her stomach that she might have contributed to Dagobert's unveiling. Jordan nodded with a slow smile.

"Another call for your husband to show himself, milady," he admitted, the deliberate perusal that scanned her from head to toe leaving Alienor feeling violated. "But make no mistake, Alienor, the second task was far easier than the first."

"Touch me not, Jordan de Soissons," she hissed when he stepped toward her. Surprisingly, he stopped and regarded her thoughtfully, as if vaguely amused by the horror in her eyes. "You destroyed our lives," she whispered, and Jordan smiled.

"Your husband preyed upon his people's superstitions," he argued. "'Twas only a matter of time before he was called to task."

"He did naught of the sort," Alienor shot back defensively, earning herself an indulgent tap across the nose.

"Even you, my lovely lady, were fooled," Jordan maintained, but Alienor knew that he was wrong. Their gazes held for a moment, Alienor as convinced in her point of view as Jordan in his, then Jordan turned and strode quickly from the room, pausing for an instant in the portal.

"The trial will be tomorrow morning," he told her flatly, and Alienor's heart nearly stopped, her mouth going dry now that the day was finally here. "We shall leave at dawn to attend," he added, "for neither of us, I am certain, would want to miss the ceremonies."

Alienor closed her eyes against the tears of relief that rose at his words and sagged back against the window ledge, barely hearing Jordan take his leave. One last time she should see Dagobert and she focused her mind on that thought alone, refusing to speculate on what would happen to her once her husband was gone.

The courts were finely appointed, tapestries hanging on the walls, the king and his advisers so well dressed that they, too, seemed more ornamental than functional. Alienor was oblivious to the majesty of the court, nervous as she had never been in her life. Her entire being was fixed on the tiny door that Jordan had told her concealed the stairs to the dungeons far below and she fidgeted on her seat, impatient for the trial to get under way.

When Dagobert finally appeared, the universe skidded to a stunned halt for Alienor, her shock at his appearance making her want to stand up and scream. Terrible he looked, barely a ghost of the man she had unwillingly left but twenty days past, and her tears threatened to spill over her cheeks at the sight of him.

'Twas not enough that he was gaunt and pale, his eyes red rimmed and his skin marked with the speckling of myriad insect bites, but his luxuriant mane of dark blond hair had been shaved, leaving a faintly discernible stubble across his scalp. He wore a tunic crudely fashioned of rough undyed wool that fell below his knees, his hands folded behind his back, his chin held high despite his poorly garbed state. Alienor pressed her hands to her lips to stifle her sobs at the indignity heaped upon him, agonized by her helplessness to assist him.

But it only grew worse.

The trial was a farce and she supposed she should have expected it to be thus, but she had the faith of many in the reputed fairness of this king. It seemed this issue must be close to his heart, though, for the powers in control were taking no chances that her spouse might be found innocent. Seneschals mocked Dagobert's claim as if he were a madman, to the great enjoyment of the assembled crowd, their false accusations making Alienor want to leap to her feet and hotly defend her spouse.

Jordan must have sensed her indignation for he stayed her with a restraining hand, frowning as he shook his head. Alienor sighed and settled back in her seat, knowing he was right but hating the fact that she could not change the situation, barely aware of the occasional puzzled glance her companion slanted in her direction.

Dagobert remained stoically impassive to their taunts, but Alienor saw his lips tighten when they spoke of his father in similar terms and her heart went out to him. Even silent and tonsured, he radiated a certain regal air as he stood and stared stubbornly at the floor, his face devoid of emotion, his stance tall and straight. The king watched him with a certain wariness, Alienor noted, the crowned man's eyes narrowing speculatively as he wound a ring round and round his finger.

"For his impertinent posturing, Dagobert de Pereille should be burned at the stake!" concluded an enthusiastic seneschal. Certain bloodthirsty attendees applauded this idea and the king's glance flicked to the man for the first time.

"'Tis a punishment for heresy," he commented quietly. "I have heard no charges of unorthodox religious practices against the man." The adviser flushed scarlet at the correction, but another leapt immediately to his defense.

"Is the crime not the same, milord, whether it be against the crown or the church?" he demanded, and the king threw him a thoughtful glance. A murmur of assent rippled through the company assembled and the king glanced to the crowd in annoyance, parting his lips to speak when a spectator leapt to his feet.

"Burn him!" the man cried with a fist flung skyward, his neighbors joining in his cry. Alienor clasped her hands together as the demand of the crowd grew to a dull roar, gasping aloud when an icy voice on the far side of the room brought the chanting to a decisive halt.

"Save your fagots," Iolande declared with a haughty glance over the restlessly quieted crowd. "Dagobert shares no blood with Alzeu de Pereille."

An expectant hush followed Iolande's words and Dagobert looked up for the first time, easily picking out his mother's commanding figure on the far side of the justice chambers. Why was she saying this? Never had he known her to lie willingly and he could not comprehend her intent this day.

He studied her across the justice chambers, her slim figure draped in pastel blue, her back rigid with determination, and he almost thought that he could see the combatant sapphire of her eyes. Her expression was openly defiant, and as much as he wished her safely home, a warmth spread around his heart that he had the chance to see her one last time.

His mind slipped naturally to Alienor, and encouraged by his mother's presence, he scanned the crowd for her now as he had been afraid to do earlier. His gaze seemed to light immediately upon her despite the odd fact that she did not sit near Iolande, and his heart swelled at the radiance of her complexion. Pregnancy became her, he conceded proudly, almost smiling at the knowledge that 'twas his seed taking root within her.

"Who are you?" an adviser demanded of Iolande, and she picked her way down to the floor leisurely. She strolled the length of the hall like a visiting dignitary, pausing in front of the king before she spoke.

"Iolande de Goteberg am I, Countess of Pereille, wife of Alzeu de Pereille and mother of Dagobert," she stated frostily, and the crowd jostled one another at this unexpected development.

"She speaks the truth?" a clerk demanded of Dagobert, and he nodded, still wondering at his mother's game.

"Aye." Iolande did not look to him when he answered, and Dagobert knew she was forming a falsehood in her mind before she spoke.

"A curious assertion you make," the king prompted, and Iolande lifted her chin a notch higher that he would challenge the veracity of her word.

"The boy is my son but not of Alzeu's seed," she explained flatly. "He is a bastard born, but even knowing this, my husband had the grace to raise him as his own."

"The grace or the selfishness?" demanded one of the seneschals, in clear reference to the fact that Dagobert was known to be Iolande's only child, that lady sending him a look that could have curdled fresh milk.

"Who was his sire?" the king asked quietly, and Iolande looked back to him.

"An ostler we employed at the time," she retorted flatly.

"An ostler?" one of the king's counselors demanded skeptically, and Dagobert almost agreed with him. She would call him the seed of a mere ostler?

"He was a finely made man," Iolande conceded tightly, the faint rosy flush that stained her cheeks lending credibility to her tale.

Dagobert stifled the urge to laugh aloud, knowing fully that his mother had thawed for no man other than his own sire. The bustle between the ministers behind him told Dagobert that they believed her tale and he permitted himself to wonder whether this audacious ploy might actually work.

"Who else knows of this?" the skeptic demanded, and Iolande treated him to her most frosty glare.

"For the sake of my husband's honor, the tale never left our chamber. The ostler and even the boy had not an inkling of the truth."

"And where is this ostler now?" demanded another, earning a tolerant shake of Iolande's head.

"It has been almost thirty summers since I have seen the man," she admitted. "My husband would no longer have him within the keep and he was dismissed. I know not where he went nor even the fullness of his name." This answer was clearly received less happily, but the king rose to his feet when he saw that there were no more questions.

"Indeed we must confer over this new development," he told Iolande with a polite nod of his head. She curtsied in response and excited chatter broke out amongst the observers as the king and his advisers filed into a small antechamber behind the court.

Dagobert barely restrained himself from smiling at his mother for her bare-faced lie, remembering well how she had asked him to abandon his quest. She would have him deny his sire to save his own life now, instead. Despite any qualms he had about supporting her lie, the thought was dangerously tempting. Unable to help himself, he stole another glance to Alienor.

His wife was obviously upset, perhaps uncertain what to believe, and he let the sight of her distress fill all the hollow spaces within him, daring to hope for an instant that she truly cared for his welfare.

Years with Alienor were the only temptation that could have convinced him to endorse this lie and he felt his heart sway in favor of Iolande's move. Alienor's wide eyes were fixed on the door to the ante-chamber and Dagobert took the chance to look her over leisurely, realizing that his memory had done her an injustice.

'Twas a deep gold kirtle she wore that highlighted her coloring wondrously, full in cut that the babe was easily hidden within its drape, though Dagobert had not seen the garment before. He looked to the man beside her, not a doubt in his mind that 'twould be Eustache who cared for his wife, his heart wrenching when he recognized Jordan de Soissons.

What was that black-hearted knight doing here? And standing alongside his Alienor as if he had every right in the world to be there?

Alienor glanced down to Dagobert in that moment and he had not the time to conceal his anger from her regard. She recoiled with wide-eyed surprise and took a half step backward, the way that Jordan took her arm and steadied her bringing Dagobert closer to murder than he had ever been.

The king and his counselors filed back onto the dais above him as he struggled to rein in his anger at Alienor's casual dismissal of him. That the knave bought her clothes was sign enough that she warmed his bed, the very thought that she welcomed Jordan between her thighs while he languished in prison making Dagobert want to rip the man apart with his hands. And not just any man had she chosen but the very one who had betrayed him. Suspicion crowded into the red cloud of rage in his mind and he wondered yet again what role Alienor had played in his downfall.

Would he deny his heritage for this treacherous woman? Never! Renounce his sire to spend years with a woman who insisted on betraying him time and time again? Never! Only Eustache had seen the truth of her ways and he had been fool enough to discount the man's insight. No longer! He was born of the line of kings in truth and he cared not who knew it now.

"We have reached a decision," a clerk's voice came from above, the little man jumping back when Dagobert leapt up from his place with blazing eyes.

"No decision can you make without all of the facts!" he roared, disregarding the warning flash in Iolande's eyes as he reached for the front of his tunic. "Alzeu de Pereille was my sire and well does this woman know it, for I bear the mark of his line." He grabbed two fistfuls of the cheap cloth and the fabric rent, baring his chest to all.

"Behold the mark of kings!" he cried, savoring the shock that settled over the features of those assembled.

"Milord," a noblewoman gasped from the closest bench, falling to her knees before Dagobert with tear-filled eyes and reverently pressing her lips to his bare and dirty foot. "Long have we awaited your return."

He had but laid his hand on her head before he was surrounded by masses of people brushing their lips across his toes, his fingertips, a few bold ones daring to touch the port-wine cross of his birthmark itself, others tearing snippets of his robe and stealing them away. The healing powers of kings permeate even their garments, he thought, recalling tales of old kings who had gone amongst their people and returned stripped naked.

And now 'twas happening to him.

Dagobert looked up and met his mother's horrified gaze, surprised when she shook her head with disgust and abruptly turned away, disappearing almost immediately into the press of people. He tried to spot Alienor in the crowd but could not, his heart sinking when the jailer tied his hands behind his back with a newfound roughness, and Dagobert realized the harsh blow his pride had dealt him.

Chapter Ten

"Iolande!" Alienor cried at her mother-in-law's rapidly departing figure, knowing that if she lost sight of the woman she would never again find her in this sprawling town.

"Alienor!" Jordan struggled through the crowd somewhere behind her, but she ignored his cries as they both fought against the endless press of people bent on reaching Dagobert. Her path cleared and Alienor spotted Iolande standing against the wall ahead, the older woman's tight lips easing at the sight of her.

"I thought 'twas you," Iolande said with an uncharacteristic quiver in her voice, gathering Alienor into a tight hug when the two drew close. Alienor was surprised to feel her mother-in-law trembling slightly and she hugged her tighter in silent compassion. Iolande glanced downward when the fullness of Alienor's belly pressed against her and the younger woman smiled at her gesture. "How is the child?"

Alienor lifted one finger to her lips. "Well enough, but Dagobert said to keep its existence secret," she whispered, and Iolande nodded in immediate understanding.

"Relieved I am indeed to hear that he retains some measure of his faculties," she commented dryly, her lips pulling tight once more in displeasure. Iolande flicked a glance to the people pressing against the door to the dungeons and her anger with Dagobert's impulsiveness was more than clear.

"I confess I do not understand," Alienor admitted, feeling every bit the simpleton but unable to keep herself from asking the question. Emotionally she felt turned inside out, the tempting possibility of Dagobert's freedom and his denial of that option almost tearing her apart. And she still didn't know the fundamental truth. "Who was Dagobert's sire?"

Iolande snorted in surprise and threw her daughter-in-law an indulgent smile. "Alzeu, of course." Alienor's heart leapt at this confirmation of the tale Dagobert himself had told her, her brows immediately drawing together as she tried to fathom the reason for Iolande's false assertion.

"Then why..." Alienor began in confusion, but got no further before the older woman cut her short.

"I thought to save the fool's life," Iolande explained bitterly, "but ever like his sire, he would have none of it. Too seriously indeed do men take these vows of childhood."

Alienor opened her mouth, then closed it again, uncertain what to think of Dagobert's decision. Why had he declared himself of the line of kings when the possibility of his freedom loomed so near? She recalled the blaze in his gray eyes when he had met her regard and something inside her shriveled. Was he so loath to spend his days with her?

Jordan caught up to the women then, his lips curving in a tentative smile when he saw Iolande, but she spoke sharply to him before he could greet her.

"'Tis none other than the serpent himself," she commented acidly, fixing Alienor with an imperious eye. "I had hoped that you were not in his company," she added pointedly, and Alienor felt her cheeks growing warm.

"Jordan obtained my release," she managed before Iolande silenced her with a skeptically raised eyebrow.

"And to what shadowy purpose?" she demanded archly. "Surely we all know the serpent to be a less than altruistic soul." To Alienor's surprise, Jordan met Iolande's eyes squarely.

"Had I ever a dubious purpose, 'tis forgotten now," he declared, earning a derisive snort from Iolande and a glance of open shock from Alienor. Only now she remembered his gasp when Dagobert bared his chest, and she wondered at his game.

"I knew not that the old tales came truly to life," he confessed with apparent sincerity. "I thought only that Dagobert preyed upon his people's beliefs to further his own cause."

"No understanding had you of the full measure of the man," Iolande spat, and Jordan had the grace to redden.

"Never would I have believed it had I not seen the mark of the cross myself," he added, and Alienor saw the confusion in his eyes. It seemed his entire world had been turned askew by the mere restoration of his faith in legends and tales, but Alienor was skeptical of the immediate transformation.

"An apology do I owe indeed to your house, Countess," Jordan told Iolande, the older woman's frosty countenance relaxing slightly but her tone changed not at all.

"Words have little cost and less merit," she retorted sharply, the knight managing to look abashed at her censure. "Taking my son's wife for your own lends little credence to your apology." Alienor gasped at Iolande's assumption but Jordan jumped to clear the air.

"Not a hand have I laid on her," he asserted with telling conviction.

"A likely tale," Iolande snorted, but Alienor saw that she was not entirely sure any longer.

"The lady refused my advance," Jordan admitted honestly, "and wished to remain faithful to her husband while he lived." He turned quickly to Alienor and fixed her with a bright eye. "Have I not honored your wishes?" he demanded sharply, and Alienor felt the weight of Iolande's gaze on her, as well.

"Aye," she confirmed, turning to Iolande as she explained. "The widow sees to his needs as she did before my arrival and he sleeps on a straw pallet, leaving me the bed." Iolande looked thoughtful for a moment, then turned to the knight.

"'Twould indeed seem that you change your ways, serpent, but I would still know the fullness of your intent," she commented quietly, and Jordan nodded.

"Indeed, my insult is not yet repaid," he stated. "There is but one task I may take to undo the wrong I have visited upon you and your family."

When Iolande said nothing, merely waiting imperiously for his next words, Jordan took a deep breath and plunged onward while Alienor watched in silent amazement.

"I would make amends for my part in seeing Dagobert imprisoned by correcting the wrong," he asserted. "I will help to engineer his release."

Something flashed in Iolande's eyes even as Alienor's breath caught in her throat, then Iolande was ushering them quickly out into the sunlight.

"'Tis hardly fitting to discuss the matter in such a public place," she chided, apparently unable to resist one last lash at the knight, but Alienor knew that both women's hearts were singing the same hopeful tune.

"Come stay with Alienor," Jordan offered. "The widow will be more than happy to welcome me for the fullness of the night."

'Twas two days hence that the announcement was made that Dagobert would be executed at dawn the following morning. Iolande, Alienor and Jordan retired to the room that the women shared to argue their options one last time. Time had run out on their heated dissent, and all knew that for lack of a better alternative, they would have to follow Jordan's plan. Not a one of them liked it, but all were forced to concede that 'twas the most likely to see success.

Late that evening when the city had quieted, Iolande pressed Jordan's hand between her own just before the threesome reached the palace, her gratitude finding no words in these last moments. She nodded once to Alienor before slipping off into the darkness to do her part, her darkly shrouded figure quickly blending with the shadows. Jordan forced a smile for Alienor in the darkness and she took a deep breath as they stepped into the hall and began to play their roles.

"'Tis pure folly to think you will be allowed to see him," Jordan roared as they crossed the threshold, and Alienor launched into a volley of recrimination and tears, their display immediately drawing the curious glance of the lone guard before the entrance to the great hall.

"Too cruel you are to deny me this and dispatch my soul to purgatory. My husband he is, sworn to me before God, and 'tis my duty as a wife to but bid him farewell," she sobbed, but Jordan shook his head impatiently.

"Well you know that you might have easily been accommodated earlier in the day," he snapped, but she only wailed the louder. "How like a woman to see her way clear when the timing is most inconvenient."

"But one kindness do I ask of you before we wed, and you would deny me even this simple request," she cried. "Did not the priest threaten me with purgatory if I did not do this thing? But naught of eternal damnation do you concern yourself. Only do you think of the interruption of your own earthly pleasures."

"Have I not pledged myself to your care?" Jordan demanded in a conciliatory tone, and Alienor threw him a haughty look.

"Only in anticipation of the earthly pleasures I could provide you," she snapped, and he looked acceptably surprised. "'Twill be a cold marriage bed you find, sir, should I be headed for purgatory." Jordan rolled his eyes heavenward at her petulant words and met the sympathetic gaze of the court guard. "Too cruel you are," she declared theatrically, and launched into a noisy flood of tears.

"I had no choice but to bring her here despite the hour," Jordan confessed with the air of a man driven to distraction, patting her shoulder awkwardly. "She has fair driven me mad since we supped and she heard tell of the man's fate in the tavern."

"Which man?" the guard asked with interest.

"Dagobert de Pereille," Jordan supplied ruefully, and the guard nodded immediately.

"Aye, the dawn will be his last."

"His wife she is," Jordan added under his breath while Alienor continued to sob uncontrollably against his shoulder. "At least until we are wed tomorrow." The guard spared Alienor a glance and met Jordan's eyes again with something vaguely akin to humor.

"'Twould seem the lady is attached to the man," he ventured to comment, but Jordan snorted in derision, taking a moment to brush the dampness of Alienor's tears from his tabard.

"Women," he said in annoyance. "'Tis difficult enough to understand them. Happy enough she was when first she heard the news, making me promise we would wed right after the execution and all, then *tzut—*" he snapped his fingers to make his point "—she began to cry all over our trencher." Jordan leaned closer to the guard, who was now listening with rapt attention.

"Guilt, she tells me," he confided as if he could not believe the stupidity of the claim, and the guard chuckled under his breath. "'Tis this purgatory nonsense that the good father in our parish has been feeding her and I cannot convince her to see the true way of things."

"Aye, there are many who fear the shadows," the guard agreed with an indulgent smile toward Alienor, clearly not finding himself among those ranks.

"Oho, so speaks a man who has weathered similar storms. Wed then, are you?" Jordan demanded, seeming to have found a kindred spirit, but the guard shook his head reluctantly.

"Never found a one that seemed worth the trouble," he replied good-naturedly, flicking another glance to the sobbing Alienor, now draped bonelessly across Jordan's shoulder. She whispered "Purgatory" despairingly under her breath and the two men shared a look that spoke volumes.

"A point of merit you have there," Jordan conceded with a doubtful glance to his apparent intended. "For no end of trouble has she been this day, although—" he dropped his voice to a conspiratorial whisper "—'twas her threat of a cold bed that truly caught my ear. She is a fetching wench, and should she have her desire this night, I might have more of mine on the morrow."

The guard chuckled openly. "Aye, your meaning is clear enough to me." Jordan sidled a little closer and prepared to make his pitch, pointedly shifting Alienor's weight away from the conversation as he leaned in to whisper to the guard.

"No insult would I make to an honorable man with mere coin, but 'twould be of great interest to me to see the lady's whim met this night, should you understand my meaning."

"Little enough is there that I might do," the guard replied quickly, but his eyes flew to Jordan's pocket when an indeterminate number of gold coins made an unmistakable jingle there.

"Surely you can understand that I have no desire to spend the night listening to the lady sob. Rather would I sleep in anticipation of my nuptial night." Jordan elbowed the guard and winked, drawing a reluctant grin from his potential coconspirator.

"Who should know but you and I?" Jordan demanded in a whisper, jingling those coins again, and the guard licked his lips nervously.

"She has a younger sister," he added in a lower tone. "Untouched and lovely as the dawn, she is." The guard glanced at Jordan in time to see his bold wink. "An introduction I could arrange, either by night or day." The guard cast a glance over his shoulder, leaning closer to Jordan as the spirit of negotiation began to light his eyes.

"The jailer would need convincing, as well," he argued weakly, and Jordan clapped him on the shoulder in a congratulatory way.

"Truly you are an honorable man to think so of your friends," he said warmly, and the guard dared to smile. "But in truth, she has only one sister," he confessed, prompting a wider grin from the guard.

"Our secret is that part of the deal. Show me your gold," he demanded.

"I show you but one until you name your price," Jordan countered, flipping the coin out into the air so that it flashed in the darkness. The guard caught it expertly and bit the gold between his teeth, nodding at the softness of the metal. "'Tis yours," Jordan whispered, and the guard's eyes widened briefly.

"Truly you are anxious," he commented suspiciously, but Jordan merely laughed.

"Long have I waited for this wench and I would not have the taking of her lost for a mere coin or two," he confessed, his words launching a decidedly greedy smile across the guard's face.

"I shall be but a moment," he murmured back, his eyes darting along the corridor that acted as a buffer between the great hall and the street before he turned and strode quickly away.

When the guard returned and confessed his victory in convincing the jailer, Alienor made a great show of delight in her apparent intended's success, raining little kisses all over Jordan's face while he counted out half the agreed number of coins. The two men exchanged a look of mutual tolerance and Jordan shook his head, adjusting his helmet under one arm as he offered Alienor the other.

"This way," the guard directed them, and Alienor felt a momentary twinge of fear that they had been discovered, for he indicated another darkened passageway and not the path she had taken originally through the great hall. A shadowy door lurked at the end of the corridor, the smell that rose from the concealed stairs when it was opened convincing Alienor that they were headed for the dungeons.

But were they being imprisoned themselves? Her heart pounded with the uncertainty of it all and she was sure her distress was obvious. Jordan joked amiably with the guard as they walked and apparently saw nothing amiss, the guard's casual swinging of his keys making Alienor doubt her fears. The jailer greeted them with avarice shining in his eyes and she relaxed slightly when she saw 'twas a different man on duty than had been here before. His eyes glowed as he bit and counted the first half of his gold and she dared to hope that Jordan's plan would truly work.

"Could I have but a moment alone with him?" she begged Jordan prettily, still draping herself over his arm as though he had hung the sun and the moon just for her.

"To what purpose?" he scowled as the jailer led the way toward the cell with jingling keys. "Enough trouble have I had in simply bringing you here this night for you to be asking yet another favor."

"Indeed, *chéri,* and I know 'tis foolish, but he knows naught of you, of us, and I would tell him the tale alone," she explained for their audience, and Jordan waved one hand wide in concession.

"No matter is it to me," he retorted. "Tell him or not, for 'tis of no relevance to me. Think you that I have any desire to meet the man?"

"You are too good to me, *chéri,*" Alienor cooed, pressing a kiss against Jordan's ear and letting her voice drop to a sultry whisper. "A hundred times over shall I repay your understanding." Jordan winked boldly to the jailer at this comment and the man smothered a grin, unlocking the door to Dagobert's cell and throwing it open with a flourish.

"'Tis company you have, great king," he announced as Alienor stepped into the room with a pounding heart. She jumped as the door clanged shut behind her, a gasp falling from her lips at the murderous intent gleaming in her husband's eyes.

"Did that snake bring you here?" Dagobert demanded by way of greeting, ignoring the quick shake of Alienor's head. She closed the space between them with a couple of steps, but he had no interest in whatever lies she might have concocted for him. A hundred times would she repay that scum? The overheard words burned a quick path right to his heart.

"'Tis not important," she countered, her words low and quickly spoken. "You must listen to me," she added, but got no further.

"'Tis important to me!" Dagobert growled, grabbing his wife's shoulders and giving her a resolute shake. For two days the thought of Alienor with Jordan had been eating away at him and now she had the nerve to simply dismiss that liaison as if 'twere without consequence! What manner of woman had he wed that she could so casually toss him aside?

"How long did it take you to crawl into his bed?" he demanded sharply, and Alienor gasped with indignation. "Have you shared his warmth since first you left this foul place? How many times has he taken you? How many times has he kissed you?"

"I share naught with . . ." she murmured in an undertone, but he would have none of it.

"Naught! Do you think me a fool, woman?" Dagobert shook her again, wishing he could make her teeth rattle. "With my own eyes did I see you beside him in court! With my own ears did I hear you just call him *chéri. Chéri!*" he sneered, and dropped Alienor back to her feet, prowling the perimeter of the cell like a caged tiger.

'Twas jealousy that held him captive in his grip, and though he knew the truth of it, he could not dismiss his anger. The thought of Jordan taking his pleasure with Alienor was driving him insane, the fading of his own memory of their last night together doing naught to improve his temper. Rage and love mingled in his heart, leaving him confused and disoriented, uncertain whether to murder Alienor with his bare hands or make love to her right here, right now.

To his surprise, Alienor dogged his footsteps and tried to grab his arm.

"You must listen to me," she urged, but he shook off her grip as easily as he would have dismissed an annoying fly.

"No interest have I in your explanations, no possible justification is there for your faithlessness," he snarled, turning and gripping her jaw with one abrupt move, holding her captive against the wall. For an instant, he was tempted to kiss the fullness of her lips even in his anger, to taste her one last time, the magnitude of her betrayal bringing him up short just in time.

"Faithlessness!" Alienor spat, and something flashed in those amber eyes that Dagobert had not seen since he caught her launching shoes across their chamber in Montsalvat. She twisted savagely from his grip, spinning unexpectedly and planting the heel of her hand in the middle of his chest, sending him barreling against the wall in her stead.

"Never have I been unfaithful to you," Alienor declared, the conviction in her words so effectively stealing the wind from his sails that he paused to listen to her.

"We came this night to free you," she confessed, and lost his faith in her as quickly as it had been gained.

"Truly, milady, you think me a cretin," Dagobert countered hotly, pointing emphatically to the door. Alienor's eyes widened in fear and she shook her head wildly, holding her finger to his lips, and he found himself unwillingly dropping his tone to a harsh whisper.

"No use has that one for saving my hide," he argued, punctuating his words with sharp jabs of his finger into the air, "unless he means to profit by hunting me anew. Though you might savor the sport, I for one will forgo that dubious pleasure and remain here." Pleased that he had seen through Jordan's ruse, he folded his arms across his chest and regarded his wife, intrigued when she gritted her teeth in annoyance and her eyes flashed dangerously.

"Test the very patience of the gods, you would," Alienor managed to mutter scathingly. Rosiness blossomed in her cheeks as a result of her anger, that soft pink flush undoing Dagobert's resolve more effectively than mere words could have done.

One last time. Her lips parted to make some additional argument but he resolved that he would hear none of it. There was nothing to be gained by arguing at this late date. Too much precious time had they wasted already: it should have been enough for him that she was here.

Dagobert snatched Alienor abruptly off her feet, savoring her gasp of surprise before his lips closed firmly over hers. Never an impulsive man, he had a twinge of doubt that he might have made a mistake and frightened her when Alienor fought his embrace.

To his relief, she struggled but for an instant, then softened against him, his kiss growing more demanding with his satisfaction at the way she melted for him. The taste and smell of Alienor filled his senses, the curve of her breast filled his hand and he marveled that he had been able to survive without her. No mercy would he have for any who dared to interrupt him now.

"God's blood, no intention had I that he should take her before my very eyes!"

Jordan's cry of indignation outside the door vaguely registered in Dagobert's mind, the hasty turning of the key in the lock bringing his head up with a jolt. Alienor looked as though she would say something, but he silenced her with a glance.

"I will handle this myself," Jordan told the surprised jailer when he stood revealed in the doorway, and Dagobert almost smiled in anticipation. Truly his last night was proving to be unexpectedly satisfying. The door closed behind Jordan, the dark-haired knight holding up one hand before he spoke.

He had not the time to form his words before Dagobert landed a solid right to his jaw and knocked him out cold. Jordan groaned as he fell against the wall and panicked footsteps echoed in the hall.

Alienor muttered something incomprehensible under her breath and Dagobert met the raw fury in her eyes with surprise. Did she truly care for this man? His jealous anger showed signs of reasserting itself after that incendiary kiss but Alienor apparently had no time for his tender feelings.

In amazement, Dagobert watched her hasty sign language and immediately understood her intent, if not her reason, obediently tugging Jordan's fallen form out of view of the tiny window as the jailer tapped his keys against the door.

"All's well?" he demanded sharply. Before Dagobert could answer, Alienor had clapped one uncompromising hand over his mouth, shooting him a positively lethal look before she answered.

"Oh, Jordan!" she wailed, her gaze never wavering from Dagobert's eyes and her words confusing to say the least. "Never should you have hit him, Jordan! Now I shall have to stay until Dagobert awakens. We had yet to say farewell and the priest will have harsh words for me. Well you knew that I had yet to hem my kirtle this night to be ready for the morrow."

Had the woman lost her mind? Dagobert frowned at her when she gestured that he should say something. "Act as Jordan," she mouthed, and he could not for the life of him understand her meaning, the hot look she sent in his direction while she wailed anew finally convincing him.

"No harm meant I, *chérie*," he said, managing a reasonable facsimile of Jordan's baritone, the jailer's wry chuckle and retreating footsteps telling him that he had succeeded. Alienor, however, had no words of congratulations for him, or even of explanation, so intent was she on removing Jordan's tunic.

"Your assistance would be appreciated," she commented dryly under her breath, but Dagobert merely shook his head.

"No part will I have in disrobing your lover," he argued, his words drawing another of those exasperated looks from his wife. She gritted her teeth, then took his face in her hands, leaning so close to speak to him that he could feel the softness of her breath against his own lips.

"Precious little time have we, but 'tis simple enough," she told him. "You will dress in Jordan's garments, we shall walk out of here." Dagobert felt his eyes narrow assessingly, unable to help the accusation that formed in his mind.

"Knew he that you planned to betray him?" he demanded, and watched his wife's eyes go cold.

"Should you have left him conscious, you could have asked him," she shot back sarcastically, bending to tug at one of Jordan's boots with a vengeance.

Dagobert ran a hand over his head, uncertain whether or not to trust in her word. What madness was this? Why would the man who had once betrayed him now take such pains to free him? Alienor spared a glance up at him, the apologetic half smile she sent in his direction telling him that some of his confusion must be showing.

"You are much the same size," she murmured, "and he insisted on bringing his helmet. 'Twas his own plan and not such a bad one that you should deliberately thwart it."

This last Dagobert understood as a plea for assistance and he bent immediately to help Alienor in her task. Perhaps 'twas a ruse, but he had naught to lose and much to gain judging by the way Alienor had clung to his lips only moments before. She made a great production of sounding as though she were trying to awaken Dagobert and he had to smother a laugh more than once at her clever acting, the levity dawning in his heart making it even more difficult for him to play his role as Jordan convincingly.

"I cannot take his hauberk," he argued under his breath at one point, unable to bring himself to steal the armor earned along with a knight's spurs. 'Twould be dishonorable, unthinkably base, but Alienor merely shot him a scathing glance.

"Consider it a gift," she muttered back. "'Twas undoubtedly the argument used when your own mail was confiscated in Toulouse." Still he hesitated and Alienor shook her head in unconcealed frustration.

"Little time have we, milord, and I would not have
you go abroad without a hauberk."

Dagobert summoned a small smile of agreement,
seeing the wisdom of her words when he realized that
they had yet to get out of the palace. He reluctantly
donned the garment, amazed that it fitted as well as it
did, his fingers hesitating for a minute before he added
Jordan's dagger to his ensemble. The jailer would
merely take it for his own, should it be left behind, and
well he knew it, but he could not easily shake the feeling that he was doing the other knight a disservice.

When Dagobert stood dressed in the other knight's
clothing and Jordan was wrapped in his own torn
garment, Alienor corrected his posture with a few well-
placed pokes and prods, forcing him to stand less
straight than he did usually. 'Twas true Jordan was
slightly shorter, though he knew not if he could manage to remember all her directions and walk thus all
the way out to the street.

'Twould save his life, he told himself sternly, a sudden wave of claustrophobia making him need to get
free of the cell as soon as possible.

"Enough of your pandering, woman!" he roared in
a mimic of Jordan that was rapidly improving. Dagobert pulled Jordan's helmet on with a resolute gesture and tapped his knuckles sharply against the door,
his heart leaping at Alienor's approving smile. "You
cannot expect me to sit aside while you coddle the man
like a lover! 'Tis too late to be afoot and the man
shows no signs of waking. Truly you test my patience
this night, woman."

"Aye, Jordan," Alienor conceded with apparent
reluctance. "Indeed, you have already been too kind
to me this night."

"Wait but for the morrow," Dagobert muttered under his breath, hearing the jailer's chuckle on the other side of the door. He closed his eyes, not daring to believe their ruse might work, desperately trying to recall Jordan's comments to Alienor that had so burned his heart. Somehow he must manage to play his role convincingly. The key turned in the lock and hope fluttered in his chest.

With a gesture that ripped at Dagobert's heart, Alienor bent and placed a kiss on Jordan's cheek, the other man's eyes opening at her touch. Jordan smiled groggily at her, looking over her shoulder and fixing Dagobert with an assessing glance that spoke volumes.

Truly this plan had been Jordan's idea, though Dagobert could not fathom why he would suggest such a thing, a chill running through him at the full import of the man's move. Would Jordan declare his true identity on the morrow? What price would he pay for his aid?

Well aware of the perusal of the guard upon him, Dagobert nodded curtly to Jordan, hoping the man understood the full weight of his gratitude, hoping the knight would not sacrifice his own life for his bravery.

The moment of understanding between the two men was gone almost instantly, Alienor fairly dancing ahead of Dagobert, her pretty words full of promises. She lifted a purse and counted out a shocking number of gold coins for the jailer before they left the prison. Dagobert desperately tryed to control his outrage that such a price had been paid to the man for simply turning a key as the guard accompanied them back up to the passageway before the great hall.

'Twas a different path than he had taken before and for an instant Dagobert feared a trick, his heart pounding in his ears. He felt the unsteadiness in his steps but forced himself to continue, frustrated by the limits the helmet put on his peripheral vision. Alienor seemed undisturbed by the path, however, and he allowed himself to trust her, forcing himself to relax that he didn't give them away.

"What is the wench's name?" the guard demanded as they reached the top of the stairs, his questioning sending Dagobert scrambling around in his mind for an answer.

"Which wench?" he asked, hoping he was not condemning them with his ignorance. Alienor laughed when the guard might have been surprised, turning and wagging her finger playfully beneath Dagobert's nose.

"Always the tease, he is," she confided in the guard, her tone scolding when she continued. "He asks about my sister Ermengarde, and well you know it."

Ermengarde? Who the hell was Ermengarde? The guard laughed at Dagobert's apparent jest and clapped him heartily on the shoulder while Dagobert tried not to show his complete lack of comprehension. His heart pounded so loudly in his ears that he was sure the other two must be able to hear it, the thought of being imprisoned anew so much more unpalatable for this brief respite.

"Truly for a moment I thought you forgot our deal," the guard chortled. "Indeed, you made me wonder."

"Perhaps they could meet after Mass," Alienor suggested, flicking a speculative look to Dagobert, and now Dagobert understood the transaction that was being made.

"Nay, woman," he corrected her. "'Tis not a chat before your priest this man deserves." He turned to the guard and lowered his voice slightly. "Meet me at the weaver's stall near the Temple tomorrow after vespers and you shall share our nuptial meal."

"And Ermengarde?"

"Naturally milady would not wed without her sister present."

"Indeed, sir, you are most kind," the guard gushed appreciatively, Dagobert's breath stopping in his throat when Alienor dropped another jingle of gold coins into the man's hand. He bit back his protest before it could leave his tongue, waving casually to the guard as he led Alienor out into the street. Truly the woman had yet to learn the value of a hard-earned coin.

"Before vespers," he added by way of farewell, and the guard nodded agreeably.

The heavy door closed and he stood hand in hand with Alienor in the quiet darkness of the street outside the palace, the air filling his lungs making a weight slip off Dagobert's chest. Outside they were, he marveled, and leaned back against the wall, trying to discern the stars far overhead. 'Twas a miracle, a stroke of luck beyond compare.

"What know you of a weaver's stall near the Temple?" Alienor demanded from beside him, and Dagobert smiled to himself at the skepticism in her tone.

"Naught," he admitted, and grinned down at her, "but why should there not be one there?" Alienor laughed and Dagobert dared to chuckle himself, seeing the full vista of his life spread before him once again, amazed that the simple switch had worked as well as it had.

"We must hasten," Alienor murmured as she tugged on his sleeve, and he roused himself from his early relief. Too soon did he revel in freedom while they were as yet within the king's own walls.

"Lead on, milady," he invited her, thinking that perhaps she smiled quickly before turning and setting a killing pace through the streets.

Indeed, they were far from clear and away, he realized, that thought launching the adrenaline through him again. Despite his weakened state, his fear gave him the will to match her pace, the very threat of this taste of freedom being snatched away setting his heart pounding in his ears.

No pause did Alienor give him, hurrying him toward the bridge that they might cross from the Ile de la Cité to the mainland, virtually trotting through the deserted streets toward the perimeter of town. No shouts of discovery echoed behind them, much to his surprise, and his frantic heartbeat slowed as Alienor led them unerringly through the maze of twisted streets. Clearly she had a destination in mind but he heartily doubted that anyone could have followed their meandering path.

But where did she lead him? To the site of another betrayal? The doubting corner of his mind could not leave him to trust Alienor's intent, his imagination conjuring numerous outcomes to this escape as they walked, each more terrible than the last, but still he dogged his wife's footsteps.

Though it seemed an enormous amount of time had passed, the moon had not visibly risen higher in the sky when they approached a low-slung building near the southern wall of the city. Alienor's nervous manner did naught to assuage Dagobert's fears and he silently drew Jordan's knife.

A cloaked figure stepped from the shadows and he lunged forward with the blade. Alienor cried out at the same moment as a familiarly imperious whisper brought him up short.

"Imprisonment truly has addled your wits," Iolande commented dryly and Dagobert fairly collapsed with relief. He embraced her gratefully, not resisting his mother's examination when she drew back to examine his eyes and teeth as if he were some livestock she proposed to buy. Never would the woman lose her practicality, he mused, swallowing an affectionate smile lest she thought he mocked her.

"Hungry you must be," she said, and Dagobert nodded, feeling exhaustion sweep over his weakened frame after their run through the streets. Alienor had given him his worst working in a month, and having had little to eat over that time, he was surprised he held up as well as he did. Iolande's eyes narrowed now and she gripped his chin, forcing him to meet her gaze. "Abused?" she demanded tonelessly, but he only shrugged, unwilling to confirm her fears so early.

"No more than would be expected," he conceded tightly, turning a mischievous grin on the silent Alienor in an attempt to lighten the mood. "In truth, 'tis my own wife who has run me ragged," he confessed, and Iolande snorted with laughter as the lady in question flushed scarlet.

"Had I known you would be so ungrateful, I should have left you there," Alienor shot back, a gleam in her eye, and he chuckled despite himself.

"She would be rid of me one way or the other," he murmured to his mother in a mock confidential tone, delighting in the way Alienor's amber eyes flashed in indignation.

"You—" she began hotly with a finger pointed in his direction, only to have Iolande cut her short.

"You must eat as we ride, for time is of the essence," the older woman said, herding them both into the dark stables as she continued. "You might ride together should you so wish to argue."

The very idea of holding Alienor so close lightened Dagobert's step but he quickly saw that his wife was having none of that suggestion. She pulled herself resolutely up into her saddle and urged her mount out into the street, leaving him no option but to ride alone. Iolande watched the exchange with a sparkle in her eye, but his disappointment left him in no mood for any teasing comments she might make, and once they were all mounted, he immediately spurred his own horse to a trot.

Women, he gritted out between his teeth, shooting a sidelong glance to his wife's mutinously set jaw. Would he never understand the lightning-quick changes of their moods?

Chapter Eleven

Would that she were clever enough to want to be rid of him! Alienor dug her heels into the horse harder than was necessary once they had passed through the gates of the city, not trusting herself to speak in her anger.

Seven kinds of fool was she to have fallen in love with such an exasperating man! Always did he assume the worst. Always. She had not seen Dagobert for a month, yet in the space of this one evening, he had already accused her of adultery, deceit and betrayal. Alienor almost wished that she *was* leading him into some sort of trap, for it seemed to her at this moment that he would be well served to have one of his suspicions proved true!

It helped not at all to know that she had responded so easily to his touch, when that kiss that had so enflamed her had been no more than a stamp of possession on his part. Indeed, he had been clear-eyed enough immediately afterward to throw a solid punch while she had been gripping the wall like some dimwitted idiot, simply trying to remain upright despite the chaos of her emotions. Calm and collected, that was Dagobert, she fumed inwardly, despising the fact that he never seemed to lose control of himself.

'Twas unfair that she should love a man so thoroughly who cared naught for her at all, never mind that she should break the covenants of her faith to bear him a child. And all he could say was that she must want to be rid of him at any cost. Tears of self-pity pricked at Alienor's eyes and even recognizing them for what they were could not circumvent their course.

Someone drew up alongside her galloping horse and Alienor had not to look to know 'twas her spouse. She ignored him steadfastly, staring straight ahead to the shadowy thread of the road, uncertain she could survive a casual conversation at this moment without breaking into hysterics. Dagobert spoke her name but she stubbornly pretended not to hear, surreptitiously touching her heel to her horse's flanks to increase its speed.

To her dismay, Dagobert's mount matched the pace of her own easily. Alienor watched helplessly as her husband's gloved hand landed on the pommel of her saddle but feigned unawareness of his gesture, lifting her chin defiantly and not slowing her pace. Dagobert muttered something under his breath as he reached purposefully for her waist and Alienor panicked that he might touch her. Without another thought, she jerked her horse's reins hard to one side, abruptly putting a yawning chasm between the two steeds.

Dagobert swore now with an eloquence that astonished Alienor and she risked a glance toward him. He sat rigidly in his saddle and she sensed he was fighting for control of his temper, his eyes flashing silver when he turned back toward her.

Instinctively, she recoiled, but she was not fast enough to evade his darting hand from laying claim to her horse's reins. He snatched the leather from her hands and pulled her destrier to an unceremonious halt, his movements curt and sure as he dismounted and hauled her down from her saddle.

Before Alienor could protest, Dagobert had dumped her into his own saddle like so much baggage, fastening her mount's reins to the back of his saddle with an abrupt snap. Briefly Alienor considered giving her heel to the horse and leaving him standing in the road, but he shot a dark look in her direction as if he had guessed her thoughts and she did not dare to try.

By the time Iolande had stopped her own horse and started to canter back in their direction, Dagobert had swung up behind Alienor and pulled her against him with an assertiveness that brooked no argument.

Alienor avoided Iolande's knowing smile and held herself stiffly before Dagobert, fighting her own desire to relax against him. Fool! she called herself again, annoyed that the mere warmth of his presence could undermine her determination so effectively.

Clearly Dagobert was also in no mood for discussion. Even when Iolande matched her horse's pace to that of his and rode alongside, he did not initiate a conversation with his mother. Had Alienor not been so infuriated herself, she might have marveled at the tension emanating from him.

"There is bread and cheese in your pack," Iolande commented finally, an annoyingly enigmatic smile playing over her lips as the road narrowed, and she urged her mount ahead of Dagobert's steed.

Silence hung heavily between husband and wife, long moments dragging by before Alienor, not wanting to appear churlish, leaned around Dagobert and fetched the food from the satchel hanging behind his saddle. Truly the man had not eaten well of late, she told herself as her anger dissolved. 'Twas easy enough to see by the tightening of his flesh over his bones.

When she was settled before him again, he removed his helmet, the way he shook his head as if loosening his hair drawing Alienor's attention to his baldness. He noted her inquiring expression and smiled ruefully.

"How does it look?" he demanded, his normally steady temper apparently restored, and Alienor could not help but respond to his teasing smile. She cocked her head to one side and considered his shaved pate, new stubble already casting a faint shadow over the skin.

"'Tis not so bad," she observed doubtfully, "but most assuredly unexpected." Dagobert chuckled and she smiled in turn, her heart warming when he drew her yet closer. "In truth, I think your beard grows faster," she added, and Dagobert laughed, running a hand over the growth on his chin.

"Relieved I am indeed that you do not find it offensive, milady," he jested, taking a chunk of bread from her, closing his eyes briefly as he chewed and making her wish she had better fare to offer him.

Alienor took the opportunity to look him over, her heartbeat picking up as she studied the square strength of his jaw, the noble line of his cheekbones and nose. Even without his hair, he showed a regalness of bearing, a graceful assurance in his every move that she found irresistible.

"You mean to grow it back?" she ventured to ask, and Dagobert opened his eyes again, startling her with his bright gaze.

"Unless you object."

"'Twas of great length before," she acknowledged, having trouble keeping her thoughts sorted out when he looked at her with such intensity.

"Fifteen summers did I let it grow," Dagobert admitted, and Alienor frowned as two pieces clicked together in her mind.

"Fifteen? 'Twas just so many years since you took your vow," she said slowly, glancing up as he nodded in agreement.

"Aye," he said, and winked at her boldly, prying a piece of cheese from her fingers. "Think you that 'twas coincidence?" The insinuation that she was dimwitted sparked Alienor's simmering temper anew and she turned on Dagobert with flashing eyes.

"You need not speak to me as though I were no more than a simple child," she retorted coldly, her icy tone enough to stop Dagobert midbite.

"I meant no offense," he began in a conciliatory tone, but Alienor cut him short, sick to death of his accusations and insinuations. Why on earth had he insisted on wedding her if he thought so little of her character?

"You meant no offense?" she parroted angrily. "Just as you meant no offense earlier this night when you accused me of sharing a bed with Jordan? Just as you meant no offense when you asserted that I was helping you escape only to lead you into some diabolical trap? What sort of trap did you imagine that I could devise that would be worse than your execution at dawn?''

Dagobert sat back and regarded her with something remarkably akin to astonishment, but Alienor had already unleashed her frustration and she could not check it now. Too long had she sat back and accepted the changes he had forced into her life. At least this once, she would have her say and the consequences be damned.

"*Always* have you thought the worst of me, always have you assumed that I made efforts only to undermine, betray or deceive you," she accused hotly. "*Never* have I done anything to dishonor you or your name, but no credit am I to have for that! A virgin I was when I came to your bed and even now no other man has been between my thighs but you, but what gratitude have I for that loyalty?" Alienor waved one hand at the surrounding woods, supplying her own answer when one was not forthcoming from those bent old trees.

"*None,* save only accusations of adultery when a man happens to show me some kindness, kindness that coincidentally sees to *your* very survival. 'Twas *you* who deceived *me,* milord, 'twas *you* who enacted that foolish charade that left the goat dead, 'twas *you* who took this pledge to ensure that you and all your heirs die too young."

"Alienor," Dagobert murmured quietly in an obvious attempt to soothe her, but she would not fall silent now.

"What dishonor have I given you by believing the lies you told me? What ignobility have I committed by bearing your child despite my faith, that you might have the heir you desire above all else? My very life did

I risk this night to save your sorry hide and not a word of gratitude have you for me, only comments that I wish to be rid of you! Had I the desire to be *rid* of you, milord, I would simply have left you to die!''

"Alienor," he tried again, winning only the hard prod of her index finger in his chest.

"No sweet words from you will set this aright so easily," she fairly growled, emboldened by the loosening of her frustration to make a daringly impulsive assertion. "'Tis true enough that you have no trust of me, though there is precious little basis for your fears. *No* match can be content without the foundation of trust and I would have yours, milord, if I am to remain by your side."

"What are you saying?" Dagobert demanded sharply, the warning flash in his eyes not enough to stop Alienor.

"Your child will I bear four months hence," she affirmed, taking a deep breath to sustain her now that she had gotten this far, "but should you find yourself unable to give me your trust by that time, I will leave Monsalvat."

Dagobert froze for a moment and he was so still that Alienor wondered if he yet breathed, then he shook his head in unconcealed annoyance.

"You speak nonsense and well you know it," he argued irritatedly. "Where would you go, wife of mine? Think you that another man would take you in?" Alienor lifted her chin at his unintended insult, looking him straight in the eye.

"There are those of my faith who will shelter me until I can fulfill the requirements to take my vows." It seemed to Alienor that Dagobert blanched in the darkness but she could not be sure.

"You would take consolamentum rather than remain my wife?" he demanded unevenly, but she steadfastly ignored the catch in his voice.

"Should you be unable to trust me, I would have no choice," she maintained quietly, watching as Dagobert's lips thinned to a harsh line and he lifted his gaze to the distant horizon.

"We will speak more of this later," he said tersely, but Alienor shook her head definitively.

"Naught more is there to discuss," she concluded, turning to watch the road rising before them as the realization of what she had done washed over her.

What had she done? Had she truly made such a challenge to her husband? Unlike her it was to speak rashly and now it seemed that she had thrown the fat into the fire. What had possessed her to give Dagobert an ultimatum?

Truly she had lost her mind to so casually toss aside that which she wanted more than anything else. Too late she realized that he had said naught to reassure her, that he had not even vowed to try to meet her demand. Fool! she called herself yet again, feeling those tears of self-pity rise once more, stubbornly refusing to turn and apologize to him for her impulsive words.

"All is well?" Iolande demanded quietly from the vicinity of his elbow in the wee hours of the morning, and Dagobert spared a half smile for his mother's worried frown.

"Aye," he managed to lie, making a pretense of adjusting the sleeping Alienor so that his mother might not see the truth in his eyes. The sound of their horses' footfalls filled the silence between them, the sinking moon casting ethereal shadows along the deserted road.

"'Tis the babe, you know," Iolande commented finally. Dagobert shot his mother a sidelong look and found her assessing gaze upon him. "'Twas difficult not to overhear," she confessed with a rueful smile, and he couldn't help but smile back.

"There is truth in what she says," he argued, staring thoughtfully down at the soft tumble of his wife, her relaxed fingers splayed across his chest just as those dark lashes fanned her cheeks.

"Aye," Iolande agreed, "but the growth of the babe feeds her emotions, makes her more volatile than usual. The midwives say 'tis so." Dagobert nodded, having the experience neither to confirm nor to deny this odd assertion.

"The malaise passes?" he asked, assuming he was expected to do so, not at all certain that Alienor's dissatisfaction with him could be so easily attributed to her pregnancy. She thought he did not trust her, and deep in his heart he had to admit that there was some truth to her assertion.

Perhaps 'twas the nature of his upbringing or the realities of his inherited quest, but his first response to her actions was inevitably unflattering. Perhaps 'twas because he held her so close to his heart, perhaps 'twas an instinctive response to the newfound vulnerability his love had brought to him; he knew not which, but wished heartily that he could repair the offense.

Would she truly leave him to take the vows of the Cathar perfects? 'Twas unthinkable that he should lose her, unimaginable that he should survive this last ordeal and be without Alienor. Now that his anger had flared and faded, he considered her words more thoughtfully, knowing that if the consolamentum vows were truly what she desired, he would not stand in the way of her pursuit.

But could he possibly convince her to stay?

"Usually it passes once the babe is weaned," Iolande informed him, but he was so lost in his thoughts that the words took a moment to penetrate.

"Weaned?" he demanded in shock, not appeased by his mother's delighted chuckle. "'Tis more than a year hence."

"Aye," she said mischievously, and he chuckled himself.

"Surely you jest," he cajoled, and Iolande shrugged her shoulders expressively.

"'Tis different for each," she admitted. "I sought only to make you smile." Dagobert grinned then and Iolande smiled back, but his brows pulled abruptly into a frown when he recalled a matter that had been plaguing him.

"Eustache did not ride with you?" he demanded. Iolande immediately sobered and he feared the news would not be good.

"Tell me," Dagobert urged, laying his hand overtop his mother's, knowing that his friend would not have willingly left Iolande to ride all the way to Paris alone.

"I suppose I shall have to tell you the way of things," she conceded with a reluctant sigh, her words dispelling none of her son's fears. "Montsalvat was besieged but a week after you departed."

"Besieged?" Dagobert repeated in shock, and his mother nodded sadly.

"Aye. 'Tis said there are ten thousand men camped in the valley."

Dagobert shook his head, unable to take in the news. Ten thousand men? What enormous cost to expend in attacking a fortress of virtually no value. Montsalvat had no vineyards or orchards, barely any livestock, and was in so difficult a location 'twas incomprehensible to him that anyone would bother to besiege it.

"But why?" he asked, earning a sidelong glance from Iolande.

"They demanded you," she fairly whispered, and he sat back in his saddle in amazement. "They did not believe you gone when we told them so, and *I* had no intention of letting them pass through the gate to confirm the truth." Iolande's voice grew bitter as she continued. "Barbarians they are, these Crusaders, and I would give not a single grain of wheat for the value of their word."

"So, they settled into the valley," Dagobert mused, and his mother nodded.

"Aye, but they guard only the road, the fools," she murmured condescendingly, and Dagobert smiled in the darkness.

"You came down the east face," he asserted, Iolande's mischievous smile all the confirmation he needed.

"I knew you awaited Eustache, but the knights had been unable to ride out because of the attack. I thought to warn you, but Eustache was most dissatisfied with the idea," Iolande confessed, and Dagobert grinned even wider.

"Well can I imagine. Did you drug his wine that you might escape the keep?" he teased, and Iolande chuckled in turn.

"Nay, he has grown most suspicious in his dotage and takes but a sip of even the finest wine these days."

"Dotage?" Dagobert echoed with a barely concealed guffaw, imagining Eustache's outrage if he heard himself referred to that way.

"Thirty-five summers has he seen," Iolande asserted firmly. "'Tis most elderly for a knight." Despite herself, she joined Dagobert's whoop of laughter and the two took several moments to compose themselves again.

"He acts the old man, you must confess that is so," she said at last, but Dagobert resolutely withheld his agreement even in principle.

"You, of course, drink from the fountain of youth itself?" he jested, seeing the brief flash of his mother's smile.

"Women grow wise when we age," she asserted with a twinkle in her eye, "'tis mere men who lose their vigor and purpose."

"So, he agreed to let you leave?" Dagobert asked, knowing full well that nothing of the kind had occurred but wanting to change the subject.

"'Twas Eustache I charged with responsibility for the keep," Iolande explained proudly, and he had to admire the simple elegance of her solution. "He could scarcely dispute the fact that he was best qualified for the task."

It did not take much effort for Dagobert to imagine his friend's response to his mother's neat side step and he smiled once more. With luck, the defense of Montsalvat was going well enough that he and Eustache would see each other again soon.

"The dawn arrives," he commented now, nodding toward the first lightening of the eastern sky. "We should find somewhere in the woods to settle for the day.''

It took a fortnight for the threesome to travel the distance between Paris and Montsalvat, riding hard from dusk to dawn and concealing themselves in the woods during the day. July ripened as they rode farther south and the days were hot even in the shade of the trees, the nights scarcely better despite the wind in their faces. Their meager rations put flesh only on Dagobert, giving Alienor a new understanding of what he had endured in prison as her own belly rang hollow.

She had barely spoken with him since their argument, the realization that she could not withdraw her ultimatum increasing as each day passed with only silence reigning between them. And what else could she say? Preposterous it seemed to make casual conversation with such an issue hanging unresolved between them and the issue itself had already been thoroughly addressed.

So Alienor kept to herself, barely listening when Iolande and Dagobert talked. Often she would feel the weight of someone's eyes upon her and would look up, only to find her spouse thoughtfully considering her. What was he thinking? She knew not and had not the audacity to ask.

'Twas with relief that she realized he still took responsibility for her safety as seriously as ever he did, for each day no matter where or when she fell asleep, she would awaken nestled securely against his warmth. More than once on those long days when they rested in the woods, the weight of his arm cast around her waist would bring unbidden tears that their hearts should be so far apart while their bodies lay in such proximity.

"'Tis Lavelanet ahead," Iolande commented unnecessarily as they crested a hill in the quiet hour before the dawn and the misty silhouette of a town became visible through the steady downpour of rain.

"But half a day's ríde are we from home," Dagobert agreed, squinting up through the raindrops at the darkened sky. His destrier danced sideways, impatient to continue, and he settled the horse with one hand.

Alienor followed his gesture, admiring his skill with beasts and wishing now that she had not refused his offer this night that she ride with him. Wet and cold she was, her exhaustion so great that she could slip bonelessly from the saddle did she not pay attention.

Even after a fortnight, she had not managed to change her body rhythm that she might sleep in the day and be awake at night. 'Twas not that she was tired as she had been earlier with the babe; in truth she was filled with unusual vigor during the day, restlessly awaiting their departure, then inevitably dozing in her saddle once the moon had ridden high in the sky.

"We could avoid stopping this day and be in Montsalvat before nightfall," Dagobert suggested, but Iolande shook her head.

"You forget the situation there," she argued. "I would suggest we stop at an inn here and rest properly. The way will certainly be less easy than when I left two months past."

"No coin have we for such an endeavor," Dagobert argued, prompting Alienor's memory. She reached into one pocket of her kirtle and retrieved Jordan's forgotten purse with a gasp of delight, but the other two were completely focused on the problem at hand and did not notice her gesture.

"And heartily do I doubt that any would extend their charity to us now," Dagobert added ruefully, drawing a reluctant nod of agreement from Iolande.

"We have still some gold," Alienor interjected, and her companions looked to her in surprise, a slow smile stealing over Dagobert's lips as he edged his horse closer to hers.

"So casually did you pass it out in Paris that I thought your funds exhausted," he commented, and she smiled in return, passing him the leather pouch. Dagobert tipped out the coins into his palm, whistling under his breath as he counted them.

"'Tis more than adequate," he informed his mother, throwing Alienor a sidelong smile. "Saving this for some greater purpose, were you?" he teased, and Alienor flushed.

"In truth, 'twas forgotten," she confessed in embarrassment, drawing a wry chuckle from her husband.

"'Tis but the prospect of a hot bath that loosens your purse strings," he accused, tucking the leather pouch into his tunic as Alienor laughed in turn.

"'Twould be tempting enough for me," she retorted, feeling some of her spirit return with his teasing, "but for you 'twould be more necessity than luxury. No second water will I take should you be first into the tub!"

"Indeed, she speaks the truth," Iolande laughed, wrinkling her nose appreciatively. "'Tis a fragrant companion you have been these last weeks." Dagobert bore these accusations with typical good humor, regarding his mother and his wife with mock affront.

"Am I to be given no mercy for the circumstances that forced me to this low level of cleanliness?" he demanded, and both women shook their heads simultaneously.

"'Tis but a blessing that they shaved your head and the lice had nowhere to nest," Alienor added, seeing that he smothered a smile. Barely had she the chance to wonder what he planned before he lifted the pouch of gold from his tunic with a twinkle in his eye and jingled its contents deliberately in front of the women.

"Poor judgment indeed do you show to so insult the one with the coin," he commented. "Perhaps I alone will bathe this night!" With that, he touched his heels to his impatient horse's flanks and the beast sped off toward drowsy Lavelanet, the two women laughing as they gave hot pursuit.

The three found a well-sized room in a clean inn, each of them equally torn between the attractions of the soft mattress, the steaming bath and the fragrant food being laid out before the hearth. Of course, there was no question that Dagobert would use the bathwater third, Iolande taking the first dip as Alienor deferred to her mother-in-law's seniority.

Iolande for her part examined Alienor's rounding belly with a proprietary pride when the younger woman took to the bath, patting it and declaring herself pleased by the babe's progress. Feeling her husband's perusing gaze upon her, Alienor ducked hastily into the tub, trying to cover her embarrassment with some industrious scrubbing. Similarly, she bent her attention overmuch on the food when Dagobert stripped for his bath, finding herself painfully aware of his nudity and equally determined not to cast even a glance in his direction.

When all had bathed, Iolande and Dagobert settled before the dying fire to plan their strategy and Alienor called for more water. Certain that water would be in short supply at the fortress since 'twas always thus in the summer heat, and undoubtedly supplies from outside were being curtailed by the invading troops, she methodically set to washing all of their garments, the fabric fairly choked with dust from their travels. Soon every surface in the room was draped with the wet results of her labors and she thoughtfully considered the grimy state of her chemise, trying to decide whether she should be completely without dry garments.

"Are you not tired, milady?" Dagobert demanded softly, Alienor's skin prickling as his breath brushed on the back of her neck. He lifted her loosened hair and pressed a kiss beneath her ear, Alienor's knees threatening to buckle at the simple caress.

"Nay," she managed to reply. "I have much to do."

"Indeed?" Dagobert demanded with more than a trace of amusement. He cocked one eyebrow at all the damp clothing, looking pointedly at the chausses he wore and the chemise Iolande was wearing where she had fallen asleep before the hearth. "What else do you intend to wash?"

"My chemise," Alienor declared without thinking, flushing at the knowing smile Dagobert gave her.

"By all means, do not let me interfere," he teased, the intent in his voice making her want to stamp her foot in frustration.

"You cannot," she began to protest, the glint in his eyes immediately fading as his expression turned grim.

"Aye, you need not state it fully, love," he said flatly. "Clear enough have you made the fact that you abhor my touch."

Alienor frowned, stopping her denial before the words left her lips, completely confused and uncertain as to what she should do. Did he think she cared naught for him?

"Milord," she began hesitantly, but Dagobert waved her words aside impatiently, striding to the bed and tossing himself across it.

"I have not the strength for this discussion now, Alienor," he said tiredly. "Should you wish to join me, I vow I will not force my desires upon you." With that, he rolled to face the opposite wall, leaving Alienor to ponder the unpredictability of his moods as she thoughtfully washed her chemise.

'Twas nigh midnight when they set out on the last leg of their journey, the mountain paths they took to avoid the main roads treacherous in the darkness. Progress was slow, conversation impossible as the horses walked in single file, and the relatively short distance remaining took an unbelievable amount of time to cover.

Fortunately the rain had ceased. Glad Dagobert was now that he had spent so much time playing in the mountains as a child, for these paths he knew as well as the lines on his own palms and there was no way they could have made this journey otherwise.

Alienor rode silently behind him and he felt her hurt as surely as if 'twere his own, though he could not fathom its cause. He had awakened to feel the softness of her breasts pressed against his back and he had feigned sleep a little longer that he might savor the bittersweet touch of her flesh against his own. Too soon had she awakened of her own accord and slipped away, the coldness against his shoulders in her absence but a foretaste of how he would feel when she left his side for good.

He refused to speculate any further on the state of his marriage, preferring to focus on the matters at hand. When the stars began to fade and the moon sank below the horizon, they reached the last turn and he dismounted, holding his very breath as he crept to the lip of the path and stared out at Montsalvat.

The fortress was virtually at a level with where he lay, although a great chasm filled the space between them, the bottom of that chasm rough and uneven with sharp rocks and smaller peaks. Montsalvat crouched on its peak, a peak shaped much like a sugarloaf standing on end and encircled by a chasm, then much larger sugarloaves in the same pose. The lone road snaked its way across the rough countryside, rising from the coast far in the south to the fortress itself, and Dagobert could smell once again that familiar tinge of salt on the wind.

His heart sank when he saw the myriad tents clustered around the road before it began its steep ascent to Montsalvat, their colors so numerous and distant that they could not be readily distinguished one from another.

Ten thousand men.

A defiant banner flew proudly from Monsalvat's keep and he saw now that the attackers had tried to encircle the base of the mountain, a single line of tents making a haphazard path across the uneven terrain.

Predictably, the forces had been focused on the southern face with its road and he could only surmise that the commander knew nothing of the goat paths on the mountain's east face. The ring of attackers was sparse on this side and his hopes gained new vigor from his realization. 'Twould be easy to get to Montsalvat at night and they would not be the first to undertake the journey, of that he was certain, and the thought gave him a measure of optimism.

Judging the amount of time they had left before the sunrise, he chose a suitable spot to conceal themselves in the valley below and headed back to his horse. Tomorrow they would have to proceed on foot.

"'Twill not be so difficult to manage," he told the expectant women cautiously, not missing the flicker of fear in Alienor's eyes and the assessing gleam in Iolande's. Fortunately Alienor had seemed strong lately, that fact easing some of his fears that the climb would be too much for her. Had it been any but the east face, he would not have her attempt it, for though there were ways to reach the fortress on all faces of the mountain, the other sides were arduously steep indeed.

In silence they made quick progress down this last leg of the path, reaching the place Dagobert had chosen well before the sky turned pink. The site offered more than adequate concealment even for the three horses and they settled in restlessly for the day, so close and yet so far from their destination.

That night Dagobert turned the horses loose, hoping the beasts would not be discovered in time to foil their plans. Fortunately, they had precious little to carry other than the clothes they wore on their backs.

With a smile of encouragement for his companions, he stealthily led the way to the ring of knights they must somehow cross. He was considering the relative merits of two apparent breaks in the circle when an imperious whisper froze him in place.

"Who goes there?" came the demand, and Dagobert's heart sank.

Were they to get no farther than this? He turned slowly to confront the figure crouched in the shadows to his left, noting with relief that Alienor was close behind him, astonished when Iolande gave a little gasp of delight.

"Roger!" she declared with evident relief, and the attacker's cloaked head tilted to one side.

"Countess Iolande?" he demanded in surprise, and Dagobert watched numbly as his mother crawled forward to embrace the man. Alienor threw him a questioning look but Dagobert could only shrug in response, giving her hand a supportive squeeze when she slipped it into his own.

"Still are you bringing messages to the keep?" Iolande demanded of the stranger, and he nodded importantly.

"One from the Count of Foix have I this night," he declared, and Iolande nodded her approval.

"Dagobert, you recall Roger? His mother, Adalays, lives in the village."

"Aye," Dagobert agreed, shaking hands with the man and feeling as though he had stumbled into a social call of some formality in this unlikely place. "Long indeed has it been," he added, throwing a speculative glance over his shoulder at the king's knights gathered around a blazing fire outside their tents not a stone's throw away.

"Alienor is my son's wife," Iolande supplied, and Dagobert groaned inwardly as the man bobbed his head in acknowledgment to Alienor.

"Heard tell of the wedding, we did," Roger confided, but Dagobert summarily interrupted what was sure to be a lengthy recollection.

"What word is sent from Foix?"

"Tales of support en route," Roger responded, offering a tight scroll to Dagobert after a moment's hesitation. "Seems as I could save the climb by giving this to you."

Dagobert ignored his comment, unfurling the parchment and squinting in the darkness as he endeavored to read the script in the scant light from the distant fire. Troops, food and reinforcement in but a month, he read, letting the parchment furl shut with a snap.

"Have there been other such messages?"

"Aye, Peter's son in Aragon sends tell of support in his intent to avenge his father's murder, Quéribus continues to send supplies, always Toulouse sends word of the support they rally there."

"Raimon de Toulouse?" Dagobert demanded, surprised when the little man nodded emphatically. 'Twas odd that Raimon would betray him, then offer to support the defense of Montsalvat, and he could not surmise the man's true intent. Did Raimon want Montsalvat for himself? Dagobert spared a glance up to the fortress, amazed that 'twas suddenly the focus of so much attention.

"Can you get us into the keep?" he asked sharply, needing suddenly to be home to reflect upon this puzzle. His question drew an immediate nod from Roger.

"Aye, though 'tis easier farther north," he acknowledged, gesturing to the right.

"Let us go, then," Dagobert said tersely, impatient to be on with it. Something did not quite add up and he was anxious to discuss the matter with Eustache. No sense did it make that these troops clung so vigilantly to the idea of conquering Montsalvat, especially since word of his confinement must have reached them in this time.

"I would spare my lady as much of the night's chill as we can," he added, giving Alienor's hand a gentle squeeze. Truly she was in no condition to spend another night outside and 'twas high time she had a proper mattress beneath her. When Roger looked mystified, Dagobert explained gently, "The babe comes in but three months."

"Ah." Roger nodded, casting a questioning glance over Dagobert's shoulder. "Are you just three then?" he asked, and Dagobert looked confused in turn.

"Aye," he replied, watching a frown settle between the man's brows.

"What of Eustache?" Roger demanded.

"Eustache?" Iolande repeated.

"Eustache?" Dagobert asked at the same time, unable to see his point.

"'Tis two months since he rode out to find you," Roger told him awkwardly. "I had assumed you would all return together, but it seems I speak out of turn."

"Where did he ride?" Dagobert demanded, tightening his grip on Alienor's hand even as a chill settled around his own heart. What had befallen Eustache? Unlike him 'twas to set off impulsively and send no word, and Dagobert marveled that his companion would do such a thing, especially after he had been entrusted with responsibility of the fortress. Who now guarded the keep and kept the attackers at bay?

"Toulouse," Roger supplied. "A message came from there sealed with your mark. All assumed that you summoned him thence, for he rode out with all haste."

Dagobert closed his eyes in annoyance, easily recalling the loss of his possessions on the night that he and Alienor were arrested. Raimon must have claimed his signet ring and used it in his stead. His heart sank and he wondered who else Raimon had summoned, what other messages the count had sent in the Pereille name. Vast trouble indeed could he be facing here.

"Two months past and no word has there been?" Dagobert asked, and Roger nodded in agreement. "Certain of this, are you?" he demanded, and the other man looked affronted.

"Thrice weekly do I make this climb, and more do I know of the doings at Montsalvat than any other," he shot back hotly, drawing a thoughtful nod from Dagobert. He hoped his horse had not yet wandered too far afield, for 'twas clear what he must do.

"Easily then should you see my wife and mother within the keep," he stated grimly, ignoring the startled glance Alienor sent his way.

"Milord?" Roger asked in bewilderment.

"I ride to Toulouse," Dagobert replied curtly. "See that the women make the climb safely and take special care of my wife's condition."

Roger seemed to hesitate for a moment and Dagobert recalled his statement that he no longer needed to make the climb to deliver his message. With a grimace of distaste, Dagobert dug Jordan's purse from his tunic and tossed a coin to the man, disliking the gleam of avarice that lighted the man's eyes before he winked. For an instant, Dagobert doubted his decision to leave the women with this man, but he knew that he had little choice, feeling personally responsible for Eustache's undoubtedly ill-fated ride to Toulouse.

"Aye, milord," Roger agreed, and Dagobert's eyes narrowed for an instant.

"Another two shall I have for you on my return when I see my wife safe," he vowed, watching as the man nodded assessingly.

"And should you not return?" he demanded craftily, and Dagobert slipped his arm proprietarily around Alienor's waist.

"Should three moons pass and I do not return, my lady will see to your wage," he said flatly, knowing there were adequate resources hidden within the keep to cover the payment. Roger nodded and squinted up at the sky.

"'Twill be nigh dawn by the time we arrive," he warned, and Dagobert breathed a silent sigh of relief, momentarily certain that his wager was enough to see to Alienor's safety.

"But, Dagobert—" Alienor protested now, her words cut short when he laid his finger gently across her lips. He smiled sadly down at her, seeing only her fear for Eustache and her own climb ahead in her tawny eyes. Would that her heart would stir to fret so over him!

"Worry not, my love," he reassured her solemnly, tightening his arms around her for but an instant when he kissed her forehead, unable to trust himself to say more. Before he could change his mind, Dagobert rose to his feet, meeting Roger's eyes one last time before he disappeared into the darkness.

Alienor bit her lip in combined fear and annoyance, straining her eyes to watch the shadow that was

Dagobert slip from rock to rock until she could no longer pick out his form. Relieved enough had he been to quit her side, she thought irritably, shooting a side-long glance to this Roger, who was supposed to see to her survival, and instinctively distrusting the man. She met Iolande's eyes in the darkness, seeing that the older woman was no less pleased with the situation, then took an instant to look back over the rocky expanse in search of Dagobert.

Curse him! And he rode to Toulouse, no less, the very place where they had already been betrayed! Much as she respected the friendship between Dagobert and Eustache she could not help but wish that Eustache had not ridden out to Toulouse. Well-intentioned his move had been, to be sure, but it seemed his ride and Dagobert's pursuit could only end poorly for both men. Alienor bit her lip to stop pointless tears, realizing abruptly that Roger addressed herself and Iolande.

"Lucky we are that 'tis but the east face," he confided, shooting a glance between the two women as if assessing their strength. "But the climb is still not an easy one, the paths twisted and treacherous. No fear do I intend to stir, but I would have you know the truth of it."

"Though we be mere women, we are tough enough," Iolande asserted, and Alienor stifled a smile, knowing the little man would be hard-pressed to match her mother-in-law's determination in the face of adversity.

Chapter Twelve

September 1243

"Eustache!" Dagobert took the chance and whispered his friend's name through the narrow window that gave some measure of air into the cellars below Raimon's home.

No longer could the count's domicile be called a keep, for its walls had moved outward to encompass the entirety of Toulouse, Raimon's home only a larger and finer version of the other houses in this prosperous town, though 'twas dangerously well guarded.

Darkness had fallen in the cobbled streets, the sentries on the march doing little to dissuade Dagobert from this impulsive act. Out of time, luck and money he was, and still he had learned little of Eustache's whereabouts. Raimon's cellars alone had he been unable to search these two months of ducking and trespassing, and should Eustache not be here, he would have to give his loyal companion up for lost.

It seemed to his willing ears that some sound rose from the shadows behind the barred window and Dagobert's hopeful heart increased its pace. He spared a

quick glance over his shoulder to ensure that the street
was indeed empty, then leaned down to call again.

"Eustache!" he hissed, a little louder this time.

The answering groan from below was unmistakable and Dagobert closed his eyes in relief for an instant before the realities of the situation nearly
overwhelmed him. How on earth would he free Eustache from the cellar and both of them escape from
town without attracting any attention?

"Your assistance will I need," Dagobert ventured,
grinning when the growl became clearly Eustache's
own.

"Aye, 'tis exactly that kind of help I expected,"
came that achingly familiar irony, and Dagobert almost laughed aloud.

Footsteps carried to his ears from around the corner, barely giving him time to whisper "Later" before diving into the sheltering shadows of a nearby
alleyway. Dagobert held his breath as two men paced
past, their mail revealing their role as sentries, and he
closed his eyes thankfully when they had strolled by
without concern.

He leaned his head back against the wall and considered the incoherent growl Eustache had made,
wondering for an instant just what kind of shape his
friend was in. Would he be able to ride? To run? Dagobert gritted his teeth, determined not to give up until he had at least tried.

Someone came over the wall!

A flurry of activity in the bailey in the midst of the
night sent Alienor scrambling from her bed, her heart
pounding in anticipation of seeing Dagobert again.
She fairly tripped over Giselle in her haste and met

Iolande in the hall, the older woman's concerned features thrown into stark contrast by the light of the candle she carried, her fine pale hair hanging loose down her back.

Giselle tossed surcoats over both women, tut-tutting under her breath about the chill in the air as all three hastened toward the hall. Alienor pulled up her hood and took Giselle's cold hand within her own, barely noting that the maid echoed her own sense of urgency and wondering its source for just an instant before the three descended the steps together, each certain that 'twas Dagobert and Eustache who returned.

To their astonishment, 'twas another knight who strode into the hall, a short, curiously featured man trailing in his wake. The knight removed his helmet and had barely time to run a tired hand over his brow before Alienor launched herself into his arms.

"Guibert!" she cried, and the older man immediately smiled as he discerned her face within the shadows of her cowl, his eyes widening when he noted the fullness of her belly.

"Already ripe," he said, laughing, and swung her into the air with mock difficulty, bussing her on both cheeks and straightening her hood with paternal pride. "Proud indeed must your lord be."

"Aye," Alienor responded simply, feeling herself flush at her uncertainty.

"Suits you, it does," Guibert asserted with a grin, pinching her chin as he had done when she was a little girl, and she retreated shyly into the protection of the woolen cowl as she felt herself blush.

"Oh, all men say such things," she chided with a chuckle, brushing his hand away with sparkling eyes.

"So glad am I to see you," she murmured, and Guibert's eyes filled with tears at her words.

"Aye, 'tis good to meet again," he acknowledged gruffly, pulling her into another bone-crushing hug. "'Tis well enough you are here?" he demanded hoarsely, and Alienor knew Guibert asked about more than her health.

"He is a good man, as you vowed," she managed to reply with a small smile, and Guibert grinned in return.

"'Tis good," he murmured, turning to greet Iolande. "'Tis some road that leads to your door these days, milady," he jested, and Iolande permitted herself a thin smile.

"Indeed, the path is no longer as easy as once it was," Iolande admitted. "Glad I am that you and your companion found your way," she added, her comment drawing attention to the man who had so far stood silently at Guibert's side. Short of stature he was, his hair straight and dark, his complexion uncommonly golden, his eyes narrow and tipped upward at the outer corners.

He grinned now, setting an unfathomable network of fine lines in motion across his cheeks and revealing a set of crooked teeth surrounding one gold one. Alienor wondered in that instant how old he was, noting now the slight bend of his shoulders beneath the heavy black coat he wore, his quick agility and wiry build in marked contrast to his wrinkles.

"Indeed, milady, the most difficult paths often lead to the most venerable reward," he said with an undefinable accent, bowing low over Iolande's hand. "'Tis most gratifying to make your acquaintance once more, Iolande de Goteberg." His eyes tilted impossibly fur-

ther and he sent a mischievous glance upward to
Iolande. Alienor was surprised to find her mother-in-
law completely at a loss.

"Kado," she whispered disbelievingly, and the man
grinned ever wider. Iolande reached out and touched
his cheek, her blue eyes filling with tears. "'Tis truly
you, Kado, after all these years."

"'Tis I, indeed, Iolande, even after all this time."

The two embraced and Alienor heard Giselle snif-
fle beside her, the emotion-filled reunion bringing
tears to her own eyes, though she knew not the identity of this man. Kado and Iolande pulled apart, their
expressions serious now as they studied each other silently, tracing the passage of the years on once familiar faces.

"Alzeu?" Kado asked simply, and Iolande's tears
spilled anew, their stream difficult to curb now that
they had begun to flow. She bit her lip and shook her
head and Kado dropped his gaze to the floor, shaking
his own head sadly.

"I had so hoped to see him again," he murmured
while Iolande took a deep breath to regain her composure.

"'Tis fifteen long years since he was killed," she
managed in a hoarse voice, the news apparently doing little to improve Kado's mood.

"And your boy?" he prompted after a moment,
Iolande's lips thinning anew.

"Indeed, 'twas he we expected when we heard
someone had come up the east face," she confessed
heavily, and Alienor saw those tears rising again in her
eyes. "'Tis two months since we have had word from
him and already this year the king has imprisoned him
once."

"Your news is little better than mine," Kado conceded sadly, and it seemed the full weight of his years settled on his shoulders. He took Iolande's arm and led her slowly to a table in the hall, his own eyes suspiciously bright when he turned to Giselle.

"Have you a bite and a sip for an old man?" he asked her quietly, and Giselle but nodded before she slipped away. It seemed to Iolande that Kado's glance lingered on her for a moment, but he quickly shook his head and turned back to Iolande, seating himself heavily opposite her.

"'Twas Arpais you traveled to find," Iolande stated flatly, and Kado nodded with evident exhaustion.

"Aye," he admitted, gesturing to Guibert standing awkwardly behind him. "This knight I met in a tavern in Carcassonne and a mighty listener he has proven to be." Kado flicked a smile over his shoulder and Guibert smiled back, the recollection of some incident passing between the men.

"And quick with a blade," Kado added admiringly, sending a rare tinge of red over Guibert's ears.

"'Twas but a lucky swing," Guibert argued goodnaturedly, winking at Alienor and dropping tiredly onto the bench beside Kado.

"Too modest you are, my friend," Kado teased, smiling indulgently through his obvious dismay. "Of Montsalvat did Guibert speak, though in hushed tones, and I knew then that I might find my answer here." He hesitated for a moment, then took Iolande's hand in his, blinking quickly before raising his gaze to hers once more.

"Know you the fate of my Arpais?" he demanded huskily. "I would know even the worst of it, Iolande."

Iolande cleared her throat and Alienor watched her fight for composure as she stroked her thumbs across Kado's hand, clasped so tightly within her own. Finally, she straightened her shoulders and took a deep breath before she spoke.

"'Twas Guibert who saw her die," she stated flatly, and Alienor's gaze darted to her foster father to find no measure of surprise on his impassive face. "I suspect he thought as much when you met," Iolande added slowly, both she and Kado looking to the older knight as he dropped his gaze uncomfortably.

"Likely it seemed the woman might have been the one you sought," he muttered, "but I would not burden you with such a tale until I knew for certain." Guibert brushed a hand over his brow as if he sought to free himself of some painful recollection and Alienor wondered what grisly sight he recalled.

"Uncertain I was until you mentioned Alzeu de Pereille. 'Twas but a chance I took that Iolande and you might have met before. Had I been certain earlier, my friend, I would have confided the tale."

Kado placed one hand gently on Guibert's shoulder, his fingers tightening briefly. "No doubt have I of that, Guibert. 'Twas kindness alone that convinced you to spare me the tale when you knew not her identity for certain."

"Much trouble have we seen in these parts since last you traveled here," Iolande commented quietly, and all knew she sought to bolster Kado for the truth. Kado swallowed with apparent difficulty, then flicked his glance to Guibert again.

"Tell me only that she died quickly," he demanded, relief settling over his shoulders when Guibert nodded immediately.

"Aye, 'twas sudden and without suffering, but no chance of escape had she," he acknowledged, the other man closing his eyes for a moment against his pain.

"And the child?" he asked hoarsely, his eyes brightening when Iolande smiled through her own mist of tears.

"The child she entrusted to Guibert," she whispered brokenly, extending one hand to Alienor, standing silently to one side, as Kado rose unsteadily to his feet. Alienor's heart began to hammer in her chest, the pieces of the puzzle falling into place in her mind. She barely dared to believe the tentative conclusion she reached.

"Kado, I would have you meet Alienor, my daughter-in-law," Iolande said in a stronger voice, her smile encouraging Alienor to step slowly forward. At the older woman's gesture, she reached for her hood and uncovered her hair, the delight that suffused Kado's face when he gazed fully upon her features launching her own tears. He rounded the end of the table like a man in a dream, reaching up to touch Alienor's cheek as if he feared that she would dissolve before his very eyes.

"The very image of my Arpais," he murmured brokenly, and Alienor pressed his hand to her face with her own shaking fingers, wanting to console him but knowing not how.

"Arpais," she repeated softly, and Kado smiled up at her.

"My daughter," he whispered in response, confirming her thoughts with those two simple words. 'Twas Arpais who had given her to Guibert.

"My granddaughter," Kado added unsteadily with a gentle tap on the tip of her nose, as if he could not believe the way of things any more easily than she. Alienor gasped, a torrent of tears breaking as her grandfather gathered her close to his heart.

Kado felt a lump rise in his throat as he held this woman close, this woman who so resembled his Arpais, this child he had thought lost to him forever. Hope there was then, after all. He blinked back his tears, the scent of Alienor's hair dredging up long-buried recollections. Never should he have left Arpais here, he scolded himself, too late for the resolution to make any difference. Only now did he feel the fullness of his expectation to see her again, only now when the impossibility of that showed the extent of the void her passing left within him.

How many years had he teased himself with the possibility that he would see Arpais again if he but turned his face to the west? How long had he concocted images of her and Robert, happy and healthy with a brood of children? Well enough did he know that Robert would never have willingly abandoned his bride, but Kado refused to speculate on what had befallen that knight after his own departure. Too late was it now to know the truth.

He pulled back and touched Alienor's face, wondering where the years had gone. Was this truly the squalling babe he had held what seemed only days past? No other could she be, this woman with Arpais's eyes, and he managed to summon a smile for her, seeing the questions lurking in the depths of those topaz eyes. His gaze dropped to her rounded stomach and his smile immediately became more genuine.

The two vines had tangled and borne fruit, despite the upset of his and Alzeu's carefully laid plans. The two regal bloodlines had been successfully merged.

"Naught do I know of my roots," Alienor said tentatively and Kado grinned outright at her reluctance to make demands of him, even as he knew that her curiosity must be overwhelming. Arpais, too, had been accepting of what came her way and determined to put others first. The sign of this characteristic, as much as Alienor's distinctive eyes, proved to Kado beyond doubt that this child was indeed of his seed.

"Arpais was the light of my life," he admitted, surprised at the gruffness of his own tone.

For a moment, he thought that he might never force another word past his lips, but the dark-haired girl reappeared with a tray of food before he could continue. He joined Guibert at the board with relief, knowing the hollowness of his stomach could no longer be denied and that this would give him a welcome opportunity to put aside his grief, at least for the moment. Alienor waited, eyes bright, and, out of deference to her, Kado returned to his tale as quickly as he could.

"Half Mongol are you, child, for Arpais was full in her superior blood." He made the assurance proudly, unable to stifle the curl of his lip when he considered the other half of Alienor's lineage. A fine man Robert had been, but he was not Mongol, nor even nomad, and the prejudice Kado had been raised with could not be so readily put aside.

"When her mother died, she rode with me and a finer horsewoman you could not find among our tribe." Memories stopped his words again, the vision of Arpais riding, face tilted to the wind, making that lump rise in his throat again to check his words. Too soon was it for him to speak thus of her, too soon after his hopes for her survival had been dashed, but he owed the child the tale. And well enough did Kado know not to rely on the morrow.

Alienor seemed to sense his dismay, for she immediately covered his lined hand with her own soft one, the contrast between them prompting him to smile through his pain. A great-grandchild, he mused, shaking his head in amazement as his resolve to remain for a while at Montsalvat grew.

Arpais he had left alone with her infant, granting the care for her safety to her spouse. Only a fool of a man made the same mistake twice and Kado nodded to himself with determination before he took a deep breath to continue his tale.

"A long tale is it in the telling, but rumors came to us some years past of a line of kings claiming divine selection. These kings sought their rightful heritage and were said to be secreted in the ancestral lands of the Visigoths."

Kado flicked a tentative glance to his granddaughter and saw understanding in her eyes, knowing in that moment that she was fully aware of her husband's heritage. "The khan was troubled, doubting his divine birthright when he confronted the threshold of his own demise and saw none fit to take his place. I was sent to investigate." Bitterness rose in Kado's chest unexpectedly and he was forced to look away for a long moment to regain his composure.

"Never would I have come had I known that Arpais would fall in love and refuse to return with me," he confessed hoarsely. "Never would I have willingly paid that price, even for the khan."

Silence reigned around the table and Kado saw that none would dare ask him to continue, much to his relief. Already had he revealed too much, though 'twas clear that this bloodline fared no better than his own in their quest.

Too soon was it to make alternative plans, though Kado already had an idea of the path they might take. He would bide his time, wait for Dagobert to return and realize the futility of his quest, wait for the moment when this king was ready to pass the quest to his spawn.

Kado would wait and see his great-grandchild arrive in the world, if little else.

Two months had taught Dagobert something of Raimon's habits, if naught else, he conceded to himself as he stood in the shadows below the man's second-floor window several nights later and listened. 'Twas Thursday eve, and though the sky was overcast, Dagobert could have accurately guessed the hour when Raimon's cry of sexual release carried to his ears.

He scanned the gardens left and right before quickly climbing the trellis on this side of the house. The woman would leave immediately, Dagobert knew, and the pacing of the sentries meant they would remain on the other side of the house for yet another few moments. 'Twas now or never.

The woman's skirts were just disappearing, the door swinging closed against the light from the hall when Dagobert gained the window; he smiled to himself, pleased that all was going exactly as he had planned. If only the rest could go as well. He stepped into the room on silent feet, pulling his dagger and casually toying with the blade as he took the seat beside the bed and waited in the darkness for Raimon to awaken.

Not long had he to wait, and Dagobert savored the look of panic that crossed Raimon's features when he spied him sitting calmly in the shadows. Raimon's desperate grab for his servant's bell halted midgesture when Dagobert slowly turned his blade to catch the light.

"You!" Raimon cried with evident shock, and Dagobert allowed himself a grin.

"Back from the dead I am," he commented easily, his gaze never wavering from his opponent.

"What do you want?" Raimon demanded hoarsely.

"Something of mine you have," Dagobert said in a low voice, rising to sit on the edge of the bed. He gestured to Raimon with the dagger and the other man recoiled, flicking a glance up to his face and blanching.

"Little affection have I for those who use my mark," Dagobert continued, and Raimon swallowed visibly.

"'Twas b-but a prank," he stuttered, but Dagobert shook his head determinedly.

"No jest is the imprisonment of a knight from another house," he maintained, and Raimon seemed to rally at the criticism.

"No jest is the wrath of the king against so many of our people," he responded, and Dagobert nodded in the darkness, lifting one brow when Raimon regarded him with surprise.

"Aye, you speak the truth," he observed in a low voice.

"Games do you play with me," Raimon accused, but Dagobert shook his head.

"Nay, I have tried and failed. 'Tis enough," he maintained, and Raimon propped himself up on his elbows with narrowed eyes.

"So easily do you concede the point that I can only doubt your word," he argued. "Well enough do we all know how steadfastly the line of Pereille clings to their task." His lips twisted before he continued. "Regardless of the cost."

"Aye, you speak rightly," Dagobert admitted, throwing a grin in Raimon's direction. "'Tis my wife bids me choose," he added in an undertone, and Raimon laughed aloud.

"So the woman is with child and you would have the babe pledged to the task in your stead," he accused, his tone victorious now that he had found the trick to Dagobert's reasoning. Silence hung between them for a moment until Dagobert resolutely shook his head, deciding that there was no reason to reveal Alienor's pregnancy.

"Nay, 'tis not the way of it," he murmured, lifting his eyes to meet Raimon's as he continued thoughtfully. "Well you know that she is Cathar and 'tis but for her own company she would have me abandon the fight."

"What assurance have I that you speak the truth?" Raimon demanded skeptically, and Dagobert fixed him with a steady gaze.

"You have my word that I have abandoned this quest," he said in a low voice. "Time was that that was enough between honorable men." Raimon held his gaze for a moment, then looked down at the bedclothes with a sigh of dissatisfaction.

"My father did support your claim until his dying day," he mused, and Dagobert nodded, knowing that he spoke the truth. "And I, in his stead, willingly took up the cause."

"Until they took Jeanne," Dagobert guessed, earning a sharp glance from the older man.

"Aye," Raimon agreed heavily. "Well enough should you know that I did not abandon generations of loyalty so readily as that."

"She is your only child," Dagobert pointed out softly, seeing now the impetus behind his neighbor's decision.

"She is that," Raimon said in a low voice, a frown pulling his brows together as he recalled something painful. "No easy task is it for a father to see his only child bound unwillingly to a loveless match." He sighed again and frowned openly at his hands. "Still do I bear the scars from the 'discussion' that convinced me to abandon both my support and my daughter's happiness, though the deed is more than a decade past."

Raimon snorted and swung his legs out of bed, strolling nude across the room and pausing at the window to survey the town spread out before him. Dagobert's gut clenched when the ridges of healed flesh crisscrossing his back became visible and he shook his head in rueful acknowledgment of the price that had been extolled from this man. Raimon shook his head slowly as though his thoughts followed similar lines and he folded his arms across his chest as he looked over his demesne.

"Seventh Count of Toulouse am I," he said softly, "and the last there will be with a drop of my family's blood." Raimon flicked a glance over his shoulder to Dagobert. "The Toulousain falls to the crown should Jeanne die childless," he confided. "Such was the treaty I was forced to sign, and well do all know that she will die a virgin." He spit out the window with disgust, his brows drawing together as he turned to confront Dagobert again. "No father could give the pride of his days to such a godless match without his heart tearing in two."

Dagobert nodded slowly in agreement, feeling some measure of Raimon's pain. "Why did you betray me?" he demanded quietly, and the other man sighed again.

"Well can you imagine the threats I receive when the king wants something of me. 'Tis his brother Jeanne has wed, and she lives too close to his hand for my taste."

"And the summoning of Eustache?" Dagobert asked, Raimon's shrug all the answer he needed.

"But more of the same," the older man admitted, striding across the room to retrieve a token from a trinket box. Something flashed through the air and Dagobert caught his signet ring with a snap of his wrist.

"More than this of mine have you," he pointed out, but Raimon simply folded his arms across his chest and leaned against the wall, eyeing Dagobert speculatively.

"Should Montsalvat be saved, what would you do?" he demanded abruptly, and Dagobert rose to his feet slowly. Indeed, the same question had haunted him these past months.

"'Tis unlikely the fortress will hold out against so many," he argued, but Raimon resolutely shook his head.

"Assume that it does," he argued, and Dagobert shrugged.

"I know not, for so much depends on the king. For my part, I would see to my vassals and raise children."

Raimon's eyes narrowed assessingly. "No more claims to the throne?"

"Nay, no more do I follow that path," Dagobert retorted, folding his own arms resolutely across his chest as he faced the other man, not knowing what to expect now.

Finally Raimon nodded slowly, reaching for his chausses. "Your friend is most stubborn," he commented, and Dagobert almost breathed a sigh of relief.

"Indeed?"

"Indeed," Raimon confirmed wryly, shaking his head as he tugged on a loose shirt. "Under no circumstances would he renounce the legitimacy of your bloodline."

"Eustache is very loyal," Dagobert commented carefully, earning an ironic grin from Raimon.

"Aye, and convincing, as well. I fairly had a revolution on my hands once he had made his round of the taverns."

"So my arrival here is perhaps not inconvenient," Dagobert commented with a trace of humor, and Raimon chuckled.

"Should you be able to convince him to abandon your quest, I will indeed be glad to see the last of him." Raimon shot Dagobert a sharp look before continuing. "'Tis not inconceivable that one who escaped the king's own dungeons should manage to flee Toulouse. Your unwilling accomplice, by the way, was released."

"I know not who you mean," Dagobert responded cagily, knowing that Raimon was not fooled.

"Surely you recall Jordan de Soissons? 'Tis my understanding he would say naught in his own defense, but his jaw was so bruised, the guards could only imagine he had been poorly used. Some admiration is there apparently for his unwillingness to betray the lady who deceived him." Dagobert studied the floor for a moment, not wanting to reveal any of his heartfelt relief at this news.

"That then is your price, Eustache's verbal assent?" he inquired finally, earning a curt nod from Raimon.

"Aye, and the one you have already given me."

"And what of my other belongings?" Dagobert demanded, and Raimon chuckled.

"Yours regardless. None have I in this household who could even hope to wear your hauberk."

"What of Montsalvat's battle?" he asked, watching as the other man raised one brow speculatively.

"Assistance I could gather by Yule should you truly plan to abandon your quest. Well indeed would I enjoy a peaceful neighbor." Dagobert nodded his affirmation and Raimon extended his hand that they might shake on the deal. "By Yule 'tis, then."

Alienor started at the resounding crash of another volley of rocks hitting the south wall. Never would she get used to the repetitive pounding of the catapults' loads bombarding the fortress. All the day and half the night, week after endless week, the rocks battered the heavy walls. So far, the fortress had held, but three months of sustained attack had worn even the most resistant tempers to a frazzle within the keep. And

losing the eastern face last week had done little to lift
the defenders' rapidly sinking spirits.

Her belly tightened and Alienor gripped the wall for
an instant until the contraction passed, imagining that
she felt the very stone trembling under the catapult's
assault. She took another few steps, inhaling deeply of
the autumn air, trying to walk briskly as Iolande had
bade her to hasten the babe's arrival.

Another crash echoed against the south wall and
Alienor shuddered, resolutely heading to the north
side of the keep that the sound might be somewhat
muffled. The bright yellow crescent of the waning
moon lolled on its back overhead as she rounded the
corner and she tipped her head back to gaze at it,
slumping against the wall in despair as yet another
contraction rippled through her.

The new moon cradled in the arms of the old. She
recalled the line of poetry unexpectedly, unconsciously mimicking the moon's embrace as she cradled her swollen womb in her arms and rocked on her
heels against the pain. Tears squeezed out the corners
of her eyes as she admitted that the contractions were
growing ever closer and still Dagobert did not return.

Three months it had been since he had ridden away
to find Eustache in Toulouse, three months they had
been without word of either man. Still the attackers
camped in the valley below, still the catapults launched
their volleys against the walls. Miraculously Montsalvat's cisterns had not run dry during the summer past
and autumn had brought vast offerings from the valley's bountiful harvest by covert, nocturnal shipping.

But last week the east face was lost to the hired
mercenaries and there had been no more messengers
since. No messengers and no more supplies. Finally

they were on their own, three hundred souls facing ten thousand and it took not a skilled chatelain to see that they had little enough food for the winter ahead. Ever hopeful of assistance from afar, they stubbornly endured and the fight continued, but still Dagobert did not return, and Alienor knew she was not alone in wondering the fate of their liege lord.

Alienor could not help but blame herself for driving him away with her ultimatum and she had convinced herself in the first few days after his departure that he had been glad enough of the task that would take him from her side. But why did he not come home now? Surely he knew that a mere week apart would convince her of the folly of her words. He must know that she had heartily wished she could recall her demand even before they had reached Montsalvat.

Or did Dagobert take the burden of the action upon himself that she need not actually make the decision to leave him? But had he not virtually given her his guarantee that he intended to be here for the birth of their child? Alienor gritted her teeth against the pain of another contraction and forced herself to face a chilling thought.

Had Dagobert been injured on his mission? Unbelievable 'twas to her that he would not return, despite all that had passed between them, Roger's payment notwithstanding. His death alone would explain the complete lack of news they had had from any, including the last messenger who had gained the summit.

As a widow, she would certainly take her consolamentum vows, she conceded grimly, and only now did Alienor realize how little she wanted the life of a perfect. A home and family, Dagobert at her side, 'twas this she wanted and no more, and too late she was in coming to the realization.

Anxious was she indeed to taste the fullness of life as Iolande had once urged her, but she had driven Dagobert away without ever sharing the truth within her own heart. A cruel price she was being forced to pay now for her hasty words and Alienor felt the warm trickle of tears on her cheeks that she might never have the chance to tell him the truth.

The next contraction was strong enough to drop her to her knees and Alienor cried out for assistance, barely aware of someone's arm slipping supportively around her waist through her haze of pain.

"All is made ready, child," Iolande whispered reassuringly, and Alienor nodded, draping her arm over the older woman's shoulders. Kado appeared at her other side and she gratefully accepted his assistance, as well, walking as steadily as she was able, supported between them both.

"Is there word of Dagobert?" she asked, already knowing the answer but unable to keep from asking. Iolande's lips tightened and she looked away for a moment, as if she could see through the surrounding hills to the land beyond, and Alienor's hopeful heart sank anew.

"Not yet" was all she said, and Alienor's tears spilled again, her breath catching as her muscles tightened once more.

"Always did I think he would be here," she whispered, and Iolande could only nod, her worry as tangible as the stone beneath Alienor's feet.

"I sense that he comes," Kado insisted cheerfully, but Alienor knew that he only sought to reassure her.

"'Tis more than a fortnight before the fullness of the moon," Iolande pointed out softly. Naturally, Dagobert would expect her to deliver with the full moon, but the words held little consolation for Alienor.

The midwife appeared magically out of the darkness as they hobbled together into the keep, her ruddy face pulling into an encouraging smile when she saw Alienor's tears.

"'Tis better for the babe to come a mite early," she murmured, replacing Kado with a smile and urging Alienor toward the stairs to the solar. "Less time 'tis for you to wait and a lucky woman you are in this, milady, for the first is often much more reluctant to make its appearance."

Lucky was about the last thing Alienor felt at this moment, but she managed to summon a vestige of a smile for the midwife as the three of them awkwardly climbed the stairs. A relief it would be indeed to be more steady on her feet, even to see her feet again. Another contraction more violent than any earlier clenched Alienor's belly and she fairly doubled over with the pain, her face heating with embarrassment as a warm flood between her thighs betrayed her breaking water.

The midwife wasted no more time on pleasantries, hastening her upstairs and onto the birthing stool as soon as the constriction had passed. Sweat beaded Alienor's brow, even when her clothes were stripped away and the chill autumn air touched her skin. She breathed as she was told, perched on the seatless chair, barely noticing the tingle of the coriander seed the midwife placed upon her nether lips to speed the birth.

Events rapidly blurred for Alienor, the flames dancing on the hearth mingling with her pain, the cool cloths pressed against her forehead blending with her perspiration, the repetitive pounding of the rocks against the south curtain wall indistinguishable from the relentless contractions of her womb. Through it all, she noted only the steady path of the waning moon across the square block of night sky framed by the window, watching the crescent turn from orange to gold and finally to silver.

"What mean you the east side is taken?" Dagobert demanded in a hoarse whisper, unable to believe the news Roger shared. After an entire evening of creeping from shadow to shadow in the village below Montsalvat, his patience was truly worn thin and this revelation was less than welcome. Roger's mother looked up from her tending of the fire at his sharp tone and Dagobert forced himself to rein in his anger.

Eustache apparently felt no such compunction, scowling and spitting onto the dirt floor at the smaller man's words. "A goodly sum did you receive for your trouble, I should hope," he growled, and Roger blanched at the bald accusation.

"'Twas not I!" he declared indignantly, his voice dropping to a hiss as he continued despite Eustache's open skepticism. "'Twas outsiders, Basques hired to scale the slopes, and 'twas *they* who found the paths." Dagobert's lips thinned to a harsh line at this piece of information and his eyes met the cold speculation in Eustache's gaze.

"All alone they found the way?" Eustache demanded suspiciously, his eyes lighting with surprise when the smaller man turned on him.

"A tidy business had I, and heartily do my mother and I rue its loss, despite your accusations," he snarled, and there was an undertone of truth to his words. "A dangerous turn of events 'tis to have to scale the north or south faces, and 'twill be an important message indeed that warrants *that* climb."

"Have they taken the wall?" Dagobert demanded, some relief settling within him when Roger immediately shook his head.

"Nay, only the crest of the hill have they taken, but they hide amongst the rocks all over the slope," he informed them, sparing Eustache one last venomous glare. "'Tis but enough to make the climb overly risky."

"And a misstep on the south face is suicidal," Eustache mused with a frown, his gaze lifting questioningly to Dagobert.

Dagobert drummed his fingertips on the table, frowning to himself as he turned over their options in his mind. Eustache was right about the south face, and it had been so long since he had scaled it, he doubted that he recalled the way as thoroughly as he would have liked. Too exposed 'twas to hang there considering the path, for the light of the moon would show them clearly to Montsalvat's attackers, making them easy prey for the bowmen. He glanced out the window to the waning crescent of the moon, his heart sinking with the realization that the darkness of the new moon was still a few nights away.

A sense of urgency possessed him and he knew only that he could not afford to wait three or four nights. He ran one hand through the bristly growth of his hair and scowled, imagining an awkward way into Montsalvat and liking it not.

How he wished he knew what prompted this sharp desire to be within the keep that he could better weigh the need against the risk, but there was naught for it. Too soon 'twas for Alienor to give birth, but he could not dismiss the sense that something was seriously wrong. They would have to enter Montsalvat with the first light, for he could wait no longer.

Eustache must have followed his thoughts, for the other knight showed no surprise when Dagobert leaned forward to outline his plan.

The indigo of the night faded outside Alienor's window, the patch of sky lightening to rosy pink and thence to crimson, and still she strained. Would this pain never end? Her muscles were trembling, her loose hair damp on her shoulders, her cheeks bathed in a mingling of sweat and tears. Iolande gripped her hands, the older woman's gaze compelling as she urged Alienor ever on.

"So tired am I," she gasped, but Iolande shook her head determinedly.

"The babe comes in his own time," she murmured firmly. "'Tis not for you to decide to cease the effort." She squeezed Alienor's hands and Alienor closed her eyes, feeling the strength of Iolande's will flow between them and revive her.

"The path is wide for the babe," the midwife confirmed cheerfully, patting Alienor on the shoulder. "When next the pain comes, you must push."

"Push," Alienor repeated under her breath, sparing a glance to Iolande as she prepared herself. The tightness grew in her belly, a premonition of the contraction to come, and she licked her lips, taking a deep breath and hoping 'twould soon be past.

"As I recall, 'twas most satisfying to cry aloud," Iolande commented. Alienor almost had time to smile before the pain captured her in its relentless grip and she tipped back her head to scream.

"Excellent," chirped the midwife as she peeked up from between Alienor's thighs. "Once more," she urged, the onslaught of the next contraction the only thing keeping Alienor from wringing the cheery woman's neck.

"'Tis close now," Iolande assured her quietly, but Alienor heard her not, the violence of the contraction tearing another unwilling scream from her lips.

"Clear the way, all clear for the cart," Roger roared to the crowd on the village road ahead, while Dagobert and Eustache huddled together in the wagon. Wedged between sacks of wheat they were, the unsteady lurching of the wagon almost sending the stacked bags of grain tumbling on top of them.

Would the sentries actually let Roger drive the cart of grain up to Montsalvat's gates? 'Twas almost audacious enough to work and certainly worth a try, but now as they approached the sentry on the road, Dagobert was seized by doubts in the wisdom of his plan. Should they be discovered, they would surely be slaughtered on the spot.

The wagon came to a wobbly stop, Eustache shooting Dagobert a grim look as the motion sent one heavy sack to land precariously close to his ear. Dagobert grinned despite himself at his friend's disgruntled expression, straining to hear the conversation just a few feet away.

"What have you here?" a gruff voice demanded, and both knights fingered the hilts of their swords nervously.

"A gift of wheat for Montsalvat," Roger answered quickly, his questioner's low growl not a good portent of things to come.

"Who sends this gift?"

"I was bidden not to say," Roger responded cagily, and Dagobert closed his eyes in resignation at the sound of gold changing hands. He flicked a look to Eustache to catch his friend's eyes rolling at Roger's opportunism.

Would that Roger did not find it opportune to betray them was Dagobert's next sobering thought, and he nearly drew his blade then and there. A madman he had been to trust this messenger whose loyalty was so easily bought and sold.

And what of Alienor? Had he not cavalierly entrusted her care to this same Roger? A cold fear gripped his heart and he wondered for the first time whether she had safely gained the keep, heartily regretting the fact that he had not questioned Roger about this earlier.

Something scratched nearby, the sound seeming to come from the sacks of grain themselves. Dagobert froze, his mind filled with recollections of the rats in his cell in Paris, a sweat beading his brow as he carefully looked over the sacks he could see.

Too long had the men outside been silent, he thought in sudden panic, Eustache's hand landing heavily on his arm when he would have bolted. Dagobert met the steadiness of his companion's green gaze and exhaled shakily, closing his eyes in relief as the voices rose ahead of them once more.

"A right-thinking gentleman you are, indeed, sir," Roger commented, the coins jingling as he dropped them into some place of safekeeping. His voice dropped to a whisper and Dagobert fairly scooted forward to hear his words.

"'Tis from a lord who wishes to support his neighbor without endangering himself, you understand," Roger confided, the other man grunting in resignation before another clink of gold was heard. Eustache shook his head in amazement at the little man's skill and silently rolled to his back.

"I would have his name," the questioner said grimly, and there was a heavy pause, as if Roger were considering his loyalties. Another coin seemed to decide the issue for him.

"'Twas Raimon de Toulouse who sent the wheat," Roger said, and Dagobert fairly grinned in the darkness, exchanging a wink with Eustache. 'Twas true enough in its own way, even if Raimon had not known that they had commandeered the wagon of grain. Some sort of compensation 'twas for Eustache's incarceration, for the knight had been too weak to walk the distance home and no coin had they for horses.

"Nay, it cannot be so," the other man argued. "Fifty knights did he send to the attack and such a man as he would not deign to play both sides."

Eustache rolled his eyes at the dubious accuracy of this remark and passed his hand over his brow, but Dagobert merely shot him a look, so intent was he on the conversation. Their passage hung in the balance now and 'twould be Roger's next arguments that would have to sway the man.

"'Twas a promise made to his sire," Roger explained, and Dagobert could picture him waving his hand vaguely into the air. "Great allies were the elder Raimon and Alzeu de Pereille."

"Unlike the present count 'tis to nurse a guilty conscience," the guard declared suspiciously.

"Aye," Roger conceded, and his voice dropped to a conspiratorial tone. "Oft have I wondered during this ride whether the wheat was tainted in some way."

"Aye, that new healer has he in his ranks," the other man admitted doubtfully, and the wagon fairly bounced with the vigor of Roger's nod.

"Aye, 'tis whispered that he knows the ways of the East," he confided, and the other man seemed to take a step back. "And 'twas rumored that some of the less supportive vassals died mysteriously this summer, just after the wheat harvest," Roger added pointedly, a rustle of cloth and jingle of mail betraying the guard's hasty crossing of himself.

"Truly?" he demanded in a voice filled with awe. "Many a black art is there to be learned in the East."

"Indeed, and the less I know of such doings the better," Roger said darkly, earning a grunt of assent from the guard.

The burlap stretched over the contents of the cart rustled, and the gazes of the two concealed knights met as they pulled their knives silently. Cloth tore, followed immediately by the sound of wheat kernels spilling out onto the road, and the man laughed harshly.

"Aye, wheat 'tis," he pronounced, slapping the stack of sacks with a heavy hand that set the bulging bags shifting and Eustache's eyes widening in dismay. "But I'll be eating none of it. On with you and get yourself back before midday."

"Aye, that I will," Roger agreed, clicking his tongue to the tired draft horse hauling the cart.

The wagon jolted forward again and Dagobert dared to release the breath he had been holding, grinning at Eustache at the success of their ruse. A sack threatened to topple on them and they grabbed at it simultaneously but too late, the weight of wheat landing on Dagobert's chest, forcing the air from his lungs abruptly and prompting Eustache to smother a chuckle.

The cart labored up the steep road to the gates, men shouting to stay the catapults until they had passed. Moments later, a chill shadow fell over the cart and Dagobert knew they passed between the towers on the outer gates. He exchanged a significant look with Eustache, the expression in his companion's eyes telling him that Eustache was as surprised as he that their deceit might actually work.

The road grew more level and Dagobert closed his eyes, picturing their progress across the narrow causeway that spanned the distance to the main gate, wishing he could flip back the burlap and gaze out upon the view he loved so well. But another few moments until they were out of the archers' range.

The shadow of the main gate had barely cast its cool length over the cart when a woman's agonized scream rent the air.

"Alienor!" Dagobert cried in instant recognition, leaping to his feet and casting the burlap aside with one smooth gesture.

"No!" Eustache shouted, grabbing to restrain Dagobert and missing his friend. Dagobert dived from the cart and the knights of Montsalvat drew their blades, determined to dispatch this unidentified invader.

"Hold your blades! 'Tis Dagobert!" Eustache yelled in desperation, and the surprised inner guards fell back from Dagobert's path. A cry came from beyond the barbican towers signaling that the attackers had also heard his cry and now understood what had transpired.

"To the gates!" Eustache cried instinctively, and the knights ran to do his bidding, the portcullis between the outer towers falling shut with a resonant clang. The wall on Eustache's right immediately shook with the impact of a load of rocks and he ran one hand through his hair, taking the situation quickly in hand.

"Welcome home," he muttered dryly, and smiled despite himself when the closest knight stepped forward, shaking his hand vigorously and clapping his back in hearty greeting.

Eustache glanced to the portal to the keep, his smile breaking into a full-fledged grin when he spied Giselle standing there, her hands raised to her lips in astonishment as she stared back at him. She stood but for a moment regarding him, then turned and disappeared within, the glimmer of tears that he had seen in her dark eyes making him feel as frisky as a new pup.

Aye, 'twas good indeed to be home again, he told himself, turning to bellow orders for the defense of the walls.

Chapter Thirteen

"**I** can push no more," Alienor maintained, her tone bordering on desperation, tears blurring her vision of those around her.

"You must," Iolande insisted gently, but Alienor could only shake her head weakly.

"'Tis too much."

"'Tis very close, milady," the midwife asserted with false bravado, and Alienor spared her an ironic glance.

"'Twas what you said at dawn," she muttered through her teeth, and the woman smiled easily.

"Oftentimes the first makes his way slowly into the world," she confirmed sweetly. Alienor would have made some comment about this being the arrival of her *last* child, but another contraction stole her breath away, leaving her sobbing on Iolande's shoulder.

"In truth, I can fight no more," she argued quietly, barely noticing the agitated whisper that rippled through the assembly of women in the solar.

"Milord, you cannot," the midwife began inexplicably, but 'twas Iolande's gasp of surprise that finally made Alienor look up at the disturbance.

"I can and will," Dagobert stated flatly, shedding helmet, coif and gloves as he strode grimly across the room, casting them carelessly on the floor, his attention focused entirely on Alienor.

Her heart leapt when she saw him, but she could make no sound in her amazement, so convinced had she been that he must be injured or dead. His gray eyes were filled with concern as he squatted down before her and she noted the way his new growth of hair stood on end, his fingertip beneath her chin so unbearably gentle that Alienor started to cry.

"How long has she labored?" he demanded of the midwife without averting his eyes, his gaze running over Alienor's flushed and wet countenance.

"Since the moon rose," came the pert response, and Dagobert nodded slowly, one hand dropping to touch Alienor's stomach with a feather-light stroke.

"'Tis close," he commented, giving Alienor an encouraging smile that warmed her very heart. Their gazes locked and held and Alienor felt the barest wisp of a smile dawn through her mist of tears. Dagobert was alive, he was here and he was regarding her as though his entire world revolved around her.

"Just as I was telling her, milord," the midwife began, but Dagobert interrupted her with a curt gesture.

"Fetch her some cool water," he commanded, and the woman sniffed indignantly before trotting to do his bidding.

"The babe is large, I fear," Iolande interjected, and Dagobert flicked a glance to his mother, giving her a little nod before he returned his attention to Alienor.

Even for that instant she missed the warmth of his gaze, his very presence convincing her that she could now finish the task before her, his survival giving meaning to their child's arrival once again. Alienor would have told him as much, but another contraction seized her and she gritted her teeth against the scream that rose in her throat.

"Push, love." Dagobert's hands gripped her shoulders and she heard his gentle command even through the pain. She struggled to do his bidding, her fingers digging into his arms as she fought to work with the spasm. When the strain had passed and left her panting, Alienor met his eyes timidly, embarrassed that he should see her thus, eminently reassured by the tenderness in his eyes.

"Indeed, you are early, milady," Dagobert murmured for her ears alone, brushing his lips across her forehead, and Alienor melted against his chest in relief. "I was hard-pressed to witness my son's arrival." The warmth of his hand slipped beneath her hair to massage the tension from her nape and Alienor wrapped her arms around his neck, drinking in his strength, needing to tell him the truth in her heart before the pain came again.

"Dagobert, I truly have no wish to leave." She whispered her confession without looking up, her heart nearly stopping when she felt his fingers tighten on her neck for an instant.

"Nor I to let you go, my love," he whispered against her hair with conviction, and Alienor pulled back to look into his eyes once more. Dagobert brushed a damp strand of hair back from her face with a fingertip, smiling tenderly as he cupped her chin. "A long talk must we have," he assured her softly, and she smiled in return at his next comment, "but I would see first to my son."

"Well could it be that I bear your daughter," Alie-nor chided him gently, not wanting him to be disappointed, but he shook his head with confidence.

"Nay, love, from the very first I have known the babe to be a boy."

A boy. The son he desired above all else. No wonder he was so pleased with her. Alienor's breath caught as her muscles tightened once again, the room spinning dizzily around her as Dagobert scooped her up, seating himself behind her on the birthing stool, much to the returning midwife's shock.

The midwife's response fed Alienor's agitation and she twisted around, meaning to protest Dagobert's presence, but his very stillness was a welcome relief from the flustering of the women. He merely whispered reassurances in her ear and she felt herself relax against him, his strong hands smoothing her tightened belly muscles ever downward, her protests forgotten. When next the pain came, she drew strength from his serenity, pushing now as she never had before, feeling the babe move downward with his soothing encouragement.

Each contraction now brought steady progress, Dagobert holding a cup of cool water to her lips and bathing her face between contractions, the solid strength of his presence making the task no longer seem insurmountable. The rest of the room and its inhabitants faded away for Alienor as the contractions became so close as to seem without cessation, but always did she cling to the low sound of Dagobert's words. When the babe finally dropped into the midwife's waiting hands, his arms tightened around Alienor in relief and he pressed a kiss into her ear. The child hollered and the midwife threw them both a proud grin as she deftly cut the cord.

"'Tis a boy," she announced, and Alienor almost laughed, drooping back against Dagobert in exhaustion, her eyelids drifting closed despite herself. 'Twas done, was all she could think. 'Twas done, and Dagobert had his son.

"You spoke aright," she whispered happily, feeling him nod before he lifted her easily into his arms and stood up.

"Aye," Dagobert acknowledged, his breath fanning her ear as he laid her atop the bed in the corner.

"Dream of his name, love, for the choice is yours," he added with a gentle kiss to her cheek, then he was gone, the midwife's hands briskly washing Alienor as she slumbered. Soon the considerable weight of her son was laid on her stomach and Alienor smiled in her half sleep, her arms closing instinctively around the softness of her dozing child. Tall he was, she mused to herself, tall like his sire, and she marveled that the realization could please her so.

Dagobert descended the stairs to the hall slowly, feeling as though he had had every scrap of strength dragged from him even as he felt himself smile. A boy 'twas and Alienor was fine. He breathed a silent sigh of relief, letting the fear he had never acknowledged slip from his shoulders now that the ordeal was over and she was simply sleeping. Talk to her he would, her heartfelt confession that she did not wish to leave convincing him that they would soon eliminate whatever obstacles remained between them.

"Well?" demanded a vaguely familiar voice, and Dagobert glanced up, his grin growing wider.

"Guibert!" he exclaimed, shaking the older knight's hand with pleasure. "Good indeed 'tis to see you here."

"And Alienor?" Guibert inquired, no small measure of concern in his eyes.

"Asleep she is, as is the boy she just delivered," he confirmed, watching Guibert's eyes light with pleasure.

"A boy," he repeated with pride, gesturing to a small man seated before the fire whom Dagobert had not noticed before. "A great-grandson you have, Kado," Guibert declared, the other man's face drawing into a ready grin as he clambered to his feet to shake Dagobert's hand.

"Iolande's boy you are," he asserted, and Dagobert nodded with surprise, seeing an echo of something familiar in the man's foreign features. Something Guibert had said triggered his mind and he made an educated guess as to the man's identity.

"Arpais's sire you are," Dagobert murmured as Kado gripped his hand, and the little man gave him a sad smile.

"Aye," he confirmed quietly. "Too long did I wait to seek her out again."

"Alienor knows?" Dagobert demanded, looking between the two men and relaxing when Guibert nodded.

"A month have we been here," he confirmed.

"A fine woman she is," Kado asserted, and Dagobert smiled in response.

"Aye, a pearl to be treasured," he agreed with affection, drawing an answering grin from the Oriental man.

"A good choice we made," he confided to Guibert in a mock undertone, and that knight grinned in his turn.

"Aye, this one will do," Guibert conceded, clapping Dagobert on one shoulder.

"'Tis a boy!" Iolande cried from the top of the stairs, and all assembled turned at her words, an excited babble rippling through the household at the news. Dagobert found his hand being pumped by dozens of familiar souls and accepted a chalice of wine, good-naturedly realizing that 'twould be hours before he could find his own sleep. 'Twas Alienor who needed the rest more, he acknowledged to himself with mingled love and pride, his thoughts ever straying to the emerald-draped bed upstairs.

Alienor awoke to find her back luxuriously warm and sighed with contentment at the way Dagobert had curled around behind her. The keep was virtually silent in the predawn hours and she listened to the regular sound of her husband's breathing, amazed at how much she had missed simply lying with him. His arm lay across her waist and she savored its weight, shivering with delight at the way his breath tickled across her nape. So good 'twas to have him home again.

She opened one eye to find her own hand resting lightly on the bundled form of her son and she snuggled the sleeping babe closer to her breast, suspecting 'twould be but a few moments before he awoke. A marvel he was, Alienor thought to herself, tracing the plump curve of his cheek with maternal pride, smiling when his little fingers gripped her fingertip.

Hopefully she would manage the task of nursing more effectively than she had the night before. A tre-

mendous amount of sucking had there been but not
much milk came from her breasts. Iolande had
warmed goat's milk for the infant, but he had shown
precious little taste for it, seeming to prefer nuzzling
Alienor even without just reward.

The baby gurgled unexpectedly and opened his blu-
ish eyes wide, Alienor hoping that Iolande and the
midwife were right when they assured her that her
nursing would only improve. She knew 'twas but a
matter of moments before he hollered fit to wake the
dead.

Alienor sat up carefully so that she did not disturb
Dagobert's slumber and took a deep breath to steady
her fears. She lifted the babe tentatively, pulling her
hair away from her bare breast and jumping a little
when he latched on to her nipple with unerring aim
and determined vigor.

A curious sensation filtered through her from that
point and the babe seemed to calm and suckle less insistently while Alienor looked down at him in wonder. His eyes drifted closed in pleasure and she knew
without doubt that he was getting milk. 'Twas working!

Incredibly pleased with her accomplishment, Alienor flicked a glance to Dagobert, the color rising in her
cheeks when she found him watching her.

"Naught had you to worry about," he assured her
with a smile, and she was certain that she flushed to
the tips of her toes under his warm regard.

"Pleased you are then with your son?" she asked,
feeling the question hopelessly foolish but unable to
think of anything else to say. Dagobert grinned briefly,
sitting up beside her and draping one arm over her
shoulder.

"Well would I have been pleased with daughter or son," he told her gently, and Alienor glanced up at him with surprise. So sure had she been that he desired only a son that his words made no sense at all. He cleared his throat and met her eyes again as though he were uncertain of himself, the seriousness of his expression nearly making her heart stop in her throat.

"In truth, 'twas your welfare that concerned me most of all," Dagobert murmured, tracing the curve of her jaw with a fingertip, and Alienor's entire world skidded to a shaky stop. Had she heard aright?

"You jest with me," Alienor countered, turning her attention back to her son that he might not see the way her eyes were filling with tears. How could he tell her such lies now?

Dagobert's grip closed surely on her chin and he forced her to look at him, the raw sincerity in his gray eyes lodging the first seed of doubt in Alienor's mind. "Always did you want a babe," she argued weakly, but he shrugged one shoulder as if the point were of little merit.

"Always did I want to love my wife," he corrected in a low voice, and Alienor dared to believe him.

Dagobert inhaled deeply and blinked as if he cleared his own vision of tears, giving Alienor a crooked smile before he continued in an unsteady voice. "Make no mistake, love, for proud I am of this little one and his ten fingers and toes. 'Tis indeed a fine boy you have wrought, but 'tis his mother I would cherish before all else."

"Afraid you are that I will leave you with the infant," she accused quickly, but her heart was not in the protest. He shook his head in denial and Alienor felt her heart begin to pound with new vigor. Was this but a long-awaited dream to hear Dagobert utter such words?

"Afraid that you choose your faith over me," he acknowledged now with a sad smile, and his voice grew uncharacteristically husky. "For the boy I could find a wet nurse, but for me, there could be no other than you, Alienor." He cupped her chin in the palm of his hand and stared down into her eyes with an intensity that left no doubt of his sincerity, and Alienor thought her very heart would burst.

"Should you prefer the vows, I would not hinder you," he pledged hoarsely, "but I would have you know the truth first. I love you, Alienor, and there is naught I can do to change the way of it." Alienor felt her tears rise and she reached up to touch his jawline, unable to believe what she was hearing.

"I sought to leave only because I could not stay beside you and know you cared naught," she whispered. "Long have I loved you, Dagobert, and gladly would I remain at your side now that I know the way of things."

Something flashed in Dagobert's eyes but Alienor had only a glimpse of it before his mouth closed over hers, his kiss hungry and possessive as it had never been before. Her passion rose to the fore immediately, an untimely complaint from their son the only thing that drew them apart.

Alienor turned the babe so he could suckle her other breast, certain she had never been so awkward with anything in her life, but Dagobert watched her every move with love shining in his eyes.

"Tall like you he is," she murmured self-consciously, and her husband smiled affectionately, cuddling her against his side once more.

"But not like you?" Dagobert teased, kissing her with a gentle thoroughness that left her breathless. "Sure you are?" he whispered one last time with solemn eyes, and Alienor nodded quickly.

"Aye," she responded huskily, and he grinned fully now, his reckless kiss making her tingle in recollection of the babe's conception despite her body's exhaustion.

"Have you decided on his name?" Dagobert asked when he eventually lifted his lips from hers, but Alienor could only shake her head.

"More fitting it seemed that you should name him," she demurred, pulling back the blanket that enfolded the infant so that Dagobert could see the replica of his own birthmark on his son. She thought for an instant that he stiffened beside her at the sight, but when she glanced up he was frowning at the wall as if deep in thought.

"A good companion we lost two years past, name of Thierry," he finally said. "A fine knight he was, a man loyal and true. Thierry, Eustache and I always did travel together." Dagobert paused and Alienor did not force his recollection, knowing the man's death could not have been easy to prompt such a response from her spouse.

"'Tis a fine name," she pronounced when she realized he would say no more. "'Twas Thierry or Theriadoc?"

Dagobert smiled down at her and gave her shoulders an appreciative squeeze. "Simply Thierry."

"Thierry," Alienor murmured, addressing the babe with his new name as if to test the fit. Her son opened his eyes, seemingly accepting the name, and she smiled, speaking her thoughts almost absently. "In truth, I had expected you to name the babe for one of your ancestors,'' she commented softly, the way Dagobert straightened beside her making her wish she had held her tongue.

"Nay, 'tis better thus," he maintained stonily, and Alienor had not the courage to question his meaning.

"His eyes are like yours," she mused, taking refuge in discussing their son, and Dagobert leaned over her shoulder, seeming to have sensed her sadness that the babe so little resembled her.

"Aye," he agreed quietly, "but he has your golden skin and dark hair." He ran one hand over the shock of hair on Thierry's head and the babe flicked an unfocused glance his father's way. Alienor watched Dagobert smile at his son's antics, catching her breath when he suddenly looked to her with that same loving expression.

"Well does it suit me that none have magnificent eyes such as yours," he murmured, his fingertips brushing reverently across her cheekbones before he bent and kissed her once more. Alienor sighed contentedly beneath his caress, secure in the knowledge of his love and the family they had begun together. 'Twas everything she had ever desired and it seemed the fates had indeed been kind to her.

Only when the sun rose and the catapults started their daily assault on the south wall did Dagobert reluctantly rise to tend the keep, leaving Alienor alone with the realization that her husband was still a hunted man. She shivered despite the heavy blankets draped over her shoulders, wondering how long they would have together before the king claimed Dagobert once more.

* * *

"We received Foix's support just before the attack on the east wall," one of the household knights confirmed as he led Dagobert on a survey of the state of the keep. The catapults launched volley after volley of rocks but already Dagobert was managing to ignore the sound. He flicked a glance over his shoulder to find Eustache frowning in concentration as he listened to the knight, as well. Already Eustache was looking healthier, the light of suspicion as bright in his eyes as ever.

"How many within the keep now?" Dagobert demanded quietly, running his gaze over the apparently unmarked length of the curtain wall. Amazing 'twas what good masonry could withstand.

"Three hundred and forty, including the women," the knight responded promptly, and Eustache whistled appreciatively under his breath.

"'Tis a lot of mouths to feed," he commented, and the knight nodded ruefully in agreement.

"Aye. The storeroom is full but I fear 'twill not last much past the Yule."

"Raimon de Toulouse has promised support before Yule," Dagobert told them, watching a hopeful light settle in both men's eyes.

"We might yet win the day," the knight said with surprise. "'Twill be a tough enough winter camped in the valley and I suspect that many will head for the comfort of their own hearth with the first snow."

"Aye," Eustache agreed, squinting off into the distance. "Should their numbers lessen, 'tis possible Raimon's forces and ours could regain control of the road together."

Dagobert nodded thoughtfully. "'Tis our only chance," he said, unwilling to air his own doubts about Raimon's dependability just yet. "We must hold on until Yule and stand ready to fight." He drew a deep breath, welcoming that familiar tinge of salt into his lungs, and cocked one brow to the knight. "I would see the extent of the stores."

"Aye," the knight replied with a nod.

"No one has been over the wall since the east cliffs were taken?" Eustache demanded as they strode back toward the keep, and the knight shook his head in confirmation.

"Scattered over the hills the Basques are, and 'twould be nigh impossible to avoid them all."

Dagobert nodded in agreement, his frown lifting when he caught sight of Alienor stepping out into the bailey. She turned as if seeking someone, his heart leaping when she spied him and he saw the flash of her smile. He noted that she carried something red as she headed purposefully toward him and he left the men to meet her halfway.

"I thought you resting," he chided gently, inordinately pleased to see a light in her eyes once more. Still tired was she from the birth, but she smiled at him as if he were the only man in the world, making him marvel anew that she loved him and that she would indeed stay by his side.

"'Tis too dull abed without you," Alienor jested, and he chuckled as she flushed at her own audacity. Unable to resist, he bent and kissed her soundly, the calls rising from others around them in appreciation of his gesture making Alienor turn absolutely scarlet.

"You did that apurpose," she gasped, but the delightful sparkle in her eyes undermined her indignation.

"Aye, I did, love," he confirmed, emphasizing the last word deliberately, the way her lips softened at that almost making him forget her convalescence. Alienor giggled, seemingly having seen the way of his thoughts, and shook one finger under his nose.

"A month must you wait," she chided, and Dagobert made a great production of sighing with dissatisfaction.

"Hasten back to bed and make it but a fortnight," he cajoled, and Alienor laughed anew at his antics.

"I shall do my best," she promised, pressing the red cloth she carried into his hands. "Truly I came only to bring you this."

With a frown of confusion, Dagobert unfolded the samite, his mouth dropping open in amazement when he realized what he held.

"'Twas this you stitched in the solar," he declared, and Alienor nodded in excited agreement.

"Unfurl it," she demanded, and he did as she bade, catching his breath at the fine work before him. "'Tis your insignia," Alienor added unnecessarily, but he did not tease her, too amazed was he that she had taken the time to create such a gift for him.

'Twas a banner of red samite, as long as his arm on its short side, three times that in the other direction. A white unicorn lay placidly amidst the red field, looking back over his shoulder, the detail of his fur lovingly embroidered, his yellow eyes glinting with something that could have been mischief. A garland of spring flowers encircled his neck, and a golden crown set with red rubies rested atop his head, the pearly spire of his horn rising nobly above. All around the perimeter of the banner wound a twisted garland of grapevines ripe with fruit, their dark green leaves fairly glistening against the crimson.

"'Tis beautiful," Dagobert murmured, sensing that this was the moment to tell her of his decision but not knowing how to start. "Alienor, I ride out no more to battle," he began, but she interrupted him.

"Giselle told me that you did not crusade," she informed him quickly, and he shot her a smile.

"Aye, love, no more crusades for any cause will there be," he affirmed, waiting to see if she caught his meaning. Her eyes widened for an instant as if she dared not believe, and Dagobert nodded quickly before she could dismiss the idea.

"'Tis truly so, Alienor," he asserted. "Already have I fulfilled my pledge to my sire, for I have tried and failed to regain our legacy. 'Tis your efforts alone that spared me from certain death, and 'twas my thought that 'twould be fitting recompense to inflict my presence upon you in return."

"Dagobert," Alienor breathed, and he laughed as she launched herself into his arms with unmistakable joy. "So afraid was I," she began, but he cut her words short.

"Be not afraid, love," he told her firmly, gripping her chin so that those tawny eyes were forced to meet his. "No need have I for such worldly responsibilities when already I have you by my side. With the grace of God and the king, we will raise our children here at Montsalvat and tend to our own affairs, for together we each have all that we need."

"Do this not simply for me," Alienor urged unsteadily, and he saw that she would support his quest despite her own desires, should he wish to pursue it still. A marvel she was and he felt blessed once more that she was his bride, letting his conviction show when he shook his head.

"I do this for both of us, love," he assured her firmly, waiting while she studied him carefully, almost as if she dared not believe him. "The task passes now to Thierry, for by all rights, I should have died in my attempt."

Alienor smiled slowly and he saw with amusement that her tears were rising yet again. "I should have you weep into the cisterns," he teased, and she flushed, pressing a heartfelt kiss to his lips.

"'Twould but turn the water there to salt," she retorted, and he chuckled.

"Aye, that 'twould," he agreed, brushing an errant strand of hair back from her brow. "What then shall I do with you, love?" he mused, and Alienor chuckled in turn.

"Accept my token," she demanded with dancing eyes, and he looked to the banner again, not quite knowing what to do with such a fine piece of work since he did not intend to ride out under a banner.

"Let it fly from the keep," Alienor suggested, and Dagobert grinned at the appropriateness of her idea, scooping her up for a triumphant kiss.

"A new banner to herald the arrival of my son," he declared happily, hugging his wife so tightly that she laughingly begged for mercy.

"Men on the walls! Awake! Men on the walls!"

The cry in the night sent the entire keep scrambling from the warmth of their beds in early November. Dagobert was already shrugging into his hauberk when Alienor struggled out of a sound sleep to the call.

"Take your warmest pelisson," he commanded her tersely when her eyes ventured to open, and she noted that he buckled on his sword. Still disoriented but sensing the need for haste, she rolled out of bed, dressing quickly and gathering Thierry to her in fear. Shouts rose from outside and her heart pounded in fear that they would lose the keep this night and 'twould all be over.

Giselle appeared out of the darkness with her wool mantle and shoes, but Alienor could only watch Dagobert's grim countenance while the maid tended to her with shaking hands. He frowned as he tugged his mail coif over his hair and threw the two women a sharp look.

"To the storeroom with you," he ordered, and Alienor nodded in immediate agreement. Truly he expected the worst if he would send them all there. "Take all that cannot fight and stay there until we return." He bent and pressed his lips to hers, brushing one hand across his son's brow before he turned and was gone.

"God bless," Alienor whispered, almost certain that Dagobert had turned to look back from the top of the stairs, but in the darkness 'twas hard to tell.

"May they come back to us," Giselle whispered beside her, and Alienor dismissed her own fears, knowing that the others would look to her and Iolande for strength. She took her maid's cold hand in her own and gave it an encouraging squeeze, summoning a vestige of a smile when Iolande strode into view.

"Come, we must get to the storeroom," Iolande said quietly, and Alienor followed her mother-in-law along with the other women.

The storeroom lay beneath the hall, burrowed out of the rock underlying the keep itself. As the women reached the hall, the men's shouts grew more clear, the clang of steel on steel ringing terrifyingly close, and they hastened of one accord to the stairs. Someone had the foresight to snatch a lamp, and its flicker easily illuminated the cramped space with its rough-hewn walls, now filled with anxious faces instead of winter provisions.

No way was there to measure the passing of the night, Alienor guessing the time by the number of feedings Thierry demanded, others undoubtedly watching the oil slowly disappear in the base of the lamp. The muted sounds of the fighting raged above them, first louder then more distant, the keep finally filling with an eerily expectant silence. The women eyed one another cautiously, wondering what had happened, footsteps in the hall above bringing a gasp to more than one pair of lips.

The oil chose that inopportune moment to run out and the storeroom was plunged into inky darkness.

Countless footsteps, Alienor corrected, her heartbeat beginning to race. Thierry dozed, oblivious to the tension around him, and she wished she could share his insouciance. Did the attackers come to claim the spoils? Had all of Montsalvat's knights been lost in the night?

The trapdoor to the hall swung open overhead and Alienor blinked in the sudden light like a mole confronted with the relentless glare of the sun. The other women must have been struck similarly for they made not a sound. The dark shadow of a man came down the ladder into the space and Alienor swallowed a scream as he reached for her.

"'Tis safe enough to go up," Dagobert murmured, and Alienor fairly collapsed in relief, scanning his shadowed features carefully as her eyes adjusted to the light. Unscathed he seemed but 'twas hard to tell in the half darkness. "Tell me that you did not sit in the shadows all this time," he teased, and the women exhaled as one, laughing amongst themselves as they recognized their liege lord.

"Are you hurt?" Alienor demanded under her breath as Dagobert pulled her to her feet, his quick head shake of denial all the answer she needed to finally relax. He glanced to the others awaiting his response and gave the women a reassuring smile.

"Nay, there are but four casualties amongst us, all of them honorable losses," he confirmed, stepping into the little group and quickly clasping one woman's hands within his own.

"Corba, I give you my most sincere regrets, for Philippe was amongst the four," Dagobert told the woman solemnly, holding her hands steadfastly as she gulped against her tears. When she had composed herself, he reached out to another woman, her plump face dissolving into tears before he spoke.

"Always did Guirand and Philippe fight back to back," she sobbed, evidently anticipating his news. Dagobert nodded sadly and the two new widows embraced each other in their sorrow.

"And thus they fought to the last," he added, "for the end came quickly to them."

"Have they..." the first woman began, and Alienor's heart ached with pride when Dagobert spared
her the need to complete the request with his quick
nod.

"Aye, to the chapel they have been brought. Wait
but a while before you go there," he cautioned, and
Alienor understood that their deaths had been brutal.
The two widows seemed to understand that, as well,
each clutching the shoulder of the other in their sorrow. Dagobert turned to the expectant sea of faces and
ran one hand over his hair.

"The other two were knights hired to the house and
unwed—Arnaud de Montlaut and Guillaume de
Lombers." The remaining women breathed a collec-
tive sigh of relief, a subdued ripple of conversation
passing through their ranks as a number of women
reached out to the two newly bereaved.

"Hasten yourself, Forneria! Do you like that hole
so well?" called an impatient man from above, and
one of the women giggled in embarrassment, hurrying up the ladder to the hall and her husband.

"How went the battle?" Alienor murmured when
Dagobert pulled her aside to let the other women climb
out first. He did not meet her eyes, his lips pulling into
a wry grimace, and she expected the news was not
good.

"Lost the barbican, we did," he admitted, and
Alienor gasped unwillingly, surprised by the magnitude of the loss.

"The outer gate?" she demanded, biting her lip
nervously when he nodded assent, gathering Thierry
tighter to her breast. "'Tis so close," she whispered
fearfully, and Dagobert nodded again.

"Aye, but the stretch of road there is narrow and easily defended," he said with a determination that did not fool Alienor. True enough, the outer gate blocked only the road, the way the land fell abruptly on either side leaving no means to build a wall, but the stretch of road between the two gates could be no more than fifty strides.

"They will move the catapult," she guessed intuitively, and Dagobert glanced down at her in surprise.

"Indeed, they already have," he admitted, and her heart sank at the news. Was it only a matter of time before they gained the keep itself? Grievous indeed 'twas to suffer such a loss after so prolonged an attack, and she wondered why this had not happened sooner. Surely there were even fewer men camped below than there had been the previous summer.

"But how did they suddenly come so close after all this time?" Alienor demanded impatiently. Dagobert's expression grew even more grim and forbidding.

"Up the south wall they came."

"'Tis a sheer cliff," she exclaimed in disbelief, but he nodded curtly, his reticent tongue finally loosed with a vehemence that surprised her.

"Aye, a tough climb 'tis, and no coincidence that the moon is new this night. They were in the tower afore we knew it and the four knights standing sentry there were the sum of our losses. Nary a chance had they in the face of such surprise." Alienor hugged him tighter, sensing that he felt the loss of even so few men keenly and wishing she had the words to ease his pain.

"Why would they wait so long to attack thus?" she asked finally.

"It can only be that they knew not the way," Dagobert confirmed grimly, "and I will find the one who showed them and committed those four good men to their death."

Iolande stepped up to him then and he said no more, gathering his mother into a hug before he handed his family up the ladder, the weight of his responsibilities heavy on his brow. Perhaps 'twas the sight of that concern that prompted Alienor to end her month of convalescence after Thierry's birth a week early. When they returned to bed in the wee hours of the morning and the keep fell into restless silence once more, Alienor curled up close to Dagobert and whispered a suggestion in his ear.

"'Tis too soon, is it not?" he demanded, though Alienor saw that the thought had its appeal.

"A week more than the fortnight you granted me," she retorted, and Dagobert grinned, the shadows in his eyes already being dispatched.

"Feeling fit, are you, love?" he murmured, rolling onto his stomach beside her. Alienor smiled, her heartbeat accelerating at the knowledge that 'twould take but one move of the hand toying with her hair to slide her beneath his weight. He tangled her dark tresses around his palm to his lips, his smoky gaze fixed upon her.

"Aye," Alienor responded, feeling suddenly that there was not enough air in the solar.

"'Tis said a new mother needs her sleep," he teased, pushing the blankets down and baring her breasts to the cool air. Alienor closed her eyes as her nipples beaded, feeling him move beside her and sighing when his breath fanned those turgid points.

"No sleep do I need," she confessed, and Dagobert chuckled, the warmth of his hand landing on the
smooth expanse of her stomach.

"Nor do I, love," he whispered. "Nor do I." His
fingers tightened around her waist and Alienor smiled
to herself as he slid her beneath him. She breathed
deeply of his scent with satisfaction and opened her
eyes, smiling at his evident fascination with her. She
reached up and ran her fingers through his hair affectionately, ruffling the thick shock that no longer stood
upright.

"Too short 'tis," she teased, loving the way his teeth
flashed in the darkness.

"Too long has it been since I saw you thus," Dagobert growled, bending to nuzzle her neck.

"Aye, too long, indeed," Alienor said sighing,
melting beneath his kiss, trembling when his thumb
slipped across her nipple with slow deliberation.

Chapter Fourteen

The sky turned to flat gray over the brilliant banner still flying defiantly from the keep, the days growing ever shorter and a new bite in the wind as winter settled around Montsalvat. True to Eustache's expectations, some of the Crusaders did leave when the first blanket of snow covered the land, but those in the keep were still vastly outnumbered. Weeks passed without any word from the outside, only the hammering of rocks launched from the catapults signifying that there was a world beyond the curtain walls.

Kado looked down over the assembled troops in the chill of the morning air, his eyes narrowing speculatively. Time was running out and any fool could see that even though Dagobert might have abandoned his quest, the king had no intention of abandoning his hunt.

And only good sense did that make to a warrior like Kado, for too easy would it be for another generation to rise in this fortress to challenge the king, even if Dagobert would lay the family legacy aside. The blood royal ran hot and carried the burden of obligation, though he would not as yet speculate on the path his great-grandson would choose.

But time enough 'twas to lay the way that the boy might have an opportunity to set a path, rather than be slaughtered here when Montsalvat inevitably fell to the invaders. Kado hunched his shoulders against the bite of the winter wind and tugged his collar higher over his ears.

Time enough 'twas to speak to Iolande and begin to lay their plans.

Alienor awoke one chilly morning, disappointed to find Dagobert gone and the sky growing vaguely pink with the first light of dawn. She rose to fetch Thierry before he cried, spying her husband in the bailey, pacing off a distance from the east wall and scowling up at the sky. Curious, she paused by the window to watch.

Dagobert climbed the sentry tower in that corner of the wall and Alienor could barely discern him scanning the road far below. She watched in puzzlement as he climbed down and repeated his pacing time and again, the trail in the snow showing that he consistently reached the same spot, the expression on his face evidence enough that he did not find what he sought. She frowned to herself and tended to Thierry, certain that she would learn more of Dagobert's concern later, and, indeed, she had only to wait until the evening meal.

"'Tis the solstice tomorrow," he announced grimly at the board that night, Iolande's quick nod telling Alienor that her mother-in-law had expected the news.

"Our Yule meal will be sparse, indeed," Iolande commented darkly, echoing the pessimism that had seemed to grow of late within the keep.

Eustache leveled a glance down the table to Dagobert and Alienor watched her husband's lips thin to a harsh line, making her wonder what had gone amiss. He glanced up in that moment and must have caught the curious expression on her face, for he smiled and slipped one arm around her waist as she finished burping Thierry.

"Already has Alienor brought us the greatest gift this year," he asserted gallantly, chucking the babe under the chin. Predictably, Alienor felt herself flushing in response to his praise and he tapped the end of her nose affectionately as he reached for his son.

Iolande smiled as Dagobert scooped up Thierry and lifted the chortling babe high above his head, settling him into the crook of one arm and tickling his feet. Alienor smiled herself at her son's pleasure, feeling the knot of tension pass, but not failing to notice that Dagobert's laughter did not reach his eyes.

When Dagobert rose to pace the perimeter of the walls as was his wont now in the evening, Alienor passed Thierry to Iolande and scurried in her husband's wake, determined to know what was amiss.

"Stay warm," he scolded Alienor when he saw that she followed, but she shook her head stubbornly, gathering her pelisson tighter about her.

"I would know what disturbs you so," she insisted, and he regarded her silently for a moment. Finally he sighed in acquiescence and smiled crookedly down at her, slipping his arm around her waist as they crossed the threshold and matched steps across the freshly fallen snow. They walked without speaking for a few minutes and Alienor tipped her head back, watching a few snowflakes meander down to them out of the still indigo of the night sky.

"Aid was promised me by Yule," Dagobert confessed finally, and Alienor looked to him in surprise.

"From whence?" she demanded, and he cast her a sidelong glance as if he dreaded her response.

"Toulouse."

"Toulouse? Raimon de Toulouse?" Alienor asked sharply, and Dagobert spared her a sheepish grin.

"Aye, the same."

"Your trust did you put in the man who so readily betrayed us?" she demanded in open disbelief, but Dagobert shook his head adamantly.

"Nay, Alienor, I put but my hope in his promise, for there was no other source of hope." He sighed and pulled her into a hug in the middle of the bailey, tipping his head back to look at the distant stars. "Always did I fear that 'twould be thus, but the others drew hope from the thought of assistance. And well you should know that hope can give a man strength, even when all appears lost."

"Could Raimon not have been delayed?" she asked hopefully, and Dagobert shrugged. "Perhaps trapped behind the outer gate?"

"Possibly," he acknowledged, but she heard the conviction in his tone. "But my heart says nay. Either way, it matters not as long as the barbican is held, for he could not reach us by the road."

Alienor leaned her cheek against his chest and breathed deeply of Dagobert's scent, finding his mere presence soothing to her nerves. "What do we do?" she finally asked, the way his arms tightened around her telling her that he had anticipated her question.

"We may have to abandon Montsalvat," he admitted reluctantly, and Alienor could not begin to guess what the thought alone cost him. Dagobert's home this was, and though life here was not easy, she could well understand his affection for the place. Something magical was there about Montsalvat's perch atop its mountain, high above the doings of men as if it aspired to dwell in the heavens themselves. Always was the air clean and crisp, the raging of the elements and cycle of the seasons more closely tied to their lives here.

"When?" she asked simply, and felt him shake his head.

"I know not," he confessed, and Alienor hugged him ever tighter, wanting to do something to make this leave-taking easier for her spouse.

"Thierry should take his name at Bema," she insisted, and Dagobert drew back to look down at her.

"'Tis three months away, and long ones will they be with so little food," he pointed out warily, and Alienor nodded with determination.

"Aye, but I would see him take his name in your ancestral home ere we leave." She stared up at him, watching the emotions war in his eyes before he touched one finger tentatively to her cheek. Even though he vowed to have laid aside his quest, she knew this ceremony would be important to him.

"Much would it mean to me, for I know not where we go," he confessed unsteadily, and Alienor watched the tears rise in Dagobert's eyes. Adequate time had they to decide where to make their home, and no doubt had she that they would find some safe haven.

This one ceremony they would have before they departed, though, for Alienor had learned the full import of the ceremony of naming their son. 'Twas when Thierry took his name that he would be anointed the next of the line of kings. A full knight he would have to be to take the pledge to continue the fight as Dagobert had, but 'twas now that the family would recognize him as the heir apparent. Only fitting 'twas that that ceremony take place at Montsalvat, where similar ceremonies had taken place throughout the centuries, and Alienor was determined that Dagobert should have this last rite before they abandoned his home. The vernal equinox, signifying the rebirth of the sun, was but three months away, and a more apt time there could not be.

"So then shall it be," she vowed, stretching up to kiss him in silent reassurance before his arms tightened like steel bands around her.

The plan to abandon Montsalvat was put into motion with astonishing speed. Within days it seemed to Alienor that everyone was committed to the task. The men of the keep were fairly standing in line to assist in the task of excavating the storeroom, but Dagobert answered Alienor's questions about the digging with naught but a mischievous smile.

By the middle of January, a trove of gold of considerable value had been unearthed, and Alienor alone was amazed when it was hauled up into the hall. The vast majority was in minted coins, but there was an assortment of jewelry lavishly set with brightly hued gems as well as a group of blades with beautifully wrought hilts. Many hands set immediately to the packing of the gold into a pair of sturdy and nondescript leather sacks while Alienor stood in openmouthed wonder.

"'Tis the legendary treasure," the redheaded priest she recalled from her wedding day confided over his shoulder, and she nodded slowly in acknowledgment. Clearly that was what it was, but she could not decide whether she was more amazed that she had heard naught of it in almost a year of living here or that the mythic treasure actually existed.

"'Tis a Cathar treasure of which you speak," Alienor corrected, more out of a desire to irk the man who had wed her to a goat than anything else, "and no Cathar are you."

"Oh no?" the Celt demanded mischievously. "Seen me at the Mass, have you, these past months?"

"No Mass is read here," she pointed out, distrusting the twinkle in his eyes.

"Aye, and well do I know it. But think you that a Roman priest would not protest the lack of crucifix in the chapel?" he asked with a merry twinkle in his eyes, and Alienor laughed aloud. The Cathar refusal to acknowledge the crucifix was indeed a sore point with Rome, though truly 'twas their conviction that evil had triumphed over good when Christ was killed that prompted their denial.

"Briefly did I wonder about that at the time," she recalled, "but in truth, there were more troubling matters afoot." The priest laughed and propped his hands on his hips.

"A more vexed bride I have never seen, though 'twas soon enough you met the man behind the beast," he jested, cocking a brow to Thierry nestled in Alienor's arms, and she flushed.

"So, 'tis Cathar you are, then?" she accused to change the subject, but the priest shook his head slowly in disagreement.

"Nestorian, should you wish to be exact, but precious little difference is there twixt the two to most eyes." Before Alienor could ask anything further, Dagobert appeared beside her and addressed the priest.

"Ready then, are you, Connor?" Dagobert demanded with some measure of urgency, and the man nodded eagerly.

"Well do I know the path and the packs are ready," he confirmed with a nod to the bulging leather sacks of gold now at their feet. "Of my companion only do I see no sign."

"Ready enough am I," Guibert growled as he strolled across the room, and Alienor's heart sank at the realization that he would be leaving. Enough it should have been for her to see him safely away from the fortress, but she could not help but fear she would not see him again. He pulled her close in his usual gruff way and she knew 'twas no coincidence that he was so late in coming to the hall.

"Be happy, child. 'Twill be soon enough that our paths cross again," he said now, and Alienor could only hope that 'twould be so. Her eyes filled with tears and she forced him to endure a longer hug than usual.

"Be safe, Guibert," she returned as she stepped away, resolutely blinking back her tears. Guibert steadfastly avoided her gaze, making a great pretense of checking that his pack was securely closed. Dagobert pulled Alienor tightly against his side and she welcomed his support, suddenly seized by her fears for the future.

"Godspeed to you both," Dagobert added, reaching to shake hands with each of the men. Guibert and Connor shouldered their packs with a bit of difficulty, pausing to shake hands with certain of those assembled before they strode out the hall. Darkness was falling and Alienor blinked back her tears, hoping against hope that they would make their way clear of the fortress.

"Fear not, love," Dagobert whispered into her ear, and she turned immediately into his encouraging embrace. "All will be well in the end," he murmured, and Alienor could only hope that he was right.

"'Tis steady progress they make," Eustache announced grimly, and Dagobert was forced to concede the truth of it. The fire burned low in the grate, the rest of the keep long retired, but still the two men sat before the dying blaze in an effort to decide what to do.

But three weeks left until Bema and the attackers chose now of all times to renew their assault. Little certainty had Dagobert that they could hold off the attack long enough to celebrate Thierry's naming, but Alienor had seen aright when she had guessed how much 'twould mean to him to have his son named at Montsalvat. 'Twas a conundrum and he could not for the life of him see his way clear of it.

"I know not what to do," Dagobert mused almost to himself, but Eustache did not miss the low words. The older knight stood to toss another log on the fire, turning to sit down heavily beside him, and Dagobert knew Eustache had something to say. He cocked an inquiring brow and his friend smiled wryly in acknowledgment before he spoke.

"'Tis you they seek," he began, and Dagobert nodded in immediate agreement. "And mayhap Thierry." A cold hand closed around Dagobert's heart at that thought and he forced himself to face the truth of it, disliking yet again the legacy he had brought his son.

"Think you that the rest would be spared should we leave?" he demanded despite the tightness in his chest, and Eustache threw him a speculative look that spoke volumes. Dagobert lifted his gaze and the two men regarded each other silently for long minutes before the crackling flames, each recognizing the truth when they heard it.

"I know not, but it seems a chance well worth taking," Eustache acknowledged finally, and Dagobert nodded slowly.

"'Tis my suspicion, as well," he admitted, "though I am loath to leave this old keep untended."

An understatement that was, for the abandonment of Montsalvat was not half the problem, but Dagobert noted gratefully that Eustache was apparently willing to let the explanation lie. No need had he to explain that he knew not where to seek a safe haven to raise his family or that he was reluctant to leave before Thierry's naming. Only the crackling of the fire filled the air between them until Eustache at last cleared his throat.

"There are those that would tend this keep should you go," he muttered, and Dagobert threw his friend a look of complete surprise, wondering if he had misinterpreted the words.

Never had he considered that Eustache would not go with him, for they had been virtually inseparable since Alzeu's death, and only now he considered the fact of that. Incomprehensible it seemed that Eustache would want to stay behind when there was adventure to be had of any kind. A quick glance revealed Eustache looking suitably sheepish and Dagobert smothered a smile.

"Know you any who would take on such a burden?" he asked innocently, watching Eustache's ears redden in embarrassment. Had he not known better, Dagobert would have guessed that his skeptical companion was nursing tender feelings for some wench.

"Iolande saw fit to entrust its care to me once before," Eustache began unevenly, his lack of confidence amazing Dagobert. Indeed, the man had felt the bite of Cupid's arrow. Eustache inhaled deeply and flicked a nervous glance Dagobert's way. "'Tis true I erred in going to Toulouse myself, but the lesson has been learned, and 'tis my belief that none other could so surely see to the care of Montsalvat," he said all in a rush, his confident words undermined by his tone.

"Indeed, there is no other to whom I would entrust the task," Dagobert agreed smoothly, not missing the grateful glance Eustache shot his way, "but in truth, your choice surprises me. Unlike you 'tis to choose the hearth over the road." Had there been any doubt in Dagobert's mind as to the validity of his theory, the way that Eustache flushed furiously now dismissed every last question.

"I would ask you permission to wed, milord," Eustache mumbled, his use of the formal address betraying his nervousness.

"The lady has agreed?" Dagobert demanded, not having the heart to tease his friend in the face of his discomfort.

"I thought to have your word first," Eustache confessed, and Dagobert nodded in the firelight.

"'Twould ease my mind to entrust Montsalvat to the care of you and your lady," he agreed, and Eustache grinned with relief as he reached to shake Dagobert's hand. "Who is the lady?" he demanded in an undertone, smiling himself at the covert glance Eustache shot toward the stairs.

"Giselle," he murmured in reply, and Dagobert's eyes widened in a surprised gesture that Eustache evidently did not miss. Did Alienor know anything of this? "Aye," Eustache added with a solemn nod, "'tis long indeed I have held her in high regard, and the lady has recently given me cause to be encouraged."

"Indeed, I would wish you luck," Dagobert said, sobering when he considered his own plight once again. Well indeed 'twas to know that the fortress would be maintained by hands he could trust, but that was but the first of many problems to be solved.

"As future master of the keep, I would ask your advice to holding the gate until Bema," Dagobert demanded quietly, watching Eustache's eyes narrow as he stared into the flames.

"'Tis clear they will take the gates in less than a fortnight," he acknowledged thoughtfully, drawing a nod of agreement from Dagobert. Eustache's eyes brightened as a thought occurred to him and he leaned toward Dagobert in his excitement. "What think you of a truce? We care not if the gate falls after Bema, for you will be gone and I cannot think that they will harm any others in your absence."

Dagobert leaned back in his chair and frowned into the fire as he considered the idea. "Think you that they would agree to a truce now with surrender of the keep to take place *after* Bema?"

Eustache shrugged. "We can but try." He pulled his chair closer as the idea seemed to form more clearly in his mind. "Consider that we offer to surrender the day after Bema, that we agree to surrender all Cathars to the Inquisition on the condition that the others walk free," he proposed, and Dagobert shot him a skeptical look.

"Already do we know that they do not seek Cathars," he argued, and Eustache shook his head.

"'Tis you and your avowed followers we discuss when we say Cathar and they know it as well as we," he shot back, and Dagobert nodded slowly. 'Twas remotely possible that this idea could work.

"We would simply have to leave during the night, sometime after the ceremony," he mused, flicking a glance to Eustache in sudden recollection. "Remember how Thierry climbed down the west wall that summer when we said 'twas impossible?" he demanded, and Eustache's eyes lit up in turn.

"Aye, aye, a fine dare 'twas," he agreed, the conviction in his tone growing as he spoke. "Knotted ropes he used, and should we remain within the keep, they could be untied after your descent. None would know how or when you had gone and you would be halfway into the mountains before they sought you. 'Tis perfect!"

"Thierry would take his name here and we would be gone in time that all those remaining would not be endangered further. 'Tis indeed a workable plan," Dagobert agreed, nodding to himself as he worked it through in his mind.

Never had Alienor been a frail creature and these last nights had proved her more than healthy again. That thought made him smile to himself and consider retiring. He had not a doubt that she could accomplish the task of scaling the wall. The babe could be strapped to one of them and they would be on foot afterward, but there was still a measure of gold within the keep and they could buy horses in the first town they reached. 'Twas only a chance, but 'twas a good one, and he permitted himself a grin, refusing to think any further about their destination.

"If only we can convince them to take the truce," Eustache mused. "Let me negotiate this," he urged, and Dagobert's brows rose in surprise at his friend's insistence. "Be seen no more on the walls, neither you nor Alienor, and let me negotiate this. When Bema is past and they find you gone, no clue will they have how long has passed since your departure.''

Dagobert nodded, seeing that Eustache's ploy could buy his family time should the attackers reason that he was so long gone that 'twas not worth their effort to give pursuit. "Take my banner from the keep on the morrow, for I would take it with me," he ordered, and Eustache nodded quickly, his eyes betraying the fact that he was already thinking ahead.

The almost forgotten peace that surrounded Montsalvat during the following few weeks of truce improved the spirits of more than just its human inhabitants. The goats, whose milk production had steadily declined over the winter, now showed marked improvement, the cessation of the catapult assaults and the first onslaught of spring together resulting in an enormous number of new kids being born in the stables. The few children remaining in the keep delighted in the little creatures, the women breathing a sigh of relief that the availability of milk would now improve.

Alienor took Thierry to see the frisky newborns, squatting down with him in her lap when he seemed unperturbed by the animals so that he could see the little goats at eye level. The smallest of the kids stumbled forward on awkward feet and Alienor almost laughed at his unsteadiness until his yellow eyes met hers with surprising familiarity and that knowing expression cut her laughter short. Telling herself that she saw meaning where there was none, she reached out to scratch the little creature's silky ears, biting her lip nervously when she felt only one nub gracing his brow.

Thierry chose that moment to chortle with glee and the small goat started at the sound. He scurried immediately for the safe haven to be found beside his own mother, leaving Alienor wondering whether her fingers had felt aright as she watched him trot away unsteadily.

Bema dawned unseasonably warm and sunny, the weather lightening the hearts of all as they hurried to finish their preparations. A great feast was being laid for the evening meal, the sum of all remaining provisions being used in some concoction or another, and the smells rising from the ovens had every stomach growling before the sun had even reached its zenith.

Wood was stacked in the bailey for a huge bonfire, some of the boys scrambling on the cliffs outside the walls for additional kindling during the long afternoon. Trestle tables were set up in the hall, kegs of wine secreted away for the event rolled in from their hiding place in the stables and placed ready to be opened. More than one inhabitant came to Alienor for needle and thread to patch a favorite garment, all determined to look their best for the naming of their lord's son, all aware of the import of the ceremony.

By the time the sun was glowing red over the mountains in the west, everyone was assembled in the bailey and Alienor looked around the assembled faces with affection, knowing she would miss them all before long. Well she knew that she and Dagobert had no choice but to leave so that the rest might be safe, but she regretted in some part of her heart that they had not been able to remain amongst these loyal souls. Had it only been a year ago that she had come here for the first time and thought Montsalvat forbidding? 'Twas hard to believe. Alienor caught Dagobert's eye and smiled, knowing that this night would be even harder for him.

The sun dipped beneath the line of the hills, plunging the countryside into darkness for but a moment before the men touched torches to the pile of wood. The tinder caught with a crackle, tiny flames beginning to glow at the root of the pile before larger ones leapt upward into the night sky.

"Light triumphs anew!" Dagobert shouted the expected words and the company responded in flawless unison.

"Blessed be the Light!" A loud cheer followed, an infectious air of celebration catching them all as they applauded the rising fire and broke into a traditional refrain. Dagobert grinned and extended one hand to Alienor, the other to Iolande, leading the two women and the company into the hall for the festive meal.

Hours later the mood had noticeably sobered when Dagobert waited in the shadows of the portal to the hall. The inhabitants of Montsalvat had feasted like kings this night and gathered expectantly now around the bonfire, their stomachs full and faces happy.

Eustache paced off the distance from the curtain wall and gazed up at the full moon, and in that moment while he awaited his friend's sign, Dagobert felt the full import of what he and Alienor proposed to do. No more would they see any of these faces or feel the security of such walls around them, and he doubted his decision before he recalled that he had had no choice.

His gaze flitted from one happy face to another, remembering the old ostler's first efforts to teach him to ride when he had been but a child, the cook's tendency to slip him a morsel from the kitchens in the midafternoon, the midwife's perky chatter when Alienor labored with Thierry. He smiled, the sight of

Iolande laughing with Kado stealing the smile from his lips as he realized how much he would miss his head-strong mother.

And Eustache. A quick glance to his friend earned him a curt nod, signifying that the time was upon them. He looked out to the bonfire, panicking with the feeling that time was slipping away too quickly for him, catching his breath when he found Alienor's regard upon him.

She wore her wedding kirtle, the crimson and gold making her a picture of bronzed perfection in the warm light cast by the fire, and she smiled now, that look all the encouragement he needed to step from the shadows.

Together they would find a way, Dagobert told himself, reveling in the strength of the love burning in his chest as he strode toward his wife. Easily now did he recall his first sight of her as she strode down the aisle of the chapel with her chin held high, that same dress swirling around her ankles, and he found himself seized by an urge to pledge himself to her anew on this night.

With a private smile for Alienor, Dagobert took Thierry into his arms, beginning the ceremony with newfound confidence, cradling the boy aloft that all might see him. "More than a year past, we blessed the vine," he reminded the silent company, reveling again in the familiarity of all these faces etched in firelight. "And the vine has borne fruit yet again."

"Blessed be the fruit," chanted the assembly, and Dagobert lowered his son in his arms. Thierry was awake, his gaze steady as he met his father's regard.

"Aye. Blessed indeed be this fruit," he murmured, feeling Alienor smile with pride and opening Thierry's garments with gentle hands that his birthmark was exposed. "The mark of his lineage does he bear," Dagobert told the crowd, seeing out of the corner of his eye that Iolande had come to stand beside him. She bore the pewter chalice last used on his wedding day, the cup and stem carved with twisting grapevines ripe with fruit.

"As do I bear the same mark," he added, seeing Iolande gesture to Alienor. Alienor stepped forward and reached to unfasten Dagobert's tabard, sparing him an encouraging smile when his mark lay bare, and a rebellious thought suddenly occurred to him.

He could not, he thought dismissively, but the persistent idea still tempted him.

"Blessed be the fruit," Iolande intoned, dipping her thumb into the wine and tracing the mark on Dagobert's chest with the red liquid. She flicked but a glance to his eyes and he was surprised to note her lack of distress, immediately reminding himself that Iolande had always hid her thoughts well.

She repeated the blessing with the company joining in and dipped into the wine again, tracing another cross on his forehead. Finally Iolande lifted the cup and Dagobert sipped of the wine, his gaze meeting his son's blue regard as he swallowed, something in the infant's stare lending credence to his stubborn but errant thought.

'Twas madness after they had waited so long for this ceremony, but Dagobert could not shake the fundamental sense of rightness that the idea gave him. Fitting it was that he should make this choice, and his thoughts skipped wildly ahead, as he tried to see all the repercussions in the brief stretch of time he had to make the choice.

Dagobert felt the weight of the company's attention, their confusion and Iolande's frown of disap-

proval prompting him to dip his thumb into the chalice
without another thought. He made to trace Thierry's
birthmark, meeting the babe's eyes once more and
stopping midgesture.

This choice he had and he would leave it to his son.

Dagobert wiped his thumb on his tunic to the shock
of all and drew Thierry's garments closed against the
slight chill before he looked up at the assembly. "I do
not pass the quest to my son," he said simply, drawing a gasp from all around him. Iolande raised her
blond eyebrows high but said naught, and Dagobert
took a deep breath before he explained.

"The quest of my father and his father before him
has brought many changes to my life," he began with
a growing certainty in his tone, "events that would
have been beyond the experience of most men. I saw
Alzeu killed before my own eyes for his quest, saw lust
for vengeance in the eyes of a trusted neighbor, sampled the hospitality of the king's dungeons and barely
escaped the bite of the executioner's blade, but I
would not take back my vows, even had I known all of
this would be my destiny."

Dagobert reached and took Alienor's hand, lifting
her fingers to his lips and pressing a kiss there, barely
noting her tentative smile. "Also did my vow before
my father bring me a bride like no other, and for the
love of this woman alone would I endure it all once
more."

The crowd murmured to themselves in approval of
his words and he shot a look to Alienor, not surprised
to find her eyes glazed with unshed tears. He smiled
and gave her hand a squeeze, her responding smile
sending a pair of tears cascading down her cheeks.

"A strong son this woman has given me in but a
year—" Dagobert raised his voice to continue "—even

while the king's forces await outside the gate to destroy all those who would take the pledge to regain the birthright of our bloodline. To pursue the quest now means almost certain death, and having tried my hand, I would consider my oath satisfied, for 'twas but the wits of my wife and my mother that spared me from the executioner.

"Too heavy a burden is this for me to choose for my son before he can choose for himself. I would give him the chance to grow to manhood before he swears to take this path, give him the chance to live as a normal man, whether he ultimately takes that chance or no. My son is he and I claim him as my own, naming him Thierry de Pereille that he might have whatever protection may come from my family name on his path ahead."

Dagobert took the chalice from Iolande's hands and lifted it aloft for his final words. "I bid you welcome Thierry de Pereille as a son of the Light, son of mine and fruit of the vine!"

"Thierry de Pereille!" the crowd shouted as one, and Dagobert drained the chalice in one draught as was the custom, choking when Eustache thumped him unexpectedly on the back.

Iolande plucked the chalice from his hand, filling it and passing it to Alienor, taking of the wine herself in turn, then starting it on its path around the assembly. Dagobert stared down at his son, realizing the full import of what he had done, barely hearing the congratulations of those clustered around him until a familiar voice pierced his thoughts.

"Are you sure?" Alienor whispered, and he threw her a cocky grin, never having felt so certain of anything in his life other than his love for her.

"Aye," he said firmly, watching her smile at the conviction in his eyes before she reached up to kiss him. Dagobert wrapped one arm around her waist and held her tight, his heart thumping as he hugged his family close to his chest. Just the three of them were there now and 'twould be more than enough.

Somehow they would find their way.

The sounds of revelry continued unabated in the bailey as Alienor and Dagobert changed into their traveling clothes in the solar, their finery from the evening squeezed into the already bulging packs. Thierry had fallen asleep after his feeding and Alienor helped Dagobert slip the dozing baby into a strange pack slung tight against his chest that Eustache had devised.

"'Twill be safe enough?" Alienor fretted, earning an encouraging smile from Dagobert that eased her nerves a little. Most surprised she had been by his choice tonight, but he seemed convinced that he had done aright and she would not argue the point. Perhaps they could indeed break free of the king's judgment and find a haven to raise Thierry. She had not asked their path once they escaped the keep, telling herself that she wanted no risk of any overhearing their plans but secretly suspecting that Dagobert had not decided.

"'Tis most secure, love, and he will likely sleep while we risk our necks," he teased, and she smiled back at him. Alienor scooped up her pack and slipped the straps over her shoulders as she cast one last glance at the draped bed that had served them so well.

"We shall find another on which to make merry music," Dagobert whispered mischievously in her ear, and she giggled, feeling herself flush even as she turned to swat him. He pointed to Thierry with twinkling eyes, implying that she would wake him up, and Alienor shook one finger at her husband in mock disgust.

"Now the truth is known about this ploy," she teased in return. "No gallantry was it to insist you carry both babe and bundle, for you mean to use him as defense."

"Grave offense do you give me with your accusations, milady," Dagobert shot back, and Alienor laughed anew, knowing that he jested so that they might both find the leaving easier to bear.

Iolande appeared at the door and Alienor immediately sobered, knowing that the time of partings was now upon them. To her surprise, Iolande was dressed in dark traveling clothes, as well, her blue eyes sparkling with some suppressed merriment.

"Kado, they have not crept away without us," she called over her shoulder, much to Alienor's confusion, her grandfather's appearance in his travel-stained cloak doing nothing to clarify matters.

"What nonsense is this?" Dagobert demanded quietly, but Iolande merely lifted her chin a notch higher.

"Navigators are we," she declared archly, launching a look of confusion between Dagobert and Alienor.

"I do not understand," Dagobert confessed, and Iolande smiled.

"Aye, for you know not where you go," she retorted, and Alienor looked to Dagobert to find the confirmation to that in his sheepish expression.

"We shall find our way," he insisted, but his voice lacked his usual conviction and she knew he had not decided where to head. Truly she had been unable to think of a suitable destination, either, and Alienor stepped closer to Dagobert, slipping her hand into the breadth of his to show her support.

"Why not find my way?" Kado demanded abruptly, and Alienor blinked with surprise, not missing the way Iolande quickly smothered her smile.

"Your way? But where do you go?" Dagobert asked. Kado threw back his head and laughed at the question, pointing a triumphant finger at the younger man.

"Finally someone asks!" he crowed with evident delight, clapping one hand over his mouth when he recalled the sleeping babe. Kado's voice had dropped to a whisper when he continued. "Four months have I been here and none have asked why I came, when or where I return."

"You came to find Arpais," Dagobert supplied with evident confusion, and Kado nodded quickly.

"Aye, but *why* did I come for Arpais?" He folded his arms across his chest and regarded his granddaughter and her husband with an indulgent eye. "Only Iolande thought to ask me this and so we have made our plan." He waited expectantly and an awkward silence fell in the solar.

"Why did you come for Arpais?" Alienor asked when it became clear that Kado was not going to enlighten them.

"Blood of my blood she is," he said, and Alienor saw Dagobert nod at the same time as she did. They knew this, she thought impatiently, wishing Kado would get to the point. Already they had wasted too much time in departing from the keep.

"Your blood is important?" Dagobert said, his doubtful tone revealing that he was guessing.

"Aye!" Kado practically shouted, leaping forward to shake Dagobert's hand. "I should have known that you of all people would guess the truth," he mused almost to himself, "for does not the knowledge of these things run in your own veins?"

"I do not understand," Alienor commented sharply, "and the night is slipping away. Of what import is your blood?"

"Impatient, she is," Kado whispered to Dagobert, and Alienor watched her husband suppress a smile even as his grip tightened momentarily over her fingers.

"Always," he agreed, but before Alienor could ask again, Kado turned a bright eye on her.

"Have you not guessed the truth?" he whispered, evidently enjoying the fact that neither she nor Dagobert had. "Arpais was sent with me to make an alliance with these hidden kings." Kado dropped his voice so that they had to strain to hear. "A *blood* alliance."

Alienor's brow puckered in a frown. "But why Arpais?"

Kado leaned forward. "Half brothers were the khan and I," he confided, and Alienor felt her eyes widen in shock. She was related to the khan? "And Arpais's mother was the khan's cousin. Strong was the blood royal in Arpais's veins and we thought to begin a new line of kings, to fortify the fading of both lines."

Kado grimaced, flicking a telling glance to Iolande who seemed to be suppressing a smile. "Little did the khan expect that Alzeu would have an inconvenient aversion to planting his seed in any woman other than his wife."

He turned ruefully to indicate Dagobert and shook his head. "And their spawn was as yet too young to suit our purposes." Kado sighed and frowned in recollection. "While I tarried here at Montsalvat, hoping to change Alzeu's mind, Arpais met Robert. The rest of the tale we all know well enough, I wager."

Alienor glanced to Dagobert in amazement, somewhat relieved to find him looking as astonished as she felt. Their eyes met and she saw that the pieces were fitting together in his mind, as well. She lifted one hand tentatively to their son, dozing peacefully against Dagobert's chest, and they looked of one accord to Kado again.

"Aye," he confirmed with a smile. "The two old vines have borne new fruit. Only time will tell if he is strong enough to withstand the obstacles set against him, but would you not give him a chance to try? Well you know that here the three of you will be hunted down like dogs, but there is another choice." Kado leaned forward, a new urgency in his tone and Alienor dared to be tempted by the promise in his dark eyes.

"Come East," he urged, and Alienor's heart took an unsteady lurch. "Take not this babe into a life of hiding—give him but a fighting chance to live out his destiny."

"You know not what awaits us in the East," Alienor protested, but her heart was not in the argument, especially when Kado arched a brow mockingly.

"How much worse can it be than certain death?" he demanded, and she could not help but agree. "Well you know this king will not be satisfied until you all are gone. And despite the chaos in the East, reverence continues for those who carry the khan's blood royal in their veins."

"You would be safe there," Iolande interjected softly and Alienor dared to lift her gaze to Dagobert's. She saw a faint ray of hope in those silvery depths and knew that this could offer them the haven they both desired for their child.

And well enough did she know that a life spent hiding would be bound to wear down one so proud as her husband.

"What say you to a new life, love?" Dagobert whispered. Alienor watched excitement dawn in his eyes and knew this was the opportunity he needed to begin his life anew.

The opportunity that he longed to give Thierry to make his own choice.

The chance to live out their days together in peace.

"You would leave everyone behind?" she asked, but Dagobert had not the chance to respond before Iolande answered.

"Kado and I will go with you," she confirmed. "For there is naught remaining for either of us here. And we already arranged for Guibert and Connor to meet us on the road." She laughed aloud at Dagobert's shocked expression and wagged one finger beneath his nose. "Always did I ensure that you were a most sensible thinker," she charged, and Dagobert grinned outright at her evident assumption that he would agree to their plan.

That Guibert would be with them resolved the matter for Alienor and she glanced up to her husband to see not an iota of doubt in his eyes, though still he awaited her approval of the plan.

"To the East," she affirmed, laughing when Dagobert swooped down to kiss her breathless.

To the East and the new life awaiting all of them there.

*   *   *   *   *

COMING NEXT MONTH

#227 MARIAH'S PRIZE—Miranda Jarrett
In this installment of the *Sparhawk* series, a desperate Mariah West
convinces jaded Gabriel Sparhawk to captain her sloop, never guessing
at his ulterior motives.

#228 THE HIGHLANDER—Ruth Langan
Scottish chieftain Dillon Campbell abducted Lady Leonora Wilton as an
act of revenge against the English. But one look into Leonora's eyes and
it became an act of love.

#229 SIMON'S LADY—Julie Tetel
The marriage between Simon de Beresford and Lady Gwyneth had been
arranged to quell a Saxon uprising, yet the Saxon bride has much more
than *peace* on her mind.

#230 SWEET SONG OF LOVE—Merline Lovelace
When knight Richard Fitzhugh was called to battle, he left behind a meek
child bride given to him by the king. So who was the curvaceous beauty
who now greeted him as *husband?*

AVAILABLE NOW:

Fifty red-blooded, white-hot, true-blue hunks
from every State in the Union!

Look for MEN MADE IN AMERICA! Written by some of
our most popular authors, these stories feature fifty of the
strongest, sexiest men, each from a different state in the
union!

Two titles available every month at your favorite retail
outlet.

In July, look for:

ROCKY ROAD by Anne Stuart (Maine)
THE LOVE THING by Dixie Browning (Maryland)

In August, look for:

PROS AND CONS by Bethany Campbell (Massachusetts)
TO TAME A WOLF by Anne McAllister (Michigan)

You won't be able to resist MEN MADE IN AMERICA!

Harlequin Books requests the pleasure of your company this June in Eternity, Massachusetts, for WEDDINGS, INC.

For generations, couples have been coming to Eternity, Massachusetts, to exchange wedding vows. Legend has it that those married in Eternity's chapel are destined for a lifetime of happiness. And the residents are more than willing to give the legend a hand.

Beginning in June, you can experience the legend of Eternity. Watch for one title per month, across all of the Harlequin series.

HARLEQUIN BOOKS... NOT THE SAME OLD STORY!

Looking for more of a good thing?

Why not try a bigger book from Harlequin Historicals?

SUSPICION by Judith McWilliams, April 1994—A story of intrigue and deceit set during the Regency era.

ROYAL HARLOT by Lucy Gordon, May 1994—The adventuresome romance of a prince and the woman spy assigned to protect him.

UNICORN BRIDE by Claire Delacroix, June 1994—The first of a trilogy set in thirteenth-century France.

MARIAH'S PRIZE by Miranda Jarrett, July 1994—Another tale of the seafaring Sparhawks of Rhode Island.

Longer stories by some of your favorite authors.
Watch for them this spring, wherever
Harlequin Historicals are sold.

DESTINY'S WOMEN

Sexy, adventurous historical romance at its best!

May 1994
ALENA #220. A veteran Roman commander battles to
subdue the proud, defiant queen he takes to wife.

July 1994
SWEET SONG OF LOVE #230. Medieval is the tale of an
arranged marriage that flourishes despite all odds.

September 1994
SIREN'S CALL #236. The story of a dashing Greek sea captain
and the stubborn Spartan woman he carries off.

Three exciting stories from Merline Lovelace, a fresh new
voice in Historical Romance.